Erotic Interludes

TALES TOLD BY WOMEN

Edited by Lonnie Barbach, Ph.D.

A PLUME BOOK

For David, My Love

PLUME
Published by the Penguin Group
Penguin Books USA Inc., 375 Hudson Street, New York, New York 10014, U.S.A.
Penguin Books Ltd, 27 Wrights Lane, London W8 5TZ, England
Penguin Books Australia Ltd, Ringwood, Victoria, Australia
Penguin Books Canada Ltd, 10 Alcorn Avenue, Toronto, Ontario, Canada M4V 3B2
Penguin Books (N.Z.) Ltd, 182–190 Wairau Road, Auckland 10, New Zealand

Penguin Books Ltd, Registered Offices: Harmondsworth, Middlesex, England

Published by Plume, an imprint of Dutton Signet,
a division of Penguin Books USA Inc.
Reprinted by arrangement with Doubleday,
a division of the Bantam Doubleday Dell Publishing Group, Inc.
For information address Bantam Doubleday Dell,
1540 Broadway, New York, New York 10036.

First Plume Printing, June, 1995
20 19 18 17 16 15 14 13

(The following page constitutes an extension of this copyright page)

"Berlioz & the Ghetto Blaster" by Valerie Kelly
A want ad brings a lonely woman a young, rugged motorcycle-riding handy man who can fix lots of things that are broken—and kiss whatever hurts to make it feel better.

"The Scavenger Hunt" by Nisa Donnelly
The ultimate fantasy of lesbian sex comes true when Randi enters a bar and meets a stranger—the perfect dream lover who has a game she wants to play.

"Auto Erotic" by Sharon S. Mayes
A young woman finds sexual initiation in the backseat of her favorite car . . . and begins a wild, hungry ride that races toward the thrills she longs for.

"A Long, Long Time" by Carolyn Banks
A conventional American music teacher is picked up by a gorgeous young man in Florence, Italy, and discovers that the language barrier is no obstacle to unconventional, uninhibited sex.

. . . AND 17 OTHER TALES OF LOVE, SEX, AND ULTIMATE PLEASURE

LONNIE BARBACH, Ph.D., is a nationally known psychologist who is on the clinical faculty of the University of California Medical School in San Francisco. She has received numerous awards for her groundbreaking work on sexuality, and has written many bestsellers on sex and relationships, including her most recent, *The Pause: Positive Approaches to Menopause* (Dutton/Signet) and *The Erotic Edge: Erotica for Couples* (Dutton). She lives in Mill Valley, California, and has a private practice in San Francisco.

ALSO BY LONNIE BARBACH

The Erotic Edge: Erotica for Couples
For Yourself: The Fulfillment of Female Sexuality
Women Discover Orgasm: A Therapist's Guide to a New Treatment Approach
For Each Other: Sharing Sexual Intimacy
Pleasures: Women Write Erotica
The Pause: Positive Approaches to Menopause

BY LONNIE BARBACH AND DAVID GEISINGER

Going the Distance: Finding and Keeping Lifelong Love

AUDIOTAPES BY LONNIE BARBACH AND DAVID GEISINGER

Secrets of Great Sex

BY LONNIE BARBACH AND LINDA LEVINE

Shared Intimacies: Women's Sexual Experiences
The Intimate Male: Candid Discussions About Women, Sex, and Relationships

VIDEOTAPES BY LONNIE BARBACH

Falling in Love Again
Sex After 50: A Guide to Lifelong Sexual Pleasure

AUDIOTAPES BY LONNIE BARBACH AND BERNIE ZILBERGELD

An Ounce of Prevention: How to Talk to a Partner About Smart Sex
American Health: Sex in the 80's

REGISTERED TRADEMARK—MARCA REGISTRADA

LIBRARY OF CONGRESS CATALOGING-IN-PUBLICATION DATA

Erotic interludes : tales told by women / edited by Lonnie Barbach.
p. cm.
ISBN 0-452-27398-6
1. Erotic stories, American. 2. American fiction—Women authors.
3. Women—Fiction. I. Barbach, Lonnie Garfield.
PS648.E7E7 1995
813' .01083538—dc20 95–2766
CIP

Printed in the United States of America

PUBLISHER'S NOTE

These stories are works of fiction. Names, characters, places, and incidents either are the product of the author's imagination or are used fictitiously, and any resemblance to actual persons, living or dead, events, or locales is entirely coincidental.

BOOKS ARE AVAILABLE AT QUANTITY DISCOUNTS WHEN USED TO PROMOTE PRODUCTS OR SERVICES. FOR INFORMATION PLEASE WRITE TO PREMIUM MARKETING DIVISION, PENGUIN BOOKS USA INC., 375 HUDSON STREET, NEW YORK, NEW YORK 10014.

Acknowledgments

This book would have never been written without the efforts of some very key people.

I would like to thank my agent, Rhoda Weyr, for her clear thinking, creative problem-solving and consistent willingness to support and stand behind me during the twelve years we have been working together. I also greatly appreciate the assistance of my editor, Loretta Barrett, who has not only provided me with astute feedback in the process of writing the five books we have done together, but has managed to get a mainstream publishing house to publish female erotica—no small feat. I often feel quite invincible with these two very wonderful lionesses in my corner.

My assistant, Danee McFarr, was invaluable in carrying out the massive administrative details: inviting over two hundred authors, keeping up with where each writer had recently moved, whose agent required which additional clause, and ultimately, making sure that everything was in order for the final draft. I remain touched by and grateful for her considerate, concerned, unflappable personality, which made working with her a pure pleasure.

I am grateful for the time and energy generously offered by Ray Rosen, Julian Davidson, Paul Goldsmith and Bernie Zilbergeld in substantiating the psychological framework upon which the Introduction was built. And as with my past few books, I continue to appreciate the fine editing skills of Cherie Martin Franklin, who always manages to find time in her busy schedule to help me with my final drafts. I've grown rather attached to this last-minute ritual.

And finally, during the struggle to conceptualize the book and bring the details together, I am indebted to the help of David Geisinger. Not only did he conceive the title, but with loving patience he listened to my endless theories, helped me weed out the wheat from the chaff, and gave me support when I felt the most discouraged.

I thank you all.

Contents

Introduction

The initial idea to create a volume of erotica written by women writers grew out of the numerous requests I received from women in my therapy groups for erotic material to read during their sexual-arousal exercises. The vast majority of the literature available was written by men from a male perspective. Because the sexual experiences related in the literature were usually quite different from women's erotic experiences, women did not find their own needs addressed or their sensibilities awakened, and therefore had genuine difficulty responding to them. Consequently, I put together *Pleasures,* an anthology of real-life erotic experiences written by twenty-eight women writers.

In editing *Pleasures,* I wanted not only to provide material that could help women create an erotic frame of mind, become orgasmic, and increase their level of desire, I also wanted to legitimize this important aspect of women's lives in general. Unlike other emotions—fear, sadness, anger or tenderness, for example—sexual feelings expressed by women have been neither commonly nor comfortably represented in our literature. Traditionally, in fact, sexual feelings have been considered base, unacceptable, degrading or the more or less exclusive province of men. This negative attitude toward female sexuality has created serious problems for women in our culture for centuries.

Hence, I was both relieved and delighted when the response to *Pleasures* was so overwhelmingly positive; it seemed to indicate a real cultural shift in the direction of a greater acceptance of women's enjoyment of their sexuality, and it encouraged me to explore the area of female erotica even further, eventually leading to the compilation of this current volume, *Erotic Interludes.*

Clearly, the interest in female erotica exists—not just among women, but among men as well. Some women who seek female-oriented erotic writings want something to stimulate their sexual desire, are curious about the experience and attitudes of other women, and find that reading about these helps them become more accepting of their own experiences. Other women simply want to have more fun with sex, to play, fantasize and, in general, unleash the positive power of their sexuality. Men, on the other hand, are curious about what women think is important when it comes to sex. Some want to know what turns women on and how they can be better lovers. Other men just want the vicarious adventure of enjoying the sexual experience through a woman's eyes.

In the process of compiling *Pleasures,* I developed a deeper understanding of the kind of sexual experiences women enjoyed, and in particular I learned much more about the elements that made those special moments in women's lives truly erotic. For women, the most significant ingredient in creating the erotic was the quality of their emotional relationships with their partners. The sheer physical experience, the anticipation, and the context in which it happened appeared to be secondary in importance.

And the added excitement of the erotic experience being either unique or forbidden seemed to play a lesser role.

I found myself wondering if this hierarchy would hold with erotic fiction. What would women choose to write about if they had no restrictions, if they could create any kind of a story they wanted? I was curious not so much about the kinds of sexual fantasies women have (although some of these stories clearly represent the sexual fantasies of the writers) but about the kind of fully developed short stories female authors would consider truly erotic. I wondered how the writers would feel about writing fictional erotica as opposed to writing about real experiences, and how female erotica would differ from sexually explicit material authored by men.

To begin with, I found major differences between fictional erotica and erotic stories based on real experiences. First of all, the fictional stories are far more complex than the real-life experiences. They are more carefully honed, have deeper levels of meaning, and often reflect a wider variety of approaches to the erotic than did the nonfictional ones. Unfortunately, the complexity of the stories makes categorizing them into clearly defined and discrete areas virtually impossible. The female characters in the stories are diverse: some are heterosexual, others lesbian, some young, some old, some married, some single. And the themes are diverse as well: some pieces are like typical romance stories, with happy endings; others are bittersweet, with lessons to be learned. Some involve long-term intimate relationships, while others center around a one-night stand or a group sexual experience. And while some of the stories are well within the realm of every reader's experience, others are so unique, including one science fiction erotic story, that no reader is likely to have ever experienced anything even remotely similar.

Most of the writers, when interviewed, indicated that their stories were based, at least in part, on real-life experiences—with certain liberties taken for dramatic impact. However, a few of the stories had absolutely no grounding in the authors' realms of experience, but were totally a projection of the perfect partner, the perfect romance, the way they wished things could have been, or a fantasy of the most illicit experience imaginable. What became clear in putting this project together is that *virtually anything can be eroticized.* Certainly, from my work as a psychologist and sex therapist, I know that people eroticize different parts of the body —there are "leg men," for example, and "breast men." There are also people who are turned on by shoes, and others who are most aroused when there is the possibility of being caught. Some things are considered erotic by such a large number of people that the word itself connotes the erotic—like *lingerie.*

One thread, however, seemed to run through all of the erotic fiction I received. The eroticism was based on identifying with the main character's physical experience, the stimulation of the five senses. And what seemed to intensify this physiological experience was some element of the unknown. In no story did the writer find the predictable to be erotic. No one wrote about a long-term relationship in which the sex was good but virtually the same day after day; instead, it was the mystery, the newness, the adventure, the uncertainty of how a partner would respond or what the next moment would bring that was emphasized. This sense of being "on edge," the air of expectancy or anticipation, seemed to be fundamental to creating the charge of erotic tension.

Carolyn Banks describes an incident that occurred at a horse show which she felt embodied this quality of the erotic: "An ordinary encounter that turns into something totally unexpected is what I think is really exciting. One day I was by myself and sitting next to a stranger at Madison Square Garden. A young couple was sitting in front of us. Suddenly the young man buried his hand in the young woman's hair and pulled her head over to him. He did it with such passion and it was so unexpected that the man next to me and I just looked at each other. This one simple, unexpected, passionate movement created enormous erotic tension and we were both feeling it."

Themes of the unexpected, the new, the not quite attainable, the mystery and the forbidden came up repeatedly in the fictional erotic stories submitted by women.

I found myself wondering why this might be so; why should the unexpected heighten our erotic feelings?

When I reviewed the research* in the fields of psychology and physiology, I discovered that many diverse emotions can produce almost identical physiological responses in the body. Increased pulse rate, blood pressure and muscular tension, as well as hyperventilation and other physiological reactions, occur when a person is angry, afraid, anxious or sexually aroused. While each emotion has distinct attributes, they have in common this general activation of the sympathetic nervous system. And in general, the greater the activation of the nervous system, the more intense the emotional experience.

In one very interesting research study, subjects were given epinephrine, or adrenaline, which almost perfectly mimics the discharge of the sympathetic nervous system. The subjects were then placed in two different circumstances: one specifically designed to produce anger, the other to produce euphoria. The subjects reacted emotionally in ways appropriate to their situations; however, their reactions were more intense than those of subjects who were placed in the same situation but had not been given the drug. The increased adrenaline in the blood excited the nervous system and produced a heightened emotional response. This study reflects what is sometimes called "the jukebox theory" of emotion. By putting in a quarter you activate the machine; the button pushed (or the nature of the context the person finds himself or herself in) determines the specific song (or emotion).

Even more interesting, however, is that a heightened response can be transferred from one context to another. A person's nervous system can become activated out of anger, a competitive game of tennis, anxiety about a confrontation, for example, and

* Cantor, Joanne R., Dolf Zilman, and Jennings Bryant. "Enhancement of Experienced Sexual Arousal in Response to Erotic Stimuli Through Misattribution of Unrelated Residual Excitation," *Journal of Personality and Social Psychology*, Vol. 32, no. 1 (1975), pp. 69–75.

Schacter, Stanley, and Jerome E. Singer. "Cognitive, Social, and Psychological Determinants of Emotional States," *Psychological Review*, Vol. 69, no. 5 (1962), pp. 379–99.

then if the context directs the person toward sex, the lovemaking that follows can be much more intense. Probably the most familiar example of this is having great sex following the resolution of a fight.

Danger, challenge, the unexpected, the unknown, anxiety, fear —all excite the nervous system. Too much fear, anger, anxiety, etc., will, of course, decrease the erotic response, but as long as the emotion remains within certain limits, a nervous system that is primed or activated through any of these emotional experiences and then directed toward the erotic can result in the intensification of the sexual and erotic feelings. It is no surprise, therefore, that themes which produce this emotional activation play an important part in the women's stories. Intuitively, these writers are utilizing a natural physiological process to heighten the erotic, something that science is just beginning to explore.

Most often, in these erotic stories, the unexpected or unknown is expressed through adventure, where there are inherent risks, both psychological and physical, that increase the production of adrenaline and excite the nervous system. But adventure comes in many forms.

There is the obvious adventure of embarking on an experience with a partner who is barely known, following a fantasy rich with chemistry and possibility. There is the risk involved in relating to a partner who is not quite committed, and with whom there is no security for the future, only hope and the highest expectations. Even within the familiarity of marriage there can be a sense of adventure as new and unfamiliar territories are broached and where reactions cannot be predicted. There is the heightened sense of risk that results when we express our innermost thoughts, weaknesses, fears, jealousy and anger. The deeply satisfying sense of surrender that can occur when trust and tenderness are highest can only come from risking the exposure of our real vulnerability. In long-term relationships, the coming back together again after periods of distance often contains the charge that was missing when everything was going smoothly. And from professing one's love without assurance of its acceptance comes the experience of a kind of vulnerability that also heightens the sexual tension.

Most often, the partners of the women in the stories have an aura of mystery about them: they have a dark side, are unpredictable, come from the other side of the tracks, or may even seem a bit dangerous at times—the stranger, the "other." A partner who does not allow the woman to have the upper hand, the one she cannot control, is the one who keeps her on edge and hence is usually the most exciting. Intriguing as well are partners who reveal facets of their personality that are totally unexpected, given their outward appearance: the macho man with tremendous sensitivity, the demure housewife who turns into the sexual siren. In fact, many of the contributors talked about how important it was in their own long-term relationships to maintain a sense of mystery, to leave room for spontaneity and discovery in order to preserve sexual vitality. One author said, "Nothing is as deadening to good sex as boredom. Not only is some newness or variety necessary in bed, but being able to discover new aspects of a partner out of bed as well, is essential to a fulfilling relationship."

The forbidden is another very common element present in these fictional erotic stories written by women. The physical rush that comes from breaking a taboo, from transgressing accepted norms, has been associated with the erotic from time immemorial: the adolescent facing her first sexual experience, the extramarital affair, group sex, the exhibitionist exposing herself in wanton abandon, the voyeur, who, being apart, is the more excited by it all, unique and unusual experiences that are just far enough out of the mainstream that they pique our curiosity and awaken our passions.

In addition to these major areas, there are some other elements of the unknown that showed up again and again in the stories. Anticipation turns out to be an essential aspect of the unknown that creates excitement. In the early stages of a relationship, passion is enhanced by the tension that develops as the couple wind their way toward the possibility of their first sexual experience. Flirtation and innuendo create a healthy anticipation that remains relevant at any age; during adolescence, delicious anticipation is often the entire event.

Perhaps the most profound eroticism is that which encompasses a spiritual quality as well. A number of the authors describe sex as a transformative or transcendent experience in which a combination of the overpowering forces of attraction and trust can lead to an abandonment of defenses that culminates in a sense of unity and even what might be called a "cosmic expansion" during the most intimate moment of coupling. For some, a healing process of the highest form takes place when two people become lovers.

In looking over the stories, there are several other qualities that contribute to their capacity to excite erotic feelings. In some cases, the pace of the writing captures a rhythm or tone that in itself is erotic. Contrasts also seem to be important: strong against weak, metal against skin, the full moon rising above the water of a lake. The ability to convey the actual sensory experiences of tastes, smells, and physical sensations that are comprised in the physical lovemaking, is essential to erotic provocation. Whether or not these physical experiences are heightened by the unknown or unexpected, they remain, in and of themselves, the cornerstone of the erotic, for it is primarily the identification with the experience of the characters in the stories that will stimulate erotic tension in the reader.

Given my concern with a variety of aspects that affect sexuality, I felt it important to include a few stories that are not only erotic, but address some sensitive issues in the area of sexuality as well. A few of the stories deal with menopause, disability, aging, in such nontraditional ways that they provide new insights into certain strongly held but often unconscious prejudices and misconceptions.

These stories written by women differ from those published by most male writers in a number of ways. The stories by women seem to be "softer," the sex more sensual and relaxed—passionate and intense but not violent, harsh, or painful. I received only one story that had any sadomasochistic quality to it whatsoever, and in none of the stories were women raped or molested, a frequent theme in material written by men. In these stories, women are not degraded or portrayed as masochistic, as is often the case with male authors. Instead, the women celebrate their sexuality with appreciation and joy. In stories written by women, there seems to be more concern with nuance—the subtle textures of not only the lovemaking experience, but everything that surrounds it. And while some men may say it takes women entirely too long to get down to what they feel is the main event, many men prefer this kind of erotica, finding their own sensitivities more in tune with the sensual than the hard-core.

The women writers of this anthology consider the erotic a very important aspect of life. Marilyn Kriegel said, "I don't see the erotic in any way separate from my life. Many years ago I abandoned a rather predictable, stoic existence when I suddenly realized my life and everything in it had lost the sensual. Since that time the erotic has guided me in my life. I actually look to it first when making decisions."

The twenty-one authors who contributed to this volume spent their formative years in many parts of the country, both urban and rural. However, the majority of the authors currently live in California. The women range in age from twenty-three to fifty-eight. Only two women are in their twenties, six are in their thirties, which means the vast majority, thirteen women, are over the age of forty (and two of the women in their thirties are thirty-nine). The exceptionally high percentage of women over forty may indicate either that it takes most writers until their middle years to develop their skills sufficiently to write something as difficult as erotica, or that it takes this long for a woman to become comfortable enough with her sexuality to write erotic material.

The contributors are as varied in their marital backgrounds as they are in age. Five women are currently married, five are single, five are either living with a partner or are committed to a person they are not living with, and six contributors are divorced. While fourteen of the authors are heterosexual, six identify themselves as lesbians, and one calls herself bisexual.

In *Pleasures,* it was quite understandable when eleven contributors preferred to keep their real-life experiences—and hence their real-life partners—protected by anonymity. I was quite surprised, however, when a number of these writers of erotic *fiction*—five in all—chose to remain pseudonymous. Their reasons were varied. Since one of the authors regularly writes erotica under a pseudonym, it was logical that she wanted to continue to use the name with which her work has become identified. Another author always uses her great-grandmother's name when she writes feminist material, as a commitment to women's history. I was unprepared, however, for the reasons given by the other three women. One recently received a prestigious scholarship which contains a clause about the acceptable moral behavior of its recipients. She feared the conservative trustees would find her name in this book unacceptable and she would risk losing the award. Another woman is working on her first novel, and while she feels that writing erotica is important and shouldn't have negative associations attached to it, she herself is afraid of a future publisher's response and hence is unwilling at this time to put her name on her piece. And the last, blaming some of her feelings on the fact that she is fifty-eight years old, worries that the people she works with will express disapproval. "I'm afraid certain people will think I'm not the polite, well-brought-up lady they thought I was, and I also worry about embarrassing the organization or hurting their image," she said.

So I suppose that in some ways we're moving ahead a little more slowly than I had hoped. And while the majority of the contributors were glad to receive credit for their writing, the ambivalence some women felt about attaching their names to erotic writing suggests that negative feelings still abound in the culture in regard to open expression of female sexuality.

It should be noted, however, that the three women who were concerned about using their real names were publishing erotic stories for the first time, whereas the women who remained anonymous in *Pleasures* and who had a story accepted in this book as well were *all* willing to sign their pieces this time around. So possibly, as with other areas of sexuality, comfort grows with experience.

Additionally, comfort seemed to grow with experience in the actual writing process. Authors writing erotica for the first time were surprised at the difficulty of the task. One woman talked about how hard it was to think of enough different words to describe the explicit aspects of lovemaking. "I had to send friends out searching for new names for old appendages," she said. Another found it difficult to discover a vocabulary that had not been appropriated by male pornography, or to find a tone that wasn't flippant or phrases that wouldn't make her giggle. Still another said, "While I don't think of myself as prudish, it was hard to write about sexuality so frankly." The twelve women who had previously written stories for *Pleasures* found that the experience of writing those first stories facilitated the writing of the stories for this volume. Almost all these women agreed that writing the erotic passages was easier the second time around. And while one member of this group of twelve felt that there was absolutely no difference between writing a true erotic story and writing a fictional one, the remainder felt otherwise.

In general, the women found that the real experience they chose to write about tended to be so powerful that it virtually wrote itself. For many, the writing of it proved to be a cathartic experience. However, in the fictional pieces, the women were aware of how many decisions had to be made. Structuring the plot was, quite naturally, a more demanding task when invention, rather than reportage, was the basis for the story. As one woman said, "The real experience flowed from the heart, the fictional from the head."

While constrained by reality in the first go-around, some of the women felt overwhelmed with their choices in the second. Some even had a number of different stories going simultaneously before deciding which one to polish and submit. But overall, most authors felt relieved to have the freedom to embellish a real experience or to totally fabricate one from fantasy. Hence, they found the writing of the fictional experience more interesting. As Susan Griffin said, "It freed the artist in me."

A number of women argued for the reality that exists in fiction. According to Signe Hammer, "Fiction is as truthful as anything else, maybe more so." Tee Corinne concurred: "This fiction is more realistic for me than the true-life story because it is more like my own reality, which moves back and forth between fantasy and dreams, the present and past." In many instances, when the fictional story was based in reality, a woman would turn a mixed experience into one with a more unmitigatedly happy ending. One woman said this helped her to work out an unhappy love affair. Another felt that the writing provided her with personal insight. In creating her fantasy relationship she was able to define characteristics that she wanted in a man of which previously she had not been aware. In addition, by analyzing her story she realized the kind of qualities she needed to develop in herself in order to attract the kind of man she was looking for.

But, most important, the women who contributed stories for *Erotic Interludes* enjoyed doing so. One woman called it "a wonderful experience. It's about being out there and not hiding, not holding back any feelings. And it's great to know that this story will be out there turning on all these people. It's like having one massive love affair."

In this spirit, we all hope you enjoy the stories in this anthology. We hope they liven up your day and bring some added joy to your sexuality and your sexual relationship. Have fun with them, share them with a friend. And maybe something new and surprising will come out of it.

I

Adventure and Risk

The theme of adventure and its inherent risks seems to play a central role in creating eroticism in the majority of the stories written by women. The fear of being caught dates back in most people's lives to adolescence, when the accelerated heartbeat that accompanied the newness of sexual exploration was coupled with the fear of parents arriving home unexpectedly, or of a policeman shining a flashlight into the fogged-up windows of a car. Later in life, many people report heightened sex when there is the possibility of being caught, no matter how improbable: making love in a secluded area outdoors, walking into an airplane lavatory to meet a partner, or even making love with one's spouse when overnight guests are down the hallway. In all these cases, the fear or anxiety, while at a very low level, still produces some added adrenaline. This heightened physiological state intensifies the erotic experience.

Adrenaline pumps just as hard in response to emotional risks as it does when physical risks are taken. Whether a relationship is brand-new or decades old, emotional risk-taking can intensify the sexual experience. The risk can range from a feeling as universal as the worry about being judged a bad lover by a new partner, to the kind of psychological vulnerability that takes place when deep feelings are revealed, or when the expression of certain thoughts or emotions leaves one open to rejection.

In "The Private Life of Mrs. Herman," Udana Power writes about a fifteen-year marriage with all the sharing and trust that develop over time. Yet, Mrs. Herman's risk-taking is very real. No matter how secure a relationship may be, a break from the expected always entails the possibility of criticism.

According to Udana, "I've noticed that women who have a lot of sexual energy have a tendency to be categorized as tramps or whores. I wanted to create a woman who is giving and tender, while also highly erotic and willing to lead her man into uncharted worlds of sexuality." So with no encouragement from her husband, Mrs. Herman makes a decision. Instead of taking the sexual energy that has been lying fallow and expressing it with a new and therefore inherently exciting lover, Mrs. Herman steps out of character, and abandoning all inhibitions, opens herself to focus her pent-up sexual energies on her husband. The added potential risk of the possible affair coupled with her husband's nearly discovering it, all blend to create the kind of suspense and intrigue that build high erotic tension.

"The Private Life of Mrs. Herman" also illustrates a wonderful way to keep a long-term relationship from becoming sexually boring or flat. Udana shows that the real thrill is deep intimacy and how that thrill can be rekindled by taking the risk of exposing who you really are and trying something new.

Marilyn Kriegel deals with risk in quite another way within a long, upstanding marriage. For her main character in "Love Letters," the adventure comes in the form of an open sexual relationship. With a secure relationship at home, she is at liberty to travel through Europe with no responsibilities, no expectations, living from moment to moment with total freedom. At the same time, the nonmonogamous agreement she has with her husband pushes the limits of her marriage, thereby creating a tension that heightens the emotional and sexual feelings. Marilyn believes, "Every adventure has potential risk. And it is, in part, the potential danger to the relationship that makes the story so erotic. The relationship is constantly challenged, never taken for granted. There is also the inability of the woman to control her partner, and the inherent danger involved in his sexual liaisons as well, which makes it all the more exciting." Also, "Love Letters" illustrates an enormously useful technique for maintaining the sexual vitality of a relationship when one person travels.

The elements of risk and teasing are developed quite differently by Signe Hammer in "Strangers in the Universe." According to Signe, "Eroticism is a dance of coming together and moving apart. Sometimes you come together and it doesn't work so you move apart and when you risk coming together again, something different happens. It has a sense of teasing."

Her story features a relationship that is not charged with sexual intensity from the start, but is one in which both members of the couple are fearful of their own passion. And Signe creates a tension from this uncertainty. The anticipation and vulnerability of these two people form the basis for a more tender erotica. The risk pays off as we see them begin to come out of their shells and, with some tentative playfulness, start to trust that they will not lose themselves as they grow closer to each other.

Another kind of risk occurs when one person chooses to be completely open with another. In "Games," Grace Zabriskie fashions two people who, unlike the couple in Signe Hammer's story, jump headfirst into a relationship. Both man and woman are willing to explore the unknown together, at the risk of looking silly or weird, and this openness and consequent vulnerability elicits an erotic passion that goes far deeper than the usual initial infatuation. "There is a kind of vulnerability and intimacy that develops when both people can go together to a space they create jointly in fantasy," explains Grace. "This couple trusted each other enough to be able to explore the child in each of them. It is this special place, this exploration and vulnerability, that I find deeply erotic."

In addition, we have the unusual erotic potency that accompanies early sexual or presexual experiences. Often, the eroticism of these experiences creates far more powerful memories than later experiences, regardless of how intense or unique the more recent memories may be in comparison to earlier ones.

Also, the humor and fun that can be a part of sex are an important aspect of "Games." The contrast between passionate sex and light, playful lovemaking creates the kind of continual surprise that adds intensity to the eroticism.

In Kim Chernin's story, "An American in Paris," we experience the adventure and risk inherent in exposing one's infatuation with no assurance that the feelings are mutual. In this story, the erotic builds out of the uncertainty as to whether these two women will transform their friendship into a sexual relationship. Consequently, every gesture, movement, glance takes on a heightened significance, and with each the erotic tension builds. "What I find so erotic," says Kim, "is being attracted to someone and not knowing at all how they feel about me. There is the uncertainty and the knowing that at some point, there will be the risk of total self-disclosure and potential shame and embarrassment."

The degree of risk involved in offering oneself to another is heightened in lesbian relationships. In most heterosexual relationships, both the man and the woman know when the moment for declaring their intentions has arrived. With another woman, however, that moment is less evident. One may not be sure the other is a lesbian, or whether the other considers it only a close platonic friendship, rather than a sexual love affair. The declaration, therefore, becomes a very high moment. Someone has to declare herself if the relationship is to progress in that direction, and this risk creates enormous tension and a real vulnerability that intensifies erotic feelings immeasurably.

Sometimes, however, the adventure and concomitant risk have nothing to do with the real-life acceptance or rejection by the partner but, rather, involve opening oneself to the intimacy and potential hurt of love. In "Berlioz & the Ghetto Blaster," the main character finds her safe and secure little world suddenly called into question. Author Valerie Kelly builds erotic tension by pitting this artist, with her strong resolve to be independent and self-sustaining, against an unlikely macho handyman with a strong, sensitive, thoughtful side. As the main character begins considering even the thought of the possibility of a relationship, we can feel the enormous backlog of passion starting to find its way to the surface.

So much of the eroticism of Kelly's story comes from not knowing if the handyman will be able to break through the woman's barriers. "What is erotic is the romance of it," says Valerie. "I like the idea of someone crashing through the barriers and walls built up for self-protection. Usually it is the man who is locked in and the woman brings him out, but in this story, the man does it and I like this unexpected role reversal. I like the idea of a man who enjoys hot baths, listening to classical music, and surrounding a woman with flowers, yet can still fix a leaky roof, ride a Harley and fight through a storm to get groceries."

In "The House of the Twin Jewels," Gayle Feyrer has created a high-intensity erotic adventure. In an epic fantasy set in another universe, the woman warrior sets out in search of new experience. But the intensity of the experience results as much from an internal adventure—the conflicting desires of lust and love, the dangers of betrayal and of trust—as it does from her exploration of another land.

For Gayle, intensity and contrast create the dynamic of the story and its eroticism: "I find erotic the contrast between the woman warrior and the male slave, the dark against the light, the mixture of sounds, textures and smells of this exotic place. For me the essence of the erotic consists of the emotional intensity that comes from the blending of love and of sex—the meeting of body and spirit." And in her story it is the exploration of the world of self and other, a situation filled with confrontation and turmoil, that heightens its intensity.

Adventure and emotional risk-taking, a sense of being off-balance, a feeling of vulnerability, not knowing for certain where the next step will lead—all create a heightened level of anticipation and excitement that take the erotic and move it to a more intense level. The seven stories in this section have that sense of adventure and its inherent risks, which become inextricably involved in creating the eros.

The Private Life of Mrs. Herman

UDANA POWER

Amy Herman was anxious to get the kids off to school. It was Thursday, and Lilly, eight years old, would be picked up by her grandmother and taken directly from school to ballet class; Mac, ten, would go to swimming class at the Tocaloma Club.

Her nipples hardened under the soft white cotton dressing gown as she thought of the day ahead of her.

The school bus sounded out in front. Lilly and Mac, Jr., gathered their books and ran to the front door, still munching on the toasted waffles.

"Those are my children," she thought, watching them struggle with their backpacks and food as they ran energetically down the front path. They had come from her womb. They had entered the world from between her legs. Oh, God, the thought was unnervingly erotic. She felt her crotch getting wet as a surge of warmth flooded through her body.

Amy had forgotten all these feelings. They had fled illusively away as soon as the kids came and her husband, Mac, Sr., got promoted. Or was it when they got the new house and all those bills? . . . . She couldn't remember. Maybe it was after Lilly came . . . no . . . she was still definitely in touch with all those feelings when Lilly came She would never forget that. Mac had helped her give birth. That old surge of passion and intense love flooded into her pelvis as she remembered the dimly lit room.

Mac had been helping her breathe and push and had been talking intimately into her ear for the entire five hours of intense labor. The memory of that blinding pain had faded over the years, and now all that seemed important was the memory of Mac's voice saying softly, "Come on, sweetheart . . . yes, darling . . . Oh yeah, you're doing great, honey."

His voice had filled her whole consciousness, flooding her chest, and seemed to move inside her womb to help push little Lilly out into the world. Amy didn't realize how hard she had been gripping Mac's large hand and what strength he had been pouring into her until it was over. As the pain subsided, Amy loosened her grip, and Mac, with the help of the midwife, picked up their tiny daughter and laid her on Amy's stomach.

"Oh, my God," thought Amy, exhausted, as she watched the small glistening creature that was her daughter struggle to claim her place in this new world on her mother's tummy. Almost faint with fatigue, Amy reached down to the infant and gently guided it up her belly to her waiting breast. As the infant's mouth reached the brown nipple and started sucking, Amy felt a surge of tingling heat flood from her breast to her vagina. Astonished, she looked up into Mac's face . . . it was wet with tears and helpless with love. One hand on her shoulder, the other protectively on her hip, Mac was in awe of the miracle of his wife and new baby.

"Mac . . . oh, darling . . ." She struggled to stay awake.

As he leaned in closer to hear, she felt the strength of his male energy pouring off his muscular body. Its nearness soothed and comforted her.

"My darling Mac . . ." she whispered, as the baby sucked deeper on her tit, making her feel wanted and needed by existence itself. "I think I'm going to come. . . ."

And Mac knew what to do. He moved his head in closer and, surrounding his nursing wife and child with his left arm, he moved his right hand to cover her crotch . . . that exquisite entrance to eternity that he had been lost in so many times.

Amy groaned with pleasure as his large hand cupped her gently and his third finger felt delicately inside the swollen folds of her passion flower. It came to rest on the one sweet spot he knew so well.

As he touched it she felt an electric current flow from his hand into her. His energy swirled inside her till the whole universe seemed to start spinning around.

"Ohhh . . ." she cried weakly as the orgasm began to overtake her.

Seeing her start to go over the edge into ecstasy, he delicately vibrated his finger on her clit the way he knew she loved, and pressed his own erect cock against the side of the bed.

She felt it come up from the base of her spine. It was as though a door opened and allowed all of life to surge through her. The spinning sensation rose up and flooded her whole body, pushing at the boundaries of who she thought she was . . . pressing . . . pressing . . . pressing . . . Finally, unable to hold the energy back any longer, she let it explode through every cell in her body, cleansing her with light and pulsating out into the room. Her child . . . Her husband . . . Here in her arms . . . The happiness was so great she thought her heart would break with it. For a moment she knew what rapture was. Then everything faded to a comfortable black.

Standing at the doorway watching the kids rush off, Amy wondered at those memories. The magic of all that sex and love. Where had it gone? Why was it coming back just now? And with another man?

"Hey, honey," Mac called as he bounded noisily down the stairs like the ex-football player he was and headed for the kitchen. "What's for breakfast?"

He never really cared what he ate for breakfast, he just liked to make a loud entrance. High-spirited and somewhat thoughtless, it was his way of revving himself up for the corporate wars he headed into every morning.

The corners of Amy's mouth curled up irresistibly as she thought of this crazy man she had married. He was strong as a bull, loud, caring and steady. A little overweight, yet still hard as a rock. Sometimes boring. Sometimes intrusive. Always there for her and the kids. And lately so engrossed in all that male-competition crap that an invitation to sex became: "Hey, honey, how'd ja like a big Mac?"

" 'Big Mac,' my ass," she thought, wondering why she was grinning. A flicker of warmth surged into her cunt. She laughed out loud to herself as she closed the front door and headed back to the kitchen.

Glancing at herself in the hall mirror, she saw a pretty woman with thick brown hair that fell loosely around her shoulders. Her blue eyes sparkled with intelligence, and her round face, which she had never liked when she was young, now seemed to keep her looking eternally youthful. She grinned at herself in the mirror, realizing that she was finally willing to accept that she didn't look like a model, would never be perfect, and so what? She was an attractive woman in her prime, and for the first time in years her passions were flowing again, all because of Christopher, the young karate instructor at Mac, Jr.'s, school.

She didn't know him well, but whenever she went to pick up her son from karate, the energy between them crackled. She had taken to getting there early. He had taken to teaching with his shirt off. One thing led to another. A phone call. A flirtatious invitation. An invented meeting at her house today which they both knew would end up with making love. She felt nervous, exhilarated, worried, happy, totally turned on by it all and downright scared.

Mac hadn't really noticed her in years. She had lost weight, let her thick brown hair grow, wore sexy leotards around the house, short-shorts in the backyard and nothing at all in bed, but for some reason Mac seemed immune to her subtle invitations and very real needs. By this time Amy definitely had no qualms about getting her needs met by a nineteen-year-old boy with a gorgeous body. This little affair certainly wasn't going to break up her marriage.

As she walked through the dining room she felt the soft folds of the light eyelet-embroidered cotton move gently against her skin. It felt seductive and earthy. Oh, how she longed to make love right now, to feel the smooth head of an engorged penis playing tantalizingly around the wet mouth between her legs.

But Mac was always so busy and preoccupied, especially in the morning. "He might reject me. Make me feel silly . . ." she thought tentatively.

But *this* morning the kids were gone and she had a lover coming at ten-thirty. She felt like starting her foreplay now, at eight forty-five, with her husband. Who was *he* to tell her what to do with her own sexuality? If he rejected her, so what? She had a backup at ten-thirty. She definitely had no intention of moping around today feeling bad about her eroticism.

"As a matter of fact," she decided, "If Mac gets turned on, I'm not going to let him come. I'll just let him feel what it's like to be 'left undone.' "

She smirked her own secret little grin and undid the sash that held the little cotton cover-up together in front. It fell loosely open to reveal her molded tummy and the soft mound of fur where her legs joined. Oh, the sweetness of that gentle ache in her vagina as it longed for a cock inside . . . she intended to enjoy that sweetness, to extend it, to savor it. Let Mac know it was *hers*. "I'm a woman," she thought to herself as she stopped in the doorway of the kitchen. "I'm thirty-six. Sexual, loving and erotic, dirty and fuckable. All this energy is mine. If I don't enjoy it now, then when?"

Putting her hands on the doorjamb, she looked at Mac; his

stocky body was bent over, his head in the refrigerator. She let her cotton robe open a little more to expose her left nipple and the full length of her left thigh and leg. She was glad her body felt so tight and slim from all those aerobics. Mac hadn't really noticed except to grunt once in a while. This morning he would notice.

"Morning, sweetheart."

"Hi," he mumbled, not looking up as he moved aside the ketchup bottle, then pulled out last night's casserole and put it on the ledge next to the fridge with the milk and butter. She almost asked him what he was looking for, but decided not to engage in his morning routine of finding this and that . . . she resolved to stay with her own delicious feelings.

Surprised at her silence, he glanced up at her, then back into the fridge and said, "Have you seen the Reddi-Wip? It was here last night."

She moved up next to him and silently knelt down beside him. Opening the vegetable drawer, she reached behind the lettuce. "I was hiding it from the kids."

She held it out to him in a seductively mocking way. He absently gave her a quick kiss on the forehead, stood up and went over to the table, joking, "Good thinking, honey. All the more for me!"

And with that he grinned happily and squirted an enormous blob of whipped cream into his cup of hot coffee.

"Mmmmm . . . perfect," he groaned, lifting it to his lips.

Amy stood up and calmly closed the refrigerator door, assessing what her next move would be, then turned to her husband and just watched. He looked like a big kid with his head buried in the paper and a white point of whipped cream on the end of his nose.

Her nipples got hard again as she let her gaze fall down to his muscular neck and shoulders. He still had strong arms and massive hands. She began to enjoy looking at him as though he were new, not the man she had married, not the man she cleaned up after, not the man who worried about finances and investments and corporate strategies and braces for the children. No, this morning Mac was just a man with sandy hair and a broad face full of life that somehow managed to be handsome even though his nose was thick from being broken several times. And he still had a raw maleness about him, even behind that fancy shirt and tie. And she felt like pure woman. Powerful. Seductive. Juicy. And willing to let it all out.

The phone rang. She had no intention of answering it. Mac glanced up. "Telephone, honey . . ."

She nodded and smiled, saying, "Yes, I know . . ." and didn't make the slightest move for it. Instead she lifted her left foot and let her toes rest lightly on the edge of the kitchen table, holding her left leg high. The little cotton dressing gown fell open completely, revealing two small round breasts with hard brown nipples, a lovely torso that molded into a small waist and then flared out again to accommodate her generous hips and a thatch of brown curly hair that stood guard over a red and purple passion flower between her legs.

The phone rang again. She didn't move, just gazed steadily at Mac. He looked up; the Reddi-Wip on his nose made him look ridiculous. She couldn't help but giggle . . . while she just stood there exposing the whole of her womanhood.

Mac's jaw dropped. He couldn't even say, "Honey . . ."

The phone rang again. He stood up to get it, bumping the table, almost overturning the chair and all the while unable to take his eyes off his wife. Staring at her, he groped for the receiver, picked it up and said, "Hello," into the phone.

Amy's heart was pounding with fear and excitement. She had never done anything like this before. What if Mac got mad? Totally ignoring her fears and who the phone call might be from, she let her left fingers trace delicate circles around her left nipple. It got harder as gooseflesh arose and she felt soft melting energy warm her insides.

Then she let her hands start roaming over both breasts while her mouth instinctively opened just enough to allow her tongue to play delicately in the air around her lips.

"Where's Amy?" she heard Mac repeat to whoever was on the phone. He looked at her pleadingly, in utter confusion. It was the first time she had ever seen him not know what to do. It didn't occur to her to help him. She was having a wonderful time exploring herself.

Desire had softened her face and was causing her hips to move gently. She let her right fingers come up to play with the wet saliva on her tongue while her left fingers traced light circles along the insides of her thighs and softly over the furry patch of dark hair. Warm currents of electricity seemed to spark up from the base of her spine and vibrate gently all over her body. It felt free and good to be playing with herself in front of her husband, especially while he was caught in a phone conversation. She felt a surge of power when she realized how totally distracted she was making him.

"Amy?" he repeated into the phone. "Oh, yeah, she's here somewhere." He continued staring helplessly at her like a man stunned. Pretending to call to the other room, he shouted, "Amy?" and then just stared blankly at her, waiting for some kind of signal.

Amy took her two wet fingers and brought them down between her wide-open legs. The left leg on the table gave her a chance to support her whole body and yet tip her hips up enough so that he could clearly see all she was doing.

Opening the folds of her labia, she let her right fingers slip gently into the wetness between the inner folds of her pussy. Oh, God, that felt wonderful. Wet and warm. She spread the folds out so that Mac could see the beautiful redness, all swollen with passion.

Dumfounded, he brought the phone back up to his ear and said, "I don't know where she is. She can't come to the phone right now. Call later."

He groped to hang the receiver back up, finally found the cradle and clicked the phone back in place.

"Stay there," she commanded hoarsely before he could move toward her.

She didn't want him to touch her. Not yet. Only to look. She felt so pretty. So sensual. So happy and free. Like a living work of art.

She could see the bulge rising in his pants as she continued to spread the wetness around the opening of her vagina. The phone rang again. She paid no attention. He couldn't decide whether to answer it or not. He instinctively cupped his hard cock with his right hand as he watched her start vibrating her fingers inside her cunt. He groaned involuntarily, picked up the receiver, said, "Call back later," and hung up.

He turned to Amy. His voice broke as he whispered almost politely, "What are you doing?"

"I'm ruining your breakfast," she teased softly.

"Oh, no . . . yes . . . I mean . . . Oh, God, Amy . . . what are you doing?"

"I'm making love to you," she whispered huskily, then let her hand push two fingers up into her vagina. Her hips tilted up involuntarily and she felt like her legs were going to melt. Her head rolled back as her eyes closed and she groaned with pleasure.

"Oh, God," repeated Mac again, aching to move over to her, yet unwilling to go against her command for fear she would stop. He quickly unzipped his pants and, letting them fall over his hips, held his strong, hard cock with his right hand. His eyes stayed glued on Amy.

She lazily opened her eyes to see Mac slowly massaging his penis up and down. Little spurts of milky fluid were moistening the head of it.

Her heart skipped a beat. She felt so vulnerable and so incredibly erotic watching him masturbate as he gazed at her. His face was filled with wonder, fascination, love, sex and her. She loved to see his passion this way. His maleness. In the twelve years of their marriage she had never seen the heat of his desire so clearly.

And he loved her. That was clear. He loved her.

"Oh . . . Mac . . ." she cried as her legs started to buckle underneath her. "Oh Mac, I'm going to come."

Her eyes closed as she felt energy melt up from her cunt into her breasts and up through her throat. As a husky cry escaped from her lips she felt his strong hands holding her torso, supporting her back. He was always there for her.

Opening her eyes she saw the raw intensity of his need flashing in his green eyes just before his lips met hers.

His lips were filled with hunger and love. As soon as they touched hers, she felt a bolt of electricity enter into her like a shock. A thrill swept through her as his large hand pressed her pelvis against his. She seemed to be melting into him.

Dizzy, she felt like she was being flung off a great cliff into ecstasy. "I'm in love with this man," was all she could think as she abandoned herself to his hot kisses.

He was all over her . . . needing her . . . wanting her, and gently laying her back down on the kitchen table. Her legs dangled to the floor, surrendering the wet place between her legs to him.

He pressed two fingers gently into her vagina, causing her to arch back and groan. Then she felt the smooth head of his cock pressing gently on the sensitive folds just at the mouth of her vagina. She could feel the intensity of his need on the tip of his cock. Every time it touched her clit a magical spasm thrilled through her. Then he pressed his cock inside her just a little, then pulled it out again. As he pressed it in and out again, everything else in the world disappeared. Children. Telephones. Kitchen tables. They were male and female energies fusing, suspended somewhere in eternity, as he thrust his hard cock deeper and deeper to her center.

The passion exploded in her heart first and overwhelmed her with hot tears of love and joy. The heat swept to her genitals and exploded again in another burst of energy.

"Ahhhh . . ." she heard him groan as he felt the impact of her orgasm on his pulsating penis deep inside her body.

She felt his hands holding her torso steady as he thrust his cock into her again and again. His whole being seemed to move deeper and deeper into hers until she couldn't tell where her body stopped and his body began. Then she felt something she had never felt before. It was as if his orgasm leapt out of his body into hers.

He cried out as it poured out of him, filling her with large currents of energy. They were melting together. There was nothing else in the world. Not him. Not her. Only this incredibly sweet orgasmic blending. He cried out again as he pushed deeper into the center of her warmth and love.

The walls of her vagina seemed to suck at his cock, gripping and kneading, pulling it deeper and deeper into her. Magic sparks seemed to explode from the tip, melting her heart, melting her soul. Another orgasm leapt up from inside her groin, flooding throughout her body. His body shuddered as he felt it pour through her.

They were both helpless as the waves of energy rippled through them again and again, fusing them together into one blazing light of love and sex, then tossing them out into the infinite.

He sank his torso over hers and held her close as his chest shook and heaved. Putting her arms around his strong back, she held him close as his tears flowed hot and free. She felt as if she were tucking his heart somewhere inside her soul. This man was home. His arms, his cock, everything about him was, for her, the center of the universe. Forever and ever. This was all she ever needed to know about God.

They stayed there for a long time. Her back on the kitchen table with her legs dangling over the side, his cock inside her and his chest bent over hers with his arms around her—protecting her fragileness from the world.

They didn't move. She felt what she could only describe as her spirit spinning somewhere with his. It was as if they were both floating outside time and space in a peacefulness that didn't exist on earth.

They remained fused like that till the phone started ringing again. Mac rose up and gently took her radiant, tear-stained face in his large hands and kissed her again and again. Then slowly, ever so slowly, he began to disengage his energies from hers as he pulled his penis gently out of her body.

She wondered at the miracle of it all. The phone was ringing in some distant world she was only slowly coming back to.

She heard Mac say, "Let me take a message . . ." and she knew she didn't have to think just yet. She could take her time coming back to this planet, this reality, this time and space.

She gently raised herself up onto her hands. Her cotton housecoat was falling loosely at her sides. She looked at the face and sweaty shirt and soft penis of this man in her kitchen talking on the phone in some distant language. His eyes were on her. His face was filled with sweetness. Totally unguarded. All she saw was his love for her. He hung up the phone and moved back to the table to hold her.

She felt his strong arms surround her and pull her close to his chest.

"That was Christopher Somebody . . . Mac's karate teacher. Something about canceling the ten-thirty class . . . You know what that means?"

Amy grinned as she held him tight, letting her face press into his sweaty shirt, leaving makeup and mascara all over, and said, "Yes. I know what it means."

Looping her legs around him, she pulled him closer and said, "It means you definitely can't go to the office like this. We have to turn off the phone and take a bath together. Maybe you'll get there by twelve. Maybe not at all . . ."

Mac picked her up in his arms and, holding her close to his chest, said softly, "I like the 'Maybe not at all' . . ." then carried her upstairs.

And together they spent the day discovering each other anew and anew and anew . . .

Love Letters

MARILYN HARRIS KRIEGEL

To Be Opened the Evening of May 29.

Dearest L.,

I will have left by now. First to Chicago, then to Amsterdam. By the time you read this I will be in Holland and though you will just be getting ready for bed, I will be starting a new day.

Whenever we are about to separate, in spite of our long history, I begin to drift toward mild paranoia. I conjure up women lurking in shadows, just waiting my departure to crawl into your bed. You do not resist them. And I, of course, would not want you to.

This time, my love, I began to plot ways to ensure that whoever we were loving during this time of separation, we would also spend time loving each other. I have come upon a brilliant idea.

Instead of dutifully written postcards scrawled hastily between adventures, we can share these letters, copies of which I have taken with me. They will remind you of my love. And, when I read them, from time to time, from place to place, they will excite and delight me as well.

Like our passion, these love letters must have their own rhythm. There is not one for every night. Open yours evenings when you wish to be aroused and your curiosity overwhelms you. Perhaps you will fall asleep with my spirit wrapped around your soul.

My own copies, I will open in the morning. Some of my days will begin with the taste and smell of you in my heart. Maybe at times we will read these letters at the same moment, like those outrageous occasions when unexpectedly, as if by chance, our bodies fly together and we come as one.

Knowing that we will share these love letters has already given me great pleasure. And if you reflect back to our shared passions the month before I left, you will understand how writing them gave pleasure to us both!

Dear L.,

Will I miss you? Will you miss me? Remember when we first confessed that we didn't "miss" one another when we were traveling? How frightening it was to admit that most of the time we are apart we are happily engaged in our own experience. Knowing our love can include these separations has given a special excitement and made us free to journey through the world without guilt or recrimination.

Now I am away, no rules to follow, traveling uncensored. Ready to discover, I am myself like uncharted territory, a map of possibilities.

Walking down strange streets I wait to explore and be explored, and yet I find myself thinking that I never look more sexy or desirable than when we have just made love. Men and women admire my fullness then. They are charmed by the sparkle in my eyes, by the hidden wetness so recently deposited between my thighs. I know that when I read these letters on the road they will engender the same radiance in my eyes. I will be exploring the world, and the world will know I am loved.

Dear L.,

One hardly needs to travel to find passion and romance. Last week I was in town shopping and I met a man who took my breath away. He was so beautiful. I would have been content to stare, but he flirted with me. He was quite good. Long penetrating looks, kind of soulful with just a bit of a twinkle. I was instantly a teenager again. I could hardly speak in his presence. I loved the way I felt. The world seemed dangerous and full of possibilities. I felt vaguely stupid and inadequate in the presence of my own lust. He was with his wife. (I wondered how they handled situations like this.)

Driving home, the freeway seemed to me like one giant singles bar. I flirted with every driver I passed. Old ladies, teenagers, gay guys, gorgeous women, and bless them all, the truck drivers. Driving over the bridge was ecstasy. My cunt all atwitter, beating steadily with the sound of my heart.

Gently I placed my fingertips in my blouse and played with my nipples. I turned onto the small road and continued up into the hills, through the wildflowers. What an outrageous spring this has been, I thought, with the hills more lupine blue than green. Pulling into the car deck, I was greeted by the black curliness of Monty Wool, wagging and jumping as if she could tell how ripe I was, her nose searching for evidence of my afternoon's activities.

The ocean, pounding against the sand, sounded as if it were breathing close to my ear, and the smells of the sweaty kids, huddled by the television, their adolescent perfumes of popcorn and baseball leather, seemed absolutely decadent.

I fell into our bed. The earth seemed to sigh as I touched myself through the wetness of my clothes. Coming mingled with laughter and joy. And I sank into a light blissful dream before dinner.

Pleasure comes in such unexpected ways. I wonder where we will find our delight over the next month. What adventures will we have to talk about? And when you see me what secrets will I have to tell?

Dearest One,

I think of you climbing into our rumpled bed. I can smell the sheets, musky against the salt air. And I imagine your body, golden in the lamplight. On summer nights you look like a hero in a Renaissance painting. Your muscles, like gilded mountains, slope gently into soft valleys. Your pastoral valleys contain the secret curves into which I love to curl and hide my body. The dark places into which I dare sneak my toes for warmth, the slightly wet corners, where your knees bend and your arms curve—all are part of the landscape for my love.

How fortunate I am, that I can simply lie by your side and stare at the glow which is you, which is my lover. My friend. I will dream of your warmth and the familiarity of your body, the safe place you have made for my lust, my love, and my laughter.

Dear L.,

I will think of you at the beach house being lulled to sleep by the foghorns. When it is foggy, when the moon is deeply hidden and the lights from the city, distant reminders of the civilization that surrounds us, cannot be seen—it is at these times that I make love to you with my ears. Each time a foghorn blows, its sound, the long low moan, is carried deep inside me. When we are making love, when the light is gone and only our breathing and our touch guide us, the foghorn plays through my body, showing me all the untouched places for our passion to expand into and fill.

Sometimes I imagine that we are adrift and lost at sea. I pretend that only the sound of the horns keeps us from crashing into the rocks, and our lovemaking seems perilous and fraught with danger. I hold you tighter. I stretch my legs and arms around your body to enfold you. You can only move with me as one. My legs grow flexible and long, my arms become strong around your back. The foghorn moans, this time a reminder of life's sharp edges. And we, reckless and wanton, fuck in the presence of disaster. Later, cooled by the moist air, lying side by side, as if washed up by the tide, the fog making each sound of the waves louder than ever before, we sleep. Those nights awakened abruptly by the cold's having crept into our bones, we crawl beneath the quilt, vulnerable and grateful to be alive.

No matter where I am, the fog, moisture in the air, in my hair, on my face and on my fingertips will remind me of our sea-swept love.

Dear One,

Sleep on my side of the bed tonight. If it is clear, look up through the triangle window over the door. Down in the lower corner is a bright star. I do not know her name, but she watches us night after night. She is there every spring and remains through summer. It is strange to be watched so carefully and faithfully, year after year. She has watched us fight and attempt to pull apart. But have we ever made it through a whole night without one of us reaching out? I think she knows how deeply we love each other. When you are on top of me I see her over your shoulder. She twinkles.

Sometimes she reminds me to make love. I go to bed tired and empty and glad not to be touched and then there she is. "Oh, fuck him—go ahead." She is quite a lascivious star. Her magnitude increases with our quickening breath.

Try it. Make love to yourself and dream of me. As your cock begins to throb, watch her. See her grow in brightness. And please, love, thank her for both of us.

Dearest L.,

Look on the top shelf over the bed, there is a bottle of wonderful coconut oil. It smells of the tropics—hibiscus flowers—and warmth. I brought some with me. Imagine me opening my small jar of oil and massaging my breasts. Both nipples standing firm, I can picture your hand on your cock . . . hard and smelling of the same sweetness that will fill my nose. I will not wait long before I spread this fragrance to my wet cunt. If I am very quiet and focus carefully I can feel you inside of me, moving softly, gently, silkily until I come to your song, my toes spreading in ecstasy and release.

Hello My Love,

And good evening to your feet! You have the widest feet, shaped more like mysterious continents than feet. I love your feet. I especially like running the top of my foot along the bottom of yours. Either foot. Your feet are always warm. I don't understand what miraculous chemistry could have produced such warm feet . . . what wondrous circulation. I love your feet. I also love curling up against you and carefully tucking my feet into your crotch and holding your warm cock between them.

I love that when one of us comes to bed late after the other it is our feet that say hello. Even out of a deep sleep they reach for each other. "I'm here." "Glad to feel you." I think we don't love your feet enough. I will bring you something wonderful for them. I will search for some lovely gift for your feet.

Dear L.,

Remember before I left how much we had been talking about asses? I delight in your hands cupping my ass and holding me tight. I think it must date back to those first dances when someone was brave enough to hold my ass and all my repressed and untouched sexuality poured forth. Having my ass held is like being sixteen and ripe. I think one of the first men to hold my ass was my date for my senior prom. He was a guy named Allen and I met him at a Princeton mixer. I never saw him again. I don't remember his last name. But I do remember how he held my ass. We should thank him.

We should also thank some guy I met at the Y on a Wednesday night in '54, who tried to get me to hold his cock in the parking lot of the White Castle. I managed to fight him off, but in the process I touched his hard—oh my it was exciting—cock. That fight, the terrible rift between my curiosity and desire on one hand and my parents' and society's values on the other, have made holding your penis a sweet delight and a continual victory!!!

It is perhaps revealing of the true nature of the universe that every man I have known has added to our pleasure. And my dear you must wait for my return to reap the benefits of this trip.

Dear L.,

I have been thinking about foreplay. I have wondered if reading these letters might not be the foreplay for some yet to be discovered joy, the exact, right gesture to open us up to love that might have otherwise remained hidden and unrecognized.

Foreplay.

Our hike to Steep Ravine. The hot day, the arduous walk up the coastal trail and then the descent into the cool lushness of the creek, the ferns, the redwoods. Walking slowly for hours we become one in spirit. It is our bodies' longing for the same closeness as our souls that catapults us into each other's arms at the end of the day, even when our legs ache for rest.

Foreplay.

Breaking for lunch. Hearing about your morning's work. Sharing our doubts and fears as we indulge ourselves in your latest pasta creation. Laughing about how miraculous it is that we are able to live and do the work that turns us on. Turns us on. Our work becoming a source for our lovemaking.

Foreplay.

Sitting down to make the schedule for the week. The grocery

list, Little League games, who will cook and who will clean and who will get the mail and take the car in to be fixed. And oh, yes, I'll do the laundry and in the middle of the mundane events of our life, folding your yellowed T-shirts and pairing up your socks, my juices flow, my heart beats more rapidly and I know we are likely to make love again soon.

Foreplay.

As you read this letter I am slipping and sliding around Europe, imagining your support for my adventures and whimsy, for my work and my play and the freedom we give each other. Freedom: It is a rare form of foreplay. I love being your mate. I love being able to turn you on across these great distances.

Dear One,

On the morning I read this I am going to think of you and make myself come. I am going to regale my body from top to toe. And then, I am going to continue this good sex out into the world. It is a game we've never talked about. I love to play it: Fucking the world. Orgasm around town. Here are the two rules.

1. Make sure to feel everyone you touch. The waitress at breakfast, the butcher when he hands you change, your friend at lunch when you shake hands hello. They don't need to know you are fucking them. (Though the wisest and most aware will find a way to let you know that they know.) Just feel them, fully, completely, into your fingers and up through your ears and down into your groin, your feet, toes curling. Then just say, "How do you do?" "Just fine, thank you." It's like answering the phone while continuing to make love!

2. Assume all conversation is either foreplay or happening right after orgasm. There can be no other choices. Now listen to your voice soften. Mine becomes guttural and my mouth, with an excess of saliva, makes my lips wet. Conversations become much more interesting, encounters grow more significant if everyone is about to be or just was your lover. When I return I look forward

to hearing about how you played this game. You, who play games so well, should have some interesting tales to tell.

Dear L.,

New cities entice me. New foods excite me. New people thrill me. New beds, their smells and feel, arouse me. Can you stand it? Think of me, my darling, opening, pulsating, becoming mistress to a thousand new sounds and tastes.

What great new mysteries will I reveal to you when I return? What wisdom will I bring home? What will I have learned? Perhaps only a new dance. And, my darling, will you dance it with me?

My lover,

What miracle has worked within us? What magic has allowed us to maintain the fire when so many others have burned out?

Remember when we first met? The electric charge was so great, the memory is permanently fixed in my mind. I see the picture clearly. There we are approaching from different directions. We are introduced. We both smile, shake hands. Just one moment. One handshake. I remember looking at my hand, wondering, "What was that"? That hello like no other hello in my life.

I love remembering the passion that engulfed us. It was as if the chocolate we rubbed over our bodies to be sucked and licked off was to mask the devouring lust we shared. You were my food. My drink. My breath. Filling my mouth with chocolate with your tongue. Eating it after it was softened by your juices. What extraordinary cuisine. You breathed hard into my mouth, the air I gasped for. I melted, trusting you to breathe for me, and then not able to tell whose breath sustained which body as this single being rose to shower and wash its many legs and ears and mouths. One.

We entered each other's life as if all else ceased to exist. Only this monolithic creature, arisen from a bed of chocolate, finding its way in the world. Chocolate. Only a tiny bit of it and those ancient memories flood back. And, my darling, in my top dresser drawer there's a small package with your name on it. Enjoy it, I'll bring more home with me.

Dear L.,

The last envelope. Soon I will be home with you. Our coming together after so long apart is always filled with danger. Will you still love me? Will I, you? Or will we in our freedom have found some secret that must inevitably put an end to this union? It is the fear and uncertainty that has always made these reunions feel like first dates. Perhaps it is the same freedom that keeps us so new. We will be vulnerable again, when next we meet.

I have made a reservation for us at a great hotel. I'll have the wine with me. There is a small box wrapped in silver paper on my closet floor behind my shoes. Please bring it with you, it is a gift I prepared for us before I left. And so my darling soon we shall see.

As ever, T.

Strangers in the Universe

SIGNE HAMMER

It was raining when we drove down to the Cape, the afternoon already dark. Inside, the Corvette was a small cave full of shifting lights and reflections. Sandy drove hunched over the wheel, his long legs angled out at the knees even with the seat pushed back to its limit. I had my hand on his thigh, my arm across the black stick of the floor shift. When he reached to shift, I withdrew my hand.

We were driving into a neutral space, our first time together in a place that wasn't my apartment in the city or his little house on the side of a Vermont mountain. We carried with us nothing but a change of clothes, several bottles of wine, various groceries and a frozen duck. Held in the twin laps of the Corvette's bucket seats, peering out at the dim, blurred path of the headlights, decorously separated by the gearshift, we were suddenly travelers, innocent of context or history, drawn together against the dark outside, but secretly a little apprehensive of what we might find when we got to our destination.

The little house looked blind and still beyond the heaving windshield wipers. It belonged to nobody in particular, a cousin who seldom used it, and there was some context: Sandy had agreed to look after the roof and the gutters, and keep the pipes from freezing. We trekked inside with our bags and sacks, smelled the musty carpets, looked at the pine paneling and the twin beds. I decided to open a bottle of wine.

"I laid in some firewood," Sandy said, and went down cellar to get it. I heard the thump and clatter of a log rolling off his pile as he came back up, stamping; the wood dripped chips and leaf bits across the carpet to the Franklin stove, then thunked solidly in and burned hard. It was last winter's wood, cut when the sap was down, and weathered in the cord just visible through the kitchen window.

Sandy reached over me to take his glass of wine from the counter, ducking his head for a brief nuzzle, his beard tickling along my cheek. I wanted to lay my hand against his beard and cheek, but shyness suddenly held me. I could feel the ugly, anonymous little kitchen opening out between us, separating us, negating all the ways we had found, slowly and painfully over the last couple of months, to approach each other.

The first night in my apartment, Sandy had sat, furious and ashamed, on the edge of my bed, so skewered by self-consciousness that he could not bridge the gap between our bodies. So I got up and cooked, and we sat on my couch and ate chicken with our fingers and talked, and I reassured him, amazed and awed by impotence brought on by terror of love, rather than by dope or alcohol or fatigue. Then, when he could come on, I in my own sharp fear had tightened up so much he could not get inside, and we had another meal and he comforted me, and finally by dint of all this we got familiar. But we had familiar places to do it in.

It is hard to come together in your own skins. Everyone contains so many familiar ways of being or not being with other people that when a new one comes along it is a shock. It's as if we are trapped and exhausted by all those other people trooping through our dreams. We need a simple routine of dailiness with someone new to distract us from the fact that we are naked, until our ways of being together merge with the others, with his two marriages and my last failed love, with his records that we listen to and my books that he reads or ignores, so that landmarks we have never seen before seem familiar, and we can make it across the sudden, shifty little gulf that yawns between us, sliding into the future on the strength of the past.

But sometimes we get stuck. The simple present opens out to unimaginable depths; there are no landmarks and no boundaries, nothing to grip in the dark. And yet we float.

Sandy stretched out in the wooden rocker near the stove, and I curled up in the corner of the couch, and we drank our wine and listened to the fire pop and the wind whistle, and after a while Sandy got up and went into the bedroom, and I could hear him pushing the beds together. He came out and stood in the bedroom doorway, and I got up and went to him, standing with my breasts just touching his belly and his chin resting lightly on my head. He put his arms around me, and we went in and made love. Everything functioned, but tentatively and at a distance, he sliding into me as if exploring a new cave, feeling his way, listening for falling rocks or echoes or the drip of water. I felt myself opening grudgingly, just enough; I was acutely aware of the rain clattering on the dark windowpane next to the bed, the awful green of the walls, and the narrow trough between the mattresses that could widen and dump us on the floor if we rolled into it; I felt the need to keep equilibrium for both of us on the narrow bed, and I breathed calmly.

In the morning, Sandy went up on the roof to see whether any shingles had loosened in the storm, and I went out to the marsh to gather cattails and grasses for a fall bouquet. The land was mauve and buff under a slate-gray sky. I looked back at Sandy as he kneeled near the ridgepole to check out the top shingles and then backed carefully down the wind-dried slate and stood on the ladder to pull leaves from the drain-spout trap. I gathered my grasses, seeing no birds but seagulls and wheeling crows. The marsh path was muddy on top, from the rain, but still frozen and crunchy underneath. The next time I looked up, Sandy had disappeared, down the ladder or on the other side of the roof. The ladder leaning against the gutter made the house look desolate. Then smoke wisped up from the chimney; it made me suddenly feel the cold, and I started back. As I climbed the slope toward the house, the smoke grew to a steady stream, and I could see flashes of movement through the kitchen window.

Sandy was taking lunch out of the broiler: open-face sandwiches piled with cheese and split hot dogs and tomatoes and pickles, with mustard in between layers. For a tall man, his movements were soft and deft; he was narrow, and light on his feet.

He slipped the last sandwich from the spatula to its plate and turned around as I came in the door. "This will take the chill off your insides," he said. The sight of him standing there with the spatula in his hand made me feel suddenly faint, and I stood still, foolishly, staring at him. His beard was going iron gray at the corners, and his sloping shoulders, made worse by the tall man's lifelong habit of hunching over to talk to ordinary-sized people, made him look very fond and familiar.

He took two steps across the kitchen and suddenly his breath was on my forehead, and his long arms were draped around my shoulders. I closed my eyes, my own arms hanging limp at my sides, and we stood there while the sandwiches got cold, touching along our fronts so tenderly I could hardly breathe. In the stillness, my nipples came up into tiny pressure points that sent electric shocks into my brain every time he breathed. He brushed his lips across my forehead, settling on each eyelid so softly and quick that the only sign was a tiny answering reverberation, the barest tickle in my vulva. It was enough; in my brain, neurons were signaling like mad, sending transmitters speeding across synapses, cell membranes opening up to signal my whole body, urgently, to open as well.

My arms went around him, and I stepped into his front, feeling his penis, his pressure point, respond. He tightened his arms, sending a jolt from my nipples that caused me to stand on tiptoe and try to mount the bulge in his pants. My face came up and we kissed, hard, and then pulled back. Left alone, our bodies would have gone on without us, but we needed to find out where we were. We both took lips to be the token of trust, or not; if they made a connection, in pressure and withdrawal, in light touch and full press and quick little beating pats, they became the medium for linking up mind and body more surely than words. I believed a woman could tell, within a single kiss, whether a man would respond to her body or merely impose himself on it; whether he would be light, dry, and deft; tense, hard, and blind; or, worst of all, thick, slack, damp, and oblivious.

Sandy's mouth had come alive on mine the first time we kissed, although it was against his better judgment. He was in the middle of a divorce, and wary of women. I had a history of miserable failures with men. Perhaps all that was why it was so hard for us to get beyond the beginning; and why, even then, each time we began to make love our first kiss was like that of lovers meeting after a long separation; a shock of recognition and then a question: *Are you still there?*

Gradually, we found we were. The tiny kitchen with its cheap knotty-pine cabinets and dimestore formica counter warmed up, the chilly landscape receded, and our bodies began to feel familiar again. I found the edges of myself in the hard flat planes of Sandy's ribs and hips. And then we were in the bedroom, stripping off the absurd chenille bedspreads, pulling down the blankets and top sheets. Sandy pushed gently until I sat down on the edge of a bed, and he kneeled in front of me. He began to roll my sweater up around my ribs while I sat, mute, only raising my arms for him to pull it up and off. He kissed my nose, then looked at me with eyes gone perfectly transparent, so that I saw myself in them. He bent to unbutton my shirt. He proceeded with gravity and delicacy, opening one button and carefully spreading my shirt open to the next one. I felt a stillness spreading out from the tension point at my center of gravity, as though I were hanging in a perfect balance, every sense poised. Sandy seemed to me to be ineffably sweet and patient, his hands unbuttoning my buttons attached to my own nervous system, his face the one I might see if I looked into a mirror that showed me from the inside out. When he revealed my breasts and bent to kiss my left nipple, lip and breast met each other like lovers parted between morning and evening, each eager to return to the warm safety of the morning's bed, the soft little tent of the covers and the safe suspension between sleep and waking, where boundaries are blurred and neither is yet aware that he is naked and alone.

The little jolts in my brain began again, and the tingling along the surface of my skin. Sandy browsed on one nipple, then the other, and when he changed from a mouthing so soft I couldn't tell his mouth from my own skin to sharper pulls and kneading, with tight little flicks of his tongue at the top of the nipple, it became too much. I grabbed the back of his head and held him to me while I lay back; he came up from his knees to bend over me, his arms making little struts on each side of me, his body a tent. And then he stepped up onto the bed and rolled me onto the sheet beside him, and I was unbuttoning his shirt and kissing his chest, tonguing his tight little nipples, and then he was pulling my pants and then my underpants down, and I was wriggling to help. His fingers found moistness when they slid sweetly into the space between my lips and he stroked forward lightly to where the smooth, soft clitoris bloomed, and I felt a melting begin. I twisted to pull down his zipper and free him from the corduroy and cotton-jersey nest, and my fingers on the sweet, tender tip, with already its bead of moisture, were the same as his fingers on me, my mouth and his the same mouth, so that when he moved to come inside I felt an opening outward begin, he was inside me but we were both inside the same skin, a great, mysterious cave, and then we were floating together in a vastness that rolled out and out to infinity, and every inch was as soft as the night air of summer under trees. We didn't know who was inside whom; we were both inside and there was no outside, we occupied all infinity and rolled together in it, our two heads like one planet orbiting a great sun that was somewhere inside the universe of our bodies. The sweet expanse of us grew and grew, a slow, silent supernova traveling light-years across the space of our cave, and we bathed in its white light and heat until the last photon expired and we tumbled out, confused and amazed, into a world of rumpled sheets and the covers poured upon the floor, where icy rain beat hard against black windows and we did not feel our bodies yet our own.

And then we did, but eerily; we had come back from a far place and wondered where we were. A sadness overtook both of us; it was not the usual slow drifting back to awareness, lying companionably and talking, touching skin to keep a link.

We had been so far together that, returned, we did not know how we should act toward each other; we had no familiar ground, no safe place in which to reclaim our separate selves. In the nasty neutrality of the little house, like a motel room, we were in limbo again.

Sandy got up, went into the living room, turned on the television set and sat down, leaning into the set to make a location, a turf. I could feel a depression starting, a loss of space and connection, yet without separation; it was as though we had stolen the other's soul.

It came to me that we needed, immediately, to be someplace else, among other people. "Let's go out," I said, and after a while Sandy agreed. We drove silently through the rain to a bar where folk music was played, where men and women talked and moved, getting up and sitting down, leaning over the bar and each other, talking, laughing, arguing, while the singer sat on a high stool and between songs exchanged jokes with the audience. We sat on barstools and drank beer and Sandy flirted with the woman bartender and talked to a bearded folkie, and I just sat and let the heat given off by all those bodies warm me up, let the lively, individual movements and snatches of conversation erode my depression. After a while Sandy and I started exchanging jokes, and then we could sit there companionably and listen to the singer, and gradually, having found to our surprise that our souls were still our own, having stretched out into all the nooks and crannies of our own bodies and felt them fit us comfortably again, and having rubbed up a little against the general outlines of complete strangers in the middle-sized cave of intimacy that is a good bar on a rainy night, we were at peace. And somewhere in the recesses of our bones the little itch began again, and when we left we thought we could find each other in the dark, in any cave or cavern in the universe, and still come out alive.

Games

GRACE ZABRISKIE

. . . *this wasn't working* . . . *no* . . .

"No," Ann sighed to Rosy's clitoris. She lifted her legs from around Bart's neck, then Rosy's legs from around her own neck.

. . . *now who was beneath them?* . . .

Ann couldn't see, but John, she supposed, and whoever the guy was who'd come with him. Regretfully, she raised her pelvis and pursed her sphincter until the dildo was expelled from her anus.

A murmur or two, soft suckings and sighings, shiftings, as delicate accommodations were made for intricate extrications; convexities slid from concavities . . . and the multi-membered and -orificed beast fell apart.

Ann made her way to the edge of the enormous, many-leveled

playpen of a bed that all five of them had been disporting themselves upon for the past few hours . . . No one objected . . . She stood and looked down at them . . . lying there at different angles to one another . . . looking up at her.

"What's happening?" asked John.

"Nothing," said Ann, with no particular emphasis . . . but they all got it. They stared at her for a while, resting. John stretched himself, extending, flexing his toes, one outflung hand inadvertently finding Rosy's navel and beginning to probe it, idly.

"Take a swim," he advised, his other hand searching for one of several small pots of fragrant oil on a nearby ledge, then dipping into it and gliding along Bart's thigh to his flaccid penis. Bart noticed Ann watching, then smiled and closed his eyes. He liked being watched, Ann realized, but none of this group had ever seemed content to do that . . . or not for long.

. . . so this was what it was like to watch . . .

As John rolled onto his stomach and slowly drew Rosy's right knee and Bart's left knee together and then began licking in a wide circular motion the sensitive sides and undersides of both knees, Ann recognized an image from an erotic dream she'd had once. In the dream she'd been watching too. So as the scene before her unfolded, Ann felt that she had lived before what she was living now.

. . . or was it that she had dreamed before
what she was dreaming now? . . .

John was urging the two bodies closer together, gently lifting the outer buttock of each, canting the pelvis of each toward the other until he could easily mouth one groin and then the other, then one, then the other, over and over, until Ann sensed what Rosy must be imagining: that she could feel John's tongue even after it had left her fragile pelvic bone to glide onto Bart's sturdier one.

. . . and this, too, was how it had been in the dream . . .

John had left Rosy's clitoris to Bart's expert care, had moved to let his hot breath fall on Bart's lengthening cock.

. . . She could feel the moist heat . . . the tension growing in her own abdominal muscles . . .

Just as she sensed that Bart's ache for it must be unbearable, John's mouth descended to close around the tall, dark shaft that was waiting . . . and she could almost feel John's hand underneath shift position, preparing to find Bart's anus.

The line between watching and doing seemed blurred, the difference between doing and dreaming obscured. And between watching and dreaming . . . that line had never really existed for her at all, Ann knew . . . though she couldn't remember ever having "watched" before.

. . . for the dreamer watches . . . the watcher dreams . . .

. . . where had she read that? . . .

She looked up.

. . . where the hell had the new guy gone? the cowboy? . . .

Her gaze shifted to deep focus, and there, through the glass doors on the other side of the bed area, she saw him watching her from the Jacuzzi, the shimmering blue of the pool behind him. What was his name? Tex, probably.

. . . maybe she would *take a swim . . . but she* was *leaving . . .*

Making her way toward him, kissing an ear, a breast, a buttock good-bye as she passed them, she realized that she felt, ludicrously enough, a little shy. She hadn't felt this way about the guy earlier, certainly, when she'd fucked him until Rosy, John and Bart had all complained—or while he'd let Rosy suck him until Rosy hadn't a complaint in the world—or while—well, she didn't think she'd felt *anything* about him while she and Rosy were loving each other.

But then, when the two women ordered tall Margaritas for making icecocks with Bart's lovely, dark, long-suffering penis, she remembered that he'd laughed a lot at that—whatever his name was—Slim? And she'd enjoyed his refusal to have his own dipped. The thought alone shriveled him, he'd claimed, inarguably.

Ann sat down on the edge of the Jacuzzi and dipped a leg into the swirling water.

"This isn't very hot," she said. "You want me to turn it up?"

"Sure," he grinned. "You didn't manage to freeze it in there, so, yeah, I think you ought to get a fair shot at cookin' it. What the hell. Turn it *all* the way up."

She shrugged and slid into the warmish water, leaning against the side of the small pool, facing him.

"I'm Ann," she said.

"I know."

She waited. "I don't know your name."

"I know."

"Well, you're difficult, aren't you?"

"No, I'm Joe. And you're leaving. Or you *were* leaving."

"I know," she said.

. . . *she felt like a kid for echoing him* . . .

"Why?"

"I don't know."

He laughed. "Yes, you do. You were bored."

. . . *well,* now *she wasn't* . . .

"It showed, huh?"

"Not really. Anyway . . . I don't think that's the only reason."

She studied him for a moment. "Are you planning to tell me what you think another reason might be?"

"What do you mean?"

"I *mean* . . . if I *ask* you . . . why you think I *really* left the . . . *orgy* in there . . . are you going to give me an *answer?*

"Ah . . . no." He was watching her closely. "I think I was planning to be mysterious . . . You had that figured out, did you?"

"Yep," she said. "Want to know what else I got figured out?"

"Yes, *ma'am* . . ."

. . . *he didn't look the least bit threatened* . . .

"You like games," she said. And smiled. "You like games too."

". . . 'too' . . . ?" he repeated, much too innocently.

"Yeah, 'too.' *I* like games . . . certain kinds of games . . . Do you?"

"Well, now, *I* like . . ." he said tentatively, ". . . what *I* like is

. . . not being afraid of new kinds of . . . essentially ritualistic behavior . . ."

He checked on how she was making out with "essentially ritualistic behavior" and saw she was still with him.

. . . *some cowboy, she was thinking* . . .

". . . because," he continued, ". . . I don't know. I like games, I guess."

"Hey, don't cop out. I won't melt. Which do you like better: games *you* make up, or games where you have to figure out what somebody else's rules are?"

"Well, shucks, ma'am . . ." he reached out for her, very slowly. "I don't even know how you can tell the difference . . ." His hands touched her slim torso, and with a world-obliterating concentration his fingers found their natural places in the taut softnesses between her ribs . . .

". . . not if you're playing right . . ."

He wasn't watching, she was to remember later, because his eyes were on her face, but somehow he seemed to know when her breasts had been sent their various messages, exactly when they contracted and firmed, precisely when her nipples began to rise up tight and hard. For it was only then that each thumb began its ascent from rib to tender undercurve of breast to sensitive nipple, barely grazing its tip, one just before the other, and then the second tip again and then again as his eyes darted there, and his head lowered impulsively to kiss it and suck it lightly.

Ann's definition of a really good game was one you could forget all about while you played it.

. . . *Is that one your favorite? she was thinking.*
The left one? You know already that it's your favorite? . . .

She clasped him to her as he knelt before her, and some part of her brain was registering an awareness that what she was receiving now was what she lived for—a new "liberation." A new "first" at any rate, and, yes, possibly another small liberation: always before, her breasts had been in a sense "jealous" of each other. Never, she realized, had one been caressed when the other had not become impatient to receive the same attention.

For a moment she reveled in her own indulgence of his momentary favoritism, her awareness that the sensation of his mouth on her breast was unclouded by any need for him to hurry on to the other. And then there was no "first," no "liberation," no indulgence, no other breast congratulating itself on not waiting for its turn. His mouth on that breast was all there was . . . for a while . . . until

. . . *There are many triangles in woman* . . .

She tried rather desperately to make the thought stop there. But the line from nipple to brain that angled to groin and then back up to breast became brilliant and real in her mind and glowed like neon from darkness. The wetness and warmth of his mouth were drawing up memories; then—as vectors of energy reversed—suckling and nourishing them as they came. She felt all the other mouths on her breast, felt breasts that her mouth had kissed. She saw herself nursing the child she'd had, saw the infant she'd been, being nursed. She felt tugs at her womb, remembered labor and birth, and then, as she began to float in the waters of the womb that had held her . . . she stopped.

This was promising to be one magnificent fuck, goddamit, but she wasn't *quite* ready to have it expanded into a "rebirthing experience," . . . not even if—

. . . *whaddaya* mean, "*not even if*" . . .

—especially *since* she was about to fucking *drown,* she realized, as they had apparently lost their footings in the pool and been wallowing about for some time under water.

. . . *had she been forgetting to* breathe, *for chrissake?* . . .

Ann sputtered to the surface, unplugging herself from his still open mouth, clutching both breasts like some threatened virgin. The right one was still slightly sore. Well, it could count itself lucky if it were still the same *shape,* after that obsessive little marathon suck.

. . . *wait a minute* . . . *why was the* right *one sore?* . . . *it was the* left *one he'd* . . .

She stared at him . . . Great . . . She had one tit about to fall off from sheer neglect, and he'd managed to contract lockjaw.

"Close your mouth," she said.

He closed it. Then opened it again.

"For that," he said.

"What?"

"I think another reason you left . . . was for that."

. . . *well, shit-piss-fuck him and the dung-colored horse he rode in on!* . . . that's *what he'd been thinking about* . . . *?*

. . . *his next conversational comeback?* . . .

How many times was she going to have to learn this lesson? Let yourself go and be totally transported by sex if you must, but don't count on its being a double transport, because it never fucking *is!* Whether you really *need* or *want* more than one other person at a time to fuck is beside the point . . . At least when you come up for air, you're not looking into just one other pair of eyes and imagining, for that one joyous second before the inevitable heartbreaking crash, that you've both been to the same place!

" 'For that'?" she repeated. "What's 'that'? . . . the indescribable interpersonal joy of the two-person sexual experience?"

He blinked. "Yeah," he drawled, grinning again. "Something like that." He glanced at her breast. "What's the matter with that one? . . . Jealous?"

Now her mouth was open with nothing to say.

". . . Maybe you do need three guys at a time . . ." he went on, taking her hand from her newly liberated and maligned breast and kneeling to draw her close to him again, nuzzling her stomach and torso, gently licking droplets of warm water from love-oil-scented skin,

". . . but we're just going to have to make do with what we've got here . . ." his hand caressed her inner thigh,

". . . for now . . ." and rose to imbed two fingers in her cunt and one in her anus, smoothly, effortlessly,

". . . unless . . ." he stopped all movement and flow of energy; a bowling ball floated across her mind-screen for one distressingly antierotic moment,

". . . unless you'd just as soon quit now and go back inside . . . ?

And before she could think what to answer, his thumb found her clitoris, his lips closed over her nipple, and the image went blessedly dark.

Later, on the airliner from Los Angeles—where they'd been—to New Orleans—where they were going—Ann slept . . . sort of . . . He'd put a blanket over their laps. Every time he made her come, she'd go to sleep for a while, but every time he moved his hand away she'd wake up. Somewhere over Texas he made her come again, but she'd been asleep this time, so her orgasm woke her up for a change.

"Joe?"

"Yeah?"

"Where are we? Is this a . . . what is this, an airplane?"

"Yeah. We're going to New . . ."

"Never mind. I remember. New Orleans . . . Joe, why are we going to . . ."

"Because you wanted to see if you could be sexually born again in your old back . . ."

"Never mind, I remember, and don't say it like that. I'm sure I never used the expression 'sexually born again.' "

"Well, rejuvenated, maybe. In your old backyard . . . And something about mudpies, with icing made from what you scraped out from between the bricks of the house next door, because you were trying to make the woman's house fall down, because she used to watch what you were doing in the yard from her window, and once she called your house to tell on you . . ."

Ann looked confused. "Oh. Well, that's just something that happened. The mudpies weren't . . . you know, part of it." She smiled at him.

There was just something about him, she reflected, that she trusted completely with the "child" in her. The real child in her, not just the "childish" part, that might want its own way about things, or want to be babied or found adorable.

Of course she wasn't exactly sure what "the real child" in her was—it had never fully emerged before . . . not with a man. Anything other than "adult behavior" seemed to irritate most men, but the alternative was worse; she hated men who encouraged her to be "babyish."

And with women—forget it! Women didn't let you get away with anything! Well, they did if they were in love with you, but if you weren't in love with them it was terrible, unless they got off on that situation, which was worse. *And* they could be horribly territorial—like cats, it seemed to Ann, who had never been comfortable with feeling sexual possessiveness toward anyone in her life . . . on the other hand, sometimes a woman could make you come for about an hour . . . Ann realized that this last thought had nothing to do with what she'd been trying to think about and decided to go back to sleep.

Joe was murmuring some gibberish about "rides"—he was on for "the whole ride," he was telling her, "all the rides," not just "the bus ride to the park." She was dreaming about throwing mudpies at buses when his hand woke her up again.

"Joe? . . . What if it's not there anymore? . . . my backyard. What if it's a parking lot? Or what if there's another house there?"

"There won't be another house there. We already talked about this. We'll manage. We'll find weeds that smell just like your old weeds if we have to go out into the country."

". . . and chicken wire, or whatever it was?"

"It wasn't. I know what kind of wire it was. Go back to sleep."

". . . Joe?" He didn't answer. "Why won't you fuck me or eat me, and why won't you let me make you come?"

After a long silence, he said, "I did fuck you."

. . . what . . . ?

She'd forgotten what her question was, but now she remembered and knew this was no answer. He knew it too. He leaned over and kissed her cheek . . . for the first time.

"I know what you're asking me," he said. "I'll tell you later, okay?"

She took his hand and kissed it . . . then began to kiss and suck his fingers until he squirmed and asked her to stop. She fell into a deep sleep, smiling.

The yard *had* become a parking lot. But nothing changes too much in New Orleans. It's too tropical. Weeds had grown back along the edges. They'd been cut down, but in the back part, where the cars couldn't really get in and out too well anyway, the weeds had taken over again.

Several tall and sexy-smelling yards of them separated Ann and Joe from the rest of the lot. They'd rented a car at the airport and on the drive in had spotted and liberated a four-foot-square section of wire fencing. Joe was now bending it into a sort of roof shape, as per Ann's instructions. It was five o'clock in the morning.

"Now what?" he said, placing the thing on the ground. Ann sat down at one end of it, breathing in the familiar smell of grass and earth and these certain weeds. He sat next to her. She tried not to love him for being so at ease here.

. . . it was important not to feel things now that weren't a part of it . . . she was ready now, to start . . .

"What time is it?" she asked.

"Five."

"Look at your watch."

"Shit, I *know* it's . . ."

"No cursing, Joe. That's 'one.' Now look at your watch."

He did. "It's five-fourteen."

"You said it was five. That was a lie. That's 'two.' " Her voice had become singsongy.

He stared at her, beginning to get the idea. "That's 'two,' huh?"

"Yep."

He took a small bottle of whiskey, courtesy of Delta, from his jacket pocket. "If I drink this, will that be 'three'?"

"No." She giggled. "Did you steal it?"

"If I did, would that be 'three'?"

"Yep."

"I stole it—off the cart when nobody was looking."

"No you didn't, Joe. You didn't drink your second drink, and I saw you put it in your pocket. That's *two* lies, *and* cursing, and *that's* 'three.' Now-you-have-to-take-off-all-your-clothes."

He handed her the bottle and took off his jacket. She sipped whiskey as she watched him take off his shoes and socks, his shirt and his jeans. He glanced at her critically.

"You burped. That's 'one.' "

"I did not." (She had.)

"You-did-too-that's-a-lie-that's-'two,' Ann." He said this with perfect seriousness, and Ann felt a small knot of excitement begin to grow in her belly.

"Okay . . . You still have to take off your underpants."

She averted her eyes as he took them off.

. . . that was the way it had been . . .

"Now lie down under the thing," she said. "On your stomach."

"You called it 'the thing'?" he asked, trying not to laugh, maneuvering himself under the wire tent and into the correct position. ". . . What did you call a cock?"

" 'That thing,' " Ann answered gravely. "We called lots of things 'thing.' "

"Oh," he quavered.

She moved around behind him where he couldn't see her.

"What are you doing?" His voice *and* ass were quivering now, and his former sobriety was highly suspect.

"I'm looking at you naked," she replied rather sternly. "I'm looking at your butt." The noise that finally burst from him now sounded like the product of physical torture.

"You called it your 'butt'? I can't believe you called it . . ."

"*You* are *punished!* You think that's *funny?* . . . You think . . ." She stopped. The sudden, repressed rage in her voice had shocked both of them into silence.

. . . Jesus, where did that come from? . . .

Both of them had thought it . . . After a moment, he realized that she'd said it.

"Annie?"

"What?"

"You're not supposed to say, 'Jesus,' Annie. That's swearing. That's 'three.' Get your clothes off and get down here."

He turned over (without permission, she noticed) and stared up at her in utterly childlike, unconfident defiance, aware that he was probably breaking some rule he hadn't yet been told about. . . . She remembered the two men and a woman lying on their backs, naked, staring up at her only a few short hours ago—all three of them bored, passive, uncurious—and she felt closer to this man, now, than she'd ever felt to anyone.

. . . except that he did *maybe have an awful lot of* hair *down there . . . good god . . . not to mention what seemed to be going on in the* middle *of all that hair as she stared at it . . .*

"You want me to try and make this go away?" he asked.

She nodded. ". . . And I wish . . ." she hesitated. ". . . I wish we could shave the hair off. See, the hair isn't . . ."

"We're big kids now," he smiled, folding his arms behind his head. "We have hair." And the rich, chestnut hair in his armpits glinted at her in the early-morning sun. His penis was fast losing pizzazz, but cocky was the only word for him. "Are you coming?"

And then, before she could think how to explain, he knew. Or seemed to. He worked himself out from under the tent, stood up and put his jeans back on. When they were fully buttoned, he turned his back on her and the tent, sat down and idly sorted through the weeds around him until he found the kind with the furry tip that would tickle and the long juicy root you could chew, and he chewed it.

. . . he knew . . . only one at a time could be naked; only one at a time could be under the thing . . . he knew . . .

Before they had left John's house, where all the "regulars" usually kept a few clothes, she had dressed in exactly what she had known she would want to be taking off now: she pulled off her T-shirt first. She'd worn no bra, of course, and when the warm, moist air hit her skin, she shivered.

. . . yes, this was right . . .

She stripped off jeans and plain white underpants, remembering that long ago when she'd been naked here, she had shivered in the heat of noon. Then, as she bent to remove her shoes, another long-buried memory almost made her lose her balance with the suddenness—the vividness—of it:

. . . *she is lying naked in the weeds* . . .

insects are stinging her butt, and a ten-year-old boy is astride her knees. With both grubby hands, he "examines" her, pinching her vulva as gently as he can and still keep hold, separating the small, smooth, slippery folds of flesh, amazed by the complications and the pinks inside. Another boy and a girl are watching. Suddenly they turn, listening. "Doritha!" they say. The very large black woman who is her family's maid is making an unprecedented voyage through the tall weeds to the back of the lot. The other children disappear, but Annie is naked. Her clothes! In total panic she begins putting on . . . a sock. Doritha is getting closer. This is crazy, Annie thinks; forget the socks. She grabs . . . a shoe. So in one sock with no shoe and one shoe with no sock, she is dragged, furious, screaming, through the lot. Invisible children can be heard laughing.

Ann was smiling as she crawled under the thing. She lay there a moment, looking up at the sky, looking over at Joe's placid back. Then the wire roof came into focus, and her entire body shivered with excitement. ". . . Joe . . . ?" she said huskily.

He rose and stood over her, his eyes widening. He cleared his throat, then spoke very softly: "What did you call your, ah . . . ?"

She could tell he wasn't sure whether he was supposed to ask a question now. "Well, let's see . . ." she said. " 'Thing,' of course, 'front,' 'peehole,' or 'pussy.' Take your pick."

"Okay . . . Now I have three more questions: why are there goose bumps all over your arms and legs and stomach and cunt, why is there no *hair* on your cunt, and WHO SAID YOU COULD LEAVE YOUR FUCKING SHOES ON?"

"I shaved my cunt in the New Orleans airport," she warbled, improvising, happy with her tune but aware that her lyric might find a limited audience, ". . . while you were renting the car.—You *know* why." She lifted a foot . . . "Forgot my shoes . . ."

He knelt and began removing them. "I got goose bumps because it's working, Joe, you know that? It's really working."

Holding her bare foot, stroking the back of her knee, her calf, he looked at her silently.

"What are you thinking?" she asked him.

"That I've never seen anything in my whole life," he said slowly. "Only what I wanted to see, or was afraid—or expected—to see." He put her foot down gently and rose up onto his knees, so that he was seeing her through the wire roof.

She waited. ". . . And now . . . ?" she asked, prompting.

"Now, too," he smiled, ". . . except for one brief flash . . ." He leaned forward, resting on the roof.

. . . soon he would have a waffled imprint on his forehead . . .

"Touch it," he ordered. "Touch your pussy." She did so. "With both hands . . . Now stop touching it . . . *Stop* touching it . . . *Ann,* Simon Says stop *touching* it . . . Now touch it the way you do when you're alone. . . . That's enough . . . Now push your pussy up to me a little bit."

She held herself still, savoring the moment before she did what she was now dying to do; her pelvis was weak with the need to arch, to rise, to stretch and display . . . and just as she wondered whether her body was going to be able to obey the order it had been given, her pelvis began of its own accord to tilt up from the fragile line of her spine in a slow, controlled, yet convulsive grind. Her eyes closed themselves. Her nipples tightened in the outreaching circles of shock from her cunt. Free of the hair that for so long had protected them, the smooth, twin mounds of her cunt, her core, her pussy, her thing . . . felt air, caressing.

. . . no triangles now . . .

just circles . . . bisected and whole . . . electric energy, pulsating, burning, boring inward, radiating out . . . every nerve in her body connected to these few square inches of surface flesh.

"I'm about to come, Joe," she said, in a slow, sensual parody of conversational tones . . . "What are you doing? . . . Are you looking at my pussy?"

"I'm eating your pussy with my eyes, baby," he said, after

clearing his throat again. "I want more of your pussy . . . What will you give me?"

"Just tell me what you want, Joe . . . Tell me what to do next."

"I want to see inside your pussy . . . all inside it . . . I want it closer to me first . . . higher . . . as close as you can get it . . . I won't touch it, I want to smell it." She could hear him inhaling deeply. "Now open it for me, so I can see everything inside . . ."

. . . what was inside, she thought, was an all too adult war . . . the ultimate war, the delectable war, the war between languor and frenzy . . .

"Why?" she asked, decimating this insurrection with a childish coup.

"Because," he answered, after only a beat, "I have to make sure everything's all right." And with that, he removed the tent.

"Open your legs a little bit, please," he intoned, all nine-year-old Dr. Casey. ". . . Annie? . . . Spread your legs."

He prodded and poked and peered and inspected . . . until she was gritting her teeth. All adult eroticism had ebbed from him now, and Ann was beginning to remember some aspects of this backyard business she'd forgotten—such as boredom and awkwardness.

"Okay, turn over now, so I can see your heinie."

"You called it your heinie?" she smirked. "That's gotta be the . . . *Hey!*" He'd turned her over, somehow—most unceremoniously. Her rear end was up in the air, and her mouth was full of squashed weeds. Of course they still smelled great and sexy and everything . . .

"Hmmm," he deliberated, parting the cheeks of her ass. "Hmmm . . . there's a hole here, Annie . . . Could be a deep one . . . Where does it go? I wonder . . . I'm just going to have to insurd my finger here, Annie . . ."

Her knees slipped out from under her, and she collapsed to the ground in helpless laughter. "You're going to have to *what?*" she finally managed. "You're just going to have to do *what?*"

She twisted herself around onto her back before he could stop her and pollywogged her legs around him, pulling, until he toppled down on top of her, laughing. His mouth closed around her entire ear. "I love you," he somehow whispered into it.

She'd been laughing and wasn't sure she'd heard what she thought she'd heard, so she pretended she hadn't heard anything.

"Who *said* that? . . . 'insurd' . . . did somebody really *say* that?"

"Sure," he said. "This kid named Cynthia said it to me when we were playing doctor in her backyard."

"Really?"

"Well, I hope you didn't think *you* invented all this shit?"

"I'd like to know who invented the buttons on these jeans . . . Help me . . . *Help* me," she insisted, even though he was kissing her face and her mouth and her neck and her breasts and she didn't want him to stop. ". . . The next thing that gets 'insurded' in me isn't going to be your finger, Doctor."

"No?" he asked. She had freed his erect cock, but he was keeping her from it. ". . . Well, I don't know what else we've got around here . . . except 'this thing,' I guess, but I gotta tell you —there's just one, and you can only insurd it into one thing at a time . . ."

She sat up suddenly. "Joe! . . . Listen! . . . Do you hear something?"

"No," he said, coming up on one elbow and dropping his guard . . . and she had him. In her mouth . . . to the hilt. He lay back down.

"You win," he said, ". . . but I'm a graceful loser."

Then he touched her hair . . . as she kissed and sucked and licked his penis and fondled his balls and touched him gently again and again and never thought of all that she knew, which was how she would mount him soon . . . soon enough . . . and how slowly she would slide onto his cock . . . and how she would rock in his arms and shiver, and play his games and go to his places and give him everything that she had, and rarely so much as look at another man . . . Then she took off his pants and explored his legs and his feet and his toes and she kissed his chest and stomach and ass, then licked and kissed him from his balls to the base to the tip of his cock . . . and stomach and navel and down again . . . till she met her own scent where she'd been before and relaxed a little, but couldn't stop trying to make him her own, make up for lost time . . .

"Joe," she said, "I love you, too."

"I thought you'd heard that . . . Did you hear me tell you I only got one cock?"

"I did."

". . . Ann . . . ? . . . if you were a cat, I'd be peed on all over by now, wouldn't I?"

. . . nothing else he could have said
would have made her happier . . .

An American in Paris

KIM CHERNIN

I keep telling myself that I am very calm, lying on the hotel bed, waiting for the phone to ring. But I am not calm. I am remembering things. Some of them from three and a half years ago. Some from today, wandering about through the piles of leaves that have not even bothered to turn yellow before they drop from the tree. Probably this happens in other places too, but I always think of it as distinctly and outrageously Parisian.

It is late fall, everyone is back in Paris. Today I went over to the cafe where I first met her and they refused to let me have a seat by myself near the window. I had spent the morning in the Turkish bath, my first morning in Paris, lying about for hours in the steam rooms before retiring to the outer chamber. If I close my eyes now I can see it all very clearly: fountain at the center of the room, the stained-glass windows; coats, scarves, clothes hanging beneath them; on the covered mattresses, legs curled up, leaning together, lying down, naked, wrapped in towels, drinking mint tea, eating pastries and fruit, the women talk together in a sprawl of purses and colored plastic bags, massage one another, sit with their eyes closed, keep an eye on each other.

Years ago I heard about this place from her, she mentioned it casually but it stayed in my mind. From the first moment she spoke of it, I thought: "Someday I'm going to come back here, it's going to happen and she will go there with me."

Today, waiting for her to get back from Zurich, I have run through everything by myself. The Turkish bath, the long, cold walk through vaguely familiar streets where I used to walk by myself, the deliberate stroll through the Luxembourg Gardens. It occurred to me, as I stood at the gate facing the cafe, the last time I had done this, leaving the garden, scanning the tables across the street, she was no part of my life. Even the idea of her had not yet come into my consciousness, because I was going to that cafe to meet someone else. She just happened to be there. And happened to know the woman I was meeting.

And then I ran across the street, found the friend who was waiting to meet me, was introduced to Anna. We had breakfast together the next day: coffee cooling, forgotten, indifferently sipped when I could manage to take my eyes from her. Both of us jumping up to hail a cab, race back to my hotel to gather my luggage, the cab waiting, so that I would not miss my plane. I thought, absurdly, putting my arms around this stranger to hug her good-bye, "How will I go on living without this woman?"

It has taken me three and a half years to risk seeing her again, to dare this offer of myself as lover. I look ten years older, I am too thin, I have come back with my pride and arrogance as a lover stripped away, I have let myself be broken in heart during these years and now I can't even say I believe in love any more, certainly not in that kind which roars and breaks into flame and feels fated to transform you and ends badly and drags you down into the most carefully hidden secrets of your past and leaves you there, howling in darkness, to work it out on your own.

I run the water for the shower, pretending to be calm, waiting to hear her voice, wondering how she is feeling, on her train back from Zurich. Is she, too, scared of what we are risking? The audacity of it? Dragging this fantasy by the hair from its dark corner to make it face reality? Is she trying not to think too precisely, as I, too, am not thinking? I remember her face, the broad forehead, high cheekbones, wide, expressive mouth, those yellow, almost slanted eyes with their warmth and intelligence and straightforwardness and provocation. She is taller than I am, more broadly built; the first time I saw her, wearing a T-shirt, her neck and back and arms filmed over with that dark tan only blond people seem to get, I thought immediately I would like to dance with her.

The phone rings; I come running from the shower, pouring with water, to grab the receiver, the shower thundering behind me, the bed already sopping as I leap on and crouch down and hold the receiver to say hello to her. Hello, Anna . . .

The taxi drops me expertly at her door. I'm all thumbs now, counting out the unfamiliar money, laughing at myself a bit too shrilly. He turns on the light to look at me, watches me fumbling with the coins in my palm, very slowly counts them out for me, refusing a tip. Standing in front of the building where she lives I can't manage to get the street door open. I push and shake at it, set my shoulder against it, stand back, feeling ridiculous. So easy to make a fool of oneself at this moment. She could so easily not be what I remember, I certainly am not what I have always pretended to be, a self-assured lover.

At the sixth floor I have trouble with the elevator doors. I jiggle the handle, get the strap of my purse caught in my hands, make use of my shoulder again and then stand there waiting, wondering if someone will come to let me out of this little glass cage.

Am I behaving like this in order to remind myself that my proud sense of invincibility was torn away months ago and can't be drawn on again as a protective cloak? I could weep with shame and embarrassment, dressed in tight pants, polished boots, scarf wound three times around my neck, Parisian fashion. I remember her riding up on her bicycle to have breakfast with me. The way she got off the bike fast to come greet me, putting down the bag of croissants on the table. The sense she gave of a vital intelligence, her face so beautiful in its animation, warm, engaged, intensely alive. I was fascinated by a grace of being, gestures you don't forget for years after, the way her smile carries a memory of earlier sadness, something in her larger than herself looking out through her. She has a way of stopping, holding herself very still, looking straight into your eyes and saying nothing; she holds your gaze, her eyes are open, she is not afraid of this silence, she is thinking, considering what you have said, gathering her agreement or disagreement, the yellow eyes hide nothing, finally she speaks.

I am no longer beautiful, I tell myself, getting out of the elevator at last to walk through the darkness of the hall. Why should this woman whose footsteps I hear on the other side of the door find me any more appealing than a hundred others who have stood waiting for her to open this door?

She kisses me on one cheek; we are awkward and embarrassed in this first moment, I have turned my cheek to receive her other kiss and she has already moved away from me. "So," I say, "it really is you, after all." "Are you surprised?" she says, laughing at me. She looks older, her eyes still yellow, she is taller than I remembered, her hair shorter. It is the same face and I feel ready to cry with the relief of it.

We sit down at the small wooden table, across from one another. She offers me a Eucalyptus cigarette, she seems calm, she leans over to light the small, tightly rolled cigarette for me. She sits very straight, she holds her arm close to her chest, hand raised, holding the cigarette to her lips, head tipped to the side, slightly. "It is three and a half years," I say. "I hardly recognize you," she answers, "you have become a different person." Whatever this is, the conversation building itself from the first moment between us, creating this series of tunnels leading to new vistas, from which we turn back into the chambers and rooms of our shared preoccupations, always in step, reaching out to take one another by the hand or arm at exactly the right moment—it is already a way of being lovers.

We have stood up from the table and gone into the little kitchen to make dinner. I wash the lettuce once only, she doesn't approve. "Just be glad I don't send you back to wash it three times," she says. We are eating rice-and-ginger soup, she dresses the salad. We are telling each other about our sisters who have died. Both of us are crying. We do not ask how we have come to be so intimate.

My hands have stopped shaking. I have my elbows on the table, leaning toward her. We have spoken about her writing and mine, women we have loved, a psychic who told her she had lived many lives before and always as a man, we tell each other about our favorite books, her childhood in Germany, mine in the Bronx. By the time she has driven me back to my hotel we have a history together, the kiss on one cheek, the lettuce I washed once only, the way she showed me to tie a scarf when I asked her: patiently, very precisely. In bed with my eyes open I see her growing out over the earlier memories and I ask myself, Will it be only friendship? She has a lover who lives in Germany. What do I bring that could make her want me?

Morning again, I walk back to her across streets with green leaves piled up underfoot. At the small bakery on the corner I buy bread and croissants for breakfast, Normandy butter, small bottles of yogurt. We are at the little table in the dining room again, drinking coffee from white ceramic cups. I look up, push back my plate and it is evening. I am very tired, far from home, I have walked on nails for two thousand years, trying to find this woman. I remember her, a young Polish boy, setting out for the first time for Paris. The way she gathered the traveling cloak around both of us, against the cold. It was not the first time she said good-bye and I never saw her again. I like the way she stands up from the table to take down a bottle of wine from the shelf overhead without interrupting what she is saying. The authority, the unintended grace of it enter me like pieces of glass. I want to lie down in her arms, my head against her breast, from this I feel desire coming, for the first time ever desire is to be taken, taken care of, to give self in exchange for this.

I am so small, so ugly, so infinitely undesirable. Is it because I've lost the fierceness that disguised this secret need to be cared for by another woman? Has that nakedness revealed a nakedness I've never risked before? And so, I tell myself, as the talk draws us out of her flat; and soon we are walking together along dusk-gathering streets, the others going toward home, fast, purposeful; this is the reason to go slowly, one could not, in the beginning of anything, risk showing that need at its fullest, not to a stranger.

Leaving the restaurant, she puts her arm through my arm. I take her hand, draw it toward me, let it go. But now I will it to return, to find my shoulder, to push back the high collar of my sweater, to expose me. It is a rare joy to walk fast in the sudden very great, dry, winter cold. We are wearing ten-league boots, scarves around our necks, long jackets not really adequate against the cold I love, she does not love it. I can't figure out how we will move from this kinship of mind to a comradeship of body. This could so easily be the beginning of friendship. Between women, as always, impossible to tell.

It has become the third day. We move to a warmer table in the back corner of our cafe, drinking cognac and small cups of espresso, our scarves and bags and coats piled up next to us. People stare at us. There is something about her that says, Love me and you will not end your days dozing at the fire. I think of high places when I look at her. Sometimes, when she gazes back at me in silence there is a hot, still land, more austere than southern, but gracious still with its hills and vineyards. "*Kennst du das Land?*" she says, reading my thoughts. And I answer, recognizing Goethe, "*Dahin, möcht' ich mit dir* . . ."

We do not speak of our relationship, will we be lovers, is there a future, do I love her? I tell myself it is too soon to know. Shall we ever figure it out? One day, perhaps, something will happen and we shall find out. Or it will not happen.

Night has come down over Paris. There is fog, and now from her window we see a light moving above Sacré Coeur, selecting this one building out of all others for our enlightenment. Perhaps we have stood like this at home together many times in some other life. In front of the refrigerator she takes my hand; for a moment there is not the slightest awkwardness between us and I do not know why it has ended, perhaps simply it moved on into the making of salad and soup. "No," I tell myself, "it will not happen." And I understand finally that I have taken it all wrong. This ease between us will make us friends for a lifetime, that is what I have come to learn from her. Intimacy, untroubled by eros.

I am saddened by this, listening to Mahler, both of us standing very still, across the room from one another. She says: "I see another person in you again. You are constantly changing. It's hard to keep up with you. But I like it. With you one never knows what to expect. This one," she stops to consider it: "this person I see now is eight years old."

"Eight years old? Really?" My voice sounds surprised but it is only an effort to gain time. I am trying to adjust myself to the quick change in my perception, something very large has been set in motion, it concerns our bodies, the way blood moves through them, tides of desire and retreat which will not ask us if we are willing. Tomorrow perhaps we shall make plans, a month from now I will call her from California. I shall have put up on my wall, across from my bed, near the door, that photograph of her I saw in her study. Each time I walk out into the hall I will touch the curls in her short hair combed straight back from her forehead. And even then we will go on pretending it is up to us. But for now, in this moment, I know. If I step forward, if I put my fingertips against her cheeks, I will have crossed a line that calls into question my entire life.

I feel it in my breath, in the quick heat of my cheeks, something fundamental to be risked here although I don't yet know the name for what it will cost to love this woman and how it will test me if it does not break me. What was it she said, with anger, of a well-known German actress? "To fall into a lesbian bed, that is not the same thing as to be lesbian."

She is standing with one arm against the table, looking at me very seriously. It is a moment of great delicacy. The words we speak can't do it justice, we have to trust to what we hear in the silence between words, the tension our bodies cast into the space between us.

"Perhaps because I'm feeling so shy? That brings out the child in me? I feel completely unnerved by this vulnerability in my body."

I observe the way her head is turned toward me and does not turn away. She holds my gaze, reading me deeply. "You give an entirely different impression," she says, slowly, as if it were very important to get it right. "You seem at ease . . ." She hesitates, looks for the word, finds it in German. "*Ja, gelassen.*"

"Calm?" I remember the word from a translation of her story we had worked on earlier in the day. "I feel . . . I'll show you." I put my hands in my pockets and push, with the toe of my shoe, lightly against the rug, looking down and to the side, the way an eight-year-old might, feeling embarrassed and awkward.

"No," she says, "I don't believe it. To me you seem completely at peace in your body."

And then we find nothing further to say. I have no more skill now as a lover than I must have had when I was a child, a tough girl playing with older boys at the edge of the woods, playing with knives. I do not dare to look at her. I can feel her breathing, as if she were standing very close to me. But she is still across the room, near the table. It seems to me very dangerous to let this moment pass. If we deny it we will not dare to arrive at its brink again. Love is lost or gained at moments like this.

I want to hold out my hand to her, but I am incapable of physical motion.

"I am at ease in my body," I say, wondering what I am going to say next. "Yes," I repeat, with a sense that my words are going nowhere at all, "with my body I am at ease." And then I realize that the way has been cleared for me. It happens and it is so simple. "The shyness I feel? That exists only because of what I feel for you . . ."

There is an infinity of silence; more than enough in which to die of shame. Suppose, I say to myself, she feels nothing like this for me? And then I notice she is no longer standing across from me. She has walked across the space between us, matching risk to risk. It is like the time I ran across the street from the Luxembourg to meet her for the first time. Now she has made the crossing to me.

But I need time for the unique desire that is my desire for her, nothing in it borrowed from an impersonal need to possess a woman, to take her, to make her mine. I don't want to make love to her, I can't possibly, I am eight years old.

"Let's stay children," I say, finally. "I am not ready for anything else."

We sit down on the little bed made for me in the dining room. Suddenly, I want to cry, with the immense improbability this could be happening, this woman from the cafe from the Paris summer three and a half years ago, about to become my lover? My body, inhabited still by its shyness, is making small gestures of contact, all I can manage, touching her knee, holding her hand, letting my hand move through that boyish haircut of hers. And now my face is being held, she has put her hands against my temples. She is looking at me with an expression that says, "Foolish one, why did it take you so long to understand?"

Someone has said—it must have been Anna—we would probably be more comfortable in the bedroom. We are taking hands, old comrades walking together the long, terrible distance. We are in that space lovers create that changes the laws of space for one another, proving two objects can be in the same place at the same time. We are sitting as much as lying, I am moving toward her, it is she who is below me, her face lifted, it surprises me, I would have imagined it otherwise if I'd dared to imagine, I giving myself, she the receiver.

I hear myself speaking. "I don't want to make love to you," I say. "Not now, not tonight. I'm afraid that way I won't get to know you . . ."

"Could you really still stop now?" She has raised her head to look at me curiously. I think: the seduction of this woman is the way she does not seduce. Her mystery a clarity so rare it becomes in the next instant a great secret, what she has been through to make it possible?

"Yes, I could still stop," I say, because I feel, growing with the inclination of my hands to close around her, an even stronger desire not to do it in the old way. "Yes, I could still stop now if you asked me."

But my hands have begun to act according to their own wisdom, opening her scarf, touching her neck with a growing certainty, her neck keeps arching back beneath my hands, in that unmistakable arc of a woman giving herself so that something in me finally moves and bends me over and I am unbuttoning her blouse.

I do not know how she has come to be undressed, on another night I will undress her, touching her skin with my mouth as her jeans are drawn down over her stomach. This first night I wouldn't have dared. Somehow her blouse is off and the black strap of her chemise has been slipped down over her shoulder and then her breasts are bare and I have my hands on them. Then she is completely naked, standing while I am clothed, kneeling on the bed. I say, taking her hand to bring her down next to me: "How do you manage to disguise it? I'd never believe it." And she, laughing at my surprise, knows immediately I mean her body. It is more voluptuous, rounder, than one could possibly guess from her short hair, wearing jeans, disguised as a boy.

There is another gap. Both of us are naked now, we are sitting opposite one another, our foreheads touching, two candles are burning on the floor below the long window and beyond Paris, inescapable, reduced now to a single, old stone wall.

And now I, with the sense that I am letting myself grow down into a greater depth of myself than I had before now known existed, draw back from her and let myself be seen. "I see a fear of death in your eyes," she says, making me understand, for the first time, what it means to be naked. "A fear of death and sadness."

I sit very still, very cold, there is sweat on my forehead, she is seeing me as a small child watching my sister die. This fear I bring to whatever I love. Something inside me shaking itself open. Tears come out of it. "You have another face too," I say. "It is more than sad; there is in it an utter despair, a bleak desolation . . . terrible exhaustion." I am terrified by what I hear myself saying, surely she will draw back now to hide this true face of the self never shown to another person?

We hold still, neither of us knowing if we see only self in the other. Or see indeed the other? The difference useless, it will later be clear to us. We can see in the other only what each is able to know in herself.

The room is dark in spite of the two candles. I look out into the darkness, not really able to believe that my eyes are open. I want to go back into hiding, into an impersonal desire, but it is too late. I know now how to smell, to taste, to touch, to breathe her in, to make her cross the boundaries of self, to enter me through every pore and sense and mouth and opening long before her fingers enter. We are whispering something, back and forth, in this rhythm we do not create, from which the new selves still not born, still entangled together here, will be created out of the promise of that hot summer day, that seemingly casual meeting of strangers. "Yes, this," she says, "tenderness, this is the way, like this, like this."

And now I come to her with the entire history of my loves and heartbreak, vulnerable, unprotected, shaking in the naked revelation of self. I know the way to make love to this woman, my hands respond now to the silent calling of her body. Infant screeching for breast, small child raped in the cellar, young girl reaching out with very cautious hand to touch the naked belly of another girl.

Stroking her under her arm, kissing her left ear, studying each place from which the quick intake of breath arises, hollow of waist, curve of thigh, asking for me. The bed is crowded now.

There is scarcely room for us here. I have brought into this room my mother, every woman I have ever wanted and feared to love. Breast against breast, how do I find her? This body almost my own, how tell her from the woman who did not call back, the woman who begged for love I could not give, the woman who grew cold, the woman who could never forget me?

My mouth feeling its way, her thighs grow from my lips. My tongue says this is what flesh means dissolving between us. Is she Lindenbaum, blue gate on its hinge, fountain overgrown with wanderer's sorrow? Will I be small enough to fit into her hands? Large enough to forget: adolescent love. Insane after a year of separation. Woman with flea powder in her hair. Woman loved and lost the eve of my wedding.

Her hands in my hair, closing around my head, her hands making their way, neck, shoulders, taking hold there, waist, hips, finding their handhold, growing up out of my skin.

We have gone back to origins, the forced passage, cave of myself in which I find her, putting my mouth to her, down in the wet salt heat of our beginnings. Woman with the name of mother.

There is no need to weep, I am wet with love, she takes me in the same act by which she gives herself to me, rocked out together on strange seas of forgiveness and redemption, forehead to forehead, mouth to mouth in this act of mutual surrender, later we call it intimacy. Tonight, falling into the self of the other, we say: Let it be love.

Berlioz & the Ghetto Blaster

VALERIE KELLY

He's probably in Arizona by now. That's where he said he was headed. I think about him all the time, especially times like now, when I'm in my bath.

He'd answered an ad I'd placed for a "handy man" and came to me with a week's road dirt on him and sorely in need of a shave, carrying a duffel bag and a ghetto blaster. And I was so cold to him then. "All I care about," I told him, "is the weeds back there and the leaking roof. Your life is your concern." I meant, stay out of *my* life, but he didn't hear that.

In spite of his careless good looks and obvious proficiency at any task I set before him, he was an annoyance to me. He smoked cigarettes, drove a motorcycle, and carried this huge portable stereo around with him everywhere. I could hardly wait for him to be finished each day so I could have my privacy once again. And my silence. Why did he always have to play that blasted thing?

When I bought this little cabin in the mountains, I had no idea it would take so much work. I was caught up in the romance of it all. Finally, I could live alone and paint with no restrictions, being long divorced, with both girls safely off to college. A New York gallery was doing wonders with promotion, and for the first time in my life I could afford to paint whatever I wanted. And I wanted to paint these mountains.

They hover over the San Fernando Valley toward the northwest. One can rise above the smog up here, and above the traffic and the turmoil of city life. One can escape. Is that what I'm doing?

That's what he told me. No; he said, "What are you hiding from?" Same thing.

My studio is a screened porch on the north side of the cabin. I don't do all my painting there, just the most difficult bits, such as the fine hairs of a raccoon's coat or the shiny dots in a coyote's eyes. Mostly I paint in the mountains behind the house.

I remember he was always asking questions. Once when I thought I was alone and in deep concentration, I felt him behind me. I turned and accused him of invasion. "Why do you paint animals?" he asked. "I like them," I shot back automatically. "You don't have any pets," he observed. I became defensive.

"Can *you* paint?" I asked him. "I don't know," he said with that grin of his. "Maybe. Ain't never tried."

That first week, he had been at the house every day and I found myself looking forward to the weekend without him. But that Friday at lunchtime, he let himself into the screened porch where I was working and sat down on the floor by my paint stand, noisily eating a sandwich.

"I got booted outa my digs today," he said, his mouth full. "So I'm gonna crash here if it's OK."

"You can't stay here." It fell out of my mouth all on its own.

"Don't see as I got a choice, Les." My name is Leslie, but he always called me Les. "You got three more days' work out there in the yard and another two on the roof. If I don't stay here, I move on and you're left with weeds and leaks."

"But I don't have room for you here," I protested.

"Lady, you got all kinds a room. What you're saying is you don't want me here." And then almost to himself: "Why don't folks say what they mean?"

Why hadn't I said what I meant? Why didn't I tell him how sorely I needed my time alone, how dearly I'd paid for this moment in my life?

He kept taking bites of his sandwich. He had a way of taking two bites at once, like a hungry boy. Then he was done with it. He rose, looked around, and said, "I'll sleep out here on the porch if you're scared." Then left for the yard. In a matter of seconds, a cello concerto screaming from his infernal machine filled the space between us.

That night I took a quick shower and darted into my bed as if a stranger were watching me. I was exhausted, but I couldn't fall asleep right away. I listened to the crickets and the old hoot owl and felt something was missing. It was the ghetto blaster. It had been going strong all day and now life seemed broken without it. Incomplete.

He was out on the porch, in my studio, stretched out on a mat in his jeans, probably,—or maybe without his jeans—with his chest bare. He always took his shirt off when he worked, even when it was cold out, so he must've slept without it too. Probably he was smoking a cigarette which he rolled himself. "If I have to go to all that trouble, I won't do it so much," he'd told me. I imagined I could smell the smoke, that it was filtering through the crack under my bedroom door.

I turned the electric blanket on and buried myself deep into my covers. What *was* I hiding from?

The next morning he was cooking. I could smell the bacon and the coffee, such friendly smells. I'd forgotten them. I dressed quickly and headed out for the front room and then stopped to put on my makeup. Just a little mascara, some lipstick.

"Good morning, Glen," I said. He squinted over to me, cigarette smoke in his eyes. I hated it when people smoked in my house.

"You like 'em up or over?" he asked.

I shrugged. "Whatever." I poured myself some coffee and sat down at the kitchen table. Glen made his eggs, bacon and toast into a sandwich and took it outside. "Better get started," he said halfway out the door. "Looks like rain." It didn't look like rain to me.

But he was right—it did rain. Glen had piled in enough wood to serve me three winters, I thought, but now I was glad he had. There's nothing in the world like sitting in front of a crackling fire in a warm, friendly room when a storm is trying its damnedest to beat down the walls. It makes one feel invulnerable, safe.

That night, when he was taking a shower, a piano sonata rose above the noise of the water pipes. Music followed him everywhere, even to the bathroom.

I was sitting on the rug, my back against the couch, nursing an Irish whiskey and watching the licks of orange flames in the fireplace. They seemed to dance in time with the music and I wondered who the composer was. I wondered if he'd watched a fire and set his music aflame with it.

In spite of myself, I was glad Glen was there. A cold, windy, stormy night makes you want to be with someone.

When he came out of the bathroom, he was rubbing his blond hair with a towel that was the same color as his eyes. He was wearing cut-offs with a worn spot near the zipper. "How come you don't use the tub?" he asked.

"The bathtub? Because I take showers, like you."

"A nice long hot bath on a night like this is like good sex. Stays with you a long time. Keeps you warm all night."

He was smiling, so I smiled back, but the mention of sex threw me a bit. I felt a chill and rubbed my arms.

"Want me to stoke this?" he asked, already poking at the fire. I didn't answer him. I didn't know what to say. He grinned up at me, set the poker against the hearth and said, "Well, I guess I'll be goin' out to the porch."

"In the rain?"

"I fixed it, remember? It don't rain in anymore."

"But it's cold out there."

"What are you sayin', Les?"

He'd caught me again. "I'm saying you can stay in here if you want to." And then, "In the living room, I mean."

"All right. I will."

And so I slept even more fitfully that night than the one before. I asked myself why I couldn't be like other women I knew. A handsome man in the next room, they would just take him, or seduce him, or at least fool around a little. Was I so insecure about my body or my looks to risk it? No. I knew that wasn't it. I was scared.

I'd worked my whole life to buy this place, this time, this independence. I didn't want to get close to a man now, not yet. And how could I get close to Glen physically without all that other stuff entering into it? And what would I do when he left? I'd be needful, dependent, something I'd spent years struggling against.

The storm raged harder the next day, and we were out of food. The muddy mountain roads leading down from the cabin were dangerous, too dangerous for Glen's motorcycle, so I volunteered to drive the car. He took the keys from my hand, and went alone, knowing what we needed.

And then I thought, "Oh, no, he's going to take the car and never come back. How stupid of me to let him have the keys." And when he did come back, I felt relief and I scolded myself for trusting so little.

By that afternoon, Glen had done all the inside work. He installed dimmer switches in several rooms, including the bathroom against my instructions, regulated the water pressure on all the faucets and spackled and painted some cracks in the walls. The house smelled strongly from paint and I began to sniffle like a child with a runny nose.

Glen made soup, from scratch, while we were serenaded by Dvořák, if you can call that intrusive music a serenade. The soup was delicious but I couldn't finish it. My stomach felt queasy and now my eyes began to ache.

"You need a bath," he said. I shook my head no. That was the last thing I needed. But he drew the bath anyway, adding scented oil and some bubbles. Then he came to the fireplace to get me.

I'll never get over what he had done to my bathroom. Glen had brought in brightly colored wildflowers from the garden and plants from other rooms to make it into a virtual greenhouse. The two small bathroom lights at the sides of the mirror were dimmed down low and there were lit candles on a shelf beside the tub. He had spread a fur rug from the bedroom over the tiles, so my feet wouldn't get cold, he said. A finishing touch was a glass of burgundy waiting on the tub rim.

"You can sip that once you're in the water," he told me.

"Are you going to undress me too?" I asked.

"If you'll let me."

I said no, I wanted to bathe alone. I closed the bathroom door behind him and took off all my clothes, laying them neatly on the table. Slowly I let myself down into the water. It was too hot and my skin flushed pink, but it felt good, too, and soon I was luxuriating in the steamy heat.

There was a quiet tap at the door.

"I thought you might be ready for some music," he said. And, opening the door just a crack, he stuck the ghetto blaster in. It was already playing a symphony by heaven knows who.

I couldn't help but laugh as I invited him in. After all, I was safely submerged in water and bubbles. What did it matter?

Glen turned the volume down on the stereo and sat down on the floor across from me, sipping his own glass of wine. "He was nuts, you know," Glen said.

"Who was nuts?"

"Berlioz. The guy who wrote this. They'd probably put him away if he lived now. But then, they'd probably put Van Gogh away too."

"Why? What did he do?"

"What all artists do. He poured his life force into his work. This one is about what happens when a sensitive guy in love takes opium—that's him—a self-portrait. He was in love with this actress, see, only she was real beautiful and important and he was just this Joe Nobody. So all he could do was want her for years. Then he finally gets this gig, you know? And he makes sure she's in the audience. He sorta peeks out through the curtains to make sure. The music—it's full of nightmares and passions and violence—all his fears about her and risking and all that."

It was the most Glen had ever said at one time, and when he fell silent, it seemed sudden.

"He could risk with his music, see, but he was scared to shit when it came to love." Glen laughed and shook his head. "Like most of us, I guess."

After some time I said, "My work isn't like that."

"It will be when you start working," he said. Then he grinned and took a long drink of his wine.

"I'm doing very well at it for someone who hasn't started yet," I replied, in spite of myself. "People buy my paintings."

"But you haven't put your self into them yet, only your talent. People buy your pictures to hang over the john. When you find it, your reason for being a painter, and you get it out—when you take a risk like this guy did—probably no one will buy them."

I had to laugh. "What an irony that would be! Then I'd be poor again."

"Would that be so awful?" he asked innocently. "At least when you're poor, you're free."

"Money buys freedom, Glen," I said. There were many ways in which Glen and I would never come together. This was clearly one of them. When the tape ran out, he popped in another one. This one I recognized. It was Mozart.

"Water feel good?"

"Yes," I breathed, sliding in deeper. "Delicious."

"Can I get in?" he asked.

Before I could answer, he was unsnapping his cut-offs. I had to shut my eyes to keep from looking. But then, just as he dropped one foot into the tub, I saw it. My guess was right, he was already hard. What was I doing taking a bath with a man I hadn't even known a week?

He bent his knees and laid his feet on either side of my hips. My legs were under his. The tub was large enough to stretch them out full and still keep my chest under water. But my breasts tended to float to the top, giving away my secret with their erect nipples.

"Can I wash you?" he asked, already soaping the cloth. The burgundy on an almost empty stomach, combined with the relaxing effects of a steaming bath, on top of being slightly feverish from whatever flu had befallen me, all served to make me woozy and drunk. I closed my eyes and listened to the music and felt the delicious strokes of Glen's hands and the rough edges of the washcloth slide and sweep all over my body.

He began with my arms, all the way from my shoulders to my fingertips. Then he washed my legs, calves first, then thighs. He spent too long on my inner thighs, then washed my feet. The soles of my feet, I discovered that night, are an erogenous zone. But Glen must have known that.

Then he washed my torso, beginning with my hips, then my waist. Then he slid across my breasts to run the warm wet cloth over my neck and shoulders. I bowed my head forward to get the most of it.

He washed my face with his bare fingers, outlining my bones, smoothing my cheeks. He had my face in both hands when he stopped moving. As I opened my eyes, he kissed me gently on the lips, licking the sensitive inner flesh. Then he continued his massage. He cupped my breasts with those warm, friendly, soapy hands. My breasts hardened under his touch. He let out a deep breath that trembled slightly. Or was it I who trembled?

One of his hands slid down and took me between my legs. It cupped my mound while pressing the middle finger between my lower lips. I longed for him to go inside with it, but he didn't.

I was leaning into his hands with my eyes closed, enjoying his attention, when abruptly he lay back in the tub, letting his head rest against the tile, and he closed his eyes. I asked him what was wrong. He shook his head. Nothing was wrong. We lay there for the last minutes of the Mozart piece and then Glen got up out of the tub. He was no longer hard.

He wrapped me in a towel and brought me back to the fire and sat me down like a rag doll. Then he slid down beside me and put his arm around me. And it began: another symphony of another kind.

This one *I* had orchestrated. After what I finally realized as days of longing, I buried my head in that lovely place between his strong jaw and his beautifully shaped shoulder and kissed him there, then higher, behind his ear, then lower, where the blond hair began swirling on his chest. I studied all of his muscles by firelight, tracing their outlines, kissing away goose bumps caused by me. My lips and tongue drew a path, down, down, down to the triangle of fur that would have led into his jeans, were he wearing them.

His cock bobbed up to meet me halfway, already moist at its tip. I felt the silky lotion with my fingers, then smoothed it over the head of his cock until it shined. His balls stiffened and drew up with a hunger. I held them in one hand and pressed gently and Glen blew out a quick breath of tension.

"You're beautiful," I told him. "Your body, it's so beautiful." With this he lay down on the floor, all but that one part of him which insisted upon remaining upright. It had been a year since I'd had a man's cock in my mouth, but I knew that was what I wanted. Slowly I let my mouth down on him and my towel fell away from my body. Glen reached for and took my breasts as I came forward to lie on top of him.

At that moment, my insides were crying to be penetrated, while the rest of me wanted desperately to hold onto that feeling, to memorize the warmth of being held, the ecstasy of being in a state of desire. And all at once I realized what I had been hiding from. *This* was my weakness. It is also my strength.

At last, he took me by my arms and laid me down. He brushed kisses on my cheeks and neck and then across my breasts. He told me he wanted me and asked if it was all right. And then he did it.

He drove his cock into me slowly, slowly, sliding past spongy walls, deep, deeper. Oh, God, I said all those things lovers say that sound so corny afterward. God, it felt so amazing, so unreal, like nothing else. Already I was coming. But he waited for me to come again, and again.

The next morning birds were singing so the rain was over. And the first thing I thought was that this would be over too, soon. Glen would finish his outside chores and be off. And I would be alone again to paint. I turned away from the window and found him still in my bed. I was surprised. I'd thought he would disappear in the night. But he was sleeping soundly and comfortably right there in my own bed. How handy.

He had grown blond stubble on his chin during the night and his dishwater hair was a mat of strings. But he looked so handsome on my pillow. I loved the shape of his jaw and chin and the way his mouth sort of curled up in the corners. And I realized I had always wanted to kiss those lips, since the first day. So I kissed them now and I ran my hand up his body, resting on his chest. And soon there were arms around me and we were off again.

When the work was done, Glen packed up his duffel bag and strapped it onto the bike and said good-bye. I was brave. I did not cling tenaciously or force him to promise to stop by again. I did not invent other chores that only he could do. I said good-bye and set out to paint something that would not sell, but that would bare my soul. A tribute to Berlioz.

And now as I lie in my bath these weeks later, I wonder if I did the right thing, letting him go so easily. Not the right thing, but the thing that was best for me. I'm always guessing myself wrong, thinking I'm this when I'm that. And Glen had some clues to me. He had a way of drawing me out and seducing me into reexamining my motives and values. He posed questions about me that I couldn't answer.

I wrap myself in a towel and unplug the tub, letting water and melancholy down the drain. Though it is night, I have left off the lights, and I sit in front of the fire with a glass of burgundy. "A toast to Berlioz," I say aloud, "wherever you are."

Outside I hear a motorbike. That will make forty-one in five weeks. One for every year of my life. This one stops, but then, so does the neighbor's bike. But the knock on the door is unmistakably for me.

And there he stands, as dirty and disheveled as he had been the first day I'd seen him, holding his helmet in both hands.

"I never played you any Mahler," he says. And strides into my living room as if he lives here.

The House of the Twin Jewels

GAYLE FEYRER

I was back from the stars, dripping gore and glory, weary of both. Fleet awarded me an increase in wealth, some decorative bits of metal and ribbon, and fourteen days of shore leave. After a debriefing at Imperial Headquarters, I flew a wingskiff from Starport to Mer'E'Kita, the Middle City, Capital of the Andromedan Empire.

I wore my uniform in the streets, as I always do in foreign territory. I find it earns me respect . . . where it does not earn me trouble. An Om'Zama warrior in the dress of the homelands is more likely to find herself challenged than a Captain of the Imperial Fleet. Still, there is always some male who will not believe that any woman, Captain or warrior, can fight better than he does. They are seldom real trouble. Real trouble is a gang of four who believe if all of them together can beat you, it proves that any one of them is stronger.

But no one bothered me as I wandered through the great bazaar, enjoying the multitude of sights, sounds and odors that assailed my senses. I loved the hodgepodge architecture, the wooden booths and bright tents of the bazaar vendors tumbled below the ancient and modern buildings of marble and fibrasteel. I loved walking the streets thronged with all the races of the Andromedan alliance, the black Om'Zama, the assorted blues and mauves of Cygnians, Vallaakarr, and triple-sexed Fllyll, the glistening green-furred Zorions. Exotic aliens were scattered throughout the crowd, the slaves and bonds of a dozen subject races, the piebald Pri'kia'ki, lizard-skinned Hssgornu, plate-faced Klunth, with their dull gray hides, and the varicolored Terrans, all busy about their masters' errands.

There were few Om'Zama in Mer'E'Kita, though here and there I saw a tall dark form stalking through the crowd. One small girlchild ran after me, and threw her arms about my leg. I lifted her in my arms. Her skin matched my own deep purple, with its faint bloom of blue, but the fine straight fall of silver hair showed her a Vallaakarr half-breed. One eye was swollen shut, and other bruises dulled the sheen of her skin. She asked me to take her to Om'Zama, and teach her to fight. I told her to have courage, the Sisterclans would take in any woman of age who came to them. She was a fierce little thing, perhaps her spirit would survive that long.

I moved slowly through the teeming streets, on my way to give homage to the Goddess. I passed through the Temple courtyard, with its pluming fountain and sacred Arra'Mi trees, the bitter-sweet fruit just swelling on the boughs, into the Sanctuary of the Inner Shrines. I had brought a gift of incense for the Protectress, exotic fragrance from an alien world. I opened the leather pouch I had brought and shook the opalescent fragments into my palm. They lay like rough jewels, red flashing bits of blue and green light. I burned a handful of the resin before the altar, and laid the bag in Her great bowl of fired clay, a womb of earth. The campaign had been hard, with no lives spared, but a whole continent, Her creation, still existed by my effort.

This is one thing I have never understood in men, though I know how to hate as well as any of them, and serve the Dark Mother more than any other manifestation of the Goddess. I have never understood how they can hate the earth itself, and want to obliterate her as they would an enemy. Once again, I regretted having so few Om'Zama under my command.

I went then to the shrine of shadow and flame, the altar of the Dark Mother, She who accepts only blood. Choosing one of the sharp blades lying before her, I cut myself and bled the bright violet drops into the bowl of white bone. I asked Her to be satisfied with my offering. The one bad wound I took was when I neglected Her service. I have taken care ever since to give Her this sacrifice.

After these gifts were made, I stayed for meditation, letting the delicate chime of the bell ring softly through my body, the ring repeating again and again, clearing all darker vibrations with its own pure sound. After the bells, I joined in the chanting, our voices faded with the sun, finishing at sunset. We climbed the steps to the roof of the Inner Temple and watched the great disk of the sun sink below the mountains. A brilliant streak of light, red as rubies, lit the horizon, firing the smoke-colored clouds with rose and amber.

It was dark when I encountered Melkon and O'Talla, the Ship's Surgeon and Chief Engineer, the one pleasantly besotted, the other wickedly sober, and accepted their invitation to The House of the Twin Jewels. That first night, I went for comradeship only. I meant to share a light meal, a glass of kavva, and to watch the entertainment. After that I would leave, perhaps fly the wingskiff to Om'Zama. I felt no urge to indulge myself in the dubious pleasures of the most extravagant brothel in the city.

Declaiming erotic poetry to the triple moons, her rich voice like honey and gravel, O'Talla guided us through the winding streets to the fabled torch-lit portal. Before us rose the outer gates of black iron wrought in the shape of mating dragons. Two giant

Hssgornu guards passed us inside the gates, through the shimmer of the force field, into the red grape arbor. A white gravel path wound through arching trellises heavy-laden with fruit, leading us to the exquisite inner doors of aged ivory. Each elaborately carved panel described an erotic scene from Andromedan myth. I recognized the twins, E'Lan and Le'Ter, sister warriors, dying the sweet death . . . T'El'Pria and the roguish kouragi Kourkus, his furred flanks pressed to her smooth skin, his sharp fangs delicately gripping the nape of her neck . . . Irakiru, the queen, and her sorcerer, Vel'tri the Mad, drowning in flames . . . the slave, Kel'Lan and his enslaved master, Sa'chame, kissing his feet. . . .

Impatient for the beauty awaiting him within, Melkor pushed open the heavy doors and we entered the lavish foyer of the Jewels. The interior was fragrant and gleaming, softly lit by musk-scented candles in sconces and chandeliers. The floors were set with an intricate pattern of colored marble, the walls covered with alternating panels of gilt-stenciled silk and polished woods . . . deep purple vour'ku, pale milkwillow, rose heddanut. The only furnishing the one great desk in the center, inlaid with the same rare woods, the geometric pattern on its surface matching the plan of the brothel's upper story. In the center of each square marking the bedrooms lay a jeweled key. Behind the desk sat The Keeper of the Keys.

At one end of the hall a glittering jet curtain was parted to show a room of silver, mauve, and blood violet. The black marble floor was circled with satin couches and low tables set with lush fruits and rich wine. In its center, seated on the round, raised stage, two soft-furred Cedealian hermaphrodites played a teasing duet on lyre and flute. Jeweled belts were locked about their waists instead of the usual bracelets or collars that might mar their wrist ruffs and fluffy white manes. No doubt they were the latest and most piquant pleasure of the house, Cedealia being a recent conquest of the Andromedan Empire. The two creatures played sweetly, delicately. It was early still, and the couches were just beginning to fill. Wilder revelry would come later, with flame dancers and a sexual performance—perhaps the hermaphrodites tonight.

At the other end of the hall, a wide staircase swept down from the rooms above. There was movement on the balcony as several pleasure slaves gathered to make their entrance, and below, as the patrons gathered to watch. I looked up as you descended the stair, and felt my whole body tense to stillness.

They understood your beauty well here, and played it. They kept you unpainted, to emphasize your savage quality, the wild and tawny beast only half tamed. Your hair fell loosely about your face, sun-streaked honey and amber. You moved with feline grace, your nude body slender, strong, and supple, the oiled muscles rippling in the candlelight. Rose-colored, flushed and softly swollen, your cock swayed as you walked toward me. Naked, your dark gold skin was bound with gilded chains—human strength frail against Andromedan Power. The strength and frailty equally enticing.

You felt my gaze and met it, level and cool, owning yourself still. A look that would have been a challenge, if not so self-contained. I stared back, entranced, while everything around you blurred, dissolved in a golden haze, a radiance. As if your body cast not shadow but light.

It would be easier if my passions were not so sudden, so total . . . so few. Better many small fires to warm the nights than a single consuming blaze. Easier still not to care at all.

I thought I had starved my heart into submission.

O'Talla was shaking my arm gently and laughing, mocking my penchant for aliens. I turned away and tried to be attentive, greeting the dark-eyed, sulky manchild she clasped about the waist. Behind me I could still feel your presence. Melkor was saying something . . . wine . . . sweetmeats . . . music. . . .

I had to look once more. You stood almost at the foot of the stairs, your eyes on the door. I followed your glance and saw S'Karrak had just entered the room. I fought with him on this last galactic campaign, and have seen him claim the spoils of war. Rape is a kind word for his pleasures. I saw from your face you knew him too . . . and saw your defiance even in fear. Then, for a moment, your eyes sought mine again, as S'Karrak moved forward to buy you for the evening. I was there before him, laying down my credits and receiving your key in return.

As I approached, you still did not smile but held my gaze. Large eyes, dark-lashed, narrowing as they assessed yet another stranger. . . . I could see the mosaic of their color now, the bright flecks of bronze, green and topaz. Then you turned and, without touching you, I followed, far enough behind to watch the movement of your buttocks as you climbed the stairs and walked the length of hallway to your room.

I shut the door behind us. You stood a moment, framed in the darkness of the full window open on the garden. Then you turned, already hard, as I was already flowing. Your response was trained with threats, no doubt—perhaps enhanced with a delicate taste of drugs. But I could see no sign of it as you approached me, your eyes were clear, fired with challenge and desire. Standing before me, you lowered that taunting gaze. Submissively, you held out your wrist cuffs to have your chains unlocked. Smiling then, ruefully. Gracefully performing a ritual abasement disguised as a ritual freedom.

It was I who stood rigid for fear of trembling, almost gasping at the first touch of your hands, Terran cool on my hotter flesh. Your fingertips traced the line of my mouth, brushed my cheek. Did they teach you this sweet hesitancy here, as they train your hardness?

"Your skin is the color of plums," you said, your voice light, husky, a voice for whispers.

Your hands rested for a moment on my throat, then moved downward. Your fingers suddenly deft, unlacing, unbuckling my armor, sliding leather and metal over my shoulder. My breasts nested in your hands, nipples centered in your palms. Your fingertips drew them out, pinching the buds to sharp points of pleasure. This time I gasped aloud.

Your hands slid down over my ribcage, over my belly, my hips, pushing the clothing before them. You eased my feet out of the leggings, removed my sandals. Slowly, your hands moved up my legs again, caressing calves and thighs. Your cheek brushed the triangle of hair, then pressed against the mound. Your head turned inward, moist mouth seeking the swollen lips, your lips nuzzling closer to part the tender fold of flesh.

The rush of pleasure filled me. My knees folded and I found myself kneeling in front of you. Your eyes were wide and faintly puzzled. Then you smiled and gathered my face in your hands. I could feel the shape of my skull, like a cup you brought to your lips. Your eyes closed as you kissed me, drinking deep. Your cool tongue bringing the taste of my own sex into my mouth. Dizzy with pleasure I let you press me back against the floor. Let you ride me, my legs falling open to receive you, the first orgasm coming with the first sweet thrust of your entry. I let you command my body again and again, like moist clay you formed and re-formed to your desire.

The second night, I arrived forewarned of your power. Our bodies began a duel, each trying to impress the other. At what point did heartless skill transform itself to heartfelt passion? The beguiling fingers begin fiercely to clench and grasp? I remember your cries . . . and mine. The slick slide of our bodies. The coolness within you, your balls tight and round in my hand. The sudden dark perfume of your musk as your body arched and shattered beneath me.

The third night I came to you drowning and pulled you down with me.

The fourth night . . . the fourth night I was late. The Keeper told me no one had claimed you—instead you were performing. I stood behind the jet curtain, half hidden by its glittering strands, and watched you taken by two massive Zorions, trapped between two dark green-pelted forms, tender flesh gripped by clawed hands. I watched your mouth swallowing one wet pink cock, your ass the other. I could see your face behind the thrusting buttocks of the one who filled your throat.

Perceiving me, you froze for a second, until the one fucking you slapped your ass sharp and loud, urging you on. Your cock, dangling half hard between your legs, stiffened then and began to rise. The audience laughed and cheered. I wanted to know if it was my eyes or his hand which brought you erect.

Magnetized, I stayed to witness the climax of your performance. I heard the harsh cries of the Zorions as they came. Watched the white sperm shoot from your cock, spurting through the spread legs of your captor into the waiting mouth of an eager participant who joined in from the audience. I turned and left then, full of nausea and desire.

For a week, wanting you, I refused to return. For a week, I prowled the streets after dark, trying futilely to stanch the open wound of lust. Above me the stars burned feverishly, a bright, speckled pox on the black skin of night. Around me, in the city of night, the city of whores, hot eyes watched me from doorways. Arms and thighs beckoned me into alleyways. Voices whispered in the dark, soft as silk sliding off skin. Harsh as silk ripped from flesh.

For a week, I hunted the brothels for fair-haired Terran slaves, trying to re-create your magic in a slanting line of cheekbone, the chiseled edge of lip, the hard swell of thigh sliding to a soft inner surface, the soft weight of balls growing tight in my hand. I tried to obliterate your gold in blue skin, in glistening black, in skin crimson as cinnabar, purple as blood. Tried to drown your earth scent in a sea of sweat. I found cocks bigger than yours to fill me, and when none fit as well, tried to erase the memory of your thrusting in the yielding wet flesh of women.

Wanting only the one, I drowned myself in the many. A delirium of sex that left me as wasted as any fever would, and as parched. . . .

Today in the gymnasium S'Karrak made a point to seek me out. He told me he had been to visit you. His hard, flat eyes fixed on my face as he described your encounter, how he wound you in your chains so you could not move, your hips raised to his entry. He said he thought, perhaps, to buy you for himself. There were certain pleasures the House would put no price to . . . fearing you damaged.

I have not asked what it would cost to buy you. I told myself the price would be too high, and paid in pride and honor. I have never been any man's fool. This gilded whorehouse has taught you certain skills to survive, forced you to live by your wits and your beauty, your strength a toy for the amusement of aliens. Why should you not use those skills against me, the enemy? I told myself you were clever enough to pretend, to practice your wiles in hope I would purchase you, blinded with passion.

I decided to return to The House of the Twin Jewels. One final visit to put you from my mind and consign you to your fate. Tonight I would remember who I am, and you would remember what you are.

The swift light in your face quickly faded. You were tense and wary as I led you upstairs by your chains. Pulling you across the room to the bed, I ordered you to kneel before me. I would have your mouth on me before I took you. You backed up a step, then faced me squarely, eyes narrowed, tense with anger and defiance.

"No . . ." you said, shaking your head in negation. "Not with you."

"You are insolent, slave," I hissed. "Kneel."

"No," you repeated, your voice low and cold. And then, "I did not choose to be a whore."

I struck you, knocking you onto the bed. The power of the blow stunned you. You stared at me, shocked, a trickle of blood on your lips, while I raised your arms above your head and fixed the chains to the central post. Next I fastened your ankle cuffs to the corners, using the heavy gold clasps kept there for that purpose. Submission is included in your price. They would punish you more severely than I, if I told them you resisted me.

There was no resistance now. You lay immobilized in your chains, completely vulnerable to my touch. I placed my hands on the taut, smooth skin of your inner thighs, and ran them up to encircle the bronze gold thatch of hair at your groin. Your cock, still soft, stirred slightly in its nest.

"Don't," you pleaded.

I took it in my hand. You averted your face, teeth sinking into your swollen lip. Your muscles tightened, rigid with denial, even as your sex lifted to my touch. I stroked the thickening flesh, letting the harsh dry friction stiffen it. Rising above you, I thrust down, driving myself onto your hardened cock. You gasped and shuddered as I covered you, the intense sensations threatening to overwhelm your control. I thrust fiercely, fighting my enjoyment to keep my dominance. You refused to respond until I neared my climax, and then the fire caught us both. I felt your body lifting to meet mine.

You cried out as I jerked myself off you. I gripped your cock like a pommel and thrust my cunt against your hardness. Cheated, you fought to pull away from me. I watched you struggle as I rubbed my clit on your cock. I knew you willed yourself to wilt in my hand, but I saw your skin flush, heard your breath quicken, felt the hardness I grasped in my hand pulse and thicken. You moaned, helplessly, your hips reaching up, sliding the hot length of your sex against my slickness. I knew you were peaking with me, and worked our bodies to a frenzy, feeling a dark wave of triumph rising within me.

On the edge of that dark peak, your body suddenly stilled beneath mine. Your face turned back to me, your eyes wide and desperate, sweat glittering on your skin like tears.

"A'Asha," you whispered hoarsely, "A'Asha, don't do this. . . ."

I did not ask how you learned my name. It would not be difficult. It should have made no difference to me to hear it from your lips. But it did. I had acted as a stranger to myself and you recalled me.

For a moment I leaned over you, panting, fighting the nausea that swept through me. That dark wave, unbroken, curled inward upon itself, rolling back, leaving behind it a bleak and bitter backwash of despair. I felt no fury of passion now, only desolation. I had tried to force response from your body, and my own, a vicious and joyless spasm. In the end I only hated myself in this futile attempt to despise you.

Your cock lay soft beneath me now, shriveled along with my

lust. I lifted myself from your hips and sat for a moment on the side of the bed. I felt drained, as if I had come to the end of myself. I only wanted to leave behind this brutal humiliation of us both. Not looking at you, I unlocked the chains and laid them beside you, then rose and crossed the room to my scattered clothes. . . .

Your hand is on my shoulder, turning me to face you. I meet your gaze.

"A'Asha," you say, "my name is Ian."

"E'Yon." I repeat the name you have given me. Acknowledging you.

"Stay with me." You kneel before me now, of your own choice. Your arms wrap around me . . . so fierce before and now you cling. You raise your face and your expression has changed again. Your smile is bitter, tremulous, mocking me and yourself. Your eyes dark and full of pain. "Stay."

My ruses, my cruelty, have come to nothing. Nothing but a lie you will not have between us. Let my touch be truth, as yours is. One last night as lovers . . . then strangers forever.

Do you see that it is the last time . . . that it must be the last time? I want you too much. I must escape, somehow, this passion that consumes me. All that remains between us now is my own fear. I could buy you, and take you into bond. Bonds, even aliens, may serve the Empire. Whatever you are now, you were a warrior once. Your warrior's spirit survives. You could fly the stars with me, shieldmate and lover.

If I did not love you too much. . . .

Slowly my fingers wind through your hair, gathering all the multicolors of metal, white gold and yellow, bronze and copper, warm colors flowing cool through my hand, cool and liquid smooth as water, faintly rustling like sand. I feel your breath on me, as it was the first night, your strong hands caressing my thighs. My center is hot and throbbing once again, turning liquid with your touch. I hear myself moan as your mouth touches me, your tongue sliding between my lips, your thumbs gently spreading them. Tender wet silk membranes, the keen edge of teeth, soft stroking muscle of tongue. You fasten on me, sucking desperately, and now I am desperate too, hungering to taste you.

This is the one thing I have yet to give you. Pulling away, I press you to the floor, smooth and sweetly chill beneath our fevered flesh. Heads bent to loins, our bodies mirror each other. Two mouths cover two straining sexes, swollen bud and shaft. Two hands shape the slope of back and mold the swelling curve of hip. I part the mounded cheeks, tease the damp curled tendrils, paired fingers seeking the moist pulsing rim that contracts, then opens to their touch. Your fingers slide over my clitoris, carry the moisture of your mouth to mingle with the flow of my womb. We enter gently, probing to reach the deepest point of pleasure. Fingers burrowing, mouths sucking, we devour each other . . . our only desire to drink each other's hearts.

Our bodies jolt and quiver with the burning current of desire. Melded we plunge deeper and deeper. Linked to form one crazed, craving creature, we drown ourselves in fire. Our flesh melting dissolving into flame, flame bursting, exploding into light liquidlight pouring from us into us . . . filling our souls with an incandescent blaze of brightness.

My senses return to me, slowly. I sigh. You reach out and clasp my hand. We lie together, exhausted, our heads pillowed on each other's thighs. Traces of rich seed linger on my mouth, potent milky wine. I lick the prodigal drops from my lips, savoring the salt sweet taste.

After a time, I feel your body tensing next to mine, and the grip of your hand tightens. I raise myself up and look at you. Your eyes are filled with questions, questions I know you are too proud to ask . . . and too afraid. The flickering bright colors fade in your eyes. You close them again, and turn your head aside, shutting what we have shared inside yourself. You release my hand, drawing one arm beneath you to cushion your averted face. The chain rustles across the floor, then lies still.

And so you say good-bye, accepting . . . demanding . . . the parting I can no longer endure.

It will cost me dear in credits to unlock those chains you wear.

Dearer still in favors, to clear a Terran bond to serve aboard my ship.

But I have spent too long in the darkness of myself. . . .

Whatever your price I will pay it.

II

Mystery

For women, the emotional relationship between two people, the love, trust, familiarity, and caring, account for making real-life sexual experiences particularly good. However, in erotic fiction, passion is often generated by the mysterious partner, the one who offers no security, a partner who cannot be totally owned. The unavailable partner becomes more exciting, more compelling, because the relationship cannot be played out completely. The mystery man is often the strong silent type who elicits passion by allowing the woman to maintain her fantasy projection while challenging her to continue to probe his undisclosed depths.

Situations in which the woman does not feel secure in her partner's love, in which she cannot control her lover's responses to her, promote a chronic state of disequilibrium. She has no place to rest or relax. She must always be ready to react, jump in, protect herself. And this state of heightened readiness, this emotional activation, when directed toward the erotic, creates a high degree of passion and erotic response.

Often, these are the passionate love-hate relationships in which the flare-ups create the kind of intensity that makes the person feel vibrant, alive. However, most frequently, these dark, passionate relationships burn themselves out. And while such a relationship may remain one of a woman's most memorable affairs, the roller-coaster ride often becomes intolerable, and a realization that certain self-destructive processes are in operation accounts for the relationship's final demise. This is true in "Birthing," by Doraine Poretz, in which the main character was never, when outside the bedroom, able to equal the intimacy and intensity she experienced with her partner during lovemaking. The man's lack of commitment, coupled with his veiled promise of more, made him even more enticing. "The complicated personality, a man with many layers, is particularly seductive to me," says Doraine. "His inability to articulate his emotions, yet his strong expression of attraction and need for the main character in the story is an inherent contradiction which I find challenging and exciting."

Many women, in a similar relationship, experience themselves as victims and bemoan their fate—vowing to never risk again. However, the main character in "Birthing" is able to step out of the relationship, take back her power, and continue on with her life, without diminishing the significance of the love affair.

In "Leaving Sasha," Susan Block writes about a woman who feels possessed by a man, in a relationship that is so compelling that it can almost be called an obsession. Try as she might, the main character cannot put out the fire created by this man. She is in his power; even his house is magical. And it is this quality of her being so out of control that even she doesn't know what her next move will be, that keeps the eroticism at a feverish pitch.

In addition, Susan is writing about the comparison between superficial sex and passionate sex. She presents us with a number of different sexual encounters filled with variety and humor, all of which are erotic and fun, but the intensity of the main character's feelings for Sasha moves the eros to another level. According to Susan, "In passionate sex you are not in the real world. You meet on another plane and are not deciding whether or not you should get married, should have children, have enough money, whether you respect the person. Judgment is set aside in favor of the intensity of the experience."

When mystery and adventure merge, we have a double heightening of emotional response. Nisa Donnelly weaves the two in "The Scavenger Hunt," the ultimate lesbian fantasy adventure story. And whereas in heterosexual situations there can be real danger in going off on a sexual adventure with a stranger, the danger is mitigated when the mysterious and unknown partner is another woman. According to Nisa, "The typical lesbian fantasy is going into a bar and meeting the ideal person. Here, Randi lives out her fantasy. And she can act out the experience with impunity, because she is going off with another woman." It is the mixture of anxiety and excitement in response to this very femme, but unexpectedly dominant, mystery woman that intensifies Randi's erotic attraction.

Deena Metzger's main character in "Blood Oranges" also encounters the dark stranger. The fear and daring she experiences in going into the unknown with him intensifies the erotic for her. He is not the safe, boring man, but a man with the kind of otherness she can barely comprehend. According to Deena, "In agreeing, in fact instigating, the meeting with this total stranger, the woman enters the unknown. And I believe all good sex has some component of the unknown in it. You must continually reveal a part of yourself, try something new, open up to each other again suddenly for the sexual experience to be truly erotic."

For Deena, mystery, the unknown, entails the spiritual. "When sexuality enters into the spiritual realm, which is its highest form, I find that the erotic experience is also enhanced. As the two characters' bodies come together, there is a sense of unification with the world and there is a healing that takes place that is far beyond pleasure."

This sense of the spiritual as being a part of the particularly erotic experience showed up in the stories of quite a number of the authors. Again, there was a sense of entering into the unknown, of losing their sense of physical boundaries and a merging with the other person and all of the universe. For Suzanne Miller, this spiritual aspect is the most significant aspect of the erotic.

In "The Hunters," Suzanne creates what she feels is a transcendent sexual experience, where, although known to each other, the man and woman are revealed anew. "Sex becomes the doorway to Eros," she says, "to the mystery which can lead to the direct experience that nothing in life is known and that everything and everyone, including oneself, is constantly changing and therefore temporary. In that comprehension, so vivid because it is felt on the physical plane, lies the freedom to act in the moment, opening the possibility for deep passion and ecstatic union. It is on the edge of the unknown that we find the true erotic."

The five stories in this section deal primarily with a sense of mystery, the mysterious partner as well as the mystery of the spiritual component of sex. And both of these aspects of the unknown are utilized by the authors to heighten the erotic experience.

Birthing

DORAINE PORETZ

An arrow of moons startled her bones. She grew thin, her flesh streaming away. She hadn't slept a whole night during the first months of their separation but instead would wake and talk to the moon. Sometimes her body heaved silently in rhythmic waves, or a cry would sound—a perfect O which reverberated through the house, circling the bedpost, the slender lamp—a cry which began from her cunt, rose to her belly, through her heart until it was arrested for one moment in the blue light of her throat.

The bird beating in her chest was still alive. For years she had felt these wings helplessly locked in their narrow cavity. Then, when the man came toward her—a powerful wind from her left side, a wind in her ear spiraling to her brain, bringing the mountains to her eyes—the bird's wings beat more fiercely. They shook the opening in her chest, making room for all the ancestral ghosts and dreams of progeny. Suddenly she could no longer live in the manufactured days of white bread and linoleum. She could hardly tolerate driving a car, bantering with her colleagues at work. The man made himself only partially known: between them was the abyss, and she lived each day on the rim.

The day was bright and hot when they met. Most of the interviewing of new students had been completed in the beginning of the week. She wondered how long she would be able to tolerate the work. She was a sculptor, not an administrator, and yet she managed to do the job. But, in the last few months, she was feeling a shortness of breath. It was a constriction so violent that at times she had to excuse herself and walk the streets around the school, looking up to the top of the pines that lined the block. When she returned to her office this one day, she was startled to find a man standing in front of her desk. He was tall and broad-shouldered, dressed in jeans and a multicolored shirt. She was struck most with his hair: black, with a blaze of white that slashed across his brow.

"Did I startle you?" he asked. "I'm sorry."

"Oh, no. Not really," she lied.

"What does 'not really' mean?" he smiled.

She laughed and shrugged her shoulders and instantly became efficient, rustling some papers on her desk, asking the man to sit down. He had a daughter he wanted to enroll in school. Could she be interviewed as late as June? She assured him, "Since the child would be a senior, and the class was presently open . . ." she kept talking, her words flipping out like a bolt of cloth that could be cut anywhere because of the pattern. She kept talking, watching him closely. And soon she began sculpturing him in her mind's eye. When he got up to leave, she gave him a brochure and was still watching, still sculpturing him.

The next day, he telephoned to ask some irrelevant question about the application. She knew why he had called.

"I had a dream about your ass" he said. "I've obviously never seen your ass, but I knew it was yours." There was a long pause.

"Ah . . . is that all?" she stammered.

"No, I would like to have dinner with you." Another pause. "I'm divorced," he added. "Miserable marriage."

"Oh, that's wonderful," she replied. "No, what I mean—"

"Saturday, my place, 7 P.M."

Driving into the canyon, surrounded by mist, she felt as if she were underwater, winding through the hills as she would reefs. Traveling up and up, she felt herself going deeper in. Into what? Where? The driveway was long, and she imagined a grand house at the end of it. Instead it was small and open, filled with dark wood and glass. Her favorite part was the stone fireplace covered with primitive icons. He handed her white wine in a perfectly clear, crystal glass and brushed back the hair which continually fell on his forehead. She watched him as he got up to cut the cheese. An instinctive regality, in spite of the jeans, shirt and sandals. She accepted another drink, and getting up, she meandered down the hall, peeking into each of the rooms. She felt oddly at home. She heard him call: "If we're to make those reservations . . ."

The Indian food scalded her tongue. She didn't say anything, just drank a lot of water. After a bit, she got used to it. In fact she began to enjoy the heat radiating throughout her body. She fingered the stem of the wineglass.

"When did you have all of yourself?" she asked.

"What?"

"You said before that you are working to get yourself back again. When did you have it all?"

"You want a little more wine?"

"No."

He finished his glass. "When I was about ten, I guess. I lived with my grandfather. He was big and warm and Irish. And he loved working in his garden, drinking his whiskey and cooking. He and I would cook together, dig vegetables out of the yard, and swap stories. Now, that was a good time. We were . . . magicians. We made soup out of weeds, we made things up, and we believed each other."

"What happened?" she asked.
"Happened when?"
"After the tenth summer."
"I grew up," he said.

He lit a candle on the nightstand and turned over to her, and in a flash she recognized him but did not remember a moment later who he was. Only that when he pulled her back toward him, stroked her hair, licked her eyes and neck, then kissed her breasts and belly—until finally feeling him deep inside her—she knew he had made love to her many times before. All the while he was drinking her in, she felt herself streaming down a corridor into a familiar place that was strange only because she had not visited there in oh so long a time. No face reminiscent of any other, but the scents, the textures, the music, were all carrying her across. The bed was a kingdom, then the inside of a cup, the night pouring in tasted like mint. A flashback of a flashback: a swing and a child's foot, the space existed, in the same instant, in his fingers, in the sheets, in her white toes, pressed like pebbles into his thighs. In the dark, she sensed light.

They fell asleep, and when she woke she found him already dressed. He asked her if she wanted to take a walk in the hills. He would bring the dog with them. She felt lazy and cold, but not wanting to be left alone, she consented. The moon was full, and she made her way easily down the drive. The night was surprisingly warm. He walked ahead of her, apparently lost in thought, the leash hanging from his hand, the dog running ahead. The scent of jasmine was wild within her, and the dark, entering her body, made her afraid. She rushed ahead and took his arm, and while they walked, she pressed him to speak about his childhood, his marriage. And while he talked, she saw a young vulnerable boy, the one who had been betrayed too many times before. She wanted to take hold of that boy, gather him in, convince him that she understood his anger, his longing. He called in a sharp voice: "Dino!" The dog obeyed and waited patiently as the leash was hooked to his collar. They walked farther into the hills. He let the dog free. She bent over to pick up some stones. "Don't move," he said. His voice was tender but strong, the timbre of it made her quiver. With one hand he took hold of her waist, and with the other lifted her full skirt and slipped his hand into her nylon panties. "Relax," he said, "relax. Let me see you in the moonlight." He brushed her skirt up to her shoulders and pulled her panties down completely. "You have a magnificent ass," he whispered. He kissed it and stroked it, his hand cool against her warm skin. Her knees shook, and she fell into the rough grass. Dried eucalyptus leaves infused her body. He kept rubbing her ass and soon was on top of her, his chest pressed into her narrow back, one hand cupping her breast, the other stroking her buttocks. "You are so beautiful, do you know that?" He pulled her up on all fours and took his cock and rubbed it against the crack of her ass. She could feel its smooth soft head growing larger. It's like silk, she thought.

"I want to fuck you here," he said.

She could hardly breathe from desire but said, "No . . . don't. Please."

"It won't hurt." He put his finger in her ass. "See how wet you are, so open."

"No," she repeated.

"All right. Whatever you want." His fingers searched for her cunt between the grass and eucalyptus. He rubbed her and pinched her, his fingers exploring, searching for entrance. "You're so wet," he said over and over, "so wet, a deep pool." And then, with no warning, he thrust into her from behind, deep into her cunt. The shock was awesome, and in one instant she was flush to the ground and catapulted toward the stars. He fucked her hard, kept fucking her, filling her up with semen and moonlight, taking them both to kingdom come as the dog looked on.

They circled back to the house. She held on to him the whole way. The hall light was on, and as they walked in, she noticed her gabardine jacket slung over the couch, the empty wineglasses, the cold bits of cheese stuck to the plates. She went into the bathroom, and sitting on the toilet, she looked at her smooth belly, her thighs, her crooked toes. The body was a touchstone: a guide, alive with sensation from the moment they had undressed in the bedroom down the hall, through the corridors of lovemaking, into the wildness of the night. But the body was changing every moment, water being released which just hours ago was being craved, skin falling away.

It was past 2 A.M. She walked into the room where they had made love: the bed was a sprawl, a brush alive with hairs, the toothpaste cap off. All the highlights of intimacy and escape. How long had she known this man?

When she walked into the living room, he was staring at the fire. He made no move toward her. She knew she had to leave. Her body wanted the warmth of his, wanted sleep, but her spirit wanted her own self back again. She put on her jacket. He looked surprised.

"You're not going?" he said.

"Yes."

"But it's so late. Stay till morning."

She wanted to interpret his invitation as desire, but a stronger sense told her it was his disappointment at the loss of control, a break in the dance he had choreographed. He walked her to her car, kissed her, thanking her for the evening. His politeness made her feel hired. Driving down the hill, she wondered if he was thinking about her.

A week passed, and he hadn't called. She wanted to forget the evening, but memory was a beast. Finally she telephoned him from her office, to give herself the illusion that the call was a business matter. He answered and was abrupt, and she felt foolish. He's wondering why I called. She blurted out: "I had this dream about you."

"Oh," he asked, "what was it about?"

"Ah . . . ," she lied, "something about you and the military."

She heard him stiffen. He analyzed the dream coldly, obviously affronted by her dream's impression of him. She hung up, fragmented and flabbergasted, then burst out laughing. That night she wrote him a note explaining the absurdity of it, confessing that she had made the dream up as an excuse to call. He phoned her immediately, saying he would not have had the courage to admit the lie. They made plans to see each other the following week.

The floor creaked. She pushed back the curtain. Her own room was bare and clean. Pine floors. White walls. The bed was brass with a beautiful white chenille spread given to her by her mother. A milk-glass vase with two blue irises stood on a wicker table. She thought about how little time she had spent in this room in the past nine months. He preferred making love in his house, in his bed. She sat on the floor, cross-legged, the sunlight from the window falling in a rectangle at her feet. She sat there, within her pure geometry, and looked out. The trees amazed her; each leaf, struck with morning, sang. They provided such refuge, these trees. She would often fling her arms around them, delighting in their rough skin, sensing the ancient mother within herself. No, she was not alone. It was odd, but often being with him, she felt alone. No, not alone—much worse—misplaced. And yet she knew she was madly in love. What was it? What was she missing? Her urge was to fuse with him, but in many ways he repelled her. In the time they were together, he never once said he loved her, and yet she sensed that his longing for communion, to have her there perfectly and utterly, was as deep as her own. She had always wanted to be in love with a man she felt knew "secret things." The others were always predictable, never poised for flight. This man was different. She remembered the way he first looked at her, carefully as a man does a woman, but deeply, with promise of sight. And when they first made love, she had cried out: "Oh, I want everything!" And pulling her head down toward his mouth he whispered: "You may get it."

They lay face to face on the bed, the room black except for a patio light filtering through the louvered shades.

"Why is it so cold?" she asked.

"The heat doesn't reach back here," he answered.

"You should get a fireplace," she smiled.

"No, I shouldn't," he blurted, suddenly annoyed.

He got up, and she pulled him back into bed. She was used to his moods.

"Stay for a moment," she said. "It's an awesome thing, lying next to someone in the dark. All those invisible worlds that whirl around, that can only be caught when you're lying still next to a lover. I was watching you while you slept. Your lips quiver when you breathe, and your hands—"

"Jesus," he snapped, "stop rhapsodizing, would you? It's just a body like any of the rest, any of the others you might fuck."

"I don't sleep with anyone else. I told you."

"Oh?" he replied, looking up to the ceiling. "And why the hell would I care if you did?" Humiliated, she turned away. "Come here," he cajoled, "don't be childish." He pulled at her shoulder. "I'm sorry. Come here. I want to taste you." She was hurt and angry, but his hand stroking her nipples forced her to turn toward him. "Such beauties," he said, fondling her breasts. And pressing them together, he put his face between them. Then, with great tenderness, his tongue began circling each nipple, moistening each one delicately, finally finding its way to her ear. Her back arched as the silent whorl resonated through her body. She could come like this, the snake-tongue exploring the inner recesses, circling, circling, drawing out the sound of the sea from her ear, covering them both with waves, eroding flesh, indicating the years, the centuries they had lain together.

The telephone rang. She hoped he wouldn't answer it. He fumbled for the light and then the phone. His voice was clear and precise. It unnerved her that he could be so composed after such passion. She knew it was his ex-wife. When he hung up, she saw deep lines etch their way into his face. She pulled him toward her, but he shook her off and got up to wash. The air had changed.

"What would you like to eat?" he asked. "I can make you an

omelette or . . . let's see . . ." She heard the refrigerator door open. "We have turkey, a little camembert . . ."

"It's up to you," she called back. He loved to cook for her. It was a major indulgence in which she delighted. No matter how simple, his meals always had an air of elegance. He cut fruits or vegetables with a delicate eye, extricating a perfectly shaped lemon wedge, slicing a tomato into thin lace circles. In his house, the glasses and crockery shone; the knives were always sharp. Ready.

She got up and pulled his terry robe from the foot of the bed and wrapped it around herself, following him to the front of the house. Scrunched on one side of the living-room couch, she watched him prepare the meal. She took pleasure watching him. Often he was dark, brooding, reading a book or staring into the fire. He would sit, hunched over, his shoulders raised, sipping a drink, and she would recognize a hawk, his intense eyes hooded by unruly brows, the mass of straight hair—feathers which shone in the firelight. At those moments he was other than her lover, other than even some magnificent bird. He was the Stranger, and she was mystified that in his strangeness he could be so attractive and familiar to her.

"That was Carol on the phone before. Tess is unhappy and wants to come here sooner."

"And?"

"And I don't want her to." He poured himself a drink and walked to the sliding glass door and looked out. "I have so much to do here," he said. "Another script is boiling, and I still have rewrites on the last one." He stood a few moments looking out, not saying anything. Then: "I'm not available, you know . . . for anyone. You do understand that, don't you?" He said this all to the glass sliding door, to the city, lit up and flickering, below.

She fingered the tiny pearl bracelet he had given her, remembering how much he delighted in slipping it out of his pocket and surprising her. He was often generous, frequently catching her off guard with some gesture of deep caring: books, flowers, praise for one of her sculptures. Yet just at the moment she felt the relationship was gaining intimacy he would withdraw, not call, treat her with an unnerving politeness. She poured herself a glass of wine.

She remembered the first months of their love affair, arriving at his house one morning, a yellow lily in her hair, her face very brown. He opened the door and cried: "A veritable Gauguin." That gave her courage for what she was about to say: that she was in love with him. And when she told him, he looked away. "That's not possible," he said, uttering it not in wonder, but as a command. She got up to leave, but he held her, would not let her go. Looking into his eyes, she caught a gleam, saw it beyond the shadows, recognized the clear lake of his soul. Terrified, she thought: such beauty should not be allowed.

"I have something to ask you," she said. "I need some advice. It concerns us."

He stopped washing the tomato and turned around. He looked on guard; his voice, however, was nonchalant: "Are you pregnant?"

"No," she laughed. "No, my love, I'm not pregnant."

"Oh," he said, relief clearly echoing in his voice. He went back to washing the tomato and then some lettuce. "What is it, then?"

"I've been offered a job, an opportunity to teach art." He turned around, lettuce in hand, and beamed. "Why, that's wonderful!"

"Yes," she nodded. "It is."

"You don't sound very pleased. What is it? The salary?"

"No, the salary is very good. Only . . . I'd be gone a year . . . in Paris."

"Paris," he smiled. "Not bad." A pause. "But a year. That's a long time."

"Yes." She circled the rim of the glass with her finger. "Well, what do you think?"

"Think? Why, I . . . think . . . it's a fabulous opportunity."

"I know, but what I mean . . . what do you think about me . . . being . . . gone?" He had already turned back to the sink, was now tearing the lettuce. "So?" she asked again. "What do you think?"

"I can't tell you what to do."

"I'm not asking you to do that."

"It's your life."

"I know. I'm just asking for—"

He shot around: "What? What are you asking for?" He was throwing the lettuce into the colander now, shaking it hard, getting the last bit of water out. Suddenly he looked pathetic. He said quietly: "I told you . . . I told you from the beginning that I . . . I . . ."

"Yes," she whispered to herself, finishing her wine in tiny, parceled sips. "You told me."

After four months of separation, she knew it was finally over. Suddenly, she felt oddly relieved. She could begin to look forward to this opportunity: Paris! A chance to be on her own, making art, making money. Everything was packed, ready to be shipped the following day. Somehow, through it all, she had managed to get everything in order. She was terrified she would fail in some way, out there, alone, but she was also excited. In the last week without him, she began to feel that leaving meant finding a part of herself that had been lost. She recalled how in the time they were together she had done very little sculpturing. So much of her time was spent being with him or thinking about him. Even their conversations had revolved around him. Not because he was eager to reveal himself, but rather because she pressed, needing to know every nuance of his emotional makeup, needing to understand him. Was that love, then? That all-encompassing need? In the last weeks, however, a new energy was infusing her life. He was no longer ever-present in her thoughts. I'm free, she thought. Free.

That is why she felt terrified when, this particular morning, she awoke and felt it again. That longing. That terrible ache making its way into her every limb. She heard it hissing along the windowsill, saw it reemerge in a rush of bougainvillea cascading down her neighbor's roof: a glut of purple that pulled her body up by the roots of her hair. And now, swaying there, through the curtain, that longing. Like a fragrant boy. Gently, gently. She could sway with it, lean into it, let it hold her around the waist, let it breathe on her neck. She could give herself over, but no! she could not . . . would not . . . let it any closer. She walked from room to room, her skin tightening.

The white-washed day stretched ahead, threatening under its soft gaze. Seven o'clock. She had gotten all of three hours of sleep. She felt the wings beating, a reverberation that forced her to catch her breath. She quickly telephoned a friend. The answering machine clicked on. She hung up. She fingered a couple of books. No, she didn't want to read. Maybe music. She often danced alone now, naked, one candle illuminating the dark. She had never danced for him. She had wanted to do a luscious strip, make him hot, have him pull a fifty-dollar bill from her cunt, but had never gotten around to it.

She padded into the kitchen and made some coffee, put a croissant into the oven. At least some of her appetite had returned. But there she was, crying again. Oh, God, she thought. Not this again. She ate and glanced at the paper, caught her reflection in the glass of the litho above the table. Jesus, she thought. Do I look awful!

When she heard the doorbell, she thought it was a mistake. A neighbor's bell. The walls were thin enough. It rang again. How could she possibly see anyone? She wiped her eyes and her nose with the back of her hand and asked who it was. There was no reply. She opened the door a crack and . . . "Oh, my god," she murmured. "No. Not now." He looked older, maybe because he hadn't shaved.

He smiled embarrassedly. "I'm sorry I didn't call, but I was driving past, and I . . ." He stopped. "I'll leave if you . . ."

She opened the door. "No . . . please . . . I'm just surprised." Her hands tightened on her robe, then flew to her face. He walked in and looked around. Several boxes were pushed against the wall.

"All packed, eh? When do you go?"

"Two weeks."

"It's good. Good you decided to go."

"Yes."

He walked into the living room, stood looking at her. She ran her fingers through her hair. "Ah . . . do you want a cup of coffee?"

"No. Thank you." He took out a cigarette. His hands looked older too. The skin dryer. "Can I . . . can I sit down?" he asked.

"Oh, oh, of course," she laughed. Nervous. She was so nervous. She asked again: "You sure no coffee? Some tea?" He smiled and shook his head, sat there smoking in front of the white-shaded window. He leaned over and ran his fingers along the back of a small clay sculpture. "I've always admired this piece," he said. He smiled again. "You're looking too thin."

"I've missed your cooking."

"You should take better care of yourself."

"I'm beginning to," she said.

After a moment he abruptly got up. "Well, I don't really know why I stopped in. I was up early, writing, and went to get the paper and passed your house and—" He stopped. In the past she would be the one to rescue him from any awkwardness, make an excuse, fill the gap. He was uncomfortable now, standing with his weight shifted to one side, looking at her, disjointed. She said nothing. Couldn't think of anything to say. Then she remembered the keys.

"Oh," she mumbled, "I've got something to give you." She rummaged in the desk and walked over to him. "The keys to your house." He waited a moment and then took them, and then suddenly he pulled her in, pressing her shoulders so tightly she heard her small bones crack. "Christ," he whispered, "I will miss you . . . I *will* . . ." He wrapped his arms around her and began to madly kiss her face, all of it, the cheeks, the chin, the nose, biting her ears, taking hold of her hair, pulling her head back so he could kiss her throat. Suddenly she was crying.

He kissed her for a long, long time, her shoulders, her breasts and then opening her robe, he fell on his knees kissing her stomach, the inside of her thighs. She stood there, her toes deep in the pile of the yellow carpet, feeling herself an accordion—waves of pleasure then fear then sadness playing her. And now, standing above him, she looked down, saw his head, the mass of dark feathered hair between her legs. His mouth was on her, sucking her up until he pulled at her buttocks, pulling her down to him. Holding her, sitting face to face, he wrapped his legs around her behind and she around his, and taking her face once again in his hands, he kissed her mouth so hard she could feel his teeth touching her own. He sucked her lips, running his tongue under the upper lip, and then the lower, surely he will devour me, she thought, surely my whole head could fit into his mouth. Her fingers began frantically unbuttoning his shirt; she felt the electric hairs on his chest coarse against her palm. She pressed her breasts against the shock of hair, igniting more sparks, and he kept kissing her as though if he stopped, she would disappear.

She fell back, and his hand found her hot cunt. While he fingered her, she thought of the deep fluted flowers that curled around her yard. Such deep shimmering throats. His fingers were wet, and he kept kneading her slippery hole, rubbing one side then the other. He was over her now, his pants off, and she reached into his underwear and grabbed his cock, thick and smooth, and rubbed him—up down, up down. Her mouth suddenly on him, licking him, sucking him, thinking: I could stay, I'll cancel the trip and stay, I don't need anything but him, just him. She fell back again, his fingers were still inside her, her legs opening. I don't need anything but this, she thought, just him, his pow— Oh, oh, oh! "Come, baby, I want you to come," she heard him say, "just like this, just for you, just come," she heard him say, "Yes," *I can't promise anything* she heard him say, "That's it, baby," *I mean, I'm not available* she heard him say, "Come sweetheart . . ." and she felt the bird flapping violently in her chest, crazy now to break through. She put her hand on his hand and guided it to exactly the right spot. "That's it," she said, "that's it . . . Oh, oh, right, I'm . . ." *a dark bird* "coming . . ." *fierce, sequined* "I am . . ." *my own, my very own powerful* "coming . . . Christ!" she cried, "yes, yes, I'm here now . . . I'm here . . . Christ!" she yelled . . . *bursting* . . . "coming . . . I'm coming . . ."

She kissed him tenderly on his cheek and promised to write. He smiled and stroked her face and left. She ran after him to give him the sculpture he had admired. Walking back to her apartment, she thought how she still had to buy some French language tapes and make arrangements for her cat. She didn't look when he drove away.

Leaving Sasha; or, The Bed Makes the Man

SUSAN BLOCK

For the third time, and the last time, I was leaving. Sex had nothing to do with it.

It had to do with power, with possession, and control, with wanting to have kids and wanting to *be* kids, with wanting to be sane and needing to get crazy. It had something to do with each of the wise opinions of all my good friends, including my mother. It had to do with running, with not looking back.

But sex? Nothing to do with it.

It didn't even have anything to do with love. Because, after all, I still loved Sasha. Even as I backed my old scar-faced station wagon packed with my life in milk crates and clothes bags out of his long skinny Hollywood driveway; even as I watched his deep amaretto eyes getting smaller and smaller through my windshield, I loved Sasha more than ever. He stood there—black, curly Cossack hair, soft flannel shirt flung hastily over strong broad shoulders (Sasha never went to a gym; his muscles developed from actually *working),* black boots, black stare—under the oddly lit entrance to his fantasy-filled gingerbread house where I had been one of his resident fantasies. I was a princess in a fairytale bed, a fanciful layer cake of mattresses piled one on top the other beneath a stained-glass portrait of the Land of Oz. A bed of dreams for a Man of Dreams. "Pipedreams," my good friends called them. Or maybe they were visions . . .

I slammed on my brakes, narrowly missing the ice-cream truck that used to wake us out of that bed every morning. No; sex had nothing to do with leaving Sasha, but it had everything to do with staying away.

Because if this third time was to really be the last time, I needed something very strong, some kind of super knockout drug for the heart, something to distract the desire, the sadness, the lost, lonely, ice-cream panic. And that something had to be sex.

And I knew exactly where to get it. Andre, the Playboy of West Hollywood (or, as he preferred to call it, "Beverly Hills Adjacent"). Find a heterosexual singles party between Fairfax and Westwood and you'd find Andre, always with a different woman; both Hefner bunnies and brilliant lady executives practically begging him to let them into his cologne-drenched Calvin Klein briefs. Ever since I'd impulsively slipped him my card, he'd been leaving steamy messages on my answering machine. Sasha despised Andre. He was so ultra-slick, so satin-lipped, so utterly *GQ.* Andre was just what I needed.

And when I arrived back at my own barely lived-in apartment, there was another message from him on my machine just waiting for me . . .

"*Rosalyn . . . Andre . . . Nicole just left, and I'm all alone relaxing in my Jacuzzi . . . The water is so . . . hot . . . and wet . . . Why aren't you here with me . . . swirling in it . . . Don't call . . . Just come . . .*"

I clicked off my machine . . . and went.

Andre, I anticipated, could teach me discipline through sex. Through him, I would learn control, how to stay on course and not look back. Everything about him was so hard, tight, so precision-cut: his athletic, Nautilus-pumped body, crisp, flaxen hair, smooth-skinned, finely chiseled features, cruelly curved mouth, perfect teeth . . .

Andre sold real estate, though he liked to tell people that he *used* to sell real estate, now being into moving more glamorous properties like feature films and rock videos. Actually, it looked as if he sold sunglasses. I counted about twenty pairs lying on his art-deco coffee table, one for each of his man-of-action sports: tennis, golf, running, snow-skiing, water-skiing, girl-trapping . . .

He trapped me as soon as he stepped out of the tub, his gorgeous golden body dripping and flushed with heat. We'd barely exchanged pleasantries before we were upstairs in his boudoir, a high-tech black-on-black affair, his super king-sized plush ebony mat raised high upon a platform like a stage. Above it hovered a bigger-than-lifesize blow-up of Andre in ski shades coursing through white powder. Discipline. Control. The man knew how to never look back.

I looked directly into the cool cobalt eyes of the "real" Andre and boldly placed my hands upon his hard, fetching little towel-wrapped butt, knowing that would make him kiss me. My eyes closed and lips opened to his luscious minty tongue, which plunged into my mouth like an experienced diver who knows exactly where the pearls are, sending sharp electric shivers down my spine. One of his hands slipped off my skirt as the other slid between my bare thighs, his finger pressing up inside me, all the while gently pushing me back upon his perfect, smooth, black bed.

Then he flung off his towel, his long, glistening cock curving back toward his flat stomach. I bent toward it, and he pushed me back, looking down at me like a skiing champion at the top of a great mountain. He paused a moment, searching my body for the "fall-line," the surest path through my slopes and curves, then down he plunged, past the starting gate, skiing right through me, so hard and fast I could barely breathe. This must be what I need —I thought as he whipped my jangled body around and traversed the "backside of the mountain"—raw sex: icy-hot, athletic, impersonal, perfect.

But here plunging turned to pumping—constant, relentless, aerobic coition—in and out and on for hours—or what started to seem like hours. At one point, Andre even jumped off me and onto his Lifecycle, biked a few rounds, then bounced from his trampoline back onto the bed for more calisthenic pumping on me, his newest piece of exercise equipment. And the man never tired, never stopped, never even came.

As he gained control, I lost consciousness. Just nodded off somewhere between the in and the out. Hours—or maybe minutes—later, I got up, stumbled into his black and gray bathroom, swabbed some Vaseline around between my aching thighs, slipped on my clothes, and took off.

I drove away thinking of Sasha, about how he'd sometimes whisper, "Oh, Baby, I belong inside you, you know I belong inside you," as he'd push through the soft folds of fleshy feeling, how he'd suddenly pull back and gaze at me with such tenderness, such infinite longing, and then press in farther, making us both come with an intensity that bordered on poetry.

But I was losing it, losing control. I sped down the dark boulevards like a chased woman. Other men could look at me like Sasha had, I thought. Other men could satisfy me. I just had to find them. In the meantime, I switched on the radio:

"You make me feel . . . like a virgin . . . oh ooohhoohhoh oh . . ." The only man who'd ever made *me* feel like a virgin was Rick, my first boyfriend, and that was probably because at the time I really *was* a virgin. Rick had satisfied me, and he was smart, well-mannered, responsible, Jewish; my mother had adored him. Unfortunately, he was now married with two kids in a suburb of Pittsburgh. But I knew another Rick who lived in L.A. . . .

This Rick was a dream—sweet, sensitive, and very solvent, a

little on the hefty side, but hung like a porno star. Moreover, he could cook. Within his bright kitchen was a yuppie's garden of culinary delights: bowls and pans of every size and design, gleaming knives, whirring blenders, mixers, whippers and tenderizers. A bounty of colorful fruits, meats, fresh herbs and spices simmered in pots and laid spread out upon the countertops, emitting intoxicating, exotic aromas. Fortification, I thought: Just what I need to give me strength to stay away from Sasha.

Rick grinned, a big matzoh-meal Pillsbury Doughboy, speared a succulent bit of veal and thrust it between my salivating lips. "Yummm," I groaned. This was not just a man my mother would like; this was a man just like my mother.

Supper was long, languorous, delicious: The veal was bathed in a silky French cream sauce laced with sweet, rosy apples and savory mushrooms. The pasta was luscious, the salad crisp, and the wine—Rick *knew* his wine. "Could hedonism be a reverse form of discipline?" I wondered alcoholically as Rick talked (he could *talk*, too!) wistfully about the thirty-nine-year-old out-of-work actress he'd been dating who refused to have kids until she'd starred in a major motion picture. "Oh, perfect," I thought, licking the sauce around my lips. "I want kids, Rick wants kids; everyone will approve."

I considered telling Rick about Sasha, speaking lightly of his maddening Slavic eccentricities, or perhaps even admitting to what was turning into an obsession for this man I was trying to leave. But before I could summon a word on the subject, Rick rushed kitchenward, then emerged holding two frosty pastel-peach bowls, and spooned a sliver of the sweetest, lightest, fruitiest fresh sorbet into my open mouth.

Then, before I could swallow, he dropped down under the table, pulled off my black patterned panty hose and began eating me with much more relish than he had eaten the veal. I began hallucinating that this Rick was my old Rick come back from the past to marry me, to lift me up out of my Sasha-bred turmoil and set me on a china plate swimming in a sea of French cream sauce. "Ohh . . . ahhh . . . you're verrry . . . ummm . . . goood at . . . thaaat," I gasped as he kissed it, licked it, flicked it, sucked it, slurped it like a shake through a straw. I slid off the chair, down onto the floor, he kept eating, and I started coming, gushing right into his mouth.

The new Rick didn't even want me to suck his hefty happy shlong; no, tonight he was doing the cooking *and* the eating. He picked me up and carried me into his bedroom, the banquet hall of his decadent "restaurant." Soft jazz oozed from raised stereo speakers, flattering low mauve lights flickered, Chinese satin sheets stretched across the heated water bed like a tablecloth awaiting the final course in his feast of many pleasures. I was it, of course, the last liqueur. But he chomped me like a cheeseburger —devoured my flesh, consumed my juices, then held onto me with one hand, licked the other palm and wet down his nine inches of hard, hot kosher meat. He thrust it inside me and groaned softly like a wine connoisseur discovering a particularly wondrous Chardonnay. As he pushed and pulled and the water bed rocked, I felt as if I were drowning in cream sauce, smothered in the mounds of his hot flesh. Unlike Andre, Rick (thank heaven) was not opposed to coming. He did so with another soft groan, rolled himself off me onto the water bed, and belched.

I closed my eyes and saw myself swimming nude underwater at a pool party. The other partiers were eating, while Sasha and I frolicked like dolphins, grabbing and kissing, dunking and squealing. I tried giving him an underwater blowjob, came up sputtering . . . and triumphant . . .

"Rick?" I said softly, hoping he might help me regain control, perhaps "eat" away my invading thoughts of Sasha. But he didn't reply, just snored peacefully, a baby whale after a big meal.

The next night, I decided to give it a rest. Perhaps what I needed was mind control, my mind over Sasha's matter. With that objective, I flipped on my machine and took a trip to the posh Century City offices of a highly respected, consequently expensive psychic medium. There I spoke to a spirit from another (probably asexual) dimension named "Dr. Peabodies" who "came through" the personage of a rather good-looking ex-

BMW dealer named Pete. Briefly, I wondered what sex with a medium might be like. Would Pete hump while Dr. Peabodies howled? Surely doing it with a doctor from another dimension would utterly obliterate Sasha, a mere human, from my psyche. It would lift me high above my obsession; only, this time I wouldn't be on an elevated sexercise mat or swimming in a plate of French cream sauce. I would be flying high on the spiritual plane. A woman possessed by "the spirit" could never be possessed by any man . . .

I didn't dare propose such an intimate extra-dimensional idea, however, but simply exhaled and asked the inevitable: "Should I stay away from Sasha? Or maybe—should I go back?"

"My dear, oh my dear, my dear," pronounced Pete / Dr. Peabodies in squeaky, singsong East Indian Brooklynese. "The mere manner in which you have phrased your question reveals your answer." Dr. Peabodies cleared Pete's throat and smiled slyly. "Should you 'go *back*'? Ah my dear, never go backwards! Always go forward! Grow and prosper! God bless you!"

Aha! I thought, the spirits supported me. I had been *meant* to leave Sasha! I was a chess piece en route to my next square. I was running fast, flying high, moving in the right direction. "Never go backwards! Always go forward!" I repeated like a mantra, and vowed that I would never again conjure images of Sasha when I slept with another man.

I decided that the best way to do that would be to play out—to the hilt—a fantasy of sexual power so strong, so completely overwhelmingly compelling that there wouldn't be room among my brain cells for images of Sasha. I called Michael, a short, divorced, dirty-minded director of issue-oriented TV movies-of-the-week. Several times, Michael had offered to assist me in acting out my wildest fantasies. At this point, I was ready.

"Okay, Michael, here's what we'll do . . ." I said, already assuming control.

"Love it," he replied. "Absolutely love it." (Men like Michael, who take charge all day, adore being told exactly what to do when it comes to sex.) "I'll put my secretary on getting the set together tout de suite."

This time, I would re-create myself into a paragon of voluptuous might. I frizzed out my long, straight hair into a jungle of curls and ringlets, covered my body with oil and rust-colored streaks (for the "wounded" effect), slipped on a tiger-tooth necklace, wrapped one leopard-print scarf around my hips and another around my chest. Then I looked in the mirror and saw a ravishing, radiating savage: Hippolyta, Queen of the Amazons.

When I arrived at Michael's I noticed that his secretary had indeed set our scene: His big, airy beach house was strewn with green leaves and branches and smelled like mangoes. "Jungle Love" played from a hidden stereo, wrestling mats covered the floor. A tangle of nets and ropes lay waiting for action in one corner of the den. And in the opposite corner, looking ever so dapper in khaki and pith, lay Michael—my very own Great White Hunter.

He pointed a camera right at me as I charged through the door like an angry elephant. "I know the meaning of that magic box, White Man Devil!" I trumpeted in my version of Royal Amazonian Broken English.

"It's just a camera, Queen." He grinned, getting into the game.

"No! It is an instrument of power!" I corrected, stalking him slowly so his lascivious brain could fully register my fabulous costume. "White men use it to steal the souls of their women." Somewhere in the back of our heads, we knew we sounded like a laughable old Tarzan movie, but we weren't laughing; we were *into* it. This was fantasy; this was Hollywood. Mind control through suspended disbelief.

"You will not steal my soul, White Man Devil!" I declared, picking up the rope and whipping it around him, snatching the camera and tossing it into the heap of nets. Slowly, I removed my upper leopard-print scarf, revealing my oiled brown breasts, tooth necklace dangling dangerously between them. Then, cheetah-quick, I tied the scarf around his open mouth. He struggled against the ropes, but I held them fast, loosening them just enough so we could wrestle like lion cubs all over the mats.

"O Queen, how might I satisfy your royal pleasure?" my Hunter inquired ever so timidly as I pinned his shoulders to the mat, rubbing my body up and down, up and down over the rock-hard bulge in his safari shorts. I jumped up and flung myself into the large chair in one corner of the room. From there, I felt I could survey the whole jungle, my Queendom, that steaming realm of unconscious urges buzzing with dragonflies, dancing natives, winding, raging rivers of death and desire, and the beat of an ancient drum. Down in the pit (on the mat) lay a beautiful white man, my Hunter, my Slave, writhing in my ropes, a captured snake.

"Come to me," I commanded. "Come kneel to me at my throne." He crawled quickly to where I sat, my legs spread wide, glistening. I untied the scarf around his mouth and guided it to the quivering source of the Amazon that boiled and bubbled between my thighs. "Drink of my secrets, and you will be strong," I intoned, and he drank obediently, though *not* with much relish (unlike Ravenous Rick, Michael wasn't much of a cunnilingus connoisseur). But I, being Queen of my own Pleasure, needed only the slightest flick of the white man's tongue to make me come like the River Goddess, flooding the entire jungle, making the natives and all the animals run roaring and screaming in terror.

"Now my power is yours, White Man Devil!" I cried, and he ripped off his safari shorts, mounting me on my throne, pounding me like an animal skin, stealing my Indian treasure like a ruthless conquistador, all in just a few blinding seconds before he fell back, spent, upon the mats (Michael never could stay inside me for more than a minute before he came).

I closed my eyes, floating down the Amazon, then opened them only to see what I was sure was a mirage: a little China doll, a beautiful, olive-skinned, young Oriental woman clad in nothing but jade-green eye shadow. "O Queen, how might I, your humble servant, be of service to Your Majesty?" she asked in her tiny doll-voice.

"That's Liana, my housekeeper," Michael explained, breaking the mood only briefly. "I thought an extra character might make our scene more fun."

"Oh?" I was one speechless queen. Liana laughed and squeezed into the throne beside me, her long black hair brushing my skin like a shower of petals. She looked up at me, her shining dark eyes expectant, awaiting my "command." "Make love to me," I whispered, shocked and delighted by my own shameless nerve, and she caressed my body with hers, her warm skin melting me like butter on steaming rolls. I felt a terrific surge of sensual strangeness, my limbs locked around this tiny, lovely replica of my own female form. Her hands were delicate and exploratory like mine, but smaller; her breasts firm and round like mine, yet so exquisitely petite. Our lips touched, two soft, cool feminine mouths, two gentle, inquisitive tongues. Liana was the little sister I'd never had; we were Amazon warrior women at play, two Vietnamese whores performing for the American soldier who masturbated as he spied on us. She sucked me with her tiny mouth, her ladyfingers touching me as I came to her, laughing like bubbles rising in champagne, rising above all that ever tied me down. Then I dove to her pretty, silken-haired womb, uncertain at first as to how to go about doing this, then reveling with power as I realized that I knew her pleasures as I knew my own, could almost feel myself being licked as I licked her, innately understood her rhythms and desires as I never truly understood any man's. She was my geisha, my doll; I controlled her as I had been wanting to control myself. As she moaned and sighed, tensing toward release, I felt I knew exactly what she was feeling, every roll of her slim hips, every luscious flutter of her vaginal walls. I sucked my sweet geisha-doll, pushed even farther as I felt Michael's stiff maleness suddenly thrust inside me from behind; for then she was coming in front of me and he was coming in back, the two of them coming right through me toward each other. I was the conductor of this electrifying sexual charge, both giver and receiver at once, in total control and out of my head. We all shrieked, then giggled, and collapsed.

Drifting into sleep, I congratulated myself on having just had great sex without thinking even once of Sasha. I had gained control, I was running free, I was playing hopscotch all over the chess board. Sasha would never catch me now . . .

Suddenly, Michael was shaking me out of my throne, his chair. "Nothing personal," he announced. "But I cannot stand to have a woman sleep over in my house . . . ever."

The geisha Liana was gone. The grandfather clock, encircled by a bright green plastic jungle vine that now looked pretty silly, said 3:15 A.M. "It's just a little problem I have with women sleeping over in my personal bed. Please don't take it as a rejection," he said.

"Oh, no, I don't take it as a rejection," I replied sweetly, trying to focus both my eyeballs in the same direction. "I take it as a royal pain in the you-know-where." I picked up my saliva-drenched leopard scarf. "Well, go make me some coffee," I commanded.

"I don't have any coffee."

"No coffee? Jesus." I wondered how Queen Hippolyta would handle a guy like this.

"I've got Perrier . . . papaya nectar?"

"Forget it, Michael." I grabbed my coat and stumbled down the steps into the chill ocean air, feeling vaguely like an overworked, underpaid whore.

I cruised south on the Pacific Coast Highway, calming myself by counting beds, considering how the bed makes the man. There was Andre's elevated brute black sexercise bed; Rick's water bed, satin-sheeted for orgiastic feasting, Michael's mats (he wouldn't let me near his precious, "personal," undefiled-by-woman bed). And then there was Sasha's bed, our Princess and the Pea fairy-tale bed that had whisked me to heights I was beginning to think I'd never reach again . . .

"Don't look back!" cried the voices in my head, the sensible voices of my friends, my mother, Dr. Peabodies. "Take control!

Why, you just aren't being thorough enough. You are dating—and screwing—haphazardly, indiscriminately. What you need is to begin a focused methodical Mr.-Right Hunt. Place personal ads, try video-dating, computers, friends of friends, friends of your mother's friends. You won't even have time to think of Sasha. Anyway, there are other Sashas out there—better Sashas, taller Sashas, richer Sashas, smarter Sashas, and yes, even sexier Sashas."

I drove straight home, sat down, notepad in hand, and clicked on my answering machine, determined to begin my "Mr.-Right Hunt" by listening to *all* my messages, not just running out to take on the first semienticing one: "Hey, Rosy-Q, Arnie here. The word on the local grapevine is that you're a free woman again. Congratulations! Let's celebrate! Gimme a call." . . . "Hi, Rosalyn, uhhh, my name is Jeff, um, I'm a friend of Sandy's, and well, she suggested I call, so, I'm a lawyer, I enjoy racketball, old movies, ummm, I just got divorced, well, separated, and ah, we can get into all that later, I guess, so my number is 345-2222, call, ahhh, whenever you feel like it." . . . "Ros? Ros? Are you there? Aren't you *ever* there? Where *are* you all the time? This is Peter. Call me." . . . "Rosy, this is your mother. Just checking in to see how you're doing on your own now." . . . "Rosalyn . . . Andre . . . I'm in the Jacuzzi again . . . hot and wet . . . for you . . . Don't call . . . Just come . . ." . . . "Hello, Roosaleen? Thees Salvador. I meet you at thee deesco last week . . ." . . . "Rosalyn, I miss you, please come back." It was Sasha.

I wondered, as I took the familiar route from my place to Sasha's, why I was doing it—going "backwards" instead of "forward," as the wise old disembodied Dr. Peabodies had warned me against. I *did* feel like I was moving backwards through time, driving down the old streets, taking the turns of my past, pulling into the long thin driveway, stepping under the white Grecian arch, onto the cobblestone path, through the wrought-iron gate, into the fantasy garden strewn with colored Christmas lights and classic statues of naked women. I could sense the ancient spirits of Sasha's house coming out to greet me, the lights blinking, the statues stretching their smooth stony limbs, the eighteenth-century painted ladies lifting their skirts and leaping from their picture frames, the busts and gargoyles yawning, puckering their lips for a kiss. The whole scene seemed to emanate from Sasha's strange, unyielding passion. But it's *too* strange, I thought, this is another world; it's not the real world. There's a reason I left, a good reason. I turned to the gate and started to run—back to the "real world" of one-night stands and disembodied doctors and car radios turned up full blast to drown out the sound of my dreams.

Sasha was standing in front of the gate. In the blinking light, he looked like one of his statues, his dark Herculean brow arching fiercely, his broad, strong chest peeking out from his open robe, his hair curled around his head like a crown of black pearls. He looked sad, yet peaceful, standing there stroking Astarte, the cat, in his arms.

"You can't keep me here!" I cried like a petulant child.

"Rosalyn," he said in that rich deep baritone that had me mesmerized, even from my answering machine. "I'm not keeping you here. You're in control. You came here yourself. And you can leave right now if that's what you want." He stepped aside, leaving the iron gate open to me. Defiantly, I rushed toward it, then looked back at him once more, glimpsing those amaretto eyes gleaming in the Christmas lights, freezing me where I stood.

I tried desperately to conjure images of Rick's eyes, Andre's eyes, Michael's, Liana's, my mother's, anybody else's eyes, yet it was hopeless. Sasha's eyes, even the tiny, tired creases beneath them, pulled me out of the "real world" and into his warm, strong arms.

We held each other, just held each other, tight and close, as if a storm were raging all around us. And when the storm quieted, he kissed me, sweet pliant lips pressing lips, not a feminine kiss like Liana's, but soft, softer than any man's, so soft I felt as if the storm had turned into a gentle spring shower raining all over inside me. "Come on," he whispered, leading me back through the garden, past the stone lion spouting water, up to the huge oak door of Capricorn Castle. I could see the fire flickering, beckoning through stained glass, telling me that I was home.

I followed him into the funky, half-finished kitchen, watched him feed Astarte and rinse off his strong, workingman hands. He reached for a towel and looked up, catching me gazing at him. "Missed me?" he asked, betraying just a touch of vulnerability. I nodded, wanting to say something clever or meaningful like I'd say to any other man, but all I could think of was how I longed to fill myself up with him, his hardness, his softness, his soul. Our eyes lingered upon each other from across the kitchen for just another moment before we threw off hesitation like an old cloak in springtime and rushed at each other, embracing, feeling every part, every inch of beloved flesh that we had missed so much, that we had thought we might never see again.

"Oh, Sasha," I sighed, "I feel so good with you. Now I know why I left, why I slept with all those other men, so I could appreciate—"

He grabbed my shoulders so hard I shuddered. "You disgust me," he whispered with hushed ferocity. "You and your games, your sexual adventuring."

All the sweet intoxicating movement of the moment screeched to a shattering halt. There I was, whisked out of heaven and dropped down into the defendant's chair. "Sex had nothing to do with it!" I blurted. "It had to do with power, with possession and control—"

"Words, Rosalyn, psychobabble."

"Oh, Sasha." I smiled sheepishly. "You know me—"

"No, I don't know you." His eyes shot arrows. "What's worse is you don't know yourself. You don't know what you want. You act like you do, but you don't."

"Oh, and you know everything, don't you?" My head boiled with hate. *This* was why I left, I thought, *this* was why I should leave right now, run fast and never look back.

"I know I love you," he whispered, his harsh grip softening, cracking what little cover I had, pouring love into hate, making the two seemingly disparate emotions whirl together in a maelstrom of mounting passion.

"I love you, too," I responded, longing to melt, yet hardening. "But there are things I need to find—"

He roughly released his grasp, pushing me backwards into the living room. "I had thought we both had found each other," he said. "That we didn't need to look anymore." He turned and disappeared into the back of the house, letting the big kitchen door swing creakily behind him.

He's crazy, I thought, really crazy. Possessive. Dangerous. *Bad* for me. My friends are right. My mother's right. Dr. Peabodies. Everybody says he's crazy. I must be crazy for coming here.

Once more, I ran for a door. But I felt the mischievous, eerie spirits of that house surrounding, possessing, converging upon me. Here I was back in fantasyland, being courted by strangely lit gargoyles, the portraits of Sasha's White Russian ancestors, the wizards and bears and motley art objects. For a moment, I thought I heard the ice-cream truck clanging down the street in the middle of the night, promising me that I could find anything I wanted right here if I just stopped running . . .

Perhaps I was not Hippolyta Queen of the Amazons, after all, but Atalanta the mythical Greek princess who could run faster than any man. Each man who sought to possess her she outran, and all losers were sentenced to death. Atalanta was the champion, always winning, always in control, but each time she "won," she killed another man, and so killed off a part of herself. Finally, one young man fell so deeply in love with her that he *had* to race her, to make her stop running with other men, to possess her completely, to win her love—even if the race cost him his life. This young man wasn't even a very good runner. But he challenged Atalanta anyway, and, with the help of three golden apples given to him by the Goddess of Love, he won. Of course, Atalanta *let* him win. After all, she was getting tired of all that killing and racing against strange men. Moreover, she felt that this young man's love for her was so strong and so compelling that she had no real desire to run away from it. So she *looked back* at his gleaming golden apples of love; she let herself lose control. In losing the race, she was winning his life; in losing control, she was gaining *amour* . . .

Sasha had offered me his golden apples, I thought. Perhaps I should pick one up, taste its power.

And there he stood, naked in front of the carved medieval knight on his bedroom door, watching me struggle with myths. "Ros," he said, "I'm sorry."

I kicked off my running shoes and went to him, silencing the Furies in my head, stopping the race, at least for the moment, looking back. I looked into his eyes and saw the intensity of pain and joy that I had so deftly avoided feeling all week, the pain of living and dying alone, the joy of making love together.

We made love beneath the image of Oz on his bed of many mattresses, his flying carpet into imagination. We imagined that we were the only two people in the universe and the universe was ours to create. And we made love, truly *made* love, as a potter makes a pot, as a tree with the sun and rain makes leaves; we were making, molding, melting, squeezing, slapping, sucking and breathing life into something between us that was somehow different from our cranky, lonely, male and female selves, something miraculous and crazy, something I could never explain to my mother or disapproving friends, something dark as blood, yet starry bright, something utterly out of control.

And I could feel it shooting through him—this wild thing we were making—through his smooth flesh gone all goose-pimply as he pounded, passionately pounded, making the love that possessed us both, that whirled inside me like the tornado carrying Dorothy up to Oz. It twisted and howled through the shivering caverns of my womb, through the screams of my mouth, through his bellowing in my ears, through the briny hot tears in my eyes, through all my openings, exploding like the end of the world, or a new beginning: A sperm entering an egg, a thousand tiny UFOs visiting a round, lush, glowing Earth; a biochemical-interplanetary mating vision, an Emerald City.

Losing control has won me a vision, I realized as we lay there drifting to the music of our heartbeats, riding our magic mattresses across green, green galaxies, spinning through heavenly bodies.

Later, as the night wrapped its dark shawl around us, I noticed how utterly relaxed I felt, a little disoriented, but peacefully powerful, warm, at home. I turned to Sasha (who always awoke when I did) and said, "What do you think—has my leaving you again improved our sex life?"

"Ros," he replied, yawning like a bear. "Wasn't it you that said, 'Sex had nothing to do with it'?" And he winked and tickled my ribs until I was gasping and giggling and kicking off the sheets.

The Scavenger Hunt

NISA DONNELLY

Bars, by their very Saturday-night nature, were not Randi's kind of place. Too much sweat and confusion, laughter and music, tears and dramas all swirling, heaving, conspiring to pound out migraines that would hang on for days. Deadly mementoes of bad judgment.

Randi was beyond it all, or thought she was. Late-night fantasies that only burst like dime-store balloons in the dust of day were for other women, those who still knew how to dream. And Randi knew dreams littered the floor at Babe's as surely as abandoned rubbish huddled in the gutter in front of the bar.

Fleeting fantasies, fragile as gauze, were best kept tucked away next to the vibrator, saved for lonely nights when solitary pleasure was the only kind around. Maybe for some, the bars offered hot sex, but never for her. Better to leave the bars and their promises of ecstasy to the true believers; Randi no longer chased floundering visions through futile fantasies.

Only the promise of cigarettes was enough to lure her into Babe's, which, at least, was safe; nobody would stare at her leather jacket, her cropped hair, or worse yet, call her "sir."

So, Randi charged through lavender shadows that bathed the street in softness, sending out nightly promises of temporary paradise, of secrets lurking just beyond the blazing purple neon sign that burned away the blackness. "Get in, get out, go home," she promised herself, pushing the door open and instinctively narrowing her eyes against the smoke-shrouded dimness. In one corner, shadowy webs of light illuminated the cigarette machine and the pay phone, where a tall blonde half-held the receiver to her ear, waiting, Randi assumed, for an answer to her call.

The blonde's bold eyes narrowed, then dropped to Randi's chest, circling, probing the depths of the black-leather vest that hung open over a T-shirt that stretched taut across full breasts. "Nice," the blonde muttered appreciatively, the eyes lingering shamelessly before beginning their slow ascent, tickling Randi's earlobes, licking at her mouth. Aqua eyes, shadowed in dark rainbows, rimmed in heavy lashes, finally ported, hard and even, in Randi's. This was the woman Randi had always dreamed of, standing before her, dressed in black satin and velvet. Long blond hair dipped perilously close to one eye before continuing an unencumbered journey across naked shoulders dusted with silver stars. Lace-mitted hands, tipped with long, red fingernails, toyed with the phone cord. The woman's gaze never flinched. Feeling suddenly naked, exposed, Randi blushed; the woman smiled knowingly and turned back to the phone.

Unnerved, Randi quickly turned away, rummaging through her jeans to discover a button from her favorite flannel shirt, an empty cigarette pack, and twenty-three cents—eight of it in pennies. "Don't want that, do you?" she asked the cigarette machine, which winked an almost obscene reply when she crumpled the empty cigarette pack on its surface. Pulling a pair of bills free,

Randi squeezed into an opening midway down the bar's long expanse of mahogany and mirrors, laughter and soft backs. Leaning into the cool hardness of the railing, she dangled the money across the bar. "Nothing attracts bartenders quicker than money waving in the breeze," she announced half to the woman at her left.

"It all depends on how much you're waving," a voice whispered from her right shoulder. Startled, Randi raised her eyes to the mirror and there, behind her own familiar reflection, was the woman from the phone. Just as the bartender's fingers plucked the bills free, long, red-tipped fingers moved down Randi's shoulder, extending a pack of cigarettes: Randi's brand. But as she reached for the cigarettes, muttering, "Thanks," the fingers coiled around the gold-and-white package and tucked it into the soft-melting crevasse between a pair of delicately full breasts. The bartender jingled a handful of change into Randi's still-waiting palm, which automatically closed around the coins. Mesmerized, Randi was powerless to break her gaze from this woman, whose hot breath kept tickling her earlobes. Luminous eyes shot into the mirror then rebounded into Randi's soul. Randi's breath came short. Closing her eyes, Randi blinked hard, looked again. The vision stared back and smiled.

A lifetime might have passed, although the hands on the little clock imbedded in the belly of a mermaid who was beached by the cash register hadn't moved at all. "That machine doesn't have what you want, but I do," the voice whispered, slipping in under the music, the noisy bar clatter. Randi turned to feel warm words brush past her ear. Shivers spilled down her back. "I drink Southern Comfort. On ice. With a piece of lime. Bring it over there." The vision pouted at her reflection, smiled brightly, then walked away—never looking back.

"Southern Comfort, on ice, with a piece of lime," Randi parroted to the bartender. "And a beer, no glass." The looking glass exposed Randi's hungry eyes following the vision to a tiny table in a darkened corner where the woman watched and waited. Randi felt those eyes skimming her legs, defining her ass under wallet and keys, sliding across her shoulders, down to her breasts, until her cunt began to warm. All the while, delicate fingers tap-tapped the half-exposed pack of cigarettes. On any other woman, the actions would have been absent-minded, innocent, nonchalant. But with this woman, every movement, every whisper was nothing less than a deliberate promise. A bright-pink tongue determinedly rimmed lips that waited patiently for the smooth sweetness of Southern Comfort, of Randi.

The music, the noise, the crowd fell away until there was no one else in the bar, maybe in the world. "I've been waiting for you," the vision whispered when Randi finally reached the table. Tiny shadows, urged on by flickering candlelight, chased across the dark lady, as Randi had named her since their meeting by the phone. Randi began to speak, but something in this strange woman's eyes muted her. A black high heel nudged the empty chair a little more open, as Randi sat the drink down. When the leg pulled back, a flash of naked thigh gleamed, a personal invitation.

Sliding onto the vinyl chair that wobbled from too many Saturday nights, Randi sat as if there were no place else she would ever want to be again, as if there were no tomorrow, no yesterday. Tapping a cigarette free, the woman lit it, then extended it, filter first, toward Randi's mouth. "Better?" she asked. Randi nodded, almost afraid to breathe, to talk, for fear the vision would fade into the smoke.

"These are yours." The dark lady pushed the cigarettes toward Randi. "And this, of course, is mine." She raised the glass and looked hard into Randi's dark eyes. "And that, of course, will be mine too." The eyes forged a trail down the soft curve of Randi's chin, along her neck, across her chest, before settling where Randi's eager nipples stood on end, betraying her already prickling flesh. Randi wondered if her dark lady could see beneath the leather, the fabric, and was watching those shameless nipples harden. A piercing throb jarred Randi's belly, then slammed between her legs. She didn't want to control the sensation, couldn't, even if she'd tried.

"How did you know about the cigarettes?" Randi asked finally, trying desperately to find something to say to this woman whose eyes kept rummaging under the T-shirt, tickling, licking, nuzzling the ever-hardening nipples. Finally, with a little sigh and a longing last look, the dark lady raised her eyes. "I notice things, it pays to notice things. I noticed you the second you stepped through the door." Randi could almost feel little demon tongues dancing over her burning skin, licking, sucking at her hidden secrets.

The dark lady smiled, very sweetly, very innocently, then the very tip of her tongue darted up across her lip. The effect wasn't wasted, Randi's heart exhaled then plummeted to her cunt, where it lay pounding incessantly in time to her too-quick breathing.

"Actually, I'm on a bit of a scavenger hunt." A sparkling fingertip traced the edge of her glass. "That's why I'm dressed like this. I ordinarily wouldn't go out to a bar, all alone on a Saturday night, dressed in satin and lace. But I was at a party and there was this scavenger hunt, and so here I am." Brightening, her eyes kissed every line, every detail on Randi's broad face.

"I don't understand." Randi was trying to ignore the throbbing between her legs, the tiny voices that kept prodding her to run back to reality, to the predictable safety that was her life, before being consumed by this smoldering fantasy that had remarkably become real.

"Everyone else had a partner for the scavenger hunt." The woman looked very innocent. Except, a single finger kept circling and dipping into the cocktail glass. Except she kept bringing that finger to her lips, slowly licking off little droplets of Southern Comfort. The eyes never flinched. "There's a truly wonderful prize . . . for the one who comes with all the things she's supposed to. But I don't have a playmate—I mean teammate—so I have to do it all alone. And what if I lose? I don't like to lose." The full mouth pouted slightly, reminding Randi of a doll in a toy-store window.

"So you came here to find somebody to do it with?"

"Exactly. Want to play?"

"Oh, I couldn't, really." Randi fidgeted in the chair, deciding to leave before the dream exploded in her face. For Randi, loving strangers, especially exotic ones, wasn't something that was likely to happen in real life. Better to go home, watch the late movie and turn her dark lady into a full-blown fantasy, courtesy of the ever-faithful vibrator. "I've got things to do." Randi jingled her keys for emphasis.

"So do I." The dark lady exhaled in frustration, pursed her red lips, and then very patiently, added, "That's why I asked." She smiled again; Randi's heart exploded. "You're really not interested in playing with me? It's a truly wonderful scavenger hunt. And we can party after it's over."

"I don't like parties much," Randi admitted, embarrassed.

"You'll like this one. Here, I'll even show you what I have so far . . . from the list, you know. I only need one more thing and then I'll win. You don't want me to lose, do you?" Randi shook her head.

"This is my list, pay attention." A naked pinup girl, frozen on a greeting card, pouted at Randi. "Cute, huh?" Randi nodded. "She reminds me of you," the dark lady winked, "around the tits." Randi blushed, thankful for the bar's shadows. Watching the dark lady read, Randi imagined kissing those soft lips that moved with the words: "A feather fanny, to finger the leather, that unfingers the lace, that whips it all into shape, ties it up for a present, and . . ."

"And what?" Randi's curiosity peaked and she reached for the card, only to have it snapped back, just out of reach and tucked away. "And . . . that's what I have so far," the dark lady ignored Randi's hungry fingers.

"What else is there?" Randi asked, suddenly very aware of the dark lady's foot rising up her leg, probing behind her knees, slipping between her thighs, on a determined course to her throbbing, gushing cunt. The dark lady only smiled in reply, tossed off the last of the Southern Comfort and extended her hand, "Come with me, we'll go get the rest." And Randi, hypnotized by her very essence, obediently let herself be led across the room, out the door, onto the street, all thoughts of leaving as abandoned as the empty cocktail glass on the little table.

"My car's right here." The dark lady stood by a black sports car. "But I have a car here," Randi protested, "I mean over there." Leaning against Randi, the dark lady opened the passenger door, then trailed breasts and naked shoulders across Randi's back. "Which would you rather be in, that car or me?" A low groan answered for Randi, who sank into the car. "Good girl," the dark lady answered, slipping beneath the wheel, letting the skirt rise high and easy on her legs.

"The last thing will be at my place. We'll go there first and then party." Randi wasn't listening; instead her ravenous fingers inched toward the naked shoulders only to have her errant hand caught midair. Soft red lips sucked each of the fingers, nuzzled Randi's hand, moved into the soft warmth of her neck, nibbling, licking. Finally, the dark lady kissed Randi, hard and long as agile fingers rummaged inside the T-shirt, teasing, tormenting, until the nipples rose, pulsating, electrified.

So slowly Randi thought she would explode with desire, lace-covered hands moved to her waist, loosening, probing, exploring the coarse hair and soft skin just beyond the buttons. Finally, one long finger slipped into Randi's wet, aching cunt, moving slowly, back and forth, up and down almost in time to the music that crashed from the car stereo. Randi could think of nothing but fingers, greedy, hungry fingers exploring her innermost secrets. Sliding farther down in the seat, a low, soft moan escaped as she raised her gushing cunt to devour the finger which exited as deftly as it had come. Raising the finger first to Randi's lips for a moment then to her own, the dark lady licked the dampness slowly, patiently, like a little girl seeking the very last traces of ice cream on a stick. "See, you really are a very good girl, and I really do like good girls." Randi felt her dark lady smiling.

"I don't even know your name." The words came soft, quiet, when Randi's power of speech finally returned. "Ah, but I know yours," the dark lady was checking her eye shadow in the rear-view mirror, "that woman at the end of the bar told me. Said you don't come to Babe's often, that you don't like the bars much. Is that true?" As she turned from the mirror, night shadows traced Lydia's delicate features, and Randi coveted every moment.

"I'm whoever you want me to be: Regina or Yvette or Nicolle or Natasha or Lydia. Do you like any of us?" Randi nodded, not daring to speak, fearing it would break the spell. "Good, because I'm Lydia. Much better than Natasha, don't you think? I was Natasha at the last scavenger hunt and I lost." A tiny cloud furrowed Lydia's brow, prompted by the memory of losing. But before pulling the car from the curb, a lacy hand darted across the seat, took one of Randi's eager nipples and turned it slowly, while an anxious tongue sucked and licked at her neck until the tiny hairs there shuddered erect. "Aren't scavenger hunts fun?" Lydia demanded, sending the car into the night.

Yet, each time Randi stretched nearer to Lydia, she was nudged away. Instead, Lydia's hands stroked her own soft thighs under lavender stockings caught by black lace garters. Shimmers of streetlights sent strange shadows shooting up her raised skirt. Randi's cunt pounded for want of Lydia; her fingers hungered for the naked shoulders. Mindless of the path they followed, Randi imagined Lydia touching her, of Lydia forgetting about the stupid scavenger hunt, the party, of Lydia making time stand still. Finally, the car stopped by an eerie Victorian mansion with a dozen mailboxes on the porch.

"Come with me." Lydia's first words since the drive began jarred Randi back to reality. Without a backward glance, Lydia slid out of the car, leaving Randi struggling to button her jeans. The sound of Lydia's heels moving across the vine-covered porch echoed faintly through the night's silence. Finally freeing herself from the car, afraid Lydia would vanish into the labyrinthine recesses of the house, Randi took the stairs two at a time, hurled herself through the unlocked door, then charged ahead, following the scent of Lydia's perfume, the sound of her heels.

"What kept you?" Lydia demanded when Randi reached her, although only moments had passed. She was turning her key in the lock so slowly Randi could almost hear the tumblers move. "I don't like to be kept waiting."

"Lydia, I'm sorry." Breathless, Randi hung across the banister, gasping for breath, exhausted from her flight to the very top of the manor.

"You are a very bad girl. I'm very disappointed in you." Lydia never turned from the latch to face the agonizing Randi. "You really should be punished, you know?" The husky voice was modulated, as if she were discussing the weather on a perfectly clear day. "If I'm late I'll never win the scavenger hunt." Sure that Lydia was about to send her away, Randi turned to the stairs, cursing herself for her stupidity: she'd walked into Babe's by accident, miraculously got picked up by a fantasy and now she'd blown it. "Don't worry," Lydia called after Randi's unspoken thoughts, "we still have time." And she laughed, the sound of wind chimes just before a storm.

Stepping into the darkened room, Lydia lit candles along her way, before slipping into a black satin chair, rousing a sleeping black cat, who growled in indignation. "Don't mind Miss Snooty Feline," Lydia said, draping a long leg across the chair's soft arm, studying Randi, pleased at her good fortune.

Glancing around the room, Randi's eyes lingered on the four-poster bed, complete with gauzy curtains that shimmied in a soft summer breeze. Illuminated by the candlelight was a gallery of nudes. In one, Lydia lounged by the sea, naked save for boots and a riding crop. A horse grazed in the background. "Somebody's idea of me," Lydia's voice followed Randi's hungry eyes.

Embarrassed, Randi turned too quickly from the painting and leaned against the wall, a miserable attempt at nonchalance, for she had realized immediately that except for the bed and the chair Lydia occupied, there was nowhere to sit. Self-conscious, she looked pleadingly toward Lydia, who was admiring her red fingernails. "There's champagne in the refrigerator and glasses in the cupboard. Get them." Lydia rearranged herself on the chair, apparently mindless of Randi's discomfort.

Once in the kitchen, her favorite part of every house, Randi hummed and puttered, her breathing finally normal at last. Finding towels and glasses, even a little mirrored tray, she selected a bottle of champagne from the half dozen that kept company in the refrigerator with a brown head of lettuce and a dried-up, half loaf of bread. Trying to avoid the menacing eyes of the cat, who watched from a cupboard sentry post, Randi opened the bottle, losing only traces of the foam. "How's that?" she asked the cat, who only closed its eyes in contempt, feigning sleep. Carrying the bottle and glasses into the next room on the little tray, Randi composed a symphony of small talk and wit, all for Lydia, who, she imagined, was settled in the satin chair, smoking, waiting for champagne. Randi had already decided to sit on the floor at Lydia's feet so she could caress Lydia's thighs, slide her fingers into that sweet, pink cunt. She smiled in anticipation.

But the chair was empty. Lydia, instead, lay on the bed, a sequined mask hiding her eyes. The velvet top was gone, snow-white and pink breasts, that Lydia tickled with a feather fan, peeked through a black-lace corset. A forgotten cigarette fumed in a crystal ashtray. "Oh, you're back." The fan teased the pink nipples erect. "I was waiting for you, but you're late, so I started without you. Too bad, it really was you I wanted." Randi's hands shook until she was sure tray, glasses, champagne and confidence would all spill across the floor. "I'm sorry," she muttered miserably, ashamed that she had, once again, spoiled the moment.

"Stay there." Lydia's voice pierced the night as she slid off the bed. Taking the tray, Lydia filled the glasses, then began to peel away Randi's leather vest. "Such a bad girl, making me wait for you, making me want you, leaving me here all alone with nothing but my feather fanny. A bad girl, who needs to be taught a lesson."

"Yes . . . I mean, no . . . I don't know." Randi stuttered, staring at the floor then dragged her eyes to Lydia's commanding face. "That's my good girl," Lydia whispered, lowering her face to Randi's chest, to nibble and suck on the fabric that encased nipples throbbing from want. "You like that, don't you?" Randi moaned; Lydia turned, looked slyly over her shoulder and picked up a glass. "You may unfasten my skirt—carefully."

With shaking fingers, Randi tried to loosen the zipper, but the same fingers that could dance a carburetor back into shape had turned to wooden stumps. Her jeans, damp and coarse, rubbed against her burning cunt. Fingering the satin, the skirt finally fell open and Randi reached inside, only to have Lydia pull away. "No-no," she scolded, as if Randi were a naughty kitten into some new mischief, "not until I tell you." Lydia reached up, gently caressing the side of Randi's face before burying her lips in the soft, waiting throat until Randi moaned, trembled, gasping for breath.

"Please, oh, please, Lydia." Randi closed her eyes, begging, praying for Lydia's fingers, her tongue, wanting desperately to please her dark-lady fantasy.

"Just stay there, stand there." And Lydia slipped out of the skirt, exposing gleaming thighs against lavender stockings held high by their lacy garters. She smelled of roses, incense, champagne. Lydia stepped close to Randi, licking her neck, trailing her breasts across Randi's shirt. Lace-covered hands freed Randi from the T-shirt that clung mercilessly to her damp skin. Their nipples touched, hard, exploding, and Randi's legs trembled. Lydia then caressed Randi in earnest, teasing her magical tongue over each taut nipple until Randi arched her back, groaning. Still, Lydia's demanding tongue continued to torment the aching nipples, pulling them through insistent teeth before allowing them to all but escape again, then calling them back, harder each time. Curious fingers probed, explored, delighted the hidden niches of Randi's body. Tremors coursed through her veins.

Teasing and tempting, a thousand fingers seemed to circle and flutter in Randi's damp jeans as Lydia's persistent mouth forged on, following the beltline. Lydia pressed into Randi's back, licking, biting, until Randi felt her skin go hot then prickle as if she had been too long in the sun. Reaching back to caress Lydia, Randi's hungry fingers were guided across the corset up to petal-soft breasts, only to be brought back to reality by the snap of cold steel gripping her wrists.

Dancing in front of her prisoner, Lydia kissed Randi softly, silencing the moans. Toasting her own handiwork, Lydia's tongue caught droplets of champagne before moving the glass to Randi's nipples that grew only harder from the chill. Persistent fingers slid down Randi's belly, unfastening the jeans' buttons, one by aching one. Sucking and biting the exposed skin, Lydia kept drawing Randi closer and closer to passion's brink. Randi groaned, the sound rose from deep in her cunt and spilled out her aching throat. "You must be very quiet. We don't want to wake the neighbors. And I have lots of neighbors, all very grouchy, very mean." Licking Randi's navel, the jeans slumping to the floor, Lydia buried her face in the soft down of Randi's belly. The floor seemed to convulse and Randi's knees buckled in answer to the ultimate call of gravity, of passion.

Only then did Lydia lead Randi to the bed. Settling her captive on its edge, Lydia lay back against dark satin pillows. Shadows wrought by flickering candles illuminated Lydia's fingers that piloted a waiting vibrator to her own cunt. All the time, Lydia's eyes burned into Randi's. Lydia pushed the buzzing vibrator between her legs until the tiny lace panties teased her clit. Arching her back a little, a low moan escaped, and Randi, mesmerized, moved closer, her own cunt dripping. Gartered thighs tensed from the vibrator's harsh demands. Randi leaned into Lydia, took a neglected nipple in her own eager mouth and sucked. Electricity snapped from Lydia's flesh; stark passion exploded across the bed. Moving her head down along the lace corset, Randi nibbled until she reached Lydia's soft, lace-covered mound, where the vibrator purred. Lydia's breath came hard and swift as she rose to Randi, hurtled ever higher by the vibrator, moaning, tensing, pushing against the gush of orgasm that threatened to consume them both.

Finally Lydia switched off the vibrator and slipped free of Randi. "You really are a bad girl, aren't you?" She stroked Randi's hair, whispered against her temples. "I told you to stay there and here you are moving around, probably wanting to slip your fingers into my hot, juicy, throbbing cunt." Standing then, Lydia stepped out of the wet lace panties and angled her soft, rounded ass toward Randi, smoothing each silky stocking.

Lydia's breasts brushed Randi's face. Dancing feathers fanned Randi's breasts; indignant goose bumps marched in cadence. "You like that, don't you?" Randi's eyes pleaded, begged for just one of the pink-tipped breasts that hovered out of her eager tongue's reach, for just one of the red-tipped fingers to dip into her anxious wetness. Inch by painful inch, a soft nipple moved toward Randi's eager mouth. Randi's cunt pounded out its own demands as Lydia's fingers guided hungry mouth to hard nipple. A silk scarf, the color of midnight, teased Randi's forehead, then grew taut across her temples. A determined finger circled lightly, stirring dampened secrets. Randi breathed only through gasps and moans. Fingers stroked her belly, tickled the soft mound that protected wet treasures.

Turning Randi on her belly, the fingers teased the ultimate depths of desire until the soft skin there trembled in anticipation. "You want me, don't you?" Lydia asked, although she needed no answer. Lydia's finger rimmed Randi's lips and when her tongue reached out, she tasted her own dampness there, smooth and cool. She sucked the finger—a kitten suckling from its mother for the first time. Lydia tickled her back, her buttocks, startling them with flicks and tremors, making them rise to the touch, then quivering there, waiting for more. Wanting Lydia to consume her, to quiet the aching throb that pounded relentlessly in her cunt, Randi trembled. Wetness gushed from her convulsing cunt. Hidden secrets exploded. Tremblings of release rippled through her throbbing body.

The feeling ravaged her, teased against her, slapped her exploding ass. Aching for more, her cunt tightened, her ass rose. She was nothing now but throbbing, pounding, demanding cunt, ravenous cunt, screaming for more. She wanted to come, moaning, pouring herself out across Lydia's bed, yet she wanted to wait, to prolong the passion. Randi buried her face deep into the pillow savoring the scent of Lydia. Strong fingers moved against her clit; firm, persistent fingers kneaded the exploding wetness. Lydia knew Randi's body better than even Randi knew it.

In the distance, Randi heard the gentle hum of bumblebees, calling her to their hive on a summer afternoon. The hum moved closer, buzzing against her clit, along her ass, until she could no longer tell vibrations from fingers or tongue. As full and hot as she had ever been in August on the relentless prairie, she was only cunt, ass, tits, all aching and gushing, throbbing, beating, crying for more, for release, for ecstasy itself. Filled with the tingling, the pounding, Lydia relentlessly pushed her toward an abyss Randi had never known before.

Eagerly, Randi slipped into it and then fell, jerking and trembling, into the chasm, hurtling across time and space until the sky and ocean exploded into the universe.

Finally, she lay sweating, trembling at Lydia's touch, her very breath. Bumblebees silenced, her cunt was slowly emptied. Metal-on-metal tinkled, sounding very far away, freeing her wrists; her hands fell limp. Fingers tousled her hair and then moonlight crept across the bed. Drained, empty, void of movement, she lay quiet, her breath shallow. Sweet tears, borne of ultimate passion, consummate pleasure, spilled into the pillow. Damp warmth caressed her skin and she smelled peppermint soap, felt warm towels against her back, her ass, her still-tingling cunt, as Lydia washed and dried her gently, kissed her, pulled the covers up around Randi's shoulders.

Through sleep and passion-dimmed eyes, Randi watched Lydia undress: the stockings, the corset, the mask, all discarded on the satin chair. Watched her brush out her long hair, then move toward the bed, where she slipped in next to Randi, pulling her close, protecting her against the night.

"You really are a very good girl," Lydia mumbled, wrapping herself around Randi, stroking her hair, petting her to sleep.

"Can I ask you something?" Randi turned toward Lydia, as much afraid of the question as of the answer. Lydia kissed her hair, hugged her tighter. "What was the other thing you were supposed to get for the scavenger hunt?"

Lydia smiled. An almost silent, not-quite-breathless chuckle escaped. "You, my darling. Didn't you know?" The whisper stole into the night. "You were the scavenger hunt." And Randi slid into sleep, safe in Lydia's arms.

Blood Oranges

DEENA METZGER

> "In me it is not fit, holy things to bear.
> Red as I am with slaughter and new from war;
> Till in some living stream I cleanse the guilt
> of dire debate and blood in battle split."
>
> *Aeneid*

I like to think that I belong to a great lineage; like Buddhists, I can trace the teachings back for centuries, as far as Ishtar, Queen of Heaven, Goddess of Love and Ecstasy, The Great Whore, Mother of Harlots, you recognize her name, don't you, in Esther, whore for the children of Israel, who saved them from the viciousness of Haman, by sleeping with the Persian King, at the behest of her uncle Mordecai, the first holy pimp of Judeo-Christendom.

Surely you know the story from the Old Testament. When I was a young girl I loved the festival of Purim, because we were encouraged to put rouge on our cheeks and wear lipstick, the darker the better, while we vied to see who was the most beautiful, who would reign over the festivities as Queen Esther. I won it one year when my father laid down all his pennies in my name.

You see, I was raised to believe in the Bride, in the Shechina, the female aspect of God coming down to earth every Sabbath, the man and woman ordered to retreat to the holy bed and everyone in the community in the great clusterfuck of love calling the holy spirit down into their bodies with cries of ecstasy, "O God," the entire planet roiling from the rhythm of it. To prepare for the Sabbath, I change the linens, perfume the bath, rouge my nipples. I wait. She comes down gleaming; I can't resist her.

Christopher likes to tease me, saying he's surprised that I've never walked the streets, since I act as if I have a calling. "I never thought I'd meet a woman who claimed polishing her nails was a sacred act," he pretends to scoff at me, and I smile as he stands beside me clearly fascinated as I slowly stroke red polish onto my carefully filed oval nails, covering the delicate white moons. Before a wedding, the bride and all her handmaidens stained their fingers with the juices of dark berries in order to protect themselves from the evil entrances of demons. At night, the bride left dark streaks upon her new husband's back, staking out her territory.

Christopher knows what I like; if I am peeling blood oranges, I get his attention as the deep-orange rind is peeled back and the delicate blood-red pulp exposed. He licks the juice from my fingers. It is a blood bond between us. He brings me dark sweet fruits, pomegranates, blueberries, blackberries; I like raspberries, we eat them one by one, examining the pink circle, spreading the delicate red pulp, sticking our tongues into the small open center before we bite down. You can get lost in the globe of a raspberry; it is a miniature world. The best raspberry I ever ate, he passed to me, as if it were the holy sacrament, from his mouth where he had carried it, half a mile swimming down the river. It was still perfect, warm and sweet from his tongue. I savored it a long time rolling it about my mouth, imagining what it had been like for him to carry it to me, sticking my tongue where the stem once was, before swallowing. He had been watching me the entire time; as I finished I leaped into the water and swam away from him, and when he caught me, I arched out of his wet and slippery grasp, bending backwards, a dolphin in reverse, my breasts just grazing his lips, challenged him to a race, spraying water in his face and laughing as if we were innocents.

Then we made the fish together. The light seeped into him as a river moistens a bank and a new power rose up through his sinewy legs, his body melting so I could feel him being constructed from the inside out, white bones forming, then silvery muscles and tendons and then the smooth dark skin stretched taut over his frame, the hairs spinning magnetically about his nipples. We also began to spin and the crescendo of centrifugal force drew me toward him, he didn't have to move a hand, the movement was from within him. We fell down into a point upon each other, like any ordinary Ishtar joining with her common Tammuz or Aphrodite on the sea couch with Adonis and the world made one.

It was that way with Christopher from the beginning. We were drawn to each other like two desperate strangers in a tug-of-war who are thrown upon each other. In retrospect, I realize that I'd been preparing for something I didn't know was coming. One day I woke up with the desire to call all my old lovers and make peace with them, and so I tracked down the two husbands and the few lovers who had really mattered and met with them. I put my house in order, or you could say, I made the bed, turned the mattress, aligned the frame with the coordinates of north and south, smoothed the fresh linens that I had hung to dry in the spring sunlight and the morning breeze. I was an innocent again; I was clean.

After that I became celibate. It was not that I didn't feel heat, I did, a constant fire like a small pot or heated rock steaming inside me, but it didn't open to any bodies, and when a man came near me, no matter how much I was wanting, the desire turned against him and I slinked off even as I was pressing forward, my body insisting that I be alone with its heat. At that time the sight of a beautiful body or face failed to excite me and even intelligence or a great heart and overwhelming presence which had always incited an equally great geyser of desire failed to attract me, and I no longer fantasized the poetry of the bed as I came in contact with poets, did not dream of their rhetorical arms carrying me to the six heavens. I was afraid that I was becoming a nun against my will, and I remembered with a newly born sympathy my elderly uncle who'd complained to me when I'd been crazed with lust that he no longer had desire. I hadn't understood how one could miss something which wasn't there. But in these days, I came to understand this pain as I writhed in the chastity belt of my own making.

I didn't realize that the nun can marry God, that when her body turns inward the spirit enters her through the hot channels of prayer and she is not alone in her bed. Esther Harding says a virgin is a woman who is unto herself, is virgin because she cannot be compelled either to maintain chastity or to yield to an unwanted embrace. I had become a virgin again, almost growing the membrane back so that if and when the proper time came, the entrance would not be automatic, we would both be aware of the gravity of opening the door even to the bridegroom God. Sometimes I took comfort in the thought I might never open the door again; in those times, I restrained my own hand from slipping down toward my thighs and entering what had become a sanctuary. I stayed outside like one who is locked out of prayer under the image of Sheila na gig, the Irish goddess, her hands on her labia, spreading herself wide open across the holy portals of the early churches, the entrance to my own nave past the pubic bone mysteriously forbidden even to me. And still the fire burned, steadily, even intensely, but nothing external could feed it, the curse of an eternal flame which insisted on its own fuel.

One night I was having dinner with a woman friend in a mysterious restaurant set in an adobe dome, a cavelike structure, lit with real candelabras. Flaming cylinders of white beeswax, set on great iron hoops suspended from the curved ceiling, created flickering patterns on the muted natural-dyed woven rugs and tapestries hung on the sand-colored walls. I was seated facing the door, fascinated by the great shadows cast by the entering guests. Martha and I had not seen each other in a long while, so we chose our meal with as much attention to the time it would take to eat it as to the food itself, and after we had very slowly dipped the individual leaves of an artichoke into a delicate fennel-flavored butter, scraping the pulp between our teeth, we were served a series of Ethiopian dishes, tender lamb stew and pungently spiced lentils, the food, to be eaten with our fingers, gracefully spread on a thin cloth of bread.

We were talking about being alone, as women so often do in this decade, marveling at both the joy and the horror of it. "It surprises me," she was saying, "that I contemplate living alone, that I think I may volunteer for it." She had a luminous integrity which inhibited penetration and I imagined her lover experienced with her what others must have felt with me, the presence of an invisible force, an insistent but imperceptible motion outward imitating the dark crawl of an indomitable glacier driving out all opposing motion in its path. She pulled me toward her; she held me at bay, I could only go so far. We would always have a table between us, this boundary of sociability. The pull and the resistance, the call and the denial, was like a draft on the flame inside me, and I felt the fire within flare up so suddenly I opened my mouth to exhale the intolerable heat.

The door of the restaurant opened across from me, the candles flickered, the shadows danced, and then a great swath of darkness was thrown against the far wall. Maybe a candle or two were blown out by the wind, something startled me so that I looked up and found myself caught by his eyes, unexpectedly trapped, as if shining metal teeth had grabbed my ankle. I couldn't look away and realized without understanding it that he was also caught by me. I could see nothing but his eyes; I don't know what he saw of me. I forced myself to look away, to drop my eyes; it took enormous effort. Martha noticed my distress, I may have even whimpered; she asked what had happened, wondered if I were suddenly ill. Maybe I was. I was burning everywhere and the color blazed on my face. "I'd say you'd seen a ghost," Martha said, "except you're not at all pale. But you're shaking."

I had to tell her. I couldn't. What was there to say? I had no words. He continued to stand there, it seems there was a wait for his table. He dwarfed the men who surrounded him. He had the fierce passion one finds in ugly men. He commanded attention with his presence, as his face did not serve him. As for his body, I couldn't see it for the force of his personality, except that he was tall, broad and dark. It was his energy that nabbed me. I couldn't breathe. He had to have known what was happening, because he looked at me again; he had gotten free enough to laugh. It was not what I expected as he threw his head back, emitted, almost but not quite, the laugh of conquest. If initially it was arrogant, it soon became very sweet, had a startled quality, as if he was as unnerved, startled as I was.

Neither of us was young. If you had asked me then I would have said he was a flautist, a sax player, or a young general, the kind you have in third-world countries, the cream of the young Turks, the best in the world, and the portly man by his side was his drummer or aide-de-camp. The other, skinny guys were the scum of the earth, the agents and promoters, the mercenaries, the record company representatives, the public relations scammers, the war profiteers trying to make a deal. He was a head above all of them. They stood in a claque chattering and every now and then they asked him something and if the drummer couldn't answer, he did, nodding or shaking his head, clearly disinterested. I didn't delude myself that I was distracting him, because he seemed to fall into himself periodically as if he were meditating, and then he awakened and looked directly at me, expecting to find me there, and he did. I was always turning toward him, obedient to an inaudible command. Then the maître d' appeared, and they were led away to an obscure table in an antechamber.

"What are you going to do?" Martha asked.

"Nothing," I said, trying to shrug it off. "He'll have to do something, if he wants me," I answered, certain that would end it.

"He is doing something; he must want you," Martha smiled as the drummer appeared in the archway, beckoning to us. I tried to appear lighthearted as I laughed gaily and motioned him to us in return. He turned on his heel; I sank back, relieved and disappointed. That was that.

"You'll have to do something," Martha insisted.

"Are you sure you're not the one who's interested?" I knew she wasn't and I was more than surprised by the upheaval in myself. I had thought I was immune to an affair of the heart and this one a stranger; I'd never picked up anyone in my entire life.

We finished our meal, sucking the gravy from our fingers, washing our faces with damp warm towels scented with rose water. I would have liked to pass the towel over the bones in his ugly powerful canine face, but I pushed the thought away from me and folded the small cloth precisely, aligning the damp edges, and set it aside.

"You'll have to do something," Martha insisted.

"My friend the voyeur?"

"Your friend the friend," she said softly.

"Why doesn't he take the initiative?" I asked. "Isn't that how it's done? I don't want to be an aggressive woman."

"Don't play games. He can't do anything without being disrespectful; in this you have all the power. Ironic, isn't it?"

"How do you know all this?"

"If you were sitting in my chair, you'd know it all too."

"The seat of wisdom?"

"Mmm. If you like. But you have to do something. You'll have to write him a note and send it over with the waiter."

We ordered coffee. A silence fell between us; it was not uncomfortable. I wasn't fantasizing anything, I was trying to stay in the dark. Then there was a pen in my hand, a piece of paper, and I was writing. "We'll give it to the waiter," I agreed, "but as we're leaving, not before."

Martha shrugged. Coffee came. She reached for the note as

casually as she reached for the white cubes of sugar and the pitcher of cream, but I wouldn't give it to her, afraid she'd take charge. Then I noticed that he was walking across the room. It seemed to me, he stayed in the men's room only long enough to wash his hands. When he exited, he gave me so long a look I couldn't control myself, I beckoned to him as his aide-de-camp had beckoned to me, and, without taking his dark eyes from mine, he walked slowly toward me. It was as if his spirit reached the table before his body; it pulled my hand forward to meet him. I couldn't speak, I would have liked to ask him his name, but I simply held out the paper. He took it most carefully, so careful not to touch my fingers—I could feel the heat of him on my skin—saying, "I'll think about this seriously," and turned away. I thought I had gone with him, bound to him as with rope, but I never left the chair.

"What did you say in the note?"

I wrote it out for Martha on another paper as a way of keeping it for myself. "I don't know what possessed me." The note said: "It's been so long since we've met. Shall we come together again at 10 on Friday night at the Euphrates. I'll reserve a room in my name. Angela Silver."

"I also left him my phone number."

"So he can confirm?"

"So he can refuse."

"And you?"

"I've already made a choice; I don't want the opportunity to change my mind."

At the Euphrates, you leave your shoes outside the door, hang your clothes in the closet and put on the robe and slippers provided in the alcove before you step into the inner chamber amid the smell of incense. This room had a tiled dipping pool and a statue of nymphs dancing the world into creation outside the window in the private garden among ferns and lilies. The jasmine was blooming.

The elegance of the hotel had almost seduced me when he

entered simply saying, "Christopher." I said, "Angela," and then we knew each other's voice. He put his finger to his lips commandingly, but I was not going to speak. He looked about the room, it was perfectly beautiful by any standards; there was a basket of tropical fruit on a low glass table alongside the requisite bottles of champagne cooling. He had sent those, room service had arrived a moment before he did, so I had known he was coming.

"This is the false paradise," he said. "I have been here too many times in my life." He motioned me into my clothes and we walked out of the hotel, all without speaking. By the time we reached the street, away from the theoretical safety of doormen and porters, I was trembling and he took the basket of fruit from my arms and carried that and the champagne as well. He still said nothing, and I remained under the injunction of silence. I imagined he understood my fear perfectly: a strange man, I only knew his first name and I had come, with much struggle, to the time when I valued my life. He took my arm, but very gently, to steady me and without triumph.

His car was immaculate and ordinary. That relieved me. I conjured a story for each detail. The car was white. That was a good sign. His eyes were dark and hooded; that meant trouble. I tried to memorize the license plate number, but when he stroked my hair gently after he unlocked the car door, I forgot it as I got into the passenger side.

When we had come to the end of the road—it was the proverbial end of the road—he opened the door for me, took a blanket and pad out of the trunk and walked off onto a path through fairly rough terrain up onto a grassy knoll, a circle carved out of the surrounding sage, scrub oak, thistle and hoarhound which made entrance difficult and forbidding; the moon was waiting. He turned me to him, the moonlight on both our faces, stroked my hair, then ran his fingers down, encircling my neck, his thumbs stroking the voice box, but quite gently. "Don't be afraid," he said, "we're here only because I have a broken heart."

Then I was less afraid of him, because of his voice, I think;

there could be no crime in such tenderness. I was more afraid of the fire in my body. It was so quiet between us, I imagined he could hear the flames inside me wrap about the logs of wood he was feeding me with his silent intense scrutiny, with his hand on my shoulder, with his delicacy, through his fierce wolf-like face and his demanding yellow eyes reflecting the light oddly brilliant in the darkness. These two small beacons of animal light impelled me to trust him even further.

We sat on the blanket for a long time. We could hear the moon patting across the sky on her bare feet, her way lit by stars. He looked at his hands a long time. I did not know if they were full or empty or what he had held with them. Then he looked up at me and our eyes locked as they had locked originally, and when they penetrated me, I recoiled and then I was opening and opening again and opening again, one locked chamber behind the other, opening, further and deeper than I have ever opened before, and still his eyes entered me even more deeply as if he were spreading me open with his fingers, probing the curves of a pink-shelled nautilus to its furthest point.

"Is this what it means to know a woman?" I whispered.

He sighed deeply, "If he knows her, she made it easy for him. But can she know him? Will he allow it?" he asked after a long time and looked at me again, still the wolf but caught in a trap this time, his hand tensed into a claw he would chew off. He extended the hand to me, there was something invisible on the palm, the fingers spread away in some agony. I wanted to touch his hand but I was afraid and I knew he could not touch me with it again; then I looked in his eyes, they were veiled, and I realized he was asking me to enter him, that I must be the man this time, must set out with my hands and eyes to open his steel trap doors, which were heavier and darker and more firmly locked than mine.

"I would like to know you," I said, afraid of what I had to know when he showed me both his hands, stiff and bent and agonized. I could not tell if they were contorted in pain or in threat when he grunted, "There is so much blood on them. You will never be able to enter me deep enough to make them clean; I am stained to the core. Even when one fights a good war, there is always blood on one's hands afterwards; they never come clean."

He began quoting the Aeneid; I knew the verse. He was repeating the line "Red as I am with slaughter and new from war" as if it were a mantra. He was almost in a trance, his face twisted with pain. I could not reach him and I was afraid again. I could hear the summer wind in the far trees, but it did not come close to us—was that a warning? I stood up and made a circle about the blanket with a stick and then, because I was fearful, and also because I did not know what I was doing, I walked about the blanket three times in one direction and then three times in the other—to get time, I told myself. He looked at me, the light was going out of his eyes. I had little time. I knelt alongside his rigid body.

"You have to give yourself up," I said with more bravado than confidence and took his claw and pressed it against my face. I could feel the scratch of his blunt nails. He didn't say anything and so I scraped his hand along my skin down to my throat, put my thumb on his thumb against my larynx, saying, "Because you can injure me, you must surrender." His face contorted. I felt him tremble and finally some semblance of a voice pressed out between gritted teeth.

"Didn't I seek you out?" he asked. "Didn't I give myself up?" His hand collapsed as if the blood had drained out of it. He lay there limp and hopeless as if his heart had stopped.

I reached into his shirt, and when I felt the beat under my hand, I began to unbutton his clothes. He didn't move. I was grateful the buttons weren't brass, did not have eagles on them. I removed his shirt, he made no move, was neither living nor dead. My own clothes seemed absurd. I wished I had stolen the robes from the safe hotel, but I hadn't, so I undressed and bent over him, my breasts swinging, my belly crescent like the moon.

He had given himself up, but it was as if it had killed him to do it. "I will wrap you in white flags and leave you to the birds," I said.

"Do what you want with me," he answered bitterly.

I undid the buckle of his belt and slid his pants down his hard slender hips, he was naked beneath them, his skin like dark sand, bits of mica gleaming in the moonlight. I ran my fingers down my booty as he lay perfectly still on his back, his arms and legs spread out. He was so still, I could have cut his heart out with a knife and offered it to the gods. Instead I bent over him, my head on his belly in an attitude of prayer. I had not expected to do this. His eyes were open. They were not quite the dead eyes but they were not the eyes of light. I did not know how to open the rest of his body. I prayed for a long time and then I heard a voice and realized that I was chanting and I continued, the voice breaking out of my body, and I let it soar and then it seemed to me that he joined me, that there were two voices, but I was not certain I saw his lips moving and as I chanted I saw him rise up. "I need your lifeblood," he whispered and, reaching down along my body, pulled the string between my legs until the plug was removed, and he fell back again. I slid my hands down between my thighs into the warm opening, bathed them in the blood from the conical shell, then holding my red fingers up in the moonlight, I passed them first over his eyes and then I began to write on his body.

He knew what I was doing before I did. I did not have to say, as I wrote with my menstrual blood on his lips, his throat, his shoulders, "These are the seventy-two names of God" on his entire body with my menstrual blood. **Anat, El, Shakti, Siva.** It took a long time, and as I reached his belly, **Tetragrammaton, Ely,** his sex began to rise, **Hecate, Lilith,** coiling toward my body, **Emmanuel, Magnus, Parvati,** like a cobra from its dark basket, **Auf-Ra, Mehen, Hathor, Thoth.** It took a long time, **Messias, Sabahot, Adonay,** and when I ran dry he laid me down and delicately spread my lips and licked the circle open again, his wet tongue penetrating ever so slowly, the waters dripping into me until I could place my index finger within again to find the ocher ink and write more names, **Ischiros, Primus, Novissimus, Ereshkigal,** the names of the Goddess mixing with the names of the God, **Eve, Asherah, Yahweh, Shaddai, Aries, Leo, Pania,** all the names on his smooth dark belly, hard nipples and thighs, **Filius Hominis, Pater Omnipotens, Eumenides.** The tip of the great snake, **Ptah, Python,** rose and danced toward me, **Sheba, Khumbaba,** a drop of seed appeared from the small hole, **Gaea, Propheta,** which widened like the iris of an eye, **Jesu, Pentagna,** against the press of blood, **Inanna, Sheol, Shekinah, Athanos,** I wanted the snake in my mouth, **Nehustan, Charitas, Infinitas;** they used to think that's how the serpent was engendered, **Via, Pastor, Virtus,** the woman sucking its head into her body, **Nahema, Apep,** the bite like the magic circle of the Ouroboros creating an end to time, **Nephthys, Anqet,** and the beginning of all creation, **Nammu, Ceres, Persephone, Lux, Imago, Sanctus, Ninhursag,** Christopher moved his head between my thighs, we circled and rocked in the breath of our bodies, I felt the joy born and stopped him to lick the taste of my blood from his lips, **Ariadne, Dionysus, Hermes, Aphrodite, Osiris, Isis,** and then pressed his head back again wanting that tongue in my body, feeling myself open to him as he had opened, the molten core at the base of my spine, **Seraph,** beginning to pulse and rise. At the last moment, I pulled him away from me, dipped my fingers within me for the last bit of blood, **Tammuz, Ishtar, Nahusah** and wrote the last secret name of the manwoman God ******* on the swelling serpent's head, its mouth opening deeper, showing the serpent's teeth as I cupped my hands about it, driving it toward the mouth between my legs. His eyes were wide open and I saw his heart pounding in his chest, the great Snake God slipped into me, drove up my spine, as his lips pressed against my temple and sperm spilt into me, " A living holy stream," he cried, and the words sent my own body heaving as if it were the earth from which this white fountain exploded in heat and sulfur. The tree over us groaned in the wind as the entire world untangled its beating limbs and came to rest.

After a long time Christopher wiped the tears from his face and brought the champagne and basket of fruit to our blanket. The warm champagne exploded out of the bottle, showering us with its sweet wetness. I laughed and he pushed me down again, pinned me under him while he cut an orange in four and rubbed the crescent between my legs, it was sweet and red when he bit into it and passed the other half to my mouth.

And that's how I became a priestess for The Great Whore, and on our Holy Night I join with Christopher at the moment when the Gods join as well. It's the sacred night of the body and we keep the Sabbath as religiously as it's ever been kept.

The Hunters

SUZANNE MILLER

He waited for her, loving the long moments moving past them, out toward the arched curve of mountain, out beyond to the blue-green mass of sea. In his precise patient waiting, the heated active waiting of the hunter, he saw in the hushed silence of these moments that the curving of her woman's roundness was not separate, was the same as the slight rise of hillock upon which she lay, the same great curve of the near-distant mountain, the same vast slow undulation of the farther depths of the sea. As he lay separate enough from her to see clearly, he was stunned by the organic fusion in his view, each imprinted upon the other with the woman as the core beginning, the alive touchable center.

This finally was what she was to him, what woman was: the essence of all things elemental and enduring. He was overcome with the desire to touch the fine endless center of her. To find fulfillment in the dark touch of her. He stalked this singular reality within her in his patience, the deep source of life-fire within her, the light hidden in the layered curved depths of the mountain and the final folding in of the rhythmic movement of the sea. Only through her and the touch of her could he be healed in his separateness.

Perceiving at last these truths in her, in her body, he waited and was still. She was not yet ready, perfectly ready for him. He had not yet sensed the quiver of her first subtle awareness of him, of her own felt desire to contain him and all that he is within her renewed abundance.

She held fast with all the surface of herself to the warm moistness of the mountain earth, multicolored and rich with spring. Curve for curve she met the image of herself, felt the full penetration of the earth, filling her, awakening within her the impersonal mystery of creation. She felt him near to her, very near. She felt his eyes on her, seeking her out, and she exulted in her deep sensuality. She loved the fine force of his attention covering her while she held fast to the other, surrendering the length of herself to the hard-soft surface of the earth. He felt a denial of him in her pressing to the earth, yet he was sure and patient.

They were old together. Ancients. Through her he had come to know the limitless span of the eternal, in which she traveled concurrently his past, present and future. He had learned through the failure of his forceful youth and its disillusion, that this denial of him was momentary, was necessary. His early wounds taught him the slow receptive inner yielding of the woman was certain and desirable; the wisdom come from experience to seek that and that alone past the darker moments of her denials.

Following as an artist would the lines of her body as it met the earth, he saw each rising and falling define her anew, bring her to renewal. She was nearing contentment, the contentment given by the earth. He felt her soften deeply into the passive womb-earth. She would become aware of his touch soon. The insistent flame of life's desire to renew itself would flare up, burning through her contentment, calling for a different satisfaction.

Now he felt the terrible exhilaration of the unknown. As she became more and more aware of him in her body, he became unsure. This uncertainty in him, this vulnerability, though known again and again through the years of passionate meeting with her, created a new man in him. The modern, known man fell away, unnecessary, and he became aware of his own strangeness in reaching out to her.

It was this new man who she in her instincts was hunting. For between them there was no prey, only a mutual hunting of the other; life stalking itself.

He was breathless as he watched her stirring. A restlessness began in her, a dissatisfaction with her contentment, a disturbance in the peace of her aloneness. A deepening sensation of heat began to beat up in his blood, slowly, rhythmically, the internal sound drum-primitive. He waited and was still, the instinctual hunter certain that the soul of his pure fire would touch her and begin in her the dream of him, of her fulfillment through him, matching beat for beat the sound of his own blood.

She stretched fully, like an animal. He was shocked by the great impersonal force in her. It was that which met him as he moved to touch her with his silent stillness. Finally. Perfectly. It was that which he saw so stark and vivid in her eyes as she turned to meet him, the great impersonal mystery which bound them to each other, the man and the woman; moving them beyond the known terrain of their private lives out into the wilderness of their forgotten history.

She rose suddenly and he saw that she was all bright and flamelike and golden. She moved slowly, dreamlike, toward him with a strange wildness about her, a foreignness. She turned completely to him and lay softly down, facing him, fitting her arm around his waist and moving closer, touching now her length to him, resting her head against the deep pounding urgency of his heart.

He stroked her soft hair, pressing his full sensual mouth lightly against her forehead moving errant strands of hair back as he traced with brushing kisses the lines of her beloved face, the deep-set eyes, the broad cheekbones. Her wide eyes saw him new and unknown. At last he touched her upreaching mouth with his, barely touching, moving with lingering intimate contact side to side, stopping time. All his excited waiting had been nothing compared to this silence in touching so gently, so gently. And she was lost utterly with him in this discovery, the warm rushes of their mingling breaths, this slow undemanding meeting.

The emptiness of separation dissolved in this meeting breath for breath. She touched his sensitive beautiful mouth, tracing her fingers around and in between their kissing. Her fingers searched the broad lines of his face, his high forehead and over and through his fine hair, curling and winding it around her fingers. The still touching of their lips changed in intensity until they seemed of one breath.

There was so much to find in each other. How many men and women were they? They sought within the truth of their bodies for the knowledge of who they were to each other, until finally, even that seeking, through the breath and lips and hands, ceased. For they could not know the other beyond the senses and it no longer mattered; they were surely all men and all women in this hunting of the other.

He was hard and full against her softness. A deep burning began in her, creating an opening in her once cool completeness. It had been so long since she was opened that she was startled at the intensity of the rings of fire dancing and whirling within her core. She felt she could ride the edge of the flames endlessly. He sensed her opening. Her breathing came in deep surges and her arms drew him closer in subtle command. Her body arched into him. He pulled away to see the startled look of her and moved again to her, covering her mouth and kissing the full depths of her while he caressed her curving softness down to the alive center of her sex, moving gently, circling the fiery point of her until her sweet nectar covered his searching fingers and he brought them up for them to taste and mix with their near-breathless kisses.

He looked into her clear honest eyes and moved over her with his body, molding perfectly to the curved hollow of her hips. She ran her fingers over and around his pulsing satiny hardness, drawing him into her, deeply into her. Through the time of her closing, her chaste connection with him, her inner body had become dark and unfamiliar. He pressed carefully and gently into her slowly yielding folds. There was such an aliveness in her gradual opening, that the whole length of her center clung to him as he pressed himself deeper, endlessly deeper, finally hearing her sharp muffled cry as he felt the touch of her depths on him. Her opening life to him was a miracle of pleasure.

Again they were still, still as the first touching of their mouths. He had at last found her again. At last touched the deep blood center of her. He wanted never to move again, for she fit over and around him in perfection, this eternally unknown woman who was his own among all others. She too was perfect and full, so full of him she felt she might explode utterly from the intensity of her feelings.

Time fell over their stillness until a new demand came up in them. The subtle swelling of her inner flesh, the imperceptible flowing movement, clinging then releasing, pulling him yet deeper until he could not bear his own peace and moved against her arching curved body, their increasing hunger bringing them to a pitch of active seeking until their bodies in unison gave way to a final yielding and there was no more active movement, but a common vulnerable rhythm. A rhythm of utter harmony and a movement so perfect, one breath, one beating heart, one soaring complete release into the mystery.

The sun was on them and all their brightness. They lay heavily together, still, while the last quick movements within her quieted against his softening flesh, held gently now in the full open flower of her. After a time of immense quiet, she ran her fingers over his dear body. His face was buried in her throat's hollow, where he heard the deep pounding pulsebeat of her heart.

New life was felt in her, newer even than the earth's gracious giving, a hopeful stirring deep in her center. They were part of all life around them, and all of the alive natural facets of the world glowed and glistened between them. The sweet smell of their bodies came up with a warm rush of breeze and they breathed deeply of themselves and the earth and were filled with an effortless joy. Her eyes danced for him and they kissed playfully, childlike, rocking side to side in the midst of spring's flowering all around them. They tasted the salt sweet liquid of their bodies and he rested his head against her full-flowing womb, attending to the possibility of new life.

He curved around her back now, resting, sculpting himself to her moist body, his arms crossed over her breasts. She ran her hand over the fine hairs of his arms, so lightly, not even touching his skin. She pretended she was blind, memorizing him, touching him to know him thoroughly through that sense alone. He knew she was for the moment a blind woman discovering him, imprinting him upon herself. His heart felt such compassion, for he saw how fragile they were in life; tears filled to the edges of his eyes for her, for the possible child, for the sweet abundant earth, for himself.

Finally she knew he was for her, born again for her and for this. She would know him and this truth always and yet never know him, for they were always to be together and always to be unknown. He would not leave her again and she would no more look beyond the comfort of his presence. They were committed in their bodies, known through centuries of time, their primal bond knowing no rival.

III

The Forbidden

When most people think about the unusually erotic, they think about the forbidden. In many areas, it is that very thing which cannot be possessed that is the most desirable, most intriguing. Actions that are prohibited carry the greatest excitement; the man or woman who is unavailable is often more desirable than the one who is at your side every night. And sexuality is one area in which the forbidden is most highly charged.

Sex and the forbidden are inextricably intertwined from the beginning. At an early age, many children get the message from parents that there is something naughty but wonderful about sex. Many religions preach against sex, making the taboo only more intriguing. Curiosity about sex begins at an early age and remains high throughout life, especially in relation to areas of sexuality not yet experienced. With the forbidden, in adult sex, comes the resurrection of the incredibly strong sexual feelings that accompany adolescence and preadolescence. As sexual experience increases, the forbidden moves to new levels: making love to the forbidden partner, one of another race, with the possibility of being caught, watching another couple making love, making love with more than one person. Each person has his or her own idea of what constitutes the enticing forbidden, but it is the unknown, the curiosity of what it might be like, that causes the rush that accompanies the trespassing over acceptable boundaries, that increases the erotic attraction.

For the adolescent, everything sexual takes on heightened interest, because everything is forbidden. For girls, even necking and petting are forbidden. According to Sharon Mayes, "Living in a sheltered existence in the South, with parents who were very religious, meant that sex was taboo. The most exciting thing you could do was to get a boy to drive you around on a motorcycle or in a car—driving fast and being away from parents was real freedom. There was also the power of being in control of something forbidden or taboo." In Sharon's story, "Auto Erotic," automobiles become imbued with all the eroticism of forbidden sexuality. The car, which represents status, power, danger, and freedom from parents, is itself a metaphor for sexuality. Driving, especially driving fast, can create a physical excitation. This excitation can be as easily used to heighten the readiness for a race as to heighten a sexual experience.

For most people, sexual feelings experienced during adolescence take on a primary intensity that causes even more recent memories to pale in comparison. As a result, these adolescent and preadolescent experiences frequently form the major fantasies or favorite activities for the person later in life. This is true for the protagonist in Sharon Mayes's story as well as the main character in "A Long, Long Time," by Carolyn Banks. Whereas automobiles carry the erotic content for Sharon's story, an adolescent erotic memory of museums forms the basis for the one written by Carolyn: "I remember going into museums as a teenager. The museum had an erotic quality because it was the only place I could see naked bodies. I would think about touching them and how it would be to be closed in the museum after hours and have all the statues come to life."

Carolyn's story takes this adolescent memory and builds it into the fantasy life of a grown woman. As she develops this fantasy she embarks further and further into the forbidden. He is much younger than she is, the forbidden partner. He is undressing her in front of passersby, the exhibitionist totally carried away by the sensuality of the moment. And of course, the unexpected ending keeps erotic intrigue high.

Another way to keep erotic intrigue high is to have an extramarital affair. The possibility of being discovered and the potential threat to the marriage get the adrenaline flowing. The obligatory time spent apart, longing for the beloved, keeps erotic tension at a peak. Meanwhile, every moment together takes on an added and cherished intensity due to the often complex but necessary plans and precautions required to carry out the illicit affair.

In "Humming," Sandy Boucher capitalizes on the variety of emotions that accompany an extramarital affair and create physiological excitement and heightened eroticism. According to Sandy, "It's the intrigue, the fact that the husband doesn't know, the forbidden aspect of this affair, that makes it so titillating and exciting. Every look, every moment, is erotically weighted and vibrating."

In addition, "Humming" deals with deeper issues. We have a woman who is struggling with the changes caused by menopause, and the details of this primal passage are presented in ways that enhance, rather than detract from, the eroticism. According to Sandy, "Menopause is also a spiritual opening, where one is transformed. This woman is in this intense period of transformation and she is tremendously vulnerable. Her ability to feel the tenderness, caring and trust allows her to surrender herself to her partner and this heightens the sexuality. In addition," says Sandy, "a challenge to patriarchal religious hegemony and an affirmation of ancient matriarchal roots are posed by the bold sensuality of two women making love in a Buddhist meditation room."

A forbidden partner is not only one who requires a clandestine affair; it can be someone of a different race, another nationality, a significantly different class background, higher or lower. But a person who is physically different, a person with a physical handicap, is forbidden in a different way—a way that is often both anxiety-producing and intriguing.

Rebecca Silver, in "Fearful Symmetry," creates for her main character this dilemma consisting of intrigue and fear. Despite the impracticality of the relationship—their different social backgrounds and temperaments—her immense attraction to the power of a man who is so terribly vital in the way he has dealt with his handicap enables her to confront her fears. "The eros of the story is so intense," says Rebecca, "because the woman has successfully confronted something in herself, she has overcome her fear—her fear of a different body." And this fear, this feeling of mixed approach and avoidance of the uniquely forbidden adds significantly to the erotic impact.

Finally, there is the forbidden for the sake of the forbidden. Victoria Starr creates a totally fantastic fantasy in "A Japanese Play." In this story, she has incorporated voyeurism, exhibitionism, racial mixtures and group sex. "The story is about what you cannot do, the taboo in this society," Victoria says. "The forbidden is exciting because it has been kept from you." Yet, interestingly, whereas so often erotica that is focused on the forbidden or taboo deals more with the superficial, the fantasy of the illicit, this story deals with the forbidden within the loving context of an intimate relationship. And it is this theme of the intimate relationship, at the foundation of this extraordinary event, that is essential to holding the story together and making it truly erotic. "The romantic-love theme," says Victoria, "gives the characters the relaxed atmosphere and comfort to experiment, because there is trust between them. Without it, it wouldn't be as erotic. It would be more anxiety-producing, more hard-core."

So it seems to be true that, for women, stepping out into the forbidden requires the safety of a relationship. In each of the five stories that explore the limits of the forbidden and the taboo, a strong emotional contact between the characters enables the woman to venture out.

Auto Erotic

SHARON S. MAYES

The red leather felt cool to my fingertips. Daydreaming, I slid my hand down across the seat and back to rest on my thigh. The cassette was Joni Mitchell singing, "She comes from the school of Southern charm, likes to have things her way." I always wondered why Mom named me Scarlett. "Shades of Scarlett conquering," she said, "a woman must have everything." I couldn't agree more. I smiled at the sweet memories that kept me company. Don slept in the back seat, having spent the night working in the emergency room. I insisted we spend the day at the beach in a cove I call paradise.

We used to have a jet-black Buick with red leather upholstery. The year was 1959 and I was twelve going on twenty. My father loved this car. I washed it with him, watching his strong hands lovingly stroke the hood with soapsuds. He wore his old plaid Bermuda shorts and tennis shoes with no socks. His hair, jet black like the car, fell over his forehead, and when I knew he wasn't paying attention I would spray him with the hose, giggling madly.

"Youuu little brat!" he would yell, grabbing the hose and turning it on me. We would run around the car laughing until I surrendered. Sometimes we'd wrestle on the front lawn with the black Buick shining at the curb. Dad would scoop me up and toss me into the front seat. Before I straightened myself out we'd be speeding down the tree-lined country roads, my hair blowing out the window, the warm wind flushing my cheeks. Dad lit a cigarette and stared at the road. He didn't talk much, but I adored him. We shared a love of speed, fast cars and red leather.

The drive would take two hours, not long if you love to drive. I opened the sunroof as soon as the fog had burned away. The rolling green hills beyond the bay emerged from their night-dresses, the water glittered like diamonds and the magnificent bridge loomed ahead. Another glorious day in paradise. Hundreds, thousands, millions of people lived within two hours' drive of paradise, but rarely had I met anyone in my cove. Often I was alone there with miles of fine white sand under my feet, the raging Pacific crashing against giant rocks in front of me, fields of wildflowers blanketing the cliffs behind. Deer and elk grazed and mated. The world was alive and giving birth in this place, a place to think and dream and play.

I remember the night I snuck out my bedroom window and went to my girlfriend's house to meet two friends of her brother's. They were older, maybe sixteen, and one of them had a car. I wore my pink shorts and a white blouse with a Peter Pan collar. My mother and I had had a terrible fight that very day because I wanted a bra and she said, "What for?" What for, indeed! The blond guy was sitting behind the wheel of a metallic blue '53 Plymouth. He kept ducking out of sight as Susan and I just stood there. To relieve the awkwardness, I walked around the Plymouth, sliding my hand over the roof, the fenders, the door, until I stood right next to him. "Nice car," I gestured.

"Yeah," he sort of grinned, biting his cigarette with his front teeth. "Want to go for a ride?" Susan was already in the back seat with the short, skinny guy sitting as far away from her as possible. I thought about opening the door and watching him tumble out, but.

Pridefully tossing my head back, I got in the front seat and looked at him closely. He was cute. My legs started to tingle a little and a funny feeling came over my stomach. "Let's go."

Billy was his name. He was a high school dropout. His parents were divorced and he lived in a trailer court with his mother. Susan said he worked on cars all day. I wasn't going to say anything about that. I'd never been in his part of town. I squirmed when he glanced at me sideways. The seat was covered with a wire-mesh thing that scratched my exposed thighs. I was going to tell him, but, like my father, Billy didn't talk much. I noticed that his car wasn't nearly as nice as Dad's.

Eventually, Billy let me cover the rough seats with a blanket. Every weekend when I spent the night at Susan's we'd go to a drive-in movie. I figured I could get away with it until my parents found out. Billy seemed to like me. I liked him alright, especially when he let me drive. Late at night I could speed down the back roads with the windows rolled down, the black sky rushing to meet us, the trees parting as we entered. Billy would lie down in the back seat and smoke cigarettes. Once he said he was thinking about taking me somewhere.

He put a radio in the Plymouth the next week. When he picked me up, close to midnight, he was all dressed up. I mean he had on regular pants instead of jeans. He didn't say a word. We drove for an hour toward the ocean, then when he found the place he wanted we stopped. We sat there staring at the trillions of stars and the moon lighting a path directly to us across the waves. Billy put his arm around the back of the seat and turned toward me. He looked at me funny and I looked right back at him. When he finally kissed me I thought I would melt. His hand felt hot on my shoulder. I was lost in his smell, his hands moving slowly around my waist, he pulled me closer to him until I was enclosed. Conway

Twitty's "It's Only Make Believe" blared from the radio. I wondered how long this could last.

Just as I got the hang of kissing, I felt his hand under my blouse on my back. I thanked God my mother had relented on the bra. A rush of warmth shot up my spine, but I did stop kissing him long enough to say I wasn't supposed to be doing this. He sat back and looked at me sadly. I was sorry he had taken it like that. After all, I hadn't said I wanted to stop. He put his hand on my knee and squeezed it. "Hey, cut it out, that tickles." Dad did that a lot.

"You're a pretty girl, you know that?"

"No." I was embarrassed and flattered.

"You're just a kid, you know that?"

"No, I'm not!" This infuriated me and I started to get out to walk. "Who do you think you are, anyway?" I retaliated.

"I'm nobody." He said it with such certainty. "I'm nobody you should be fooling around with."

"Oh yeah! Well, I'll just leave, then." I had my hand on the door handle.

He reached for my shoulders and turned me toward him. He kissed me hard, then lifted me up and somehow put me in the back seat. His kisses covered my face, I felt his weight on my legs and my skirt being moved up with his knee. He gently unbuttoned my blouse. His hand covered my breast and it swelled to meet him. My whole body trembled. His knee pushed my legs open and I felt something hard pressing against me. Overcome with sensations, I forgot everything in the world, even myself. I was aware of only the soft blanket on my back, the smell of him, the longing in my breasts.

Suddenly, he sat up and put his hands over his face. "I can't." I didn't know what he meant, what was wrong. He pulled me to a sitting position and kissed me sweetly on the cheek. "You're just a kid. You shouldn't be here. Come on, I'm taking you home."

I never saw him again, but I thought of him almost every night for a long time, sometimes still do. We were over the bridge now, my silver Prelude, I, and Don in the back seat. Only a short strip of highway left before we turned toward the ocean and circled around the Impressionists hills through valleys of redwoods, across treeless flats by the reservoir where the hawks fly. There was almost no traffic. I pushed the accelerator closer to the floor, squealing around the curves, letting the power of the car pull me out of the turns. My body sank back into the bucket seat. Time for another cassette, a cigarette.

After Billy, nothing much happened for a year or two. Susan and I spent many nights poring over her father's old *Playboys* while listening to the top twenty. Sometimes we rubbed each other's back, and the tingly feeling in my breasts would return. One Sunday morning I woke up covered in blood, terrified that God was punishing me for that feeling. Susan assured me it was no big deal, just a hassle that came every month. Mom said I was a woman now, but that didn't mean I could act like one.

Three new boys moved onto our block, raunchy boys named Darren, Meryl and Hotrod. I used to watch Hotrod polish his Harley-Davidson motorcycle every day. Meryl had an old junker, one of those station wagons that looked like it was made of wood.

Susan and I had the woods behind her house completely staked out; it was our territory. We had built a fort in a big maple tree where we often sunbathed nude. It wasn't long before Darren, Meryl and Hotrod were spying on us. Hotrod called us "jailbait" and tried to convince the other guys to ignore us. When we all finally got on speaking terms, I goaded, cajoled, everything except begged, to get a ride on the motorcycle. After the boys caucused, it was agreed: one ride for one game of strip poker, strip poker first, ride second. I began to think that boys weren't fair.

We assembled in the tree fort. I was ready and confident, never having lost much at games. Rings, necklaces, shoelaces—everything counted and I wore half my mom's jewelry box. Poor Susan wasn't as smart and she began to lose right away. Darren and Susan were down to their underwear when Hotrod and Meryl started going off for minutes at a time. Susan's chubby breasts poked out of her bra showing her nipples as red as her cheeks. She laughed hysterically and was happier than I'd ever seen her.

Darren, his eyes glued to her breasts, sat with his jacket over his lap. Nobody was paying attention to the cards. The red in my cheeks was annoyance. Susan was getting all the attention. It was the first time I remember thinking that losing was winning in some cases.

Just as I was about to leave, Meryl said he wanted to show me something he found in the next clearing. I followed him through the bushes. Susan and Darren were now negotiating new rules, the next person to lose had to let the others touch them any place they chose. Bored with the game, I followed Meryl into the bushes. When we got to the clearing, Hotrod was standing behind a tree with the Harley parked behind him. "Come on," he said, "you're gonna get a ride."

This was a big machine. I could barely straddle it and bend my knees, but I climbed on behind Hotrod and Meryl climbed on behind me. A surge of power ripped us from the ground. We spun around in circles before leaping into the air and flying down the dirt road. My eyes were shut, praying to God, even though I had recently become a nonbeliever. Hotrod's hair stung my face and I put my head on his shoulder. The trees raced by in a blur, Meryl pushed closer to me, his legs and arms gripping mine. His head was buried in my neck, his breath hot under my shirt. Sandwiched between them I felt indestructible. We hit the asphalt jumping over a ditch from the dirt road, dust flew wildly and I screamed. It was a physical surge of energy, totally exciting, the ecstasy of the open road.

Meryl followed me to school a lot. He was there when I got out, and we walked home together. Occasionally he brought the junker, and we drove to the amusement park to ride the roller coaster, my favorite ride. He was unbelievably nice to me for a boy. We slid into holding hands and making out when I baby-sat next door.

Our parents became friends before long. On weekends they played bridge late into the night. We stayed in my bedroom or his, ostensibly watching TV. In the spring for my fourteenth birthday both families expeditioned to the state park for a major picnic. Meryl ate ten hamburgers and ten hotdogs on a dare. After the parents were worn out from softball and swimming we snuck off to play treasure hunt. I was wearing new purple shorts and a halter top bought after months of whining and nagging Mom. Meryl ran ahead, hiding behind trees and jumping out whooping. He thought he could scare me, I even pretended that he did. We sat down under a shady oak tree to watch the squirrels. It was then that I saw someone moving in the bushes to my right. Quietly we tiptoed over to get a better view. At first I couldn't tell what was happening. I saw pink flesh moving rhythmically, legs coming out of the ground. They were moaning, but it wasn't scary. Meryl put his hand over my mouth and dragged me away. He said they were "fucking." My curiosity overwhelmed my common sense, of which my mom said I had very little to start with. "Let's watch," I whispered.

"I can show you how to do it," Meryl grinned, holding my hand tight. My hand felt connected to my stomach, that stirring ache came again. Before I could answer he was kissing me. My head fell back into the leaves, my arms had nowhere to go but around him. He kissed me with his mouth open, his tongue searching for mine. When he began to feel my breasts and inched his hand inside my shorts I felt a surge of intensity. It was like the moment the motorcycle left the ground. I didn't want to stop. I could hear Conway Twitty's song and feel Billy's car blanket on my back. I could smell his maleness, feel the muscles of his arms, the hardness between his legs. He stroked the inside of my thighs, slipping his fingers under my shorts and panties. An incredible electric shock reverberated down my legs and up into my abdomen. Meryl was trying to pull off my shorts when I saw a face in the tree. It was Hotrod standing right over us.

I pushed Meryl aside with uncommon strength. "Hey, what are you doing here! You creep." My halter top was half off and my shorts were covered with wet spots. Meryl just lay there next to me staring at Hotrod like an idiot. "You're spying on us." I was indignant.

Hotrod knelt down and casually pulled my halter down to my

waist. He looked at my breasts and smiled. My nipples stuck out, asking to be touched. I wrapped my arms around myself and glared at him. I could see his pants were swollen like Meryl's had been. He picked up a twig and ran it up and down the inside of my leg, then across my shorts and around in circles. Little stabs of pleasure mingled with my chagrin. Meryl propped his head up on his elbow and watched. His jeans were unzipped. Hotrod rubbed the bulge in his pants while continuing to play with the twig. I wanted to watch, but instead rolled over on my stomach, curious and annoyed. Meryl rubbed my back and I could hear Hotrod breathing heavily. Dad was yelling for me in the distance. I jolted up and ran without looking back.

There is a particular fork in the road where going to the right can take you only one place. I sped around the curve with no hesitation, knowing that six miles away was what I called the gate to paradise. It was really a cattle crossing with the doors always open and metal bumps in the road to slow you down. But to me it was more. There was a strong wind howling across the meadows from the ocean. The Prelude shivered in the gusts. Cows grazed lazily on either side of me, turning their heads with indifference. I could feel my breasts tickled by the cashmere sweater. Racing toward the edge of the Earth at ninety miles an hour distracted me. Don was awake now, stretching like a cat in the backseat, reaching for a cigarette.

"Here we are, approaching the gates of paradise," I joked with him.

"Scarlett, for Christ's sake, slow down." He careened back and forth trying to get a light. "Who do you think you are, Richard Petty?"

"Don't be grumpy. Look at this gorgeous day."

The sun made the meadows emerald. Wild iris formed purple streaks through the green. It was a place where I liked to run across the fields, roll down the hills or lie facing the sun feeling the Earth revolving under me. I pulled into the parking lot at the end of the road. No other cars were there. Don was assembling the pack: water, fruit, books, binoculars, sweaters. I stepped out and stretched, then put the seat forward to help him.

"Come here." He pulled me on top of him, kissing me furiously all over my face.

"Hey, what is this?" He had his hand under my jeans squeezing my bottom. His shirt was open to the waist, his brown chest warm and creased from sleep. I buried my face in it. "Let's go down to the cove first." I wanted to prolong the delicious anticipation.

He gently cupped his hands over my breasts and began to play with my nipples. The rich leather smell of the seat mingled with the sleepy smell of him. I could see the eucalyptus trees bending rhythmically in the wind. My eyes shut and our tongues tasted each other. He knew what was irresistible to me. I couldn't lie on top of him for five minutes without wanting him inside me, and he easily held me close that long.

"We've got all day, love. Now, later, in the car, in the cove, in the fields, wherever we want," he whispered and licked my ear simultaneously.

The car filled with soft heat interrupted occasionally by the cool breeze from the open door. Soon I was putting him inside me and listening for his usual murmurs of pleasure. I held on to the armrest and felt the cold steel of the door handle next to the soft leather upholstery. I was moving on top of him with my face buried in his soft neck. His hands frequently held me still while we floated in our separate ecstasies. The backseat cradled us in red like the hot flannel sheets on our bed.

In my fifteenth summer I moved far away from Susan, Meryl, Darren and Hotrod. We lived in a suburb near the outskirts of a small town. I was morose and unhappy, missing my old friends. Daily I went for long walks down the back country roads. One day, a carload of boys sped by whistling and catcalling. I envied them in their speeding car. In a few minutes they were back. I kept walking, aware of the straight skirt that molded itself around my bottom. They stopped. A tall, lanky boy got out, his brown hair sticking straight up on top and greased back on the sides. I smiled at him politely. The souped-up cherry-red '57 Chevy sat off on the shoulder. The driver rudely revving it up, throwing gravel and dust everywhere.

"Hay," this means Hi in local dialect, "you're new here, you know?" They stuck "you know" on every sentence. Agreement was always indicated.

"Yeah." I had seen him around the high school and knew he was some kind of hoodlum, as my mom called them. He played black music on his saxophone and was in a jazz band where they drank liquor. He always wore jeans and a blackT-shirt with Camel cigarettes rolled up in the sleeve. He was reputed to be the best drag racer in the county. The Chevy belonged to him.

He frowned at me. "A girl shouldn't be out here walking alone, you know." He stopped walking toward me when I stopped. "Unless you're looking for something, you know."

"Oh, yeah?" I put my hand on my hip and shifted my weight so it stuck out to the side provocatively. "Thanks for telling me."

"What's your name?" He lit a cigarette, disinterested.

"Scarlett, if you must know." I turned away as he did. "What's yours?"

"J.B."

"What kind of name is that?" Initials for a name was stupid, I thought. He apparently sensed my disdain.

"Want to go for a ride, Madam Scarlett?" He gestured like a knight bowing to a princess, his chivalry catching me off guard.

"Maybe, sometime." I wasn't getting into that car with those drooling idiots, one of whom was leaning against the car combing his hair.

"How 'bout now, Miss Snooty." His sly grin was contagious. I liked him already.

"No." I glared at the boys in the car. "See ya." Turning with as much sway as possible I started walking back toward home. My face was a fire of excitement. I was alive again, glowing with thoughts of what I should have said, fancy phrases, quick comebacks. I wanted to drag-race with him in that Chevy.

J.B. never had a girlfriend until me. The boys reluctantly accepted me, and the other girls weren't too friendly either. We were a well-matched pair, hotheaded, impatient and angry. No one knew it, but we weren't doing any boy-girl stuff. We were friends. I helped him work on his car, and he taught me to drive a stick shift. We went to the drag races every Saturday. There were utterly ridiculous rules about girls on the sidelines at the races. But when we were alone in the country he let me practice racing. One day, he said, girls might be allowed to race and I might as well be ready.

After some months he took me to a black nightclub where he was playing. Passion flowed from his saxophone. This was adventure, living as I craved, with every sense. I loved dancing almost as much as driving. J.B. was pleased. He said I was "progressing," whatever that meant. He sat with me during the break and I felt pretty important. That night he kissed me good night. It wasn't much more than a peck, but better than nothing.

I dreamt I was walking down the country road. A carload of boys with J.B. driving stopped in front of me. J.B. got out and walked up to me. Slowly he unbuttoned my blouse from the top down. He put his hand inside my bra and lifted my breast out. The other boys watched wide-eyed. I turned my head so he wouldn't see the pleasure in my eyes. He caressed my nipples, then undid my bra and put his hands around my breasts. I stood very still, letting him touch me however he pleased. He knelt down and ran his hands along my legs over my hips then back to my panties. My panties were wet. As he pulled them down under my skirt I woke up.

My legs gripped Don's body and the sensation of climbing began. In the moments before the flag is dropped at the start of a race, the urge to go, to take off, is almost uncontrollable. Once that feeling begins there is no going back. There is only the complete desire to cover every inch of the road, to make every step a part of the finish that can only be as satisfying as the accumulated and combined energy in the getting there. Crossing the finish line is magic, an ending where I apply the brakes with care. When I stopped I only wished to go back to the starting line.

Don held me tight, breathing heavily. We were still for a few minutes.

I sat up and smiled at him, his cheeks all aglow, his eyes closed. I wondered if his fantasy world was like mine, if he was turned on by memories, dreams from the past. Was there a way to talk about it? Would it ruin what we had? "Honey, what do you think about when we make love?"

"You." He said it without opening his eyes, without pause.

"Just me? Nothing else?"

"Well, your luscious body."

"Come on, you don't just think of what we're actually doing. What else? Tell me."

"You're sexy. What can I say? The actuality is all I want."

Men must be different, I thought, not wanting to upset the natural balance of things. I wasn't unhappy that he thought I was sexy.

We strolled down the dirt path, the wind whipping around us and the roar of the ocean in the distance. The sun was brilliant, but barely warm. I knew the fine sand in the cove would be hot. All these clothes would come off again. We held hands gazing together at the purple ice plants, the wild lilies and orange poppies along the trail. Don spotted a magnificent elk on the hillside.

J.B. and I went steady for a year. He never made a move to touch me beyond a simple good-night kiss. I was beginning to think there was something funny about him. We often followed the other cars of teenagers to the river to park, but all we did was talk about cars, science fiction and music. His friend Butch gave him some bootlegged whiskey one night in June. J.B. wanted to drive to a new place to test it out. He had discovered this abandoned cemetery where no one went. The road was dirt but passable and led to a sweeping meadow in which weeping willows and falling tombstones rested peacefully. It was a full-moon night, the light bright enough to see the whole valley. We gulped some of the whiskey. It burned my throat. J.B. kept drinking and I studied the stars. He followed me out of the car, bottle in hand. The Chevy gleamed in the moonlight almost like neon. J.B., unlike himself, slipped his arm around my shoulders. We stared at the constellations for a long time, not speaking, not moving. Then, out of the blue, he said, "I love you."

I felt like crying for no reason. "I love you, too, J." It was simple enough. And I think, at the time, I really did love him, at least as much as I loved the Chevy.

"Let's get in the backseat, you know."

"O.K." Already terribly nervous, my heart seemed to be beating itself to death. My legs were rubbery. I knew this was really going to be it. The magic of the moon and stars haunted me. The backseat of the Chevy beckoned.

His kisses were slow and lingering at first, then rose to a frenzied passion. The year of anticipation had heightened the desire. He seemed someone I didn't know, a stranger. I touched him for the first time, shocked to feel how big he was in my hand. My breasts warmed. He unbuttoned my blouse just like in the dream and undressed me with care. We were both trembling as we rushed on. J.B. tenderly caressed my breasts until I could feel the space between my legs grow warm and wet. His kisses were different than ever before, long and slow at first, then his tongue licked mine like fire dancing in the dark. His long, slender legs gradually, rhythmically inched mine apart. The tip of his cock played on my belly, and I couldn't resist rising up to meet him, opening my legs as far as the backseat would allow. A soft flash of red filled my vision when he entered me, his kisses wild on my face. I remember only the sense of infinite motion that followed. The stars were twinkling and falling from the sky. Afterward, we raced down the country road as fast as the Chevy would go, the windows rolled down, cooling our hot, exhausted bodies. I felt delirious.

Don was reading intently. I played with the sand, straining it through my fingers, watching my diamond emerge. The gulls had a nest in the side of the cliff to my right. They were engaged in active discussion, screeching sounds at each other, then flying away to find food for the babies. I remember wishing I was a bird when I was about four. My mom found me preparing to fly out my window and told me sternly that if I wanted to be a girl I couldn't fly like a bird. The logic of it escapes me, but I always remember this when I'm bird-watching. I don't have wings, I mused, but I do have wheels.

Don began to rub suntan lotion on my legs. His sweetness was unpredictable. "Wanna go back to the car?" He whispered intently, biting my shoulder tenderly.

"What's with you and the car today?" I asked, laughing. For the first time, I found myself wondering if he knew.

A Long, Long Time

CAROLYN BANKS

She smiled when she saw him standing so casually, weight thrust onto one hip, as if he'd been waiting a long, long time. The fading sun beat down through the skylight, but he didn't seem to notice. He neither squinted nor raised a hand to shield his eyes.

She had seen two teenaged girls pass in front of him earlier that day. She had watched their young legs, sassy stride, skirts swinging brightly, hair bobbed and bouncy, like girls out of a television commerical, Young Americans. She had felt a twinge of envy, pang of fear. They were young and he was young, and their giggles were for him, for him, an offering, a tribute.

No matter. He never glanced their way. But this alone, she realized, made him all the more attractive, made the girls even more likely to return.

Let them, she thought suddenly, as if the thought itself were a dare. *Let them,* because, of all the women, all the women throughout time, young, old, smooth-skinned and not, *he chose me.*

It was a dizzying realization, this, and because of it, Celia felt singled out. It wasn't a matter of anyone else needing to know, either. She felt that way merely by stating the thought to herself: *he chose me.* She felt it too. In fact, if she were to translate the thought into sensation, it would be as if the absolutely outermost tissue-thin layer of her skin had begun to sizzle, or perhaps to glow.

See what this has done to you, she chided herself, but not unhappily.

He hadn't seen her come in, and she was glad of it. It gave her a chance to eye him openly and without distraction. She did just that, absorbing, trying to memorize where his hair curled, where it didn't. That and every sinew, every rise, every curve.

He was classically beautiful, she knew, and in that way he was sexless as well as timeless, by which she meant that teenaged boys might well have acted just as those silly young girls had, acutely aware, in his presence, of themselves, of their yearnings, their new-stirred desires.

Wasn't that exactly what had happened to her? Hadn't she just been strolling along, minding her own business, when pricked, yes pricked, by the awareness of his presence as if by something pointed, Cupid's arrow, maybe?

It left no mark, though she expected to find one; she felt that yielding, that impressionable. There was no sign at all. She looked afterward as she had before, or— Wait, not so. Afterward she was a little flushed, a little pouty-lipped. Healthier, though not, as she'd anticipated, wanton.

But before. What, indeed, what would a casual onlooker have seen? A woman with a run in her hose, and queen-sized hose at that; no makeup, she hadn't bought any in years. Scarf tied carelessly over towel-dried though naturally curly hair. Hair in need of a cut by several weeks, if you wanted to get picky about it. And that blouse! Far too dressy for the skirt she'd grabbed that morning almost without looking.

But anyway, that's what had happened to her, to frumpy Celia, as she'd once imagined her piano students called her: she'd found herself in a room with him and she'd felt a stirring that she'd forgotten all about, a little tug *down there.* And then her skin had begun that kind of filamental tingling that she'd later come to think of as a sizzle. These were the first two signs, tug and tingle.

She hadn't yet looked at him, exactly; had just felt him there, felt that he was in the room. This is how she'd known so acutely what the teenaged girls would feel. Because she'd been one, because she was one yet again.

She would have to describe it as an exposure of sorts, a revealing of some part of her that was tender and remarkable. And, in her case, so long buried.

She thought this with no shame, no judgment. It was merely an accurate assessment, and one that made her smile.

She noted now how he stood, naked and careless of the fact. Or was he? One hip was forward, causing a ray of fading light to fall upon his genitals, spotlighting them, as it were.

His penis, she noted, wasn't erect, and that filled her with anticipation. She liked to cup his flaccid penis in her hand and feel it come alive. Or, ofttimes better, she liked to kneel in front of him, catching him in her mouth and pulling her lips along and along and along as he lengthened, grew hard. She could take all of him to the base when he was flaccid. Then—not very gradually, either—her lips would be forced to slide upward, upward, upward to the flower of his penis, the tip.

She would hover there momentarily, like a hummingbird. And like a hummingbird, she felt fragile, delicate, at moments like these.

Then she would reach for his hips, smooth as marble, with purpose. She would guide him back and forth, back and forth, a rhythm that was ancient, mindless, elemental.

She knew the sounds that he would make, knew too what each sound meant: nearer, nearer still. Then, his fingers deep in her hair, he would reach for her, urge her upward. She would pull away as she rose to see his face, his thick-lidded eyes, his satisfied gaze.

Then—he knew so little English—he would say two words, *Now you.* He would make much of the pillows and tapestries and drapes he had gathered for their bed. *Now you,* he would say, not so much placing as nestling her upon the various textures and musty smells she'd come to know.

She knew other things as well: the weight of his thighs, the touch of his fingers, the heat of his breath, the curl of his tongue.

He was so practiced! When she moved with him it was like dance, an attunement: his leg there, hers here, his back arched so, then her own. Even when they turned and tumbled so that she emerged astride him it was effortless, adept, as though done in suspension.

He has given me grace, she thought. But perhaps she had, with her heightened receptivity, absorbed it from him.

Had it been that way at the start, smooth as a sphere, an act of beauty as well as an act of love? Though the beginning had been only days before, she found it hard to remember her former self: dowdy but respectable, a frump, she now knew.

But there she was, in his presence, feeling— What was it? Ah, yes, tug and tingle. He had been a stranger, a beautiful young stranger, so beautiful, in fact, that she hadn't been able to look away, hadn't been able to keep from marveling at the glory of him.

He was slender, taut-skinned, with a ladder of muscle that rippled from his stomach to his chest. She could not stop thinking of what it might be like to touch those muscles with her hand and then with her cheek, too, and then, perhaps, the inside of her thigh.

Oh, they might very well have been there that day, those giggling girls with their short, swinging skirts. She wouldn't have known it, wouldn't have known anything once his body called to her in the deep, deep-down way that it had.

She was inside out, the soft pink tender underside of her was showing and yes, yes, yes, he knew it, knew it too.

The others in the room—not just the girls but a man in uniform and an older couple, shocks of thick gray hair, she now, as if under hypnosis, recalled—withdrew politely, or so it seemed. It might have been that they receded in her mind's eye only. What did it matter, anyway? What mattered had already been stated: that she was in a state so remarkable and that he knew, *he knew.*

She'd done the dumbest thing ever then, she'd fumbled through her purse, eyes still fixed upon him, and she'd taken out dark glasses, glasses with lenses black as pitch, and she'd stuck these glasses on, crookedly, she supposed, but she'd stuck them on and thereby felt herself safe. She could stare away, stare at him with wide appraising eyes as though unobserved.

It proved a blessedly ineffective defense.

He laughed at it, in fact, as he came forward. Celia willed herself to run but couldn't move, could only wait.

She felt an intake of breath when he reached down and removed the glasses, tossing them aside. She couldn't remember letting her breath back out. It was as if she'd held her breath through it all, right up to the present, maybe, even, was holding it still.

The glasses gone, he had kissed her, at first with little licks and nips, his lips so soft and damp across her eyelids and her cheeks. When had he unbuttoned her blouse? She wondered this as his hands and then his mouth beheld her nipples. Her eyes were shut when she felt the slick silk fabric drift across her shoulders, when she heard it whoosh behind her as he tossed it to the ground.

Her skirt fell to her feet and he moved beside her, his penis hard against her thigh. She was glad for the run in her pantyhose, glad because it helped him split them, helped him get his fingers underneath the elastic of the panties that she wore beneath the pantyhose.

But it wasn't awkward, the removing of all her garments, wasn't at all. Rather, there were fades and dissolves as there might be in a movie. Then she supposed her eyes had been shut anew, because all that she registered, remembered registering, were sensations: moist soft sweet hot hard seep slide ooze slick hard hard hot hot hot. Only later did she realize that she'd felt his penis and then his tongue and then his penis against inside her again and again and again until all of the urgency was gone and what was left was soft sweet afterplay.

At one point she'd rolled onto the soothing surface of the tiles. She thought that she might stick there, remain, like a relic, to be written up in guidebooks and viewed by tourists. She tried to explain this to him, but had to give it up as too complex, too beyond her meager vocabulary.

That first time! She'd finally realized that hours and hours must have passed and that there she was, limp and salty with sweat and his semen and her own wonderful flow. She'd leapt up, searching out the places where he'd thrown her clothes, smoothing out the wrinkles and the creases, or trying to.

Even so, after she'd left him that first time, she'd walked around the city with the smell of him upon her and within her, so potent that other women sometimes turned to look at her and smile.

She'd smiled back.

And each day thereafter she'd gone back to him, and each day thereafter there he'd be, waiting.

They didn't try to speak at all now, even the *Now you* was no longer needed. Oh, once or twice she called his name, David, though he never spoke or asked her hers. To Celia that seemed a purifying thing, rarity made rarer still, a union beyond mere social convention. She would ask him nothing and he would ask her nothing, nothing so mundane as facts would intervene, intrude. She knew all that really mattered: the way he tasted, moved, smelled.

Ah, si, amore, she heard someone say.

Weary from their lovemaking, she had plummeted into sleep. By degrees he brought her back to the now. Languidly she leaned against him, following his gesture. He was pointing out the skylight and the fact that the sun had long gone.

She stretched and stood and began dressing as he watched. She was more careful now with what she wore. She leaned against an alabaster pillar to pull the thin skein of nylon over her left leg and then her right. Sure enough, he was eyeing her. She took especial care, too, with her brassiere, cupping her breasts as she adjusted pale lilac lace. The bra was new, too.

She didn't use a comb on her hair, only raked it with her fingers in much the way that he always did. She didn't have a mirror, but she saw that he at least thought it—and her—quite beautiful.

She wondered if he knew or cared that her husband would be waiting.

And he *was* waiting too. He was slapping his hand at his trousers, and he started talking even before she reached his side. She could never imagine David in trousers like those, madras, the sort that golfers wore.

"I'll tell you, Celia, all this art business, I just can't figure it out. Here we are in Florence, Italy, for God's sake. Florence, with restaurants and shops and stuff like that and you, you," he lowered his voice, as if saying something naughty. "You want to spend all your time out looking at some dumb fucking statue."

She turned from him briefly. It was to hide her smile.

He misunderstood her reaction. "Okay, okay, I'm sorry about the language," he apologized.

She looked at him more fondly than she had in a long, long time. "It's all right," she said, taking hold of his arm and then pressing as close to him as she could. "It really, really is."

Humming

SANDY BOUCHER

How glad I am that she doesn't look like any of my three daughters. In the last years especially, in which I have pursued a meditation practice and the study of the great, elegant texts of Buddhism, often I have felt that time does not exist, or that all of it exists in this very moment, or that the space of a lifetime is no bigger than a drop of dew trembling on a petal of a flower, and as evanescent. Given this perspective, what can our relative ages matter?

Still, if Jeanine were to remind me of one of my daughters, I'd be uncomfortable. After all, I do inhabit the time-limited world of conditions. One condition being my aging body, wracked these days with the storms of menopause. Another being the old shingle house in which Ralph and I live. Rotting at its foundation and threatening to slide down the steep lawn in back, still it sits with shabby charm in the Berkeley hills. The house speaks to some people of a gracious, leisurely decade when trees were more numerous than houses up on the hill; as my presence must awake in some people a nostalgia for the late forties, early fifties, when young people were supposedly more innocent and trusting in life than they are today. I am not, myself, interested in that time of my youth, or in the years of mothering that came after.

I am really only interested in this particular moment in the big shadowy bedroom with its view of the distant Golden Gate Bridge red above the shining water. In this quiet afternoon now and then I hear the cooing of the doves who live under the eaves. A soft gray sound, from somewhere far away, it enters my mind as I look at the black curls lying flat, like a baby lamb's, wet with our sweat and a sweeter, thicker juice. Wisps of curl feather down her thighs a few inches, lie softly up against the undercurve of her belly. This bower of dark hair, thin enough that the skin is visible underneath, damp and warm, welcomes me. I lick each curl, moving to where the hair grows more thickly, the odor deepens. Odor of salty wetness that opens caves in my mind, rich odor of deep-sea secrets, of sun-warmed olives, the sunshine transmuted to a thick golden liquid in which I lie suspended. Jeanine's odor.

I stroke the tender skin of the inside of her thighs, my fingers converging at the rosy lips visible under the hair, brushing lightly over them. Her voice comes, a soft ohhhh of anticipation. I lift my head to look up at her, see her brown eyes watching me with that same intent look that takes over her face when she leans to my breast, takes my nipple in her mouth and examines it gently with her tongue, nurtures it with her lips. Such concentration, such passionate attention. My own cunt has begun to throb, my body going hot and seeming to swell, heightening my skin's sensitivity.

While the fingers of my right hand play in her hair, moving lightly over her vulva, with my left I reach to take her small, callused hand. I kiss her fingers, linger in her palm, suck her thumb, moving my tongue around it in slow revolvings. Ahhhh, she says, lifting her pelvis, offering herself. I let my breast lie against the open lips, feeling their wet warmth on my skin, my tightening nipple. Jeanine shudders, says my name, and I lower my face to brush her thigh, move carefully upward until I am kissing her outer lips. She has begun to move her pelvis in smooth, subtle circles, each coming toward me a gesture of desire, each drawing away an invitation to follow her. I do now. Slightly spreading her lips with my fingers, I place my wet mouth between them, greeting her tight bud of a clitoris, slipping my tongue down to probe the opening of her vagina, moving up again to suck. Jeanine makes a low crooning sound that vibrates through her body into my mouth. Slipping my arms under her lifted thighs, I reach up to cup her breasts, tease the hard pink nipples as my mouth answers hungrily each thrusting, seeking movement of her desire.

These same breasts I gently cradle half an hour later as we sit in the deep hot water of the bathtub. When I invited her into the tub she asked, "When is Ralph coming home?" "Not until seven, I think." Her eyebrows knotted. "You *think!*" But she got in with me, lifting short, muscular legs over the side of the tub, lowering her small ass into the water so that she now sits facing me. I soap her breasts, long breasts with nipples pointing down, while she tells me that when she loses weight her breasts hang like empty bags on her chest. I can't imagine it, they are so full now, overflowing my hands with their slippery weight. She touches mine, and murmurs into my hair, "Your breasts comfort me." "Hummmm," I say, small sound of acknowledgment, of satisfaction.

It is only in these stolen afternoons that we are able to be together. I have been married for thirty years, to three different men. Some women find marriage restricting: I find it liberating, even marriage to a man like Ralph, who runs a metaphysical bookstore and cares more about meditating than making money. He does support me. And I like the safety of marriage, the comforting routine, the coziness. My mother encouraged me to develop a practical attitude to life coupled with a vivid appetite for its pleasures. Jeanine cares about Ralph too: she does not want to hurt him. She carries her love for me like a secret treasure, folded and wrapped, close to her heart. Her desire sends flames up through her body, lighting her eyes. Sometimes those eyes catch me unawares, as when, leaning over Ralph to pour his coffee, I glance up to where she sits on the window seat, the newspaper held before her. She is not reading: her eyes are watching my movements with an attention so focused it startles me. She looks into me, and without moving an inch I feel myself falling toward her, plummeting with her down, down, deep inside to the place we visit together, the place where stillness lies, holding us.

Now, in the bathtub, we have leaned our heads into each other's shoulder; the steam rising from the water wets our faces. I don't know whether it's my rampaging hormones or the heat of the bath that causes the sweat to streak my forehead. As my hands move under the water to stroke her sides, cup her buttocks, Jeanine turns her head to nuzzle my neck. I smile, remembering my first sight of her, how impossible it would have been for me then to imagine this joy that floods through me at the touch of her lips on my throat. She was a thirtyish woman in dirty blue overalls whose black hair hung limp and straight to just below the ears. She was digging with a shovel in our front yard. I liked watching her work, her arms pushing and lifting, her back bent, then straight. Then I noticed her eyes, which are the color of old mahogany, the flash of interest that lit them when she looked at me. I noticed her mouth, with its full, pouting lower lip. On the second day, she had washed her hair to shiny softness and wore clean overalls; she sat on the porch talking to me, smiling an invitation, before she started work. On the third day I began to help her.

Jeanine and I have often giggled, since, about her having been our gardener, remembering *Lady Chatterly's Lover.* Actually we are far from the classic master-servant model of dime-store romances, for she is only taking a break from the media jobs that have supported her very well during the past five years: now she luxuriates in the physical exertion, the relative simplicity of her job as a gardener. If anyone comes from humble beginnings it would be I, daughter of a widowed mother who supported my sister and me by working as a cashier in movie theaters. Marriage was my way out of the crowded, threadbare apartment where we all slept in the same bed because there was only one; it was my ladder up out of worry and want. I climbed it gladly.

I am feeling the flat, strong muscles of her upper back and shoulders, kneading them, smoothing them as Jeanine murmurs in appreciation, when suddenly she stiffens, sending a little tidal wave of hot water across my belly. Her head snaps back, her eyes widening.

"Was that a car in the drive!?"

I listen, hearing nothing.

Jeanine rises from the tub, her body streaming, and lunges for the window that faces on the driveway.

"Oh, god, it's *Ralph!*"

The flat sound of a car door slamming rises from the driveway.

She comes back to stand next to the tub, her body arranged in odd, stiff angles of panic.

"What should I *do!*" she asks, her eyes on me pleadingly.

I sit in the hot water, surrounded by steam, and the nervousness erupts from me in a low giggle.

She's convulsed for a few moments too, and then she asks again, "But what should I *do?*" spreading her hands in a helpless gesture.

"Put on your clothes," I sputter. "Quick!" For I can hear the sound of Ralph's opening the door downstairs, his footsteps in the living room.

She's pulling on little gray socks, they look so ridiculous, then her corduroy pants, her red shirt, over her wet body.

"He's in the kitchen now," I hiss. "Go down and talk to him."

"Oh, shit, my underpants!"

"I'll hide them."

She rubs the steamy mirror to clear it, looks at her red, moist face, her tangled hair.

I am still giggling.

Halfway out the door, Jeanine turns to me, fixing me with a fierce look.

"I *hate* this!"

Then I see only the smooth white-painted wood of the door.

In a few minutes I hear voices in the kitchen, Ralph and Jeanine carrying on a conversation. He has probably offered her a drink of freshly Osterized carrot juice; she has probably asked him about a book, something mildly exotic and hard to find, like *Initiates and Initiations in Tibet,* by Alexandra David-Neel. This bibliographic communication will make a safe cover for Jeanine's suspiciously flushed appearance, for when queried about esoteric volumes Ralph loses all connection with the world about him and goes off into his mind like an ancient labyrinthine library where one title leads him to the next in contented quest for the most worm-eaten, mildew-encrusted tome ever unearthed. He cares little for the content of these books, or for their physical beings; it is the search that brings color to his cheeks.

In my steamy hideaway, I let myself go, slipping down into the still-hot water, giving myself to the shudders of mirth that contort me. Downstairs, the voices go on, or Ralph's voice, that is. I can imagine his rapt face, the excited lift of his chin. And Jeanine looking at him with big, relieved eyes.

I do not see her again until the next Sunday. Ralph and I have come to the chanting session at the Clear Light Institute, of which he is a director. I had almost decided to stay home because I was suffering the weakness and heat that accompany my periods now. I've heard other women describe hot flashes, but this is different, not a flash but a constant deep radiating heat that leaves me sweaty and lethargic. I'd been in bed all afternoon, reading, when Ralph came to ask me if I wanted to go with him. On reflection, I decided the chanting and meditating might be just the thing to cool my raging blood.

"If women had written the Buddhist canon," I told Ralph as we drove across Berkeley, "there would be special meditations for menopause."

Ralph pondered this, and then began to tell me about the *Therigatha,* a volume of poems written by the first Buddhist nuns. "They were contemporaries of the Buddha. They wrote in Pali, the ancient language. It's quite a volume . . . stories of monastic life, songs of their moments of enlightenment . . ." He went on for the next ten minutes, telling me of the various translations, the whereabouts of the original and how it was found. This recital was so thoughtfully given, with such erudition and sensitivity, that I was filled with my fondness for Ralph, and reached to rub him gently on his arm.

The meditation room of the Clear Light Institute is hung with sumptuous Tibetan paintings on silk scrolls: blue-faced demons dance before spread fans of orange flames, green-skinned goddesses wave multiple arms. The panels of the walls are painted deep red and that clear flat blue that the Tibetans love. Gold leaf climbs the pillars. Perhaps thirty people sit on pillows, eyes closed, mouths open to sing the sacred syllables, these sounds which vibrate in the belly, in the throat, connecting one up to the great sound that is always echoing in the universe. Sometimes I really do feel that merging of sound, when the chant sings me, rather than I sing it, but tonight I'm restless, impatient with the slow droning, enduring my heat and dizziness. Maybe it was a mistake to come. I consider sneaking upstairs to sit in the lobby or on the porch.

Then Jeanine arrives. I *feel* her enter. It's a sensation like a cool hand slid up my back, signal to wake up. Opening my eyes I see that she has just slipped through the door, her embarrassment at being so late obvious in the stiff way she holds her shoulders. She wears a purple, loose top and jeans; her small feet are bare. A slim gold chain encircles one sun-bronzed ankle.

Does she know I'm here? My heart pounds. It takes all my strength not to call to her, not to lift my hand. Then I realize she has settled herself on a pillow to my right, facing me. Her attention falls over me like a cloak. I feel faint with excitement, knowing she has taken that seat to watch me.

The chant stops now, the last long syllable drawn out into the room by a few deep male voices, loud under the steady higher voices of the other men and the women. And then there is silence, a silence in which the chanting still exists, in which it has built a many-layered sensitivity. I can feel my body still vibrating as I settle myself for the half-hour silent meditation that always follows the chanting.

To ease the stiffness in my crossed legs, I shift position slightly, and then I place my right hand on my knee. A simple action, and simple to describe, but the significance of it is staggering. As I begin to move my hand toward my knee, I become aware that all her attention is focused upon it. There are an excruciating few moments of held breath as my arm moves, bringing my palm-down hand closer to the round promontory of my knee. Jeanine's watching with every cell of her body hangs upon me as if I lift her with my arm and move her through space. My arm is heavy, weighted with its mission, as it traverses the distance and pauses, my hand hovering just an inch above my knee. Then, with a sound not uttered, like the fluttering ahhhh of surrender, I let my fingers sink to touch the cloth of my skirt, my palm settles gently over the curve of my kneecap. It is as if the air has thickened to solidity. There is nothing in the room now but that hand resting upon that knee. It is enormous, utterly deserving of the passion Jeanine offers it. It is magically alight, pearly with the glow of its mysterious presence. The gilded pillars, the faces of demons and people, fall back before its mystic power.

I open my eyes slightly, to see from their corners the figure of Jeanine clenched forward, her mouth slack in dazzlement. I feel how tenderly my hand lies upon my knee, like a cloud of morning mist upon the top of a hill, poised there without weight, holding us both in a condition of grace.

After the chanting, we meet in the lobby. Ralph has gone off for a meeting with the directors, having touched me on the elbow and assured me he will not be long. This gentle patting of one another's arms seems to have developed into a rite between us, expressing the affection and shared inertia that bind us to each other. Jeanine is studiously not looking at me from the other side of the room, where she talks with one of the young male meditation teachers. So it is my turn to watch her. I like how she responds, even to this young man who is being a little too proprietary with the insistent tilt of his body toward her, his gaze intent upon her mouth. Jeanine hums with a steady enthusiasm when she is with people. He may imagine that her looking full into his eyes is designed to encourage his attentions, but it is only how she looks into everyone she meets. Her hair is sleek and glistening tonight, in that little Dutch-boy haircut that I find so humorous sometimes. The purple of her shirt sets off the brown skin of her throat.

Just now her eyes meet mine, and I find myself grinning in sheer pleasure. Jeanine excuses herself from the young man: she is suddenly before me.

Still smiling, I want to give her myself, my difficult day, my weakness.

As she reaches to hug me, I feel how sticky my skin is, how my body trembles inside.

"I'm sorry. I've been sweating so much. I must smell."

Holding me, she has lowered her head to my shoulder, her cheek against the thin damp cotton of my dress. "I *love* how you smell."

The words come to me as if from her arms, her collarbones, her thighs; and something is pushed aside in me.

"Ah, why are you crying?" Jeanine cups my cheek, wipes the tears with her thumb.

"Come with me," she whispers. "I want to hold you."

I hesitate, glancing around at the people in the lobby, who are chatting quietly in small groups, seemingly oblivious of us.

"I know just the place," Jeanine mutters as she leads me toward the stairway to the basement.

We descend narrow, winding steps to a corridor into which several doors open. At the end of the hall, Jeanine pushes aside a heavy curtain to lead me into a tiny dark room like a cave, lit only by small candles on an altar. This is the room set aside for individual meditation. Jeanine pulls the curtain tight at the door and fastens it, then turns to touch my wrist with cool, reassuring fingers. "You know that when the curtain's pulled," she whispers, "no one would dare to come in."

I look around, my eyes slowly adjusting to the dimness of this familiar room. It is perhaps ten feet square, with one meditation pillow placed near the door, the altar opposite. Rugs and tapestries cover its walls, muffling the sound of the prayer wheel that turns in the corner. The wheel is a tall wide cylinder wrapped in green paper, with a flounce of vibrant red. It hums in its turning, a sound steadily insistent in the room, spinning its assembled prayers out into the universe.

Jeanine folds me into its throbbing as she takes me in her arms. She holds me gently for a time, her chest rising as she breathes deeply.

This room is as dark, as enclosed, as a womb. Jeanine begins to sing with the prayer wheel, the tone like the pulsing of blood in our veins. She rocks me, comforting my body, smoothing my burning skin. Her smell merges now with the odor of incense that permeates the room. Slowly she moves her head back to seek my lips, and I taste her smooth moistness, mint, a slight reminder of the tea she drank after the chanting. Her lips move now, seeking me, her tongue asking questions of my mouth, and my answer is a quickness of breathing that shakes my chest. She teases, probes, tantalizes my own tongue to follow her movements; and I feel a tingling in my clitoris. Abruptly I want her closer and closer to me. I want to enfold her completely, draw her inside me.

The prayer wheel sings of sunshine, bright mountain air, a many-windowed monastery clinging to a cliff as Jeanine invites me to lie down on the layered rugs. "Here?!" I whisper. "How *can we?*" Her brown eyes smile at me, brilliant with desire. "No one will come . . . not with the curtain drawn. They'll think we're meditating."

I glance around, uncertain. The Buddha sits with closed eyes on the altar, minding his own business. The silks spread under him are the color of the soft inner tissues of the body; they glow richly red and rose in the candlelight. One large scroll painting hangs on the wall. It depicts a female deity dancing. She is nude except for a rope of jewels that snakes down between her breasts and laces across her thighs. Her body is silvery, her face golden. Her eyebrows sweep up like birds above wrathful eyes. Her headdress depicts a pig carved of gold and encrusted with jewels.

But Jeanine is touching me, coaxing me, drawing me down until I look up to see the dark ceiling covered with paintings so old their colors have muddied. Now we lie breast to breast, and the heat of my body that has been so unwelcome all day intensifies. "Yes," Jeanine murmurs against my throat. "Oh, yes, love . . ." Her hands have lifted my loose dress to move beneath the cloth, cupping my breasts, her thumbs fluttering against my hardening nipples. She kisses me, her tongue moving deep in my mouth, and I feel myself opening to her, giving in to the heat of my body until it becomes a steady surge, powerful as an ocean wave. Jeanine rides the wave, swimming closer and closer to my center. Her hips move against mine, the firm mound of her pubic bone thrusting ever so subtly, tantalizing me with its pressure.

Then she pulls away a little, and I see that she has caught my heat, her cheeks flushed darkly, her eyes wildly shining. "We've got to take off your dress," she murmurs, "or it'll get all wrinkled and damp."

I glance at the curtained door. "But how can we . . . ?"

"Yes, it'll be better . . ." To convince me, she lifts her purple shirt. For a moment her arms are held high, her torso lifted, and my body trembles with pleasure at the sight of her breasts, long and full, the nipples pink tight berries. She is stripping off the blue jeans, throwing them to the side. The ankle bracelet is a fragile gold line on her nude body.

"I'll help you." She lifts the dress higher, works it up over my head. And I am nude too, the air touching my skin.

Slowly she lowers herself to lie full length upon me, one leg between my thighs, and her pelvis seems to sink into mine. I am so without resistance. I feel her heart pumping in quick rhythm against my chest.

She begins to kiss my shoulder, and moves down my arm until her mouth finds the inside of my elbow. Her tongue licks the tender skin, her lips kiss wetly. My whole arm vibrates with pleasure, and I can feel my cunt opening under the weight and warmth of her body. She moves to my wrist now, her tongue examining every millimeter of sensitive skin, until she leaves it to kiss my palm, lingering.

Deftly, she lifts herself and moves down to smooth my thighs. She leans to kiss, her cheek brushing my pubic hair, beginning a hot throbbing in my cunt. She moves down to my knee, her mouth encircling my kneecap, tongue tracing its contour. Then she sucks the muscle just below the kneecap, sending flutters of energy up inside my thigh to my vagina. She moves down again, briefly stroking my calves, and arrives at my feet, which she holds in comforting hands. She kisses my instep, and then sucks, as I begin to moan.

I have opened my eyes to find the image of the deity dancing on the wall above me. Her breasts flicker in the dim light. An arm, a foot, are raised. She tilts toward the next step, establishing a rhythm that travels from her silvery body to mine. Moving, I join her in it, my hips circling now, slowly, subtly, my breasts lifting, hands braced against the rug.

Jeanine comes up to lie upon me, her mouth seeking my breast. I close my eyes as she kisses, teases, lifts and cradles, and I see the body of the silver woman moving in her passionate dance. I recognize those breasts, those neat narrow hips, the thickness of dark pubic curls. Opening my eyes, I see her face bent to my breast, the black hair falling forward, her look of intense concentration. Her lips close on my nipple and she sucks, tentatively at first, tenderly. Our movements happen together now, our hips and thighs undulating. Letting my head fall back, I close my eyes, giving in to this dance as Jeanine sucks more hungrily, her teeth closing with tantalizing care upon my hard, straining nipple. I thrust my breast into her mouth and she takes it, sucking in as much as will fill her mouth.

Her hand has moved down between my legs, seeking in my

vagina, so wet and open. She slips her fingers into me, moving them inside, and the heel of her hand slowly rubs my tight clitoris. My clitoris is a nipple now, wanting to be sucked.

My hands grip Jeanine's back, kneading her shoulders, pressing her to me. We are slippery with sweat where we touch. My mouth is hungry to taste her.

Jeanine lifts up, turns, leaving my breast to cradle my hips, lifting her leg across me. Just before she lowers herself onto me, I look up into the dark expanse of hair between her thighs, reach to spread the small silkily pink lips of her vagina. On the wall above the moons of her buttocks, leaps the silver-bodied woman in ecstatic movement.

Then she is upon me, her mouth closing over my cunt, her breasts pressing into my belly, the weight of her hips on my shoulders, and, at last, the hot, soft opening of her vagina for my mouth to suck and stroke. Jeanine moans, moves in quick instinctive shudders as she settles on me. I receive the weight and feel of her whole body; it opens me more. My face is lost in her cunt. We have become one being, our movement taking us in an ancient joyous pattern. There is no inside or outside. There is only this movement, yet I know I grip Jeanine's buttocks, stroke her back, press her even closer inside me. Within the storm of desire are the subtle movements of the dance in our bodies, moving deep inside us, taking us to that moment of dissolution.

Jeanine hums into my vagina, the vibrations lifting my body as I hear the pulse of the prayer wheel loud in the room. We are nothing but sound now, carried out beyond the limits of our minds, as our movement becomes an uncontrollable undulation. I know only the pungent hot softness of her cunt, my face plunged into it to suck and suck. Her own sucking sends waves up through me. The urgency peaks, and there is a moment of wanting so intense it feels like pain. I thrust against her and her mouth presses on me, hard now, she'll stay with me, she'll come with me, I suck and suck.

The moment breaks. I turn my head to muffle my cries against the soft flesh of her thigh. Long high ragged sounds are torn from me. I feel her groan of completion vibrating into my cunt, as my hips jerk, my fingers twitch against her back.

And then we are free, floating outside our contours in emptiness. A stillness, a perfect stasis opens beneath us.

Peace.

I let my arms fall from her body as I lie beneath her. She has rested her cheek against my thigh, absolutely still.

Turning my head I open my eyes to see the dancing goddess once again. She has returned into her fixity, one bangled foot eternally raised. But I see that the expression of her open mouth, which I had interpreted as a fierce snarl, is instead a smile of such rending sweetness that it draws from me a long quavering sigh.

"Yes, love," Jeanine answers me. "Oh, yes, my darling," her breath hot against the inside of my thigh.

We hold each other for a long time before we are able to sit up. And then it is a while before she lifts the dress to slip it over my head, stopping to kiss me, our mouths slippery, wet with the heavy odor of our bodies. Then I watch the purple blouse eclipse her breasts, the jeans slip up over her thighs. We stand touching each other gently, hands on each other's waist, and I sink into those dark eyes, so open now, carrying me deep. The sound of the prayer wheel is a steady throb, reminding us of the eternity we have just left. As we lift the curtain to go out, I glance back at the woman whose body flashes in her dance, whose golden face beams at me.

When we stand outside the room, smoothing our clothes, we have entered another reality. A lighted corridor, blue-paneled, stretches away to the stairs. Closed doors flank us. Jeanine and I look at each other with wide open, sated eyes.

We wander off separately, I to find Ralph, who waits for me on the porch.

"You disappeared," he says, without reproach.

"Feeling better?" he asks as he helps me into the car. And as he gets in the other side he fixes me with a concerned gaze. "You look . . . hmmm . . . more relaxed . . ."

I can only nod, mutely gazing at his long serious face.

We drive beneath old trees, heavily black and looming in the dark. High above is the pale crescent of moon. The night seems ancient beyond believing.

Fearful Symmetry

REBECCA SILVER

The sun was in my eyes when I looked across the meadows. The man seemed to step right out of the sun. A slim, indistinct silhouette, but I could make out a quick, cocky bearing as he gestured and laughed with his teammates. I felt the familiar tang of that decision of the blood: *this one.* I sat up and shook the sun out of my eyes.

He settled himself on the blanket next to me, watching the game: the stars of *Lost and Yearning* were playing softball against the staff of the Lone Star Cafe; the teams looked like suburban kids romping, making less real the massive overhang of skyscrapers that had begun to cast their first shadows over the illuminated game. He watched intently: his face was oddly grave as he followed the ball's flight from hand to hand. Still a little dazed from light, I concentrated, readying myself to attract him.

His body was a young boy's, lean, slight, with an air of a short life of intense risk-taking; faded denim jacket, leather boots, a black Lone Star T-shirt, untrimmed soft black hair. I could finally take in his face, as he half turned it away from me. The extraordinarily high cheekbones and shadowless black eyes of an Indian, high forehead, hawklike nose, sculptured lips. The lines of his face contrasted with the youthfulness of his body, but they were the hollows and recesses of suffering, not of age, a deepening around the eyes and down the planes of the face. His skin was dark, dusky really, and there was a fine scar along the ridge of his cheek. I pay attention to hands, and what I saw was beautiful. His right hand rested on his thigh, strong and shapely, tendoned, expressive. I waited for him to feel the weight of my regard.

"Hey ya," he said, grinning. He held out his hand: "Lefty."

"Hi, Lefty." I shook it. It was warm, the grip firm. "I'm Sarah."

"Man, it's so *hot.*" He shrugged off his jacket. My skin flushed with discomfort. Embarrassed, before I could stop myself I looked away. On his back was a harness of canvas straps that looped over each shoulder and reached down to what there was of his left arm. The stump of the arm was fitted into a white sock that fitted the swivel of a prosthesis that ended in what could only be called a hook. The "arm" of the prosthesis had been covered in a rich brown leather that zipped up the side. He ignored my awkwardness. With a contemptuous private smile, he hooked a beer by the tab of the can and popped it open. I heard metal on metal.

I lay back again as the players trooped toward us. There was a burden of anxiety on me, irrational but overwhelming, of a "normal" person confronted at once by differentness and desire. My childhood taboos against ever showing interest in a handicap were confusing my urge to show interest in him as a man. How can I get this across? I couldn't talk with him now—his friends were lying down between us, to stretch out in the heat. I heard him say, "Damn, on a day like this all I want to do is take my clothes off and run around naked on the grass."

I heard myself blurt out, "Me too."

He looked at me, vastly surprised. There was a beat of terrible silence. I was a stranger among this group of friends, brought there by an acquaintance who was out on the field, and this was the first statement I'd made to anyone. Oh, yes, very smooth, you idiot girl. I lay back down with my arm over my face, wishing the ground would open up beneath me.

"Hey, a carousel. Who likes carousels?" It was his voice, and he was challenging me. I got unsteadily onto my feet. "C'mon."

We stumbled up the grass bank toward the little carousel, where children were jostling in a line. He leaned over to me and whispered, "Carousels are great, but they're real slow, y'know? You like to ride fast?" I nodded. "This way."

He led me quickly out of the park, down Fifth. We stopped where a massive white Harley-Davidson with gleaming chrome wheels was parked illegally on the sidewalk. "Like it? Get on. Hold on tight." Jesus Lord! I got on.

He kicked it into life, and we lurched forward. I involuntarily grabbed his waist. At once we were flying, as you fly in a dream, down Fifth, the white machine dancing through the traffic. The wind whipped my hair back from my face. My blood was pounding with the roar of the engine. The great wheels were a blur under my feet; the monster's heart that seemed to be directly beneath me generated steady throbs that swept up my thighs and shook my body. It all fell away on either side: cabs, carriage horses, the racing green of the park; we were on a concourse of our own, sailing. We had shed like a skin the clumsy movements of the mortal, pedestrian city. High, I was high! My breath stopped for a moment when I saw the speedometer hit seventy, and he took his hand off the handlebar to shift into a new gear; the only thing holding us steady was the delicate two-pronged hook. We're going for a ride!" he yelled back at me on the wind. "Lean your body with mine when I make a turn." We swept around the cloverleaf leading to the West Side Highway, and I saw the stretch of the Hudson shimmer beneath us. He leaned his body nearly parallel to the speeding asphalt. "You have to trust me or we'll go down!" he called.

"*Yes*," I yelled back, and held tighter, leaning my body as if it were part of his.

So now I know his history, I thought, as I dressed to meet him for the evening. As much as he knows mine. It was like an allegory of Privilege and Injustice meeting, as polarized as if we were representative figures carved in stone on a medieval portal. I'm a Princeton graduate, child of diplomats who had spoiled me with rather humorous adoration, petting me through a stormy adolescence and my more surefooted college years. I was in New York waiting to sail for England, where I would study Shakespeare on a scholarship to Cambridge. He had told me a grievous story that day we'd flown down the ribbon of the Hudson. We'd stopped at the side of the highway on a grassy slope and sat facing each other on the bike, talking as if we needed to lay our cards on the table fast.

He had been given up by his family at birth. "All I know about them is that she was a *puertorriqueña* named Mercedes—mercy. And he was a Nuyorican. They were very young, but they were married. And one day I saw a folder with a letter in it that said they'd given me up because of my birth defect. So I was in an orphanage till I was three. I was the little star amputee. The sisters took care of me. Then my parents came and adopted me. They're Italian. My dad was a plumber, but he's retired now and does maintenance for an old folks home. My mom had a drinking problem but now she's into AA and Jesus. The kids at school used to make fun of me a lot, so I got pretty tough and raised hell. I was even taken in a few times, as a teenager, nothing serious. I smoked a lot of pot. So now I'm a bartender at the Lone Star and a photographer. I made this attachment for my hook that fits the camera better than a hand. I had to get this make of bike 'cause it's the only one with an automatic shift. I come from Queens. You ever been there? No, I thought not. So there you have it, kid. That's me, in shorthand." He'd let out that harsh private laugh. I listened quietly, knowing that there was nothing much for me to say.

I'd been wearing a thin pink T-shirt with a flowered light skirt, and the wind from the river had chilled me. He'd gotten off the bike to lean against the low wall of the embankment, his weight on one narrow hip. "Come on over here, girl," he'd said slowly, amused. I'd slid off the bike and gone to him, half afraid. His right hand had caressed my face, his hook had slid into the waistband of my skirt and pulled me surely to him. He'd kissed me like a grown-up man, as if I were his rightful source, his own water to drink when he wanted to. His hook had held me tight in an embrace. I was frightened by its hardness, then excited, and leaned into the curve of it. His arm reached into the thick of my hair and held my head firmly toward him so he could drink from my mouth till he was full. The hook, as I was afraid it would, tangled in my long wind-roughened hair. "If I'm not careful, I'll get stuck on you," he smiled. "My hair, it catches on everything," I'd apologized, then buried my face in his salty neck, wishing I hadn't said a word.

I felt my blood warm as I remembered that afternoon. I looked at myself in the long mirror as I slid on my stockings: I am a full-bodied woman with the broad, fair face of Eastern Europe and the sleepy dark-blue eyes of my grandmother's Russia. My coarse black hair falls nearly to my waist, giving me, I know, a look of never being completely composed, even when I am most decorously dressed. There seems to be a disturbing nakedness about me always, which I try to cover with flowing skirts and high collars. I look as if I belong to the end of the last century, one of the full-blown peasant girls that stare out of rural scenes on old serigraphs. My belly is round, my hips and thighs much fuller than my more fashionable friends approve of, but I like the amplitude of my flesh; I like living in a house of softness, my bones well hidden. I like my breasts: round, heavy and low, with small, pale pink nipples. I drew up my stockings and clasped together my sheer white brassiere. I slipped on a vibrant gold cotton dress that clung to my hips and showed the shape of my legs when I walked, and slid my feet into low black sandals. A storm was gathering outside the window. I sprayed the Rive Gauche, which represented the last of my grocery money, between my breasts, on my wrists, along each thigh. Feeling fragrant and all golden, I locked the door behind me and walked onto the hot street, which shone a heavy red from the sun setting on the water. I felt like a part of the sun itself, detached from the mass of heat and light and set free to walk in human shape down Eighty-fifth Street.

He was sitting on a car on Columbus Avenue when I caught up with him. The crowds of well-dressed young New Yorkers had begun their nightly *paseo* up and down the avenue, clinging to one another, talking in hushed, excited tones. Dusk had fallen fully. The air was clean and wet. I watched him carefully from a block away, while he was still unaware of me: he looked tough, angry, lovely. He was wearing—of course—a black leather biker's jacket which gave form to his wiry frame. In contrast to the well-fed crowd flowing past him, the white kids from the richer boroughs, dressed in their pastel colors, he looked jaded and consequential and—here it was—cool. He had cool. People glanced at his hook as they passed, and some stared, but he carried himself as if they should be jealous not having one themselves. That was it, I realized: I remembered how he used the hook to gesture in conversation, to play, to tickle; he drummed it on surfaces when impatient, flicked matches for my cigarettes into flame with the sharp tip; he'd written my name with it in clear elegant script in the sand. It was a part of him, made animate. I could swear, thinking of how he'd touched me with it, that he could feel the very down on my cheek with its bifurcated point of steel. Suddenly I understood the strength of my attraction to him: The way he held that hook like a badge of courage was the essence of grace. It was debonair.

The look he gave me when he saw me made me feel beautiful and proud. He caught me by the hand and we ducked into Panarella's. It was not a place I would have chosen: Manhattan-chic, glossy, overdesigned, with neon calligraphy in the windows. He wanted to talk, and I was willing to listen. He ordered a Jack Daniel's; I asked for a special white wine that I remembered from outings to vineyards near my native Berkeley. He drank and bent toward me over the candle. I sensed what he wanted to begin with, so I began for him:

"So tell me what you remember about this orphanage."

"When my parents came to get me, I wasn't very well taken care of. I guess the sisters meant well, but they hadn't started me on a hook. They wanted me to just wear a false hand, because it was cheaper. These babies cost about two thousand dollars. All I remember is a lot of black and white flapping around, and I remember the day a sister came and told me I was leaving. I spent a lot of time when I was a kid in hospitals, getting trained. I told you, I was a real one-armed whiz kid. I remember all these experts, you know, big guys in white doctors' gowns, sitting around me saying, 'Come on, Scotty, show us how you butter your bread with a knife.' And I said—it was raisin bread—and I said, 'It's got cockroaches in it.' And they said, 'They're not roaches, they're raisins.' So I said, 'Okay, I'll butter it, but I'm not gonna eat it.' I was a real wise-ass.

"This one guy had developed a new kind of arm. I was his guinea pig. He put it on me and said, 'When we go in to see the doctors, you're going to tell them how good it feels.' And I said, 'But it hurts!' 'No it doesn't,' he said and grabbed me by the ear. 'I told you, it feels good.' So I said okay, but as soon as we get in front of the doctors, I holler, 'Get this thing offa me, it hurts like hell.' "

He'd drunk down the double shot of whiskey. Lefty was leaping from story to story, his eyes darker than ever. "Once, I was watching some kids play tennis. I was sitting on the sidelines. And this lady looks at me with this real sorry expression and she goes and *takes* the racket away from her own kid, who's like my age, and gives it to me. And the kid is giving me a real dirty look. I don't blame him. She did this in front of all the guys on the court. I could tell that look a mile away by the time I was about six. I couldn't deal . . . I just wanted to get out of there.

"So basically I'm pretty sick of this whole 'pathetic handicapped' line. I mean, I see people—I see this guy almost every day, he's in a wheelchair, paralyzed from the neck down. And he takes his fucking wheelchair through the meanest streets in New York, and through rush-hour traffic. And this guy knows, if he tips over, that's it, he's dead. But he does it. It blows my mind.

"There's this humor we use when we're alone. Like, at this handicapped ski weekend, there were the 'doublegimps,' the 'quadrogimps,' and I was 'The One-Armed Bandit.' That's why I call myself Lefty, you know? I get them before they get me.

"I hate this kind of 'Jerry's kids' telethon shit. This is what I want to do: I want to shoot a series of handicapped people who have *attitudes.* Like this skier I know with no legs, shoot him in a studio, very simple backdrop, with his skis and giving the camera that look. There's this blind guy with a little baby girl, and he takes the baby with him everywhere, in a carryall on his chest, this little newborn baby, through the streets. That's attitude. It's like, if anything hurts my little baby, you've got me to answer to. I'd like to shoot him with his kid. Just like that. Defiant.

"Anyway, here I am talkin'." He sighed, and I felt the weary focus of his eyes on me again. "Hi there, Lady." He was silent, and sat back, looking at me as if for the first time, his eyes resting on my shoulders, my lips and breasts. I felt his knee between mine under the tablecloth. He leaned closer and whispered, "You know, I see guys with all their limbs, all the parts working, and they don't know what to do with it all."

"Yes indeed," I said, smiling.

"So what I'd like to do is paint your body with my tongue."

"Let's get out of here," I replied.

My apartment was dark and cool when we got there. It was a small place, looking out on one side into an air shaft and on the other onto the street, and sparsely furnished: a futon on the floor, a jug of irises, a few straggling geraniums, an easy chair, my books. He shut the door behind me and spun me around before I was ready, forcing back my head. His teeth caught my lower lip. I fell back into the chair and he knelt in front of me between my legs. I could hear my pulse roaring in my ears. *Let me be graceful too,* I thought, knowing only then how scared I was. He sank his teeth into the softest part of my neck and I gasped. I leaned back my head and shut my eyes, feeling again as if the ground were racing out beneath me.

He rested on his haunches, looking at me with a demonic grin. I was ashamed of how flushed and tousled I must have looked. But deliberately, I held my gaze steady with his. He took both my hands firmly in his. With his hook, he traced the line of my throat down, slowly, slowly, to my collarbone. Again I shut my eyes, unable to bear it. I was conscious only of the delicate point of steel that this fierce man, darkly radiant with desire for me, was drawing down the center of my being. All reality was concentrated on that rigid point on my skin. It descended to the space between my breasts, from which I could now smell the perfume, heated and activated, rising. He hooked the metal into the first button of my dress and, with a little laugh, jerked sharply downward. The button tore open, and the next, and the next. He reached upward with the hook between my breasts, and flipped open the clasp of my brassiere. I was naked to the waist.

He stood up, and made me stand, my hands now gripped in his hand behind my back, unbelievably strong. A sudden move forward would only put me onto the point of the hook. My dress fell off my shoulders and lay in folds on my hips. Savagely, knowingly, he ran the cool steel first around the circumference of one breast and then the other. My breathing quickened. He drew the circles smaller and smaller. No touch had ever stirred me like this before. Dizzy, I moved forward, falling against his shoulder, but he jerked me back upright, hard. "Not yet," he said as he brushed the steel point against my nipple. I was wet at once. I moaned, twisting to get away, but the two delicate prongs of the hook opened and shut gently, so gently, carefully, on the nipple, holding me, that I could not have moved even if I had wanted to.

"Cold, isn't it," he said, still smiling. "Yes," I was breathing like someone who'd just been plunged into an ice-cold ocean with an undertow pulling her miles from the shore. Then he released me and, where the metal had been, I felt his mouth, so warm, opening.

Suddenly I knelt on the futon and drew him down beside me. I had to gather my thoughts, to understand why I was afraid. What will I see when he takes off the arm? Will I be repelled? The thought came with anger at myself for my fear, but civility and raised consciousness are helpless when two bodies lie down in the dark.

I thought of the first time I'd ever touched a man's penis, when I was fourteen. I'd felt exactly the same dread and terrible curiosity, and known with that gut childhood certainty that the only way to get past my fear to pleasure was simply to take a deep breath and grasp it. I was hesitant to confront what lay under the white sock of the false arm, but I knew I wanted to touch it, to get that first shock over with, and make love entirely to Lefty. *Am I really this ignorant, when it comes to laying my body on the line, to be so fearful of a body that's different? Yes. Yes, it seems I am.*

But, seeing his face in the darkness with its expression of patient amusement—of compassion, even, for me, I relaxed. He knows what I'm thinking because he's lived through this moment many times before. He raised himself on his knees, stretching. "I think it's uncool to get down with you with a hunk of metal between us. What do you say we ditch this?" Casually, elegantly, like a fencer shrugging off his tunic, he slipped each shoulder out of the canvas harness. His right hand gripped the leather-encased arm, pulled it gently off and laid it beside the futon. He slipped his shirt off over his head, opened the zipper of his jeans and slid out of them. He lay down naked beside me.

His body was a rich brown all over, and my skin seemed ghostly white beside it. I stroked his chest. It was smooth and fine, with almost no hair. He raised himself on the stump of his arm to let me caress him. I saw now how thin it was, the muscles undeveloped around the bone; it ended smoothly above the place where the joint of the elbow would be. The muscles of that side of his torso were less developed than those of his right side. I stroked the soft black hair of his armpit, then ran my hand down the arm and held it for a moment. There. It was him. It was fine.

With that behind us, he kissed me. At first gently, then hard,

hard enough, it seemed, to bruise my lips. I warmed to him, running my hands down the slope of his back, then, lightly, the tips of my nails, over the curve of his ass. "Mmm, girl, I could eat you up," he whispered wetly in my ear. He was on me now, braced by his hand, kneeling over me. His left arm was stroking my side; it slid between my legs. "Take these things off," he said, and I wriggled out of my panties and took off my rumpled dress. His mouth descended on me at once, teasing my nipples, making me moan again and again. He kissed his way, open-mouthed, down my belly, down the line of hair that led to my bush, and I felt as if a row of red poppies were blooming against me with each kiss. "Just lie back, honey child. I love this. I just love to do this. Let me." I let my legs fall open. His tongue was on me, there, right there, softly licking, savoring, slowly, like a wine taster, considering, then, quickened with thirst, drinking, drinking me in. I was lost, I reached up to meet him, *trust me or we'll go down,* I trusted him with everything I had, but still I was falling, the ground came up to meet me but it was the sky.

Morning comes bright and sudden in summer in New York. I opened my eyes to a shaft of hot light slanting into the little room. It fell over the rumpled bedclothes, the drying irises in the clay pot, the body of my lover curled beside me, sleeping furiously as a child, his arm twined in mine, a faint dampness on his forehead where the soft hair began. I kissed very lightly the scar that ran down his cheek, and smelled my own aroma on his lips. I was happy, stupidly happy. "You're just an animal, you," I whispered into his dreaming face. He woke up at once and gave me that crazy grin. "Yeah, what are you, a pussycat? Look what you did to me." He nodded toward his shoulder, where fine red lines were still visible. "Let's get up and hit the fuckin' *road!*" he yelled joyfully, and stood up, at home in his brown skin, on the chaotic bed. He was beautiful. Fearful symmetry, I thought, you can't scare me, I've got you beat. He glanced down his shoulder, rubbing with his hand the marks I'd left. "You think a few more years of sweating over Shakespeare might dilute your blood a little?

You're lethal, woman, I tell ya. Let's not shower, I want to smell you on me all day." He put on his jeans and bent down to pick up the arm. "Any more body parts lying around?" I laughed and kissed him, and went to pour the juice, singing camp songs at the top of my lungs.

When we ran down the stairs to the bike, I slipped; he caught my hand with his hook, and I left my hand there, and gently, carefully, he held my hand as we emerged into morning, the simplest light of the day.

A Japanese Play

VICTORIA STARR

I feel nervous after ringing the bell. Looking at Geoff and his pale, tense expression, I see he's nervous too. On the train riding out of the city we'd talked it over again and again, but Geoff kept falling back to the line which made us agree to do this scene in the first place: "We do it at home all the time anyway, why not get paid for it?" Why not? But wouldn't that change it, wouldn't we feel strange with somebody watching us, filming us, getting it on? Well, yes, maybe . . . but there is the awesome fact that we're in Asia and broke and trying to get enough bucks to get on with our world traveling . . . we need the money and Kikuchi will pay us well.

I'd come to see him on my own already. Kymusha, the black Ugandan maître d' at the bar where I work, put me in touch with him: "Famous Japanese artist," he'd said. "Very respectable, Vicky. He need foreign women for nude modeling, you be good . . ." Okay, at a hundred dollars a shot I could bare my tits and sit still. But Kikuchi requested some pretty pornographic poses, so I got hip quick—I raised my price. I also made sure he never touched me. Not that I could tell if he wanted to; he wasn't very direct, but I still made sure he didn't.

Now, Kikuchi isn't bad-looking. In fact, he's a handsome Japanese—on the short side, but then so am I. His face is wide and open like a triangle pointing down, with high cheekbones and pale, clear, smooth skin, dark eyes flashing from oval slits—they remind me of cats' eyes, and I like cats. He even moves like one, slinky, with this amused cunning look, as if he's after something but has all day to catch it. And his blue-black spiky hair sticks up as if someone's been scratching him between the ears. He's really rather striking, but the Japanese look has begun to bore me.

Another good reason to come to Kikuchi's: he lives outside metrapocalyptic Tokyo, in a lovely traditional house surrounded by a lush green fern garden. And he insists on beginning each session with a bath, in a glassed-in room which looks out over deep soft grass and blooming hot pink fuchsias.

I don't know exactly why he keeps asking me back . . . he wasn't getting any physical satisfaction from our sessions, and the drawings he did were pretty sketchy and poor, in my opinion. Except this time the deal is different altogether: he wants to film us . . . and watch. Geoff guessed he probably wanked the night away after watching me pose. Maybe Geoff's right. As a native Californian, I just happen to have the look the Japanese die for: white surf-color hair, long and thick with dark parts underneath, eyes of Pacific green, the changing kind . . . and my body's slim from years of action in the waves. In California it seems all the girls look just like me, but here in Tokyo I'm an exotic star.

Footsteps; he's about to open the door, and I give Geoff a final look while we're still alone. He's looking frightened, his lips tight. He's a beautiful man, tall and angular, English, with large gray Atlantic eyes, inky black lashes and fine shimmering autumn chestnut hair. He'd make a stunning woman, but it would be a shame to deprive the world of his fantastic prick—it's the only round thing about him, his prick. Oh, yes, I almost forgot, his ass, too—the very thought of it turns me on and I let him know by curling my tongue up, sending it out of my mouth, and licking my lips. His lips part, and his clasped hands drop, reaching for me, just as the door swings open.

"Vicky . . . come in . . . come in. Ah, Geoff, so nice to meet you, I hear so much about you!"

"You have?" says Geoff, firm, not very friendly as I laugh, a laugh mixed with nervousness and excitement. Geoff doesn't know what he's in for—but as long as we've come this far, I'm planning to enjoy myself.

"He's only heard the best things, dear heart, only the sexiest secrets . . ." I chuckle, teasing them both, and Kikuchi turns his quick cat-eyes from Geoff to me, smiling, appreciative of the remark. I see he feels aligned in some mythical confidence.

Geoff smiles too, secure with the knowledge I've told Kikuchi nothing at all about him, which is true. From his reaction, I wonder if he now is beginning to understand what I'd meant on the train when I tried to explain how this work feels like a show to me: an improvised drama in which I act whatever part the play demands. Right now we need someone to ease the tension. Kikuchi plays his part well.

"For you, Vicky, your usual black Russian?" I nod in assent. "And you, sir?" He speaks clipped English with polite Japanese grace.

"A scotch please, no water."

"You begin with the bath, yes? The room is prepared. You know the way, Vicky . . . I bring the drinks."

I take Geoff back to the glass room with the Japanese tub sunk deep into the stone floor. Kikuchi must be anticipating an extra-special day, as the water is strewn with rose petals, white, yellow and pink, floating on the surface, perfuming the air. Geoff quickly recovers his poise and whisks up behind me, grabbing my ass through my cotton dress. I twist and throw my arms around his neck, on my tiptoes we kiss, and Geoff sends his tongue deep in my mouth. He's getting hot—there's no room for fear when we kiss. I let one hand slide off his neck down the front of his shirt to the top of his trousers, where I slip a finger in, wiggling his clothes aside, I'm searching for his soft skin to tickle with a long nail.

"Do you want me?" I whisper, teasing him as I back away. Setting my heels on the ground, I undo his pants button with one finger.

"Yessss . . ." he groans his answer out, and I see he's forgotten Kikuchi completely. That's fine, all he wants is to watch, anyway. With two hands I unzip Geoff's trousers while he unbuttons his shirt. He loves to watch me take his clothes off, so I make the most of it, squeezing his thighs with my long fingers, loving the hard swell of his strong muscles as I push down his trousers. His bare legs are light gold, his usually fair skin well tanned from two months in Thailand.

I look up, deciding to make him jump. "I want your cock . . ." I say, giving his balls a light squeeze, pushing a round knuckle between the cheeks of his ass. "Get it down your throat, then!" he responds, whipping his underwear down with two thumbs, revealing his prick growing into a raging hard-on right before my eyes—the head straining red, his skin rolling back like a pink stage curtain going up . . . This show is on!

I laugh and get to my feet, slapping his ass with one hand, clutching his bulge tight with the other, I say "Not yet, my darling . . . We begin with the bath." Geoff watches me lean over to test the water with my hand. Knowing he's watching, I pull up my dress to give him a lovely view of my tight ass, my long legs . . . Out of the corner of my eyes I catch him rubbing his prick, pulling his skin up and down over the ridge of his cock-head. I say, "You know the longer we stay, the more bucks we make, let's take it slow today, okay, baby?" We both smile. Soon he is gracefully settling into the tub. Geoff whispers gruffly, "When we fuck, I'm gonna make you see stars . . ." and I see his hand go to his prick underwater. I love it when he says things like that, and he knows it. He watches me with a sultry "I'll show you who's directing the scenes round here" look.

I pull my dress off over my head and I'm naked, except for the white lace panties Geoff gave me ages ago. I cup my breasts with my hands and spread my hot-pink nails around my nipples like a web. Holding my tits never fails to turn me on. I grip them hard to let Geoff know how excited I am, and he smiles. I slip my panties off and get into the tub. Kikuchi will soon arrive and I don't want to shock the man. Geoff comments, "I thought he was old and fat and ugly, the way you talked about him! I was picturing someone entirely different . . ."

"You think he's attractive?" I ask, a little startled. I'd been so intent on not fucking him I guess I hadn't let myself really think about it.

"Well, he's not *my* type," says Geoff, but I catch a tension there, an embarrassment which makes me wonder; perhaps? But he finishes, "I thought maybe *you* . . ." Yes, he's definitely embarrassed. If Geoff's into this Japanese cat, then maybe I can be the one who gets to watch for a while . . . The thought turns me on so intensely I marvel I've never had it before. I picture a prick in Geoff's mouth, a man fucking him! I'm speechless imagining the delight of something entirely new . . . I cover up:

"You mean you'd like to see me fuck him?"

We hear the sound of ice clanking in glasses very near and Kikuchi enters the room. We go instantly quiet and he knows he's interrupted something. As he bends to hand me my drink, his short black kimono opens and I see a brown hairless chest with bronze-penny nipples. Not bad. He stands in front of the glass, looking out to the garden with his back to Geoff and me. He slips his kimono off and it looks like he's got one hand on his prick, and his ass muscles are clenching two sweet clefts in his soft brown bum. The minutes pass. Is he jerking off? I turn to Geoff to see what he's thinking, and I see his hand moving swiftly underwater at work on a throbbing shaft, floating. He's into it. Great.

But when Kikuchi turns around, he's not hard at all, though he's got a nice-sized cock, hanging in between two plumlike balls.

He was probably meditating. He climbs into the bath and says, "So glad you could come today. Lovely day . . ." I think, "My God, how does he manage to be so superficial?" Besides, it's gray and thick outside. Turning to Geoff he says:

"You, sir, more attractive than even Vicky say . . . I think she exaggerate when she say I must see you . . . But no, no, very nice, thank you, Vicky, you bring me such beautiful man to photograph! Two of you together make excellent picture." He nods, smiling happily. This is business; we are reminded of the job we have to do. I gulp down my black Russian. Geoff drinks down his scotch. Kikuchi has thought ahead to bring the bottles and he gets out of the tub to refill our glasses.

A few more drinks and inconsequential chit-chat and I'm ready to get on with it. I feel a little drunk, but that makes it easier. I'm thinking, what if instead of being a writer I become a porn star and fuck my way through life instead of hassling with all this intellectual bullshit . . . ? The money's better and that's a fact. I giggle at this ludicrous prospect as Kikuchi shows us to the studio . . . Geoff glances at me, the stern look returning to his face. His prick is soft again after our long soak and I can see he's wondering if he'll feel like getting it up in front of this strange man. But the way I'm feeling he doesn't have to worry.

I fling myself down on my stomach, spread-eagled on the bed. Kikuchi says: "Go ahead, just pretend I am not here and you are at home." Over my shoulder I see him settling into a dark corner where there's a camera standing, a tall watchful eye. I run my hands across the white cashmere spread thinking, "At least he's got good taste." It's almost as soft as Geoff's skin. I am hot from the bath, but the bed is warm too. There are lights strategically placed at respectful distances. No wonder Kikuchi's corner looks dark. Against the lights, I can hardly see him. Geoff is sinking down on the bed, lying nearly on top of me, just to be close. I roll over and we're belly to belly. I throw my arms around his neck as we look into each other's eyes. "This is it . . ." we're both saying silently, wondering how in the world we got here, to this bed in front of this wealthy voyeur?

From nowhere I feel the head of Geoff's growing prick tickling my thigh. Holding his eyes, I watch the change begin, very subtly at first, but distinct, tangible. It's like a storm gathering; a storm of the North Sea, hungry and a little mean, but exciting and vigorous, a wind and roar which make me feel ALIVE. His mouth whispers, "Come on, baby, fuck me . . ." and I feel the rise of the wave as if I am a pebble caught in the undercurrent, being sucked, dragged and spun under, out to sea. "I'll fuck you . . ." I hear my voice crooning the words, and forcefully I run my hands down his square sharp shoulders, tense with the weight of holding his chest above me. I want this man a little more desperately each time we fuck . . . I never know what will happen—it just gets better and better. Anticipating his prick head reaching my cunt makes me curl my ass upward, as he lifts his ass too, teasingly rising with me, like two currents of one swell. My hands crawl around his narrow hips to his ass, "What an ass you've got, you little fucker, the best ass I've ever seen . . ." I feel his cock hard, jutting into my soft abdomen like a rock. I go hard too and rub myself against him, up and down, we rub until he slides his prick to the top of my pussy. He's wet with his own juice and I feel the trail of him on my thigh, on my stomach, joyfully on the lips of my cunt! Yes, he's opening me, no, just letting me know what's to come. I guide his ass with my hand, perfect rhythm building. I feel like coming, he rubs me just right. Then, we stop, suddenly, and catch each other's eyes again. He's looking beautiful, so into our love . . . The room has disappeared. Who's Kikuchi? I don't remember him, it's just Geoff and me floating on a warm white cloud, moving on a sea.

Ah, there, it's happening, finally, he's taking my cunt on his prick. He strokes very slowly, a little deeper with each thrust. My cunt is sucking on him like a kid with a popsicle. Sounds pour from me like flocks of gulls, soft sounds, then gasping cries. "You fuck me so well!" I cry; he laughs softly, "Can you see stars yet . . . ?" He's tender, in control. But I feel him losing it, I feel it deep in my womb where the tip of his cock is kissing me, inside . . . I like to make him lose it. I like to see him go wild. He starts shoving himself in, a little harder, a little faster, he's breathing heavily and I coax him, "You bastard . . ." I whisper, knowing the sound of me talking dirty will make him come. I feel the sweat-like mist breaking out on his back. I love it, I love to feel him ram into me so his balls slap my ass, and I curve up to meet him, to stay with him, breath coming fast and sharp.

"Fuck me, just fuck me!" I close my eyes, I'm losing it too; where am I lost? Inside the rhythm, inside the sensation, rising, yes, like a beat, building—got to move with it, got to get it just right, there, yes, there, "I'm coming, you bastard, feel me!" I squeeze his cock and he pushes into me, higher, harder, we're sliding across the cashmere, my legs fly out, my nails dig into his back— He knows just when to stop but stay deep, so we each feel the waves in my snatch like ripples gliding away from a heavy stone dropped in a pool. We're pressed so close, so hot, again I feel like melting, dissolving, my cunt still beats out the first rhythm. I fall away and let my arms fly lazily over my head. I stretch out under his cock still deep inside me. I stretch, letting every nerve feel the benefit of my release. I look at his prick, piercing, he's wide and burning now, slick with my juice and dark, what a sight! We smile, lips open, wanting. Geoff follows my gaze to his prick. He slips it out and kneels over me. Grabbing it, he clenches his fist tight, the muscles of his arm stand out, sexy and defined—a body like a goddamned Greek god, that's what he looks like! There's pain in his face, holding his aching cock, "Because of you . . ." he says, meaning: I do this to him, I make him *so* hard . . .

I put my hands down to my cunt and spread my legs wide and open so he can look down into my flowering pussy. Moaning, his face goes soft, his hand flies up and down at work on himself. Holding my cunt open, my arms push together my breasts. I thrust my tongue out, wishing I could bring my breasts up to my face and lick, suck, get myself off. Geoff leans down, sucking and nibbling my nipples until . . . I can't believe what he does to me! He slides his mouth down from my breasts, over my belly, stopping to kiss that sweet mound, above the spot where I'm dying for him. Leaning upon my elbows I push his head back before he gets his tongue on me. I hold his hair in my hand and keeping his face close to my cunt, I make him watch as a curved, pink nail disappears within . . . Geoff's face is all fascination and hunger. Sliding with my juice I tickle my ass with the smooth varnished side, then give him my finger to suck.

I sit up, letting his mouth pull me and when I'm on my knees he rises too, so we're both kneeling, facing each other, eyes connected, breathing hard. A light catches my eye the wrong way and I feel blinded as if I just stared into the sun. I think, "Kikuchi's getting a good deal today." Although it's faint, I know Geoff and I are aware of his presence. We're still giving a performance, but one of our better ones, I'd say. "Let me suck you now, baby . . ." I moan. Geoff's got his hands on my tits, as I bend forward, dragging my long hair and my sweet tongue over his nipples, under his ribs, down inch by inch, down some more. He's got his hands flying all over me, pressing here, gripping there, it feels fantastic, I love it, and I want to throw my mouth down on him and gobble him up—but I don't. A good cocksucking starts slow and builds. I blow lightly on his throbbing head, now, my lips, very soft, wide, open and wet. They fit perfectly. Licking his tiny hole I flick my tongue around the rim, gently up under the edge. Geoff's sighing, light groans, he's got one hand on my breast, one holding my hair off my face so he can see me taking him in my mouth. Am I facing the camera? Yes? What a shot. I raise my ass high in the air, I know he likes to watch it move. I slip my tongue down the sides of his cock, I take him deeper, further into my mouth. He's pressing now on the back of my throat, I roll back my lips, jaw stretched—he's moving, just right, there, a little deeper, "Get it down, take me baby, take me . . ." I've got my cheek cushioned on his silky fuzz, I smell that musty-ball smell as they rise up, forcing his cock deeper down. I want to swallow him, swallow all of him. I take his balls in my hand and let him slip from my mouth and slide over my face, I roll my face in his shining prick. He tastes like me, and I love the taste of my juice on him, "I want to taste your come . . ." I slur this out, half his prick in my mouth, "Give it to me."

A huge hand playfully slaps my ass. It's not Geoff's, I can tell instantly, it's too large, but whoever owns it is sending a nice fat finger up my twat. Turning, I see it's Kymusha, the Ugandan who first put me in touch with Kikuchi. What's he doing here? Geoff and I are still, both of us looking at this man with surprise, but Geoff's cock is still jumping and straining against my cheek. And me, I can't stay still, because Kymusha's got my cheeks spread wide apart with one big black hand, and the other is expertly fingering my clit, slipping, in and out, around . . . I start to move with his hand and shut my eyes—who cares now? I've always wanted to fuck a black man anyway. I've even flirted with Kymusha at work. Looking at Geoff's face watching this black giant in between my legs with his hands buried in my pussy, I can see, yes, he thinks it's fine. And it *is* fine . . . Kymusha's laughing, a pleasant growl, fucking me with his quick heavy hands and I'm sucking Geoff's cock like it's the last thing I'll ever get in my mouth. Kymusha keeps taking me right to the edge, then letting me back down until I feel wild.

We're almost there, both of us gasping, coming together, when Kymusha speeds it up and I'm gone, shrieking, "My God, what's he doing." One hand in my cunt—finger up my ass—it feels like heaven and I'm selfish again, writhing down, crying out into white cashmere. Geoff's grabbed his prick and he's wanking, he loves to watch me come. I see two pricks, a shadow, no it's Kymusha huge and black . . . I've never seen such a big prick. The two of them wank in front of my face, I take one in each hand, they feel like poles and I use them, pulling myself up. Then I'm licking, one, then the other. Kymusha's tastes like nothing I've ever had before, delicious and black-red. I'm making him grunt, teasing his cock, slipping it down my throat then I take off onto Geoff's. I try to take them both in my mouth, but I can't, they're too big. I rub them against one another, my tongue in between. Geoff can't take it much longer, I see the tense I've-got-to-have-it-now lines breaking out in his face. He's ready, with one hand shoving his cock in my mouth, the other pushing me to roll me over on my back. Staring up at the two, two hands jerking off, "Come on my face you fucking bastard, go on!" I cry out to Geoff, but it moves Kymusha too, I see his belly grow tight. Yes! Geoff's got it—"In my mouth, on my tits, I want you everywhere!" I'm screaming, lost in feeling, and his bittersweet hot come is splashing down, on my lips, on my breasts, tickling my neck, hot and wet. I love Geoff's face when he's coming—he's in another world. One hand holds his own tit, gripping with such strength that his muscles look like they're about to jump from his skin. He's crying like trees breaking, heavy groans, practically screaming. His come flies everywhere like ocean spray smacking cliffs.

Kymusha's watching the two of us, jerking himself. With Geoff's come on my lips I reach up and take one of his gorgeous black balls in my mouth. I suck and turn my head loving the night-dark color of his thighs. I spread Geoff's come on Kymusha's prick, on my face and that does it—I roll back to take his on my tits, and mouth, he's tight and gasping but no scream. Like lightning I send the tip of my thumb into his ass and he cries out—his come flies white from his black hard-on. "You bitch . . ." he moans affectionately. It's my turn to laugh.

We all rest, vibrating like echoes caught in a valley. I scoot up the bed and collapse, tingling, just breathing. Geoff lies on one side of me and Kymusha stretches out on the other. I listen to their breathing, struggling to recover. Geoff begins to rub his come into my skin, massaging my breasts and belly with his hand, then Kymusha follows his lead; only, he's touching my face with his salty black fingertips. I'm intrigued by the pink whorl of his fingerprint, when his finger passes down my cheek I grab it with my teeth and suck on it, like a baby feeding. But he pulls away and runs the wet finger straight from my mouth down my neck over my left tit, under my ribs and down to my wet stinging clit. I sigh and spread my legs, throwing one over each of their bodies. Kymusha doesn't play with me, but he rests his hand at the top of my cunt while Geoff keeps rubbing my breasts. I've never had two men at once before. I never imagined how good it would feel to have hands on your breasts, hands in your cunt, two pricks to play with, sheer fucking magic. My sighs are happy songs.

All I hear now is the beating of hearts—pum pum paaa dum pum and over again—it seems silence after the words and deep utterings. But I hear something else, too, the whirr/shhhhing sound of a camera running, then, Click, it stops, and I remember, "My God, someone's been filming this!" and also with great satisfaction I remember we're getting paid for this! Unbelievable. I shout across the room to Kikuchi: "Hey, when it's developed can we come back and watch?" He laughs and so do Geoff and Kymusha. I turn to this black man with his gentle hand in my cunt, then to Geoff . . .

Strange, but I don't feel odd here with them at all.

IV

The Moment

There are some stories that combine the physical experience and the unknown in quite a different way to produce something uniquely erotic. In these, there is no need for danger, surprise, anxiety, adventure or the forbidden. Some erotica focuses on the physical experience so completely that it creates a vicarious physiological response in the reader. Yet in this moment-to-moment experience where there is no past and no future, we still find the unknown. The next act, feeling, smell, touch, cannot be anticipated, but is discovered as it is encountered. The major erotic tension is built through the smells, sounds, textures, sensual visuals and, in particular, the physical sensations the body is experiencing in the sexual event. However, no one particular kind of sensory input can continue too long without becoming boring. Therefore, these moments of sensation are constantly changing, constantly being formed in new and unexpected ways, until with full immersion in the erotic experience, the physiological changes can be so great that an actual change in consciousness occurs. During high sexual arousal, the electrical activity in the brain is quite different from the normal waking state, which may account for the altered state of consciousness that is experienced.

In "Cradles of Light," Susan Griffin creates the ultimate sensual experience as perceived through the body. All of the senses are alive. The light, the buzzing of voices, the sensations of touch are all erotic. By going into herself and being fully aware of the experience she is involved in, she can feel a part of everything. According to Susan, "With the erotic experience, you are reaching into your own consciousness. You are opened up, and you are widening your consciousness through the sexual experience. Totally accepting the sexual experience and being in it completely is what is erotic."

But Susan uses the erotic to do more. She uses the intensity of the sexuality to break her main character out of her mind-set. By getting beyond her own block to orgasm, she is able to accept the losses in her life, and her own imperfections. And in making love to herself, she is able to more fully accept herself and her mortality, which intensifies the experience of life—and thereby the erotic. Again, the unknown, not knowing when death will come, but knowing that it will, makes every moment precious and the experience of each individual moment a delicacy to be fully savored.

Another story that creates a thoroughly erotic experience through the bathing of the senses is Cucu Lee's "One Florida Night." The entire story centers around the sexual experience: the touch, smell, sights and sounds of lovemaking. "What is erotic to me is the touching, the sensualness of what the body is feeling, the tactile sensations, and I've tried to express these so they come alive for the reader," explains Cucu. And she does so in a manner not typical for a woman of fifty-eight years who grew up in a culture that taught her it wasn't nice to think about, much less write about, such explicit sexuality.

In addition, the ending of this simple, but very sweet, story catches the reader totally unaware. It is not until the last paragraph that we realize we have made certain assumptions that are the result of our own cultural conditioning. The story requires us to encounter ourselves at this basic level and to rethink our automatic responses—prejudices instilled by our culture.

Tee Corinne's story, "The Woman in Love," uses words to create a rhythm and pacing that set a mood and tone that are inherently erotic. Her descriptions of the South, the flowers, the food, her lover, are all so immediate, they are almost palpable. Yet, nothing is fixed. The Woman in Love and Desire come together, grow apart and resume contact. The reader is pulled along in this diaphanous world of sensuality, through the experience of the moment, with no thought of what is to come.

Tee's story is a good example of the creation of sensuality that takes precedence over sexuality. The sensual pervades the story whether or not the characters involved are actually making love. The sensual mood she creates in her writing mirrors what is important for Tee in her own life. "I am likely, in my life, to eroticize something," Tee observed. "Some people tell jokes, I eroticize a situation, an observation, a meal—not toward a genital end, but to add excitement to my life. I find beauty erotic. Softness and dancing and traditionally romantic things like candlelight create a sensual mood or tone, and it doesn't have to have anything to do with genital sexuality."

Jacquie Robb creates similar dreamlike images in her "Twilight Fantasy." Rather than a whirlwind, passionate experience, she develops the kind of slow buildup of eroticism that a couple who have known each other for a long time might enjoy. They take the time to play around, to create a slow sensuality where there is no attachment toward a goal. The main character is so completely involved with the experience of the moment, and so secure in the relationship, she can take for granted that the experience will be totally pleasurable.

In addition to this dreamlike sense, Jacquie has incorporated the unfamiliar by placing her main character in other than her usual surroundings. "For me," says Jacquie, "eroticism is the result of deep intimacy and knowledge of a partner coupled with that unknown quantity that exists each and every time they make love. The woman is in a hotel room, it has nothing to do with her regular daily life, so the intimacy has the sense of being otherworldly. It is this otherworldly sense, this being detached from ordinary concerns while being with someone she knows so well, that I find so erotic."

The detailed descriptions of the sensations that create the erotic are what distinguish each of these four stories. It is the actual physical experience of the lovemaking, the sensations coursing through the body, that fill our own, vicariously, with that same erotic sense.

Cradles of Light

SUSAN GRIFFIN

She was being changed. The sex was great in her now. She lay there thinking. It was like an inland lake. Someplace she had never been before. Only dreamt of. The evenings are warm. Certain plays evoke this feeling, certain movies. The family comes out onto the front porch. There are fireflies. The lake is near. The air has expanded so it is soft and large. Over the lake there is a swarm. Fireflies, other insects, and some other presence. They make a sound together that echoes against the purple hills. These hills are like bodies, only the inside of bodies turned outward, become like flesh and skin. The surface of the lake catches the last light. The sun is down. The sky is white. And ringing the lake, standing by the shore, or farther back, on the porches of cabins, people speak to each other, and laugh, the sound muffled and blended together with the insects into one low, nearly palpable tone. There is an incipience here. No one speaks of it.

There had not been a real lake, at fifteen, when the sex became something so distinct, but the sound was there. Just a year ago she went back, and she saw them. The young, sitting in the warm night. Twenty-five years had passed. A garage door opened. Electric lights gleamed like the lights of a refrigerator in a dark room. The dusk was filled with a murmur. On the steps of a house a young man and young woman kissed. A girl and a boy. She remembered the first boy who had lowered his body onto hers. She loved his body. But she was in love with her best friend. They slept in the same bed and spoke through the night of their lovers. This was the way they made love. Through stories of love.

They did not talk about the sex itself. She could remember the weight of him, the sway of him even against every part of her, and she, like the air expanding, becoming soft, immeasurably soft. And slow, very slow, while the blood inside her, a pulse between her legs, was quick. But the sex could not be said to be there. Nor in any place it seemed to be, her labia, the clitoris, the soft inner part of her thighs, her breasts, the flat of her chest between her breasts, the skin between her pubis and ass, nor in the place before the hair grew, not any of these places that jumped at her touch, nor in the hand touching, but in the air around, which seemed suddenly to affect her, coming over the top of her head, that place where kings and queens wear crowns, cradles of light, making every place in her body aware. She liked to watch them walk together or sit kissing, the young, who had something she remembered having once too. She could not name it.

She was just fifteen when Sammy took her into his car. He was the first one besides herself to touch her, there, on her breasts, between her legs. The sudden feeling surprised her, and seemed to grow, not by degrees, but all at once, past the boundaries of her body, as if she were resplendent, gemlike, a lake at the end of a day, giving off a creature's heat.

Why was it that, touching herself, she liked to start by hardly touching at all? So many women she knew were like this. This was perhaps like air. Almost invisible. The touch. She brushed the tips of her fingers across the place where her clitoris hid. She had let the sex grow in her for days. It was not neglect. She wanted the feeling to exist as itself. It had been a year since she had had a lover. What does it mean, lover? She had bought a card with a photograph of two women, one leaning her head against the other, one leaning over the other, one gazing up at the other, whose eyes were closed. Lovers. Why were they together? She had thought once that she knew. She had thought then it was a question of families, groups of people speaking at the edge of the lake, who would be together all their lives. When she was small and had to have her tonsils out, her grandmother had bought her some paper dolls. She could see them now, a string of arms and legs opened as if they were stretching. She loved them because they were a family. She had had to live apart from her mother and father and sister since she was six.

What she felt that she would have called loneliness was there as a need, and the need became, simply, the sensual fact itself. Her hand was light. With each motion, she felt a wave, until she could almost call out, or moan, her own voice startling her, a wish shaping inside her. She could feel herself, on the inside of her body, like the hills, like a vaulted room, a tent, bones like spans or poles, a sound reverberating in her. A place inside her like the dark car. Sammy had died. An accident. It was sudden and violent. He was married and his wife was carrying a child. And years ago, when she heard of this death, she was pregnant too. Now her daughter was the age she had been when she met him.

She had not become his lover. There was just that moment in the car. It was clear they would not be a couple. She dismissed him, caring for him only as a friend, not knowing then that the touch he gave her could never be undone, would always be part of what she remembered, indelible.

She placed the palm of her hand against herself. She was afraid of wanting too much. He had not been in her life for years, but she hated to be told about his death. She tightened herself then, against the possibility. In her wanting she knew she would begin to wish for a lover, wish that someone else were touching her. Sammy, the first to touch her, was kind, not only in his touch, but in the way he was, and this had made a difference. In Algebra class she gave him the answers. It was the way he asked, and also, a comradeship before what might, in ways unique to each of them, crush them both. What was also indelible now was that she would never have the life she was prepared to have, as one in a couple, married, staying together for a lifetime. She had had lovers and then married, divorced, had other lovers, women, lived with one woman for six years. Now she was over forty. Half her life gone. Or lived. Lived not in the way she had expected. And there was some relief to know that now there was no way to accomplish her ideal.

Her daughter had sensed a hesitation in her, unable to claim the life they had, as if it had not yet begun. As a little girl, she wished for the ideal, not forgiving the years of unmarriage. When she was eleven, they went together to visit the girl's grandmother. And they took a walk, wandering into the neighborhood of her coming of age. They walked to the high school and then beyond. Her daughter grew tired at the park and did not want to go on. She wanted to go farther, into a group of houses congregated past the park, where she had spent so much time, at fifteen. She let her daughter stay near the pond where there were children with their mothers. It seemed safe, though her daughter was not yet twelve and had the defenseless, tender look of a child about her. Later, when the dark fell too quickly, and she was four long blocks away, filled with terror, pleading against the unforeseen, she ran as fast as she could to the park. She found her daughter there at the edge, waiting, frightened by the growing dark.

Her window was open. The air was clear. And she felt herself out there, among the trees, part of the rooftops, even part of the bay. How far did she go, really, this that she felt herself to be?

She could touch herself and it seemed that what she felt, like a circle of sound, did not stop, but kept on, past where she could see, or where she had ever been. She wanted to reach some conclusion. To feel an intensity which would say to her finally, *You have what you want.* She pulled her feeling close to her, trying to direct it, trying with her hand, up inside her, then out, in circles over her vulva, faster and faster, in quick fluttering motions, to shape a sensation. As if she knew exactly what it should be.

Now, as her desire reached a high pitch, she was held at a distance from what she wanted. Her hand, which before had had a kind of grace, was graceless. She felt there was a place in her that had not been touched. And would not be. And she was left, like a crying child, outside the gate of herself.

A word came into her mind that she tried to still. Dirty, dirty, the word said, in a voice that was very young, and old, and repeated itself until she herself would take it into her mouth, forming the syllables with her lips, making it her own. She was a little girl. She had the feeling of needing to urinate. And held herself there with her hand. Until she heard her grandmother's voice saying, Dirty, that is dirty, don't do that. And she continued to say the word, until it left her.

It was late afternoon and sounds were coming in from the street below. The houses arranged like cliffs made of the space in the road a cavern from which sounds of cars and footsteps, conversations echoed. The room around her was in disorder. And she let it be.

She lay quietly for a while. Still. It was as if the noise around her were in a different world. In a world she had left. Her hand lay against her thigh. She was wet, sweating all over her body. The quiet was new to her. Not like rest or sleep. Like the eye of a needle.

She felt she had given up. It was not what she was used to, it was a virtue of hers, always to believe there was a way. An idea of what was to be, and even her idea of what her own past had been, were leaving her. Once, on a visit, her mother had brought out a shoe box of old letters. She found there a letter sent to her by her best friend. Her friend had gone off to college, and the letter came in the wake of her absence. Their friendship was surrounded by the unspoken worry that they may be in love. After she let herself know she loved women, the memory of this friendship returned to her, and she knew that they had been in love. But here was something different in her hand. On the paper, beyond the question of whether or not they had been or should have been lovers, was the love. This was what they were to each other. She loved and she had been loved, and remembered what it felt like, to have this woman's love, what it still felt like, there as she sat on her mother's couch.

There are signposts in a life. They give a sense of form. Signposts in a relationship that say, this will go on or this will end. She had learned to measure her life this way. But there is also what is. This she had learned from having a child. Her daughter would never be eleven again. Never be an infant again. And the way she was as an infant would not change now. Her daughter was the child of divorce. And this would affect her life. But beyond the question of influence, this is what her childhood had been. She had lived going back and forth from her mother's to her father's house. This was inalterably so.

She felt a stillness. What seemed to have hurt her, to have rent a hole in her, an emptiness at the far end of which appeared an edge of herself she had not known was there, was mending her, invisibly, with a swift force, like a breath.

When she touched herself again, a sweetness pervaded her body, full of richness. And then all the capability of her desire came alive in her. Like a child prevented from reaching too far across the table, she suddenly reached, she grabbed, she devoured. Whatever in herself she had given away to restraint had come back to claim her now. Faintly another self watched in fear and shame, for she was not who she thought she was, shy, forbearing, waiting her turn. Then it broke in her, and was large inside her, the air like a choir, low, a rush, in the sweet deep beginnings of her pubis, bursting like a slant of blinding light far up inside her, diffusing through her and now like a kiss warm at the base of her skull.

Outside any explanation she knew to make, there seemed to her to be a substance to what she felt. She wanted again, and then again thrust her fingers into herself, and there was a sadness pouring into her body, into the folds of her, as she shuddered, that she did not resist, it was part of her, part of what she had felt in life, even all the losses, even the deaths, just there, requiring nothing of her, but to admit it, the truth, as she reached, as if to all she ever was, to a place of depth, of more than longing, where there would be a cry sounding like grief, but being instead the sound of taking in, of having. And again and again she went into herself, and had herself, fainted back, rose, moved not even anymore out into the trees and beyond but by a different transmission, as if she were here and many places at once, in the twilight, alive at the edge of the water, mirrored in the surface, spread out in shimmering veils in the air, delicate in the green light in the needles of the pine at the shore, whispering in a conversation that surrounded her and that she had joined, she went into herself again, until again she was still.

And feeling herself wet in the sheets she curled up. There was a party. She remembered. And saw the faces of those who would go. She had not yet eaten. Her daughter would be home at eight, returning home from her first job. Who was she going to be? This child no longer a child? The air was turning cold but she liked it. She felt the toe that she had broken years ago, half asleep, falling on the stairs in the middle of the night. She would like to stay here for hours looking at the light against the wall. What would she eat for dinner? She closed her eyes and could still see the light. Just for a moment. And then the feeling again. She fainted into it, and it grew. She was drifting. There were bells, there was a sound. There was a music she must remember. There was sleep. She was changed. All she had ever seen was in her, and her mind wandered forward and backward, freed of its usual design, fashioning, embroidering, making a new garment of the pieces.

She woke to the sun descending. She rose to watch it, so red, and the blue of the water, so blue, they were like high notes. Slowly the room darkened. As she watched herself in the glistening mirror, a rose light flashed over her skin, lighting up here an arm, here a hip, her belly, the flat of her ass, a breast; then letting them disappear, these glimpses of herself, she moved into the dark again. She was not ghostlike so much as astonishingly present with that vibrancy of anything we see knowing that this alone is its moment for being.

One Florida Night

CUCU LEE

I lie on the king-sized bed, every nerve tingling, my pussy throbbing, waiting for my lover to come to me. My legs stretch languidly as I admire their smooth whiteness in the darkness.

Reflected in the glass of a large framed print hanging in the hallway, his every movement is revealed to me as I watch him undressing in the bathroom off the hall. I can see the muscles ripple in his back and upper arms as he sheds his T-shirt. Soon he will emerge, nude, his hard, erect cock telling me how urgently he wants me, desires me, is eager to make love to me.

As I switch on the radio to a music station, I suddenly remember the telephone-answering machine! My God, what if Bart calls and his voice booms out, "Get ready, baby. I'm coming over to kiss your sweet belly."

Or Peter—who always plans ahead—his clipped New England accent might suddenly announce, "Confirming Saturday, darling. I'll bring a bottle of Soave. See you around eight."

I flip the controls off, just in case.

The bathroom light goes out, and a masculine form is framed in the doorway. Giant shadows dance on the walls and ceiling from the flickering candle on the nightstand. He gropes his way down the short hall as his eyes grow accustomed to the faint candlelight of the bedroom. In the dimness I can see the silhouette of his handsome body and feel his strong hands as he reaches out for the bed, and me.

He slides onto the smooth sheet and pulls me to him, breathing his hot breath into my ear. His smell—a mixture of Irish soap, mint toothpaste, mouthwash and musky aftershave—is fresh, clean and crisp.

Caught in his embrace, I feel my entire body become warm, all my senses yearning for the promise he's offering me.

His hand caresses my back, moves to my thigh, and expertly circles forward to my bushy mound, which is becoming wet with anticipation. There, in the thick black curly nest he probes the lips and gently massages my clit. A surge of ecstasy wells within me as I eagerly squirm to his touch, clasping my legs together to capture his hand rhythmically moving into my pussy. He is kissing me, tonguing me furiously, lapping like a kitten down my neck to my breast. He takes a nipple into his mouth and runs his tongue around it, causing it to become hard. The electricity of his touch shoots through me, mingling with the fire I'm feeling in my crotch.

He fondles one breast as he softly bites and kisses his way over the other breast and down my midriff to the roundness of my tummy. Slowly, up and down, he tenderly touches my skin from my rib cage to my hips.

An overwhelming feeling of desire wells up inside me, filling me, spilling over, drenching me with warmth.

As his tongue seeks the indentation of my navel, tickling, teasing, tormenting, an involuntary flinch makes me gasp, then giggle. He laughs too, and he kisses me there to remind me that he knows where I am ticklish. His tongue inside my navel again causes another flinch.

His hands move slowly down my hips, stroking the insides of my thighs, and up the crevices outlining my pubic bone. My hips respond to his touch as I thrust my pelvis toward him, toward his probing tongue. I am panting.

His finger traces the scar on my abdomen, and he kisses it all the way up from my love mound to my navel, and stretches on top of me to clasp my face in his palms and kiss me deeply. His fingers clutch my hair as he kisses me greedily.

I feel the rigidity of his penis pressed against me, and I'm only half aware that I'm making little whimpering sounds as our tongues hungrily make love.

Like combatants in an arena we roll over and over, grasping each other tightly in a desperate embrace.

I break away first, gasping.

"You're such a good lover."

"It takes two," he responds.

I grasp his strong stiff cock in my hand and slowly move the soft covering skin up and down, up and down. He moans with delight. Like a ballet, our movements are slow and graceful, as I swing around to kiss his hard flat stomach, run my tongue over the tiny crater of his navel, and bury my nose in the fine curly light fuzz that covers his crotch. I take that magnificent cock in my mouth and slowly move up and down over it, circling the tip and flicking my tongue around its head as he groans in rapture. I am on my knees at his side, and he has reached under me and found my pussy lips. With his other hand he is grasping one breast as if it were a tennis ball, clutching, squeezing, kneading it, as he savagely thrusts his other fist against my cunt.

I am aware only of the fresh, sweet spicy taste of his prick in my mouth. I sense the Florida moonlight filtering through the curtained window, blended with the orange glow of the candle, revealing his muscular body on the bed.

The beat of the music from the radio pounds in my head. I

move my lips and hips simultaneously to the beat, as I make love longingly to that gorgeous cock with my mouth and as he explores my pussy with his fingers.

Releasing his cock, I raise my hips and bring one leg over his body, straddling him. I guide the giant tool into my dripping pussy and sit back, feeling the hugeness of his penis fill my vagina as my muscles grasp and tighten. Slowly, slowly I raise myself until all but the tip is revealed, and then I slide excitedly down the pole again, up and down, up and down, until he is moaning, "Yes, yes!" and I am joyfully riding, riding, riding.

When I bend forward, he catches each breast, which he sucks and nibbles with tiny little love-bites until I collapse on his chest, my lower body writhing with passion.

The movements excite my pulsating clit and bring my desires to a peak.

I don't want this moment to end.

I stifle a scream as there is a surge of sensation and my entire body responds to the earthquake with a shattering spasm.

He gently raises me, still impaled on that giant spear, and holds my shoulders as he thrusts upward, jabbing, stabbing his wet cock into my eager, receptive pussy. My head bends forward, my hair covering his face, and I move up and down, moaning for more.

I am drowning, his kisses smothering me. I move my tongue rapidly between his teeth, and he responds with a kiss that crushes me to him, and I struggle for breath. I come up for air, weeping with pleasure, bouncing, bouncing.

I'm riding a crest of a wave of feeling and it seems as if I'm being carried to the highest of heights. I see skyrockets in my head. Bells are ringing.

Literally.

Shrill, persistent rings of the telephone jar my consciousness into the present. Who can be calling at this hour? I glance at the luminous dial of the bedside clock—after midnight.

"Ignore it," he commands, pulling me to him, stifling my outcry, kissing me again. Six more insisting rings and I can ignore it no longer.

Still astride that flagpole, I reach for the offending phone.

"Hello?" The chill in my voice betrays my displeasure.

Twelve-year-old Kimberly lives on the West Coast. It's three hours earlier there.

"Grandma," her bright little voice comes through the receiver, "what are you doing?"

The Woman in Love

TEE A. CORINNE

The Woman in Love was born in the mind of a quiet, lonely child whose heart was fed on family tales, southern songs and country/western music. Moving in three-quarter time, she spun her dreams of an active, vibrant life, layering the images, the smells, across her senses. She watched her mother with the magnificent breasts, her Gypsy aunt and stately mother's mother. She loved them with a deep and colorful passion. Their perfumes filled her world long after they had left for one party, event, meeting or another. She would hold a glove or stole against her face, breathe deeply and slip into a dream of beautiful, graceful women who always had time to spend with her.

The Woman in Love grew amid the Spanish moss, century plants, dogwood, magnolia, orange and grapefruit trees.

The lush, moist heat nourished her, wrapped around her, insulated her, caressed her incessantly, fed and satisfied her dreams. The sun darkened her lean body, warmed the sand and water, created mirages that glittered in the distance on the midday roads.

Her world was filled with flowers: gardenias, bougainvilleas, hibiscus, jacarandas, frangipanis, fragrant, intensely colored. The women cultivated flowers, wore them, taught her their secrets and their names.

Always skinny, she ate for the sensuous pleasure food afforded, ate to fill a variety of hungers, ate pecans and peaches brought down from Georgia, figs, peanuts from her grandmother's garden, coconut milk, sweet-potato pie, avocado from the tree out back, hush puppies made from corn meal and minced onion, deep-fried, crispy on the outside, warm and steamy on the inside.

Holidays were filled with chicken dusted in flour and fried, roast turkey, leg of lamb, fresh oysters, chicken livers with thick white gravy, sauteed onions and spiced apple sauce.

Her family ate well, fished, grew, gathered, canned, smoked, fermented and drank their way through the years of her childhood. They died off quickly in her youth, leaving her rich with memories.

Out of the dreams and memories, she fashioned a life that satisfied the longings of the child that she had been and the woman she was rapidly becoming. She grew willowy and serene, fell in love with butchy, androgynous women, queer like herself, traveled and talked and rubbed against them in the warm nights of Mobile, Charleston, Savannah, St. Augustine.

Oh, seduction, that glorious ephemeral art of attraction, the drawing of one individual to, toward, into another's sphere. The Woman in Love thrived on seduction: intellectual, aesthetic, visceral. She loved meeting people, unraveling their stories, learning who they were and are.

Sometimes she was seduced by others: the way one moved her body, the turn of a head or phrase, the revealing of an exquisite piece of work. At times she was seduced by those who unveiled only hints of themselves, knowing the fragments would lure her. Usually these women did not remain to become her friends. More often she would be drawn to those who opened themselves to her, unfolding their passions, uncovering their goals.

Seduction: the art of letting another know who you are.

"Will you dance with me?" the other asked, knowing the Woman in Love melted into music. "Will you dance with me?" she said, meaning, "Come and get to know me. Let me show you who I am." The Woman in Love moved into her arms, light touching, felt the music enter her like water, enter her like wine. Part of her knew this was no ordinary dance, knew as soon as the other's rhythm immediately matched, mirrored, found her own. They danced like liquid contained in a single glass, merging, swaying, hearts soaring until the music's end.

For the Woman in Love, seduction had begun early: noticing people notice her, a lover whose eyes followed her legs, a breath inhaled with the contact between eyes, a shoulder brushed by lips. The Woman in Love adored being touched, fondled her own being, rubbed and hugged her friends. Sometimes, excited by the spirit of life itself, the Woman in Love would hold anyone in order to anchor herself to the maiden earth, grounding renegade energy racing through her torso. She knew no other way to channel her electricity, to keep from turning into pure spirit, losing contact with others, with any outside world. At times people she touched in this way thought the Woman in Love was coming on to them, expressed disappointment when the surface contact satisfied her needs.

The other drew the Woman in Love into her arms, where she breathed deep and slow so as not to cry out in her joy. For this night the other's name was Desire and her flame engulfed them both. The Woman in Love gave her lips, her mouth to the other, raised her nipples to the other's hands. She raised her mons to the other's pubic bone, the other's leg sliding through, between her own. Desire held them, drove them, rousing cravings that could not be stilled. Desire took the Woman in Love, took her with a finality that was open-ended, nourishing, invigorating. The Woman in Love curled around her lover, tensed and came, tensed and came.

Seduction: opening herself to another, allowing her hunger, her vulnerability to be known.

"Loving," she said, "always comes as a surprise, like the sunrise, even though I know it's going to happen over and over again; it always takes my breath away, opens up my memories of what is holy."

Soft vibrations of the music, flashing jukebox lights, glitter, pulse, bang along her spine. Her clit, enlarged, demanding, cries out for attention, presses against her jeans, the chair, Desire's leg. They dance dirty, standing in one place, grinding their pubes against each other's thigh. The Woman in Love breathes with the bass line, undulates, inhales the other's musk.

In the street the night is hot, a doorway near, the other's breath in her ear another kind of music, the other's need, the hand inside her pants, the reaching, raging breath. The nearby music still propels her, hungry, open, wet and wanting only to be taken, only to be freed.

The Woman in Love first encountered Desire in New Orleans in the form of an elegant butch with beautiful bones. Neither tall nor short, exquisitely proportioned, Desire, with her almost boy's body, claimed her with hips and loving hands, knelt between her legs, breathing in all her secret places, touching her in the twilight, in the half-light, late into the mornings, quietly in corners, on half-deserted streets. Desire's tapered, neatly clipped fingers stirred a longing in the Woman in Love, made her restless, dissatisfied with even that which Desire gave.

Yet music opened the doors within the Woman in Love as she moved into Desire's arms, swaying slightly. Music sent out her butterscotch-slow fingers and Desire took the Woman in Love. Was the night enough? Would any night be enough?

"I will give you this lifetime," the Woman in Love said, knowing she had even more to give. "I will give you this night, this day, for as long as love is green, fresh with new growth . . ."

"Hold me tight," said Desire. "Need me hard."

"Run off with me," the Woman in Love begged, and Desire refused, following her own road into the future.

"I'll forget you," threatened the Woman in Love, but she never did.

The Woman in Love married for sex and comfort and shortly began taking lovers: women and very young men. Her husband adored her, drew life from the fires that burned within her, loved her genius for creative solutions.

"They say my father could repair a car with a hairpin," she would say, but of course that didn't explain her abilities. For generations, though, her family had been good with their hands.

"Safely married," obsessed by the past, the Woman in Love began painting the hands of Desire, working sometimes from memory, sometimes from photographs. Although many of the canvases were realistically rendered, some were colored by passion: green in the shadows, brilliant reds, purples, cadmium edges.

Desire found the Woman in Love living in suburbia, teaching college, married still.

"Shall I go away?" Desire asked, holding herself quietly.

"No," the Woman in Love whispered. "I never did forget."

Swimming at midday in cool water, against the flow, between boulders, Desire smiles at the Woman in Love, tickles her with her toes, races her from shore to shore. Desire pulls her bodice down and squeezes the nipples of the Woman in Love, squeezes and molds her breasts, kisses her with a probing demand, a wanting that would not be stilled. Desire pulls the Woman in Love into the sand and reaches inside her suit, inside her body, pushing her want forward. The Woman in Love pushes back to meet her, to match her, to open to this mating so sun-wrapped, thrust upon her, so longed-for and feared and revered. Coming, she loses contact with all but the radiating sensations centered in her groin, in her ass. Her breath, withheld, she now expels and rocks and burrows into her lover's shoulder, into her lover's breast.

She dreams she is walking through a tunnel constructed of barrel arches. The woman beside her is tall, angular, softened at the edges. They stride in unison, in slow motion, up and down like carousel horses. Sounds form a rolling sea around them. The liquid gathers between her legs, begins its movement downward.

At that shimmering moment when they reenter sunlight, as the sounds rapidly shatter, compelling sensations race outward along her thighs. She feels herself to be both women, inside both women's bodies. The Woman in Love breathes deeply. Both women sigh.

Waking slowly to the entered evening, the Woman in Love runs her hands over her body, reclaiming the real from the dream. Conscious now, she remembers the hands of Desire, inhales slowly, feeling the cool hands move over her memory: another awakening, encoded in all her surface cells.

Arriving home late one night, the husband of the Woman in Love confronted her with "What would you do if I asked you not to see her any more?"

"Leave you," she said.

The Woman in Love returned from the beach alone, bringing polished bones of wood, blue lupine, pebbles filled with light.

Desire met her halfway with small, hungry kisses, smiles, touches soft as moth wings.

"I've decided to leave my husband," the Woman in Love said, whispered, sighed.

"Not because of me, I hope," Desire replied.

"No. No. Because of me."

Through winter and the following spring they love:

When you touch me
When I respond
Joy unfolds

You have become my text, my love; your body, your words. I have bound your letters into a volume I carry with me, read at night before I sleep, at dawn before I move into the day.

Your love is a fine spray misting my movements, mellowing my colors, lightening what might have been despair. Where your hands have been, I am yours, and your hands have been everywhere. Your words enter my soil like rain. Your memory, O love, your memory takes me suddenly, wrenches me from this world into a fairy tale where I am loved the way I always wanted to be.

A day comes when the Woman in Love knows she must move on. She must shed her past like the used branches of the white southern pine. Grow, she says to herself, I must grow into a fuller human form, become the person my heart promises, intimates, teases me to be.

Fragmentary images of magic cities drift across her mind: Montreal, San Francisco, Philadelphia, Paris, Vancouver, Cincinnati, stone buildings, arches, public sculpture. Streets speckled with sunlight. Food artfully piled in store windows.

Riding the train at twilight, her body appears ephemeral in the glass, cruising backward across the winter landscape. Entering a tunnel, her reflection becomes volumetric against the darkened window, subtly yet solidly colored. She flirts with herself, imagines sexual encounters, orgies where beloved hands excite her every sensitivity.

She squeezes her pelvic muscles, considers covering her activity with a coat, seeks out the toilet instead and comes standing, leaning against the wall, her face turned toward the mirror. A long sigh precedes her return to her seat, where she sleeps soundly, dreaming of cities.

In a glory of late-morning sunshine, the Woman in Love sits alone in a Victorian-style bar, waiting for a table in the adjoining restaurant. Yellow mums bloom at her elbow, the glass sparkles, glasses shine upside down in rows. She orders almond wine, because it's strange to her, sniffs the scent, turns the glass, amber liquid slowly moving; wooden table, parquet floors glow. A woman with a nose like her lover's slinks by in wet-look pants. The walls are green felt, fern-banked. Well-dressed women of her own age pass with their grown daughters, stately, American.

She imagines everyone undressed, fantasizes body hair, freckles, moles. She remembers a lover's evening touch, warmed with oil, sleek and even, rewarding her anticipatory thrill.

The maître d' leads her to a seat beside a window. She orders, then reads a magazine: facts, raw material for some other dream.

Later, leaving, she notices the scent of a woman she passes, sweet like the flowers of her past.

The Woman in Love met Desire again in London, sitting in a pub, slim, graying, full of stories. They returned to her flat, undressed almost shyly, excited still. Beneath the sheets they continued talking, touched slowly, hesitantly; joked about their mouths being dry.

When the Woman in Love buried her face in the other's shoulder, the hands of Desire were freed to move over her, opening her again.

"So long," she said. "It's been so long since we've been together, since it's been like this for me."

That first coming together, again and again, over distances beyond her imagination, compelled awe. The adequacy of a cheek, a touch, became fire and hunger, sweat and love.

The Woman in Love moaned.

The Woman in Love sighed.

Desire raged and washed over her. This time they both came.

In the morning the Woman in Love woke first, turned to kiss her lover, found her quiet and still. The Woman in Love feared morning would take what the night had given, touched her lover's shoulder lightly and willed herself returned to sleep. She dreamed of beaches, of walking alone on windswept ocean beaches, looking for someone.

She dreams the wind is blowing off the water, reaching through her clothes, drawing the hair from her face. Morning explodes, coral and flushed, exposing multiple horizons. Gulls flash and circle, calling to her, teasingly, to join them. She lifts from the sand, elongating her body, stretching her muscles, reaching out.

Soaring higher, she wants to thank the birds, the morning, but finds she cannot speak. The rosy gilt-edged hands of day encompass her, wrap around her, turn her, mold the furry ravine between her legs. Behind the dreamer's dream eyes, novas explode, day breaks in two, freeing shooting stars across a velvet sky. The dreamer gasps and twines her fingers in the heliotrope hair of day. An early breeze kisses her cheeks, flutters a curtain lightly across her face. Stretching, she soars again, glides and turns, coupling with the wind.

Nearing Desire, excitement rises, circles within her torso, whistles in her head. Dreaming, she crashes into the other's shore, rolls and turns across her beaches, kites and dips along the other's bony spine.

Desire erupts into a twilight sky to meet her, flowing down her own sides, winking, fiery. Warm breath, lava-flecked, encases her extended body, claiming her.

The Woman in Love awakened to find herself enfolded. Oh, those body smells! warm touch, firm hands. "Oh, God," said the Woman in Love. "Thank you, God," she said and looked into the other's eyes, liquid, calm and close.

They ate oranges in Valencia and bathed in the sea.

In Barcelona they lived in a small, cool, white room; wandered among the flower vendors until, aroused beyond propriety, they returned to their room and drank each other's body, breathed each other's smell.

Twilight Fantasy

JACQUIE ROBB

This is a story of a woman; a woman who is waiting. She is waiting for her lover in a hotel room. She has followed him south, down the coast from their home. Her lover is at a conference / in a meeting / giving a lecture; he is, at any rate, not with her now. He will return in the evening.

The woman lies on the hotel bed in a loose slip. It is hot and she fans herself with a brochure listing sights of local interest. The shopping mall. The auditorium where her lover's conference/meeting/lecture is now in progress. The brochure is for visitors, tourists. The woman is not a tourist.

The woman is not bored; she is too hot to be bored. The sun makes her . . . not fretful, but lazy. She is resting in the shade of the hotel room. She hears occasional footsteps, muffled by the deep carpeting in the hall, coming from the other side of the door. On the opposite side of the room is a sliding glass window which opens onto a balcony, a small cement balcony with a wrought-iron railing. Perhaps the balcony and railing are unpainted wood, for the woman is near the ocean.

The dull hum of the stray car passing on the street below forms an interesting counterpoint to the footsteps in the hall. The motorists are oblivious to the woman waiting in the hotel room above them.

The woman hums tunelessly. It is not a song or chant, neither is it formless. She is simply humming. The breeze from the open window touches her, cools her. The woman is in no hurry. She simply waits.

I close my eyes and try to suppress a smile as you lean toward me for a kiss. The odor of lilacs overwhelms me; I sit up, smiling broadly, cradling the flowers, forgetting that I had been feigning sleep. You kiss my cheek lightly, nuzzling my ear in the way you would have done to awaken me. Our eyes meet briefly in greeting.

You straighten and strip off your shirt, damp with a fine outline of sweat between the shoulders. You stand above me a moment, looking at me tenderly. While you undress, I start to ask you about your day. You say you held in your mind a picture of me under my umbrella by the pool and wished you were beside me. You kick off your shoes, heading for the shower.

I slide out of bed and the flowers tumble after me. I scoop them up and look around for a vase; seeing none, I settle for the plastic water pitcher in the hall which joins the bedroom with the bath. The hall holds a double sink on one side and a closet on the other. Naked but for my slip, I pad over to the faucets.

I look up and catch my reflection in the wall mirror as I fill the pitcher. With my free hand I brush my unruly red hair from my face, a habitual and useless gesture. I gaze at myself dispassionately, looking over my features as I would a stranger's. My skin is creamy; only my freckles tan, turning an embarrassing shade of green. My body is long but not thin. I have been described as Rubenesque and voluptuous by men who have desired me. I shrug to myself; by accepting my body's shape, I accept the accumulated years that have shaped it. My body is so well known to me, my gaze so familiar, I do not contemplate my form so much as the spirit for which it stands witness.

Coming out of my reverie, I place the lilacs in the water and set them beside the bed. Their aroma brightens the air, transforming the sterile atmosphere into a private retreat. I look around, admiring the effect. I feel the presence of you filling the corners of the room just as the flowers' perfume has. Filling the corners of the room, and of myself.

The steam billows from the shower stall when I open the door. You pull me under the water as I reach for the soap to wash your back. I protest, laughing, my hair flattening against my breasts, my slip conforming to my body.

I close my eyes as your arms close around my shoulders. I lean into your chest, smelling your essence. My cheek rests against the soft black hair between your breasts. The water pounds my ribs, runs down my legs; we stand, mesmerized by the water's constant force. Only slowly do we become aware of each other's pressure, the pressure of our bodies touching. I push you away then, kissing your arms as they slide from my neck.

In the bedroom again, I raise my arms to take off my dripping slip; you kneel quickly at my feet and catch the fabric in your fists. Eyes flashing, you inch the slip up my thighs while we watch the threads of water bead and trickle from the hem. Laughter catches in my throat, sounding husky. My fingers grasp your shoulders to steady myself as I lean into the tingling pleasure of your touch.

With my slip around my waist, you bury your face in my rounded belly. My breath is already coming deeper, a flush tickling my throat and cheeks. My hands move to raise you and you kiss my naked body as you slide my slip over my head.

We face each other then, and I look frankly into your eyes. I see love there, and an honesty behind the love that intimate knowledge brings. In turn, my green eyes neither seek nor hide knowledge of you. Recognition passes between us; as if we have nodded our assent, I lead you to bed.

Your erection precedes you, pointing the way. I sit on the bed while you stand in front of me. I caress your penis slowly, feel its velvet throbbing. Anticipation reflects in your eyes as my hands quicken their measured strokes to match your breath. You moan a sigh as I move one hand to your balls. I feel their weight, imagine them tightening into your crotch and feel a corresponding pressure, a tightening of my own nerves.

I kiss your satin tip and your juice springs to my lips, staining them with the familiar pungent tang. I lick you down one side, following your vein, and round the base as far as I can reach. With a groan your knees give way and you sink to the bed's edge. I wrap my legs around your calves, cradle my thumbs in the hollow of your hips. My fingers grab your taut ass as my tongue travels slowly around your point. In my excitement I am losing control; my tongue flickers and seeks the cap of your engorged member, my mouth opening to receive you.

I dive, with one fluid movement, to contain you in my mouth, widening to receive you. You are motionless, straining against your impulse to thrust. I, too, am still except for my hands clutching your hips. I begin to suck, first slowly up to your tip, turning my head side to side to feel every part of you. Then down again, to meet your pubic hair curling around your extended shaft.

Sitting up straighter, I move my hands around your buttocks to the inside of your thighs. Gently, I stroke the tightness at the base of your balls with my fingertips; gently, I move down your thighs with a shivering lightness. I move together with you as smoothly as a breath, taking you into my mouth as I inhale, allowing you to fall away with a sigh. Yet I hold back slightly; although our pace quickens, we never completely lose contact. We sway in unison and you call my name over and over, your eyes shut tightly in exhilaration.

Your body goes rigid, warning me to wait; I hold perfectly still, my mouth at your base. Then, in slow motion, completely caught up in your mood, I slip my hand around to my mouth, sharing my saliva, your leaking juices, with my fingers. You shudder in premonition. I caress your balls, slip into the crack between your cheeks, circle my middle finger around your hole. Each time my lips creep down your pulsing member, my finger slips imperceptively closer to the muscular opening.

You moan, gasping for air; I help you down until you are stretched across the bed. I lie curled towards you, wrapping my legs around one of your thighs so you can feel my warm fluid as it drips in excitement. My hips begin to undulate with the rhythm of my sucking mouth. Your hands reach for me, take my head as you strain against your desire. Your fingers move blindly over my shoulders, trying to grasp my sides while your back begins to arch.

I wriggle from your hands, wanting to concentrate on your pleasure, knowing it will be returned tenfold. I calm my pulsing heart; all of my consciousness returns to my fingertips and tongue. Once more your golden rod becomes the center of my universe.

Now we both know climax is near. In the timelessness of love's dance, neither leading nor following, our rhythm is synchronized. Both of us pause in exquisite anticipation, followed by the inevitable rush of delight, utterly new and known. With each thrust of you into my mouth, I answer with a thrust of my own, deeper to your core. Your breath comes in gasps and my body shimmers in sweet sweat as we rock.

Now both my hands go around your slippery shaft. My fingers' grip follow the sweep of my mouth, sometimes taking over while I catch my breath. When you come, with a burst and a shudder, my hands reach for your juice, seeping through my cupped fingers. I paint your belly with your sperm, trace the line of your side with my sticky fingers. We lie together, breathing heavily, until a peace settles over us.

I know it is a peace of expectation. You ask me to lie on top of you, to keep you from floating away, you say. We rest, matched belly on belly, your legs stretched beyond mine, your arms wrapped around me. I tilt my head to your chest, to your heart. The strong, steady beat lulls me; when you flip me artfully onto my back, I protest feebly. You lie above me now, bracing yourself with your arms, your hands catching mine and holding them slightly above me. I squirm, knowing you want to make me feel as good as you are feeling.

The taste of salt on my lips when we kiss is an aphrodisiac. Still holding my arms outstretched, you kiss my eyes, nose, every place you can reach. I shiver, tense to the point of abstraction, but when you find that special place on the side of my neck and kiss it with smooth, dry lips, the kisses light as a feather's touch, the playful squirming fades and I feel my body loosen to your touch.

You feel the shift in mood immediately, and with a languid move kneel between my legs. Spreading them carefully, you kiss my inner thighs. The deliberateness of your movements sends tremors cascading down my back. You stroke my legs, behind my knees, my calves, and the sureness of your caress lights me with desire. You raise my left foot to your mouth, suck on each toe in turn. My arms reach for you with a new urgency.

Your magic wand, already full, grazes my crotch; my hips move up to greet you, but you move out of reach. You kneel above me again as if surveying which limb to taste next. Your fingers trace circles around my belly, up to my breasts, just missing the nipples each time so that they strain with added anticipation. Slowly, so slowly that I succumb to the method before I realize the intent, you capture me with your rhythm, a circular, hypnotic motion, traced lightly, then in gradually deepening touch on my body.

I lie still except for the spasms that come involuntarily from deep within me. I feel as though storm clouds are racing across some internal landscape, accumulating over one precise point in my body. Your lips find my nipples and bolts of electricity flash through them; my gasp echoes like thunder throughout me. Whether you are still caressing my belly, or whether I have taken up and continued the rhythm you created I cannot tell, don't want to decide, won't stop to discover. You move from nipple to belly to throat, your hands cupping my breasts as you suck electric excitement from me. Your hands slide along my sides, slick with the heat created from the passion crimsoning my face. You are everywhere at once and I, delirious with sensation, feel the last vestiges of my earthbound, rational mind float away.

You build the pace only to stop; I'm caught mid-breath. Opening my heavy-lidded eyes, I see your gleaming face above me. You blow cool air on my neck and breasts, taking your time, smiling secretly. My eyes slide shut again; I sense, rather than see, you watch my perspiration dry, replaced by the glowing aura of ardor.

You make your way slowly down my body until you crouch between my legs once more. My still ragged breathing is slower now. You unfold yourself, stretching your legs out behind you, guiding me to the edge of the bed. Your kneel before me, studying my folds. Propped on my elbow, our eyes meet once more, lock in an unspoken understanding, promising ecstasy. Finally, the air heavy with the inevitability of pleasure, you lower your head toward my throbbing center.

You spread my glistening lips with your tongue in one smooth, sure, upward movement. My shoulders drop to the bed. Again your tongue caresses me, this time with just a hint of a flicker around my clit, and my body answers with a quick jump of the nervous system. Again the movement, a simple direct line, this time ending in a definite twist of your sharpened tongue. I catch my breath, not daring to breathe. Each stroke, never rough or rushed, promises more, assures fulfillment.

With infinitely small movements, the pattern begins to shift. Arms slide under my legs, fingers grasp my hips, shoulders press my thighs apart. Tongue, smooth chin, lips: each explore the wet inner reaches of my folds. Spelunker, I call you, diver into depths; each exploration finds new treasures of feeling, brings up fresh desire.

My hips rock as your tongue's strokes become stronger, surer. You build the pace to so high a plateau, yet each time you deliberately stop before I burst with excruciating pleasure. Each time you start again, the beginning is of such a height that I can't imagine what reaches are to come. My volition spent, I give myself over to your will, abandoning all expectation, all reason.

A hum starts low in the back of your throat, vibrates against my pelvic bone like a tuning fork, echoes through my body. The hum continues, so low as to seem not a sound but a heavy, dark object. At the same time, your tongue flicks, barely touching my ripe clit. The point of contact is so fine, yet the touch is fire and the fire is spreading.

This time the roaring comes from a hidden place inside me, an eruption that travels, white heat, through the arteries and sinews of my thighs, across my back, leaping with a cry from my throat and exploding from the top of my head. Echoes of orgasms crash through me; my body experiences and remembers simultaneously, and each memory triggers a chain reaction of new pleasure. My sweat mixes with tears that you kiss from my cheeks with your sticky, musky lips. I reach for your hand and move it to my mound, which you hold securely until the pulsations quiet.

You lie full next to me, and we press ourselves tightly together, listening to the passing storm recede. We lie very still, amazed at our creation, that our bodies are a channel for so much that must, by definition, remain unspoken.

The woman wakes. She has dozed, or believes she has. It is very quiet. She is awakened by the silence, or rather by the breaking of that silence by a familiarity she cannot at first place. She lies very still to see if she has heard what she believes she has. A key in the lock. A walk she can feel in her stomach, rather than hear. The step of her lover is a vibration in her bloodstream.

Biographies

Carolyn Banks has written four novels, the most recent of which is *Patchwork.* Her previous novels are *The Girls on the Row, The Darkroom* and *Mr. Right.* She is also a regular book reviewer for the Washington *Post.* Her short stories have appeared in *Black Mask* and *In Youth,* and features have been published in *Redbook* and *Sports Illustrated,* among others.

Susan Block, a native of Philadelphia and magna cum laude graduate of Yale University, has written for numerous magazines and newspapers, as well as for film, radio, video and the theater. She is the author of *Advertising for Love: How to Play the Personals* and a recipient of the Los Angeles Women-in-Theater Award for Outstanding Achievement. At present, she is collaborating on a book on feminine psychology with Dr. Toni Grant. Susan created and hosts her own radio show, *Susan Block's Date Night.*

Sandy Boucher is a San Francisco Bay Area lesbian feminist whose fiction and nonfiction have been published in many periodicals and anthologies. Her books include *Heartwomen*, a journey to her midwestern roots and portrait of heartland women; and three books of short stories: *Assaults & Rituals, The Notebooks of Leni Clare* and *Mountain Radio.* Currently, she is at work on a book about women and contemporary American Buddhism.

KIM CHERNIN lives and teaches in Berkeley, California. She is the author of *The Obsession: Reflections on the Tyranny of Slenderness; The Hungry Self: Women, Eating and Identity; In My Mother's House;* and *The Hunger Song*, a book of poetry. Her first novel, *The Flame Bearers*, will be published in the fall of 1986 by Random House. And she is currently completing a book about goddess worship and the New Woman.

TEE A. CORINNE is a forty-two-year-old visual artist and writer. Her published art includes *The Cunt Coloring Book* (a.k.a. *Labiaflowers), Yantras of Womanlove* and *Women Who Loved Women*, as well as graphics in *Our Bodies/Ourselves* and *I Am My Lover.* Her short stories have appeared in *Pleasures: Women Write Erotica; Penthouse; On Our Backs* and *Common Lives/Lesbian Lives.* She is a founding editor of *The Blatant Image / A Magazine of Feminist Photography* and the primary cover artist for Naiad Press.

NISA DONNELLY is a San Francisco Bay Area author and journalist whose work has appeared in a variety of women's movement publications during the past ten years. Both her journalism and fiction reflect the issues and lives of contemporary lesbians. "The Scavenger Hunt" is one of a collection of interrelated short stories dealing with lesbian life and love.

GAYLE FEYRER is an award-winning artist specializing in fantasy and erotic art. Her professional publications include the *Northwest Review, Calyx*, and *10 Point 5*, among others, and she is currently working on a new science fiction novel. In addition to sharing her life with a husband of multivarious talents, and two cats of distinct temperament, she is a prizewinning cook.

SUSAN GRIFFIN is a poet, thinker and writer who teaches and works as a consultant for creative problems in Berkeley, California. She is best known for her book *Woman and Nature: The Roaring Inside Her.* Her play *Voices* won an Emmy award in 1975. She is also the author of *Pornography and Silence: Culture's Revenge Against Nature; Like the Iris of an Eye; Made from This Earth;* and *Rape: The Politics of Consciousness.* She is presently at work on *The First and the Last: A Woman Thinks About War.*

SIGNE HAMMER has been a dance-theater and street-theater performer, book editor, labor organizer for book publishing staff and for writers, free-lance writer and magazine editor. She has published poems and articles in little magazines and commercial magazines (*Fiction, Parade,*

Mademoiselle, Harper's Bazaar, Science Digest and others). The last of her three nonfiction books was *Passionate Attachments: Fathers and Daughters in America Today*. She is currently at work on a memoir.

VALERIE KELLY has been writing erotic short stories, which have been published mainly in men's magazines, for the past six years. She has also written two dozen screenplays which have been produced for adult video and is currently working on the Kay Parker *Love Stories* line for Caballero. Her book *How to Write Erotica* was released through Harmony Books in 1986. She also gives one-day seminars on the subject through the L.A. Course Network, in Los Angeles, California.

MARILYN HARRIS KRIEGEL is a psychotherapist who divides her time between writing and lecturing in the United States and in Europe. Her most recent publication, coauthored with her husband, Robert, is *The C Zone: Peak Performance Under Pressure*, published by Doubleday.

CUCU LEE is a free-lance writer who formerly authored a weekly Texas newspaper column and regular dining and entertainment magazine features. She is a longtime television writer, and has won awards for her poetry. She is also a veteran actress, and operated her own public relations firm for many years. Currently, she lives in the San Fernando Valley and works for a major motion picture and television producer.

SHARON MAYES holds an M.A. degree in clinical psychology and a Ph.D. in sociology. Her scholarly articles and poetry have appeared in several journals: *Signs: The International Journal of Women's Studies* and *Wingspread: A Feminist Literary Journal*, among others. After ten years of college teaching, academic writing, and practicing psychotherapy, she is writing fiction full-time. Sharon is married and living with her husband in Harare, Zimbabwe, for a year, where she is working on a novel, *Immune*.

DEENA METZGER is the author of *The Woman Who Slept with Men to Take the War Out of Them; Tree; The Axis Mundi Poems; Skin: Shadows/Silence;* and *Dark Milk*. Her plays include *Dreams Against the State, Not as Sleepwalkers* and *Book of Hags*. Her article "Revamping the World: On the Return of the Holy Prostitute" has been widely circulated. She developed "Healing Stories," a therapeutic approach to life-threatening disease, and is currently writing a novel entitled *What Dinah Thought*.

SUZANNE MILLER is an artist and transformational counselor. She is the author of two books of poetry, is a contributor to the anthology *Pleasures: Women Write Erotica* and has written several plays, one of which she produced and directed in Mill Valley, California. She has also written many essays and articles, ranging in topics from child abuse to sacred dances of American Indians, and is completing her first novel, *The Life and Times of Gypsy Marlowe*.

DORAINE PORETZ is a poet, playwright and teacher who lives with her teenage daughter in Los Angeles. Her poems have appeared in numerous literary journals, and she has read her work on radio and at various cultural centers and bookstores in Los Angeles and in New York. She has published two books of poems: *Re: Visions* and *This Woman in America* and has five plays to her credit. Presently she is working on a book about the homeless in Los Angeles.

UDANA POWER is an actress/singer/writer who has starred on television and film and in theater (including Broadway). Having appeared in over 250 commercials, she has also found time to write two novels and numerous short stories. One novel and one short story have been optioned for film. Aware of a need to redefine male/female dynamics, she longs to unite eroticism with love, and strength with surrender, so that males and females can celebrate *all* of their energies together.

JACQUIE ROBB, graduate of Lawrence University in Wisconsin, has traveled extensively in North America. A poet, book reviewer, short-story and journal writer, her "The Growing Season" appeared in *Pleasures: Women Write Erotica.* She is also an administrator in private education. At present, she makes her home under the redwoods in northern California with her lover and one cat.

REBECCA SILVER is a graduate student in Elizabethan literature at Cambridge University. She received her B.A. from Smith College. Her work has appeared in *Cosmopolitan* and other magazines.

VICTORIA STARR is a young writer living and working in Santa Cruz, California. She is married and anxiously expecting her first baby. She has recently completed her first novel, a cultural-adventure love story questioning the reality of perception in the modern world, and has published short stories in *Wellspring* and *Xiachajo.* Victoria's most erotic pleasures are loving her husband and stroking her fat furry cat.

GRACE ZABRISKIE is a professional actress with numerous stage, screen and television credits. She used to make a living as a silk-screen artist. A short story, "Screaming Julians," was published in *Pleasures: Women Write Erotica.* She is also a published poet, a screenwriter and a carpenter.